Francine du Plessix Gray

World Without End

A NOVEL

Simon and Schuster
New York

C. 4

My deep gratitude to the American Academy in Rome, whose generous support and great kindness enabled me to finish this work in peace.

Published by Simon and Schuster
A Division of Gulf & Western Corporation
Simon & Schuster Building
Rockefeller Center
1230 Avenue of the Americas
New York, New York 10020
SIMON AND SCHUSTER and colophon are trademarks of Simon & Schuster

Designed by Elizabeth Woll
Manufactured in the United States of America

1 3 5 7 9 10 8 6 4 2

Library of Congress Cataloging in Publication Data
Gray, Francine du Plessix.
World without end.

I. Title.
PS3557.R294W6   813'.54   81-1493
                               AACR2
ISBN 0-671-42786-5

The author gratefully acknowledges permission from the following to quote:

Random House for Yevgeny Yevtushenko's poem *Babi Yar* from Olga Carlisle's book *Poets at Street Corners*.

Penguin Books Ltd. for the use of lines by Vladimir Mayakovsky from *The Penguin Book of Russian Verse*, introduced and edited by Dmitri Obolensky, copyright © 1962 by Dmitri Obolensky: from "Conversations with an Inspector of Taxes about Poetry," and "Unfinished."

Horace Gregory for *The Poems of Catullus*, translated and with an introduction by Horace Gregory, copyright © 1956 by Horace Gregory.

Famous Music Publishing Companies for the lyrics to the copyrighted song "That's Amore." Copyright 1953 by Paramount Music Corporation.

Miller Music Corporation for the lyric from "Down Argentine Way" by Mack Gordon and Harry Warren, copyright © 1940, renewed 1968 Twentieth Century Music Corporation. All rights administered and controlled by Miller Music Corporation. Used by permission.

Ecco Press for Robert Haas's poem "Against Botticelli" from his book *Praise*, copyrights © 1974-79.

To Ethel, Joanna, Rose

———————————

Part One

Friendship is here, my heart
Richer than love or passion.

CATULLUS

Edmund, Claire, and Sophie, friends -
and sometimes lovers - for thirty years,
travel to the Soviet Union hoping to
plan for the last third of their lives
and to resolve the struggles and con-
fusions of the previous three decades.

i

THE Russian walked with his arm linked through Sophie's, a man with soft brown eyes and a scar on his left cheek. She had been in love with him for three hours. Since childhood she'd often fallen in love with visions, strangers, ballet stars, on the occasion of a fleeting glance. She had known very great loves that lasted a day and a night. The park lay before them luminous with fog. A large romantic park, empty benches, beds of tulips scintillating with recent rain, lamplight shimmering on an immensity of moisture. The path stretched ahead of them to what seemed infinity, all end obscured, terminated only by a distant bank of vapor or low clouds. "I'd like to walk to the end," she said, "which may not exist." His glance was sentimental, swift. "We shall order it to cease existing." They had met that afternoon in Leningrad at a recital of folk dancing which Sophie attended alone. From the very beginning of this trip she'd decided to be alone some part of each day. "Where have you been you nomad," Edmund and Claire scolded her the next morning, "why do you leave us like that?" They seemed peeved, as if she were turning on some pledge. During the folk dancing Sophie had wept. Girls in early puberty veiled in white gauze had glided across the stage with steps floating and minute, their hands twining and twisting like snakes turned into flowers, like aquatic plants waving in an ocean storm. And children in black

Cossack costumes on the tremulous edge of manhood had shot across the stage like glints of coal, dancing their nascent ritual of seduction with fiery sabers, with proud and furious glances, with postures of fighters. Sophie had wept over her lost childhood, her solitude, the pain of growing up in America, the beauty of these dancing children entering like fierce swans into the storms of life. But then the next part of the spectacle upset her even more, oh the second part of it was awful. The curtain had reopened on a stage bathed in the fruited glow of Western nightclubs and an all-girl rock band singing Elvis Presley. They ranged in age between ten and fifteen, they played on synthesizers, trombones, trumpets, electric guitars, they made a din which Sophie found atrocious. They were dressed in the navy-and-white costumes of Young Pioneers, with bright red cravats about their necks; they still wore high white knee socks and flat little-girl shoes with buckles. Boom pah-de dada they sang, thrusting towards the audience their bodies made lithe by Soviet calisthenics, muscular pelvises, budding breasts. Boom dada they shook their shoulders, lasciviously trembling, winking. So perhaps Sophie wept again thinking their youth is being ruined, their civilization is just as corrupt as ours. That's when the Russian came to sit next to her asking was she alone in the city, could he help. Sophie didn't know what to say. "Stalin would die," she whispered, nodding towards the stage, "Lenin would die." He frequently smiled. He had gentle, ironic eyes. "Khrushchev mightn't have liked it either." He wore a brown shirt open at the collar, he lived in Moscow, he'd come to Leningrad to attend a congress of cardiologists. They walked together down Nevsky Prospect. When the rain started pouring they went to dinner in a large café where another band of adult men played acid rock and Sophie put her hands over her ears, saying over the platters of cold fish, "Look here this is crazy you're importing the worst poisons of our culture without taking . . ." There was a great burst of thunder, the dining room was plunged in darkness, the band stopped playing, waiters hurried about with many candles, shouting. "You have made the poisons stop," he said. For the rest of their dinner the lights wavered softly on and off as if powered by the energy of a small erratic wind. All in his face was soft and faunlike, tendrils of thick hair curling over wide temples, brown eyes that taunted hers with the flirtatious glances of bygone movie stars. "Indeed the rock music does not become you, you are more like a tango, I shall ask you many questions about your life."

"In New York I rise at four A.M.," Sophie said. "I have a two-hour television program every morning five days a week, I get to the studio at six, read the wire reports, finish the morning's script, talk to the producer . . ." "You are very famous and you earn as much as some football players and soon you will have your portrait on the cover of *Newsweek*." "I've already had that," she said. He looked amused and very tender. "Is it great freedom?" "Perhaps it is solitude," she said; "isn't great freedom also great solitude?" He shook his head at a slant, not clearly yes or no. "And what do you do in the afternoon?" "In the afternoon I go home and nap and read more newspapers still. . . ." What papers? Ah if I tell you you'll get a lesson in American geography, the *Boston Globe*, the *St. Louis Post-Dispatch*, the *Philadelphia Inquirer*, the *Chicago Tribune*, the *San Francisco Examiner*; why so many? We Americans are drunk on information, I'm beginning to think it's one of our national diseases. . . . Why have I come to Russia? Oh you ask so many questions Vladimir Ivanovich! . . . We've come to Russia together Edmund and Claire and I, best friends since adolescence, we've come here to recapture . . . we've come here to figure out how to live the last third of our lives; after forty-five there isn't much left but friendship is there, only friends will tell you the truths you need to hear to make the last part of your existence bearable. . . . Have I been in love? Oh that's been the disaster of my life. It should never be a disaster? What a flirt you are Vladimir Ivanovich! I could give you an excellent Marxist reading of romantic passion; those who still look on romance as the main ingredient of the good life are brainwashed by the bourgeois propaganda machine, victimized by a defunct capitalistic ethic that gluts on the permissive excesses of our decadent literature. . . . How's that, passing grades? . . . Do I dream at night? Yes I have primitive, simple dreams, they're often nightmares, I dream of being precisely the opposite of what I am, there are many children about and I must cook for fourteen and I'm constantly out of food and everyone shouts at me, but we must stop this immediately, in my métier I'm the one who asks the questions. . . .

He said: "I shall take you to see old friends who will make you happy." And so they had walked down the banks of the Neva to visit a small traveling circus that had just arrived to town. A thin scar ran from Vladimir's temple to his ear; in his youth he had published several volumes of verse. Sophie put more perfume on her wrists, wishing for everything with this man. The circus troupe lived near the river in a one-room trailer cabin at the center of which there was a table laden with champagne, wines, sweets. Two thin blond girls in trapezists' costumes were arranging cakes into neat little rows. The manager of the troupe kissed the doctor on the cheek and said, "I want you to meet my new juggler and hypnotist; he can put people under a spell for five days, he's cured insomnia, stopped them from smoking for the rest of their lives." "Let me also show you some tricks," the hypnotist called out, "let me show you." He disappeared into a closet and came out again in a white brocade jacket, carrying his kit. He made six orange Ping-Pong balls disappear and took them out of his mouth two at a time, he made them disappear and found them in Sophie's pockets, he made them disappear and pulled them out of the doctor's ears. The blond trapezists wore tight lavender T-shirts which matched the great arcs of violet paint on their upper eyelids; they sat on the same chair with their arms entwined about each other's waist. The juggler put his Ping-Pong balls under some dishes, lifted the dishes and said see there's nothing there anymore. The thinner girl snuggled her chin into her friend's shoulder, their faces melded together like a single head distorted in the vision of fever, their dark red mouths loomed immense in their wasted faces. "Like a Picasso," Sophie whispered. The doctor agreed. "Nineteen three, blue period." Later the Russians recited poetry, Blok, Mayakovski, the doctor's own verses. When Vladimir Ivanovich recited poetry, standing up, eyes closed, his chest rolled outwards like an opera singer's, his voice took on a different order of nature—the rolling of streams over pebbles or the mysterious language of macaws at night; he spoke his song an octave higher than his other voice and for that time the circus actors stood captive in their poses, frozen as in death, the trapezists' pale

14

long hair lay entwined like one mass of wheat above their violet bodies . . . and then after a long while the doctor-poet's eyes opened, he smiled at Sophie and talked to her in human voice again. "Oh, oh," Sophie retorted when he said Americans knew no poetry by heart, "I'll prove you wrong, I'll start with Yeats! 'That is no country for old men. The young in one another's arms, birds in the trees—those dying generations . . .' " But then she felt her tears storm up again, couldn't finish. Vladimir stroked her arm. "I have translated Yeats for our literary gazettes; for a while it was forbidden here but slowly things are changing. . . ." He was bidding his friends good night. And she went out with him again into the park.

The evening was luminous with fog, still luxuriant with her hopes for his touch. You're the victim of romantic fiction Claire and Edmund had told her for thirty years, you're like Madame Bovary; lately at every new quickening of her body she'd thought no more, I never shall again . . . "I believe in staying in my country and fighting for change," the doctor was saying; "there are little advances and freedoms which would have been silenced in the fifties; we must work step by step, like good liberals; I have a column in one of our literary gazettes every month, I plan very carefully, I try to test every limit. . . ." Scintillations of moisture still garlanded the linden trees, the empty benches seemed to fade into the gravel on which they stood. "Several times a year when I'm depressed I go to the country in the south with the Gypsies," the doctor said; "everything is let loose, it's like the Ivan chapter in the *Brothers Karamazov*, we sing and drink all night, sometimes so much that I remember nothing, but in the morning I am quite like new, reborn. . . ."

"I used to be able to do that too," Sophie said, "but no more, no more. . . ." And then she startled at the sound of footsteps in the gravel a few alleys behind her. She imagined the guide of the tourist group she and Claire and Edmund were traveling with, turned back expecting to see his stocky frame, the boreal eyes blazing behind thick spectacles; it was only an aging dog shuffling across the park. "You are so naive, so sheltered," the doctor laughed; "if you want to avoid them you must never look back! When you go out of the

Union as I sometimes do you're followed by two men, one from your own country and one from the country you're visiting, you call them . . . goons, right? I have two goons when I travel, two *doppelgängers*; it is amusing to have them meet, to set them off against each other and then reconcile them; actually they're very lonely people, they know how hated they are by everyone, sometimes I feel sorry for them. . . . Perhaps we should liberate the goons; you would say goon lib, right? But perhaps you've already had too much liberation in your country; I think everything is so permitted there that nothing is erotic anymore, isn't that true? Here we're so puritanical that men and women are forbidden to be in a hotel room together after eleven at night unless they're married, so we take many trains, much is forbidden so all is very passionate. . . ."

"We are very puritanical," he repeated flirtatiously as they continued to walk. "We have many boundaries, limitations. Trains . . . When we're very serious we take the Trans-Siberian. When all is permitted nothing is desirable; it must be very sad in your country. . . ." The fog lifted, the Neva River glimmered from under the tall oaks bordering Decembrists' Square. He went on for many hours talking about himself, like most men she'd ever desired. His therapies, his translations, his periods of censorship, his survival. Whether or not they became lovers for one night is irrelevant. "I had an extraordinary evening," Sophie reported to Claire and Edmund at breakfast. "I had a long talk with a Soviet man who goes to the Baltic States when he's in a really acute depression, Latvia, Estonia, can you imagine, those are their sanatoriums, their paradises!" "Fancy going to Riga for a breakdown!" Claire exclaimed. "I'd rather be in Moscow for mine," Sophie said. "Come my loves it's time for our morning swim."

June 1975, brilliant dawn sunlight, primeval mud of the river. Against the flank of the Fortress of Peter and Paul, once a prison for dissenters against the Russian czars, there stretches an expanse of sand which now serves as bathing beach for the population of Leningrad. The three tourists comment on the irony of the site, on the beauty of the view it offers. Above the flat indigo mirror of the Neva, Peter's city oscillates in a phantasm of

16

marble and of malachite, a prodigality of spires, turrets, coronets and eagles, of golden and enameled roofs shimmering like the variegated scales of a giant lizard. " 'It has been noted,' " Edmund reads from his guidebook as they sit beneath the fortress walls, " 'that no site in the world is less favorable to the founding of a metropolis than these 101 islands set into an impetuous river and constantly threatened with destruction by a glacial sea.' " "A despot's fantasy!" Sophie exclaims. She slips off her shoes, walks to the shallow water at the riverbank, slides her blouse over her head. Claire still lies in the shade of a tree, reading her guidebook. Edmund has thrown his clothes to the ground and stands in his bathing trunks by the riverbank, staring at the water. They are all three forty-five years old. Sophie's frame small and powerful, waist finely modeled, breasts with the ripe fullness of Titian's nudes. Claire's limbs spindly as those of a young deer's. Edmund's lithe tight body is that of a man who has a fastidious concern for aging.

Claire has turned around and stares upwards towards the fortress wall.

"Hurry up Clairsie you're the last one in as usual!"

"Thirty years of waiting for you, we're fed up!"

Edmund plunges into the river. Sophie wades in after him. Claire puts down her book and starts undressing after having picked up the contents of their satchels, which fell to the ground in a gust of wind. (In hers there is a small Victorian tortoiseshell comb mounted in silver, a biography of Mahatma Gandhi, a photograph of a long-haired teenager in a Radcliffe T-shirt; in Sophie's, a paperback entitled *Women and Sexism*, a variety of leaking ball-point pens which have colored a composition notebook various shades of mottled blue; Edmund's briefcase contains a 1915 edition of Baedeker's *Guide to Russia*, a Russian edition of the works of Pushkin.) Claire slowly slips off her jeans and wades into the river. "It's colder than the island in April!" she calls out. "Freezing," Sophie shouts, "strictly for polar bears!" She swims a vigorous backstroke, arms flailing, chanting, "I love summer, I love summer!" Claire (who has also been known from earliest childhood by the name of Pebble) keeps her arms folded over her breasts until she starts to swim. There is a rich smell of dead leaves underfoot, across the river the

Winter Palace gleams with its pale green hue of ice and verdure, death, rebirth. All is still gaiety this morning and reclaiming of childhood, all is still bathed in great playfulness. "Where is Edmund?" Sophie calls out when he has been out of sight for half a minute. "Where are you my pet?" An anguished cry here, a burst of laughter as he grabs her legs from under the water and emerges beside her to clutch her waist.

"Ah there he goes Hermes the teaser, always trying to catch us underfoot!"

"Welcome to St. Petersburg my loves!"

Sophie kisses Edmund's forehead and swims a languorous sidestroke towards Claire, her curls glinting copper in the sun.

"Best come out soon or you'll get chilled the way you used to Peb . . ."

"Like that time we first went swimming together off the sailboat . . ."

Claire: "Were we fourteen?"

Edmund: "No, no, fifteen, it was 1945!"

Sophie: "Eddem's right, forty-five."

"We used to talk a lot about reincarnation."

"Peb wished to be Saint Francis."

"Soph wanted to be Rosa Luxemburg."

"And Edmund wanted to be reborn as a work of art."

" 'Once out of nature I can never take . . . ' "

" 'Shall never take,' Sophie darling, you've gotten that line wrong since we were fifteen."

ii

Cribs, collies, playpens, golf bags, campers' tents, riding gear and even ponies, clamming equipment, picnic hampers, movie screens, radios, sand pails, bags of diapers, barbecue grills—the Nantucket ferry came in twice a day from the Massachusetts mainland redolent with tribal plenitude; its sleek-limbed families tended to be large, the one-child family was rare, the childless and the single seemed almost barred from the vessel. And at least once a day Edmund persuaded his mother to walk to the ferry to watch it disgorge its exotic cargo of American summer. Edmund and Mara were already at the landing when the ship's last horn shouted out towards the island, sounding as if the whole world had put its mouth to a whistle, staring at the vessel as if it were a foreign nation unto itself. They played a game, the kind of game often invented by two persons who share a solitude: Arguing in three languages as they observed the emerging crowds, they chose *la famille la plus magnifique* to emerge from the ferry, the one with the most children, the longest blond hair, the handsomest dogs, the tallest father, the most gleaming braces on its young ones' teeth, the largest barbecue equipment, the fullest station wagon.

They walk towards the ferry every day down hollyhocked lanes, down lustrous streets whose cobblestones impose upon traffic the stately gait of an early age, past flower vendors displaying in horse-drawn carts the splendor of red zinnias and purple gladioli.

The mother is tiny, birdlike in figure, the top of her head barely reaching her son's ears. Melancholy eyes of a Byzantine icon looming over chiseled cheekbones, black hair severely parted in the middle and carefully braided, tresses winding like a small jet crown about her exquisite pale face; and always an ornament in that hair, a feather, a tortoiseshell.

He has just turned fifteen; has cornflower blue eyes framed by very long dark lashes; wears a gray flannel vest under his blue blazer, a silk ascot about his throat; is fond of his first pair of sunglasses, which he practices putting on and off with a debonair gesture. His thick dark blond hair is worn quite long for that decade, resembling photographs of certain nineteenth-century Romantic poets.

He reads to her from a guidebook as they walk:

"*Ecoute*, listen! 'In the early nineteenth century the men of Nantucket stayed away for years on their whaling ships, hardship came frequently to these heroes of the high seas who often had to resort to cannibalism when their stores of food ran out . . . "Thar she blows, thar she blows," this was the eagerly awaited cry of the lookout, the harpooner threw his instrument with all his strength deep into the back of the huge beast . . .' "

He's stopped walking and tilts back, lifting his arm like a harpooner.

" '. . . the boat drawn by the whale bounced about in a shower of spray, the treacherous journey often lasted for many hours as the gigantic mammal swam miles across the sea, sometimes the whale attacked the boat instead of diving, it could smash the vessel with one blow of its tail or try to grab it in its enormous mouth. . . .' "

Edmund closes the book, breathes deeply, runs for a hundred yards down the street and rushes back towards his mother, waving

20

his arms with well-being. "Freedom!" he shouts in all his languages. "*Liberté! Svoboda!*"

". . . so here we were, Claire, two penniless European refugees whose only previous respite from August heat had been to spend a week in a modest inland boardinghouse run by childless Russian immigrants. Nothing much in store there for me. My mother enjoyed the proximity of an Orthodox church, and of some damp woods in which we held interminable discussions about which mushrooms were safe, how much roulette to play with this delectably free food. I can't say I wasn't surrounded by affection; the spectacle of a woman who's struggled alone to bring up a child is touching to anyone but a monster . . . a former colonel of the czar's artillery gave me tennis lessons, Moscow gentry eking out their living catering piroshki tutored me in Russian poetry in return for my painting their portraits. And the rest of the time I drew everything in sight while they gambled at their perennial game of gin rummy, which began at nine in the morning and often went to midnight. . . . Great bursts of extravagance of course, as soon as anyone sold a memoir about his days in the Cadet Corps or pawned off a family diamond there was a big party for the entire Russian community of Bridgeport, impecunious balalaika singers doubling in as waiters shuffled about very drunk, flies unzipped, as they passed the vodka. I used to think that Providence drove me towards you due to my severe case of asthma. But the fits of coughing and sneezing which seized me when I was fourteen were probably a rebellion against the fact that my only summer companions had been these dotty experts on Pushkin and Glazunov—off to the ocean the doctor told Mara unless you want your son to end up like Marcel Proust—so money was somehow found to get us a vacation on the island, ah yes she'd won hundreds of dollars at gin that spring, that was it. . . . Here it is 1975 and I can remember it as if it were yesterday, walking down Nantucket's streets towards your house in a trance, staring at all that tribal gaiety, the long-haired children swinging from oak trees, the beautiful children chasing each other down the rose-filled lanes, the shouting tribes of young running out of tennis clubs flailing their rackets, their puppy-warm shoving, whispering, sharing of edibles—childhood is a prerogative of the rich my dear; there was something both exciting and forbidden about entering your life, some kind of treason to the frugality of immigrant life. . . .

"No no Peb it wasn't guilt, it was . . . the sheer excitement of the previously denied. The few friends I'd made in school were freaks such as myself, little middle European émigrés gifted at the harp or the cello, and here we were, my God, going to lunch for the first time with what Mara had described as 'une des familles les plus magnifiques en Amerique.' I guess you and Soph had just enrolled the previous winter at her ballet school and that's how our mothers met; why didn't you phone them even earlier, I asked, we've already been on the island for a week—one must be proud in this world, she answered, one must never let the rich think one needs them; I pondered that one a long time, it may have led to many an ornery mask I chose for myself—I'll never forget the quick sly smile she gave me as she said that, and then her query as to whether I'd remembered my watercolors, a miniature set she'd given me for Christmas which could fit in my pocket, oh she'd rather starve on black bread than buy me anything but New York's most elegant watercolor set. . . ."

"That's the way I remember my first glimpse of you, brush in hand . . ."

"And I remember that just before we reached your house the ferry's horn rent the air and we ran towards it to engage in the most central ritual of our week-old island life; we ran to stare at the ship unloading its riches as if they were nourishment for our starved eyes. . . . I guess what struck us as most exotic on that ship was an entity so foreign to our own lives, the father, the American dad expostulating and supervising and explaining seabirds to his sons and reprimanding the little ones about toilet performance and overlooking the safety of every item in his bursting-with-goodness station wagon—here was Mara, orphaned when she was still young and widowed before I was ever born, and here I was the precocious monster who'd immunized himself against the possibility that there might be any better life on earth than the seclusion he'd shared

22

with his mother since birth . . . so when I met you that first day I was totally awed by the mysteries of family life, like an explorer coming to some new continent whose rites of bonding are radically different from those of his own. . . ."

"I remember how beautiful you were, and how terrified."

The ferry has spewed out its humanity, the families are driving their hoards towards the island's heart. With a sigh Mara glances at a piece of paper in her purse. Edmund puts on his dark glasses. And they walk towards a seaside street a few blocks west of the ferry landing.

"Attention at lunch today," Mara says, "you must admire this island with passion; in this country you must always admire and they have curious polite way of thanking you for admiring."

"What splendid cobblestones, what a chic horse, what a heavenly church."

"Not so sardonic please."

"What a chic church, what a heavenly horse."

"*Tishe*, quiet," she snaps in Russian. "You have great trend to irony. . . . I repeat, don't forget that proper Americans have exquisite manners. . . . I admired Fifth Avenue bus once near ballet school and Mrs. Sanford said thank you, thank you."

The Sanford house comes into sight a few hundred yards later, as hulking as the ferry that loaded nearby, equally celebrant of a confidence in childhood and in summer. Edmund stares with grave curiosity at heaps of croquet mallets lying on the lawn, bicycles of many sizes lined up against the garage wall, swings and hammocks strung from several trees, the two-foot-high cast-iron blackamoor holding out its hand for an imaginary horse.

"I protested that I have another lunch appointment," Mara says as they approach the door, "so you can meet this wonderful family alone."

"But . . ."

She blows him a kiss and disappears as swiftly as a swallow.

He stands at the front door taken aback, feigning to inspect an enormous sign in the shape of a ship's prow that wears the residence's name: SEALARK. A smiling black woman in white uniform opens the door and invites him in, church service has gone late, the Sanfords have phoned from the Yacht Club to say that they'll be a little delayed. Nantucket's bells are tolling twelve, the sunny living-room declares its owners' great enthusiasm for the animal world. Many beasts prance across its chintz curtains and slipcovers, its ashtrays and china cups strive to imitate the shapes of frogs and various forms of birdlife, a wooden merry-go-round horse serves as portmanteau for dozens of Windbreakers. Edmund walks out onto the terrace, admiring its vast view of Nantucket Sound, sinks into a chaise longue at the water's edge.

Island's church spires melting and shimmering in the noon haze like palm trees in a desert mirage, boats of all sizes and shapes pro-liferating like fireflies on the sunny water, rataplan of tennis balls, shouting of children, flap of furling sails from neighboring houses. Two retrievers run onto the terrace and start licking the span of skin between Edmund's socks and the bottom of his flannel trous-ers. He might have dressed too formally; he hurriedly unfastens the buttons of his vest; if he ever becomes rich he can wear tennis shorts to Sunday lunch. Smaller vessels bobbing like petals on the glass of the harbor, grandiose black schooner sweeping into view labeled in gold letters, *The Churchill.* Taking out his drawing pad, water from the sound, delectable sweeping of colors on thick grainy paper, melon hue over the space intended for the harbor, think of Turner's landscapes, of their melding earth sky water into one aq-ueous reality, a passage of brackish green and then of blue and brown for the shallow dun-hued water suckling at the Sanfords' landing. A sharp arch of black for the curve of the schooner gliding towards the lighthouse, struggle to suggest the harbor's activity without lapsing into literalness, each boat must fuse into the sea the way a rock melts into its forest quarry. . . . Leaning down to the terrace's edge to clean his brushes Edmund hears a rustling sound at his side. Two young girls of his age stand by the side of his chaise longue, each extremely beautiful in her own way.

From the perfect oval face, over the aquiline nose and the finely modeled, arrogant mouth, very pale eyes stare at him with a grave inscrutable gaze. Claire Sanford has already been described to him

24

by his mother—without Edmund knowing precisely what Mara meant—as "a great Puritan beauty." Her long brown hair is hugged to her head as tightly as a seal's from the perspiration of running. Her breasts barely bud under a tight little white sports shirt. And she clutches to her chest a terrified young white rabbit, with eyes the hue of crushed raspberries, whose paw is bandaged onto a wooden splint.

The other girl, full-breasted, luminous gold-speckled eyes, a curly mop of tawny hair, a powerful nose, stares with great curiosity at Edmund's drawing.

"I'm Claire Sanford," the thinner one says. "I'm Sophie Ross," says the other.

Both have extended their hands. And Edmund, startled, throws his watercolor into his lap and reaches out a hand to each of them.

"You're painting our view!" Claire exclaims.

"Do you feel any affinity to Manet?" the full-breasted one asks.

"No, more to Monet actually."

"Oh but you don't have an accent," Claire says with a pout, as if deprived of a promise. "Meet Mr. McKenzie," she says as she thrusts the rabbit's good paw towards Edmund. "He broke his leg and I put it into a splint." A curiously breathless way of speaking, fast clarion spurts.

"He's so beautiful!" Edmund cannot get his voice above a whisper as he caresses the animal.

"Thank you! You can stroke his head, too."

When shall we lose our nervousness, our habits of solitude? Edmund remains lounging in his chair, rhythmically stroking the trembling animal whose ears are glued to its head in terror at the sound of the crowd that's begun to stream into the house; oh I'm as terrified as you are Mr. McKenzie. The tribe running in from the outdoors seems to range from adolescence to late middle age, they doff their Windbreakers onto the rocking horse, help themselves to cooling drinks, swarm about with the ease of persons who have known a house since early childhood. Repeated voicings of the words "Plinker and Babsie, Plinker and Babsie"; these must be the

25

familiar names reserved for his older hosts, Claire's parents. Manners returned by the familiar sight of elders, Edmund finally springs to his feet to greet them.

"Welcome aboard!" Paul Sanford exclaims. He is a tall tanned man with burgundy pants and heavy spectacles.

"So nice so nice to have you with us!" The slight blond woman holds out both hands to Edmund. "How heavenly to have you with us!"

Even on that seaside day she stands on very high-heeled shoes which give her a frail, tottering walk. A large sun hat shelters her pale hair, her kind, drawn face. And then behind her that chattering bevy of cousins, nephews, uncles, nieces whom Edmund studies with the same curiosity he bestows upon the magnificent families who emerge from the ferry's innards. Phrases of American politeness still foreign to his ears, warm compliments on his English, his blazer and his watercolor of the harbor, what does he think of Renoir, of this first trip to Nantucket? The elders' curiously swift intimacy.

"When I was ten my father took a splendid house near your birthplace, overlooking the Rhine," he hears Mr. Sanford say. "We were four boys in the family, we had more fun that summer than any other summer I can remember."

"Do please tell your dear mother how thrilled we are with Mr. Fokine's Ballet School, and how beautifully she plays the piano there."

"My oldest brother was six foot five," Mr. Sanford adds as he hands Edmund a glass of lemonade, "he was captain of the St. Paul's hockey team, he went on to Yale and made Skull and Bones. . . ."

"Claire's older brother," Mrs. Sanford interjects, "who died three years ago, was also a promising athlete at St. Paul's . . ."

"This island is a knockout remedy for the glums," Paul Sanford cuts in, changing his spectacles; "happiness can become a way of life, young man, it must if we're to survive!" "How is your dear mother, how sad that she had another luncheon appointment." "She's frightfully busy, as always." "How attractive! What a great beauty she is!" "Thank you!" The martini in her thin-stemmed glass, the trembling of her frail hand, the ringing of a lunch gong.

"Bless us O Lord in Thy ever increasing Mercy," Plinker's voice booms over the bowed heads. "Make us plentiful in grace and strength bless those of our leaders who've helped to spread justice and peace unto the world General Eisenhower General MacArthur our great allies Winston Churchill Field Marshal Montgomery increase our fruitfulness and bring our enemies to the side of justice in order that they may enjoy the fruits of Thy bounty . . ."
Everyone: "Amen."
"How many languages do you speak?" Sophie ventures in the flurry of after grace. "Four." "Let me guess, French, German, English et quoi d'autre?" "Russian." "Oh my you could have interpreted at the League of Nations!" Sophie, Claire, Edmund and Cousin Jeff have a bridge table by the bay window to themselves. This fourth young person seated with them raises his head from a studious dissection of his chicken and stares at Edmund with particular amiability. Jeff Howell is many inches taller than the other three occupants of the table and Edmund surmises he might be seventeen years old. Crew-cut light brown hair, affable chestnut eyes, coach's whistle hanging from a string about his neck, T-shirt announcing that he attends Mr. Sanford's old school, St. Paul's. Edmund is particularly fascinated by the solidity of his neighbor's feet; as he tries to bring forth his best conversation and confines his considerable nervousness to the restless twitching of his own legs under the table he's aware of the unchanging angle of Jeff's large impeccable white sneakers, as triumphantly still as the Chippendale breakfront covering half of the dining-room wall. The revelation that Jeff is in some way related to Claire—he was orphaned at fourteen, Plinker is one of his two legal guardians—affects Edmund deeply. How privileged to be an intimate of this quicksilver creature who emanates such mystery and distance, who seems to draw a circle about herself to break the spell of her own remarkable beauty!

27

"So, how was church?" Sophie is the one who always seems the first to speak. "Impeccable I hope?" "Quite lovely really," Jeff says. "And you don't go?" Edmund asks Sophie. "I'm not Christian," she says with ease. "It's a terribly pretty building," Edmund offers. "I belong there," Claire says, eyes still cast down on the rabbit hovering on her lap. Jeff throws a wary smile at Edmund. "I saw your eyes, Jeffrey Howell," Claire cries out angrily. "When did you leave Germany?" Sophie asks Edmund in the suave adult tone of one who knows when to change the subject. "Oh the Nazis cleared us out in 1937, then we went to Paris and they chased us out of there in 1940 towards Portugal . . ."

For a time all three give their attention quite single-heartedly to Edmund. Had he been in the Blitz? No Pebble, Jeff corrects, that was Great Britain, he came from Germany and France. What town did Edmund live in in Germany before he went to Paris? Munich? Ah, the Munich Pinakothek! Sophie exclaims. Sophie's hair is like that of a marvelous feline, a lioness or tigress, its curls winding in soft tendrils about her neck. "What did your father do?" she asks Edmund. "I'm not quite sure, perhaps I didn't have one." "How exotic!" Sophie says in a throaty whisper. The other two stop eating, stare hard while he quickly asks Sophie, "What does *your* father do?" "He works with talent, he's an agent for all kinds of artists. . . ." Edmund is attacking his chicken, not visibly impressed, so she shakes her curls and adds, "I mean he's an agent for singers, dancers, playwrights, violinists, all kinds of fascinating people, oh he so loves art! . . ." Sophie speaks in a hushed, modulated, almost conspiratorial voice, she eats avidly, pausing every few minutes to scrutinize the room, whispering precious shreds of information into Edmund's ear when Claire and Jeffrey engage in one of their frequent disputes. Claire's a fabulous pianist and she's never lost a tennis match . . . Claire's refused to eat meat since the age of eight . . . Claire's her best friend in the world and she, Sophie, is not only Claire's best but her *only* friend, Claire's funny that way, very solitary. . . .

Claire wears a pale blue satin ribbon in her hair. She stopped eating early in the meal, having picked at a few mouthfuls of vegetables. Is Edmund more fascinated by her beauty or by the plenitude of her world? "At Christmas I shall visit *cousins*," she spouts upon a discussion of the school holidays, "I have cousins in Detroit, Milwaukee, San Francisco, Dallas, Philadelphia, Wilmington, Baltimore . . ." "*Ma fleur*," Sophie interjects, "You may even have cousins in Peru!" "Why, dear heart," Claire whispers, mimicking Sophie's throaty voice, "I bet I even have some in Madagascar!" She turns to Edmund and he will always recall this as the moment he first fell in love with her: the way she said "Madagascar," the little teeth as white as the first crocus and as delicate as a rodent's flashing under the glory of the beribboned chestnut hair. "Have you, Edmund, ever been to Madagascar?" she asks, staring at him with those glacial periwinkle eyes many hues paler than his. "I keep meticulously away," he answers, "from all islands which begin with the letter *M*."

The girls' laughter resounding in the room, Jeff smiling widely too. Sophie: "You speak English so beautifully, Edmund, you have only the very lightest of European intonations." Claire: "I take advanced French at Spence, and Sophie's in intermediate." Sophie: "And when we go away to Ethel Walker's next year I'll *join* you in advanced. Claire's Mademoiselle only left her last year, Edmund." Jeff: "Pebble, I remember you also had a German nurse when you were a little kid, she made the niftiest Christmas cookies." Edmund: "So you've known each other all that long!" Pebble: "Since we were born, literally." Jeff: "Not precisely that long, silly, I'm three years older than you are. . . ."

Clamor of ice in fine-stemmed glasses, a dream of crystal, whispering aprons of maids offering lemon sherbet, many voices clang over the fragile china, Babsie and Plinker, Babsie and Plinker. In the dining room's sea-struck light the adults' sunned faces are as florid as bloodstains in the snow, there are bright little yachting flags in the lapels of their jackets and shirtwaists. "Uncle Plinker are you thinking of coming to join us in Hobe Sound next Christmas with Uncle Charlie? . . ." "No sweets, actually we're thinking of going to the Bahamas now that the war is over and we can travel more freely. . . ." All this Edmund hears, observes, particularly Paul Sanford's voice booming over their heads as he

29

organizes the pleasures of the summer's last weeks, American dad supervising reprimanding counseling, is April's morning sickness better today, a little brandy after lunch could do the trick. . . . Masticate, chump, swallow he urges a four-year-old nephew seated on his lap, eat your vegerino, duck. . . . And that gastric upset of Douglas's, bicarbonate of soda, sporto, the old remedies are the only humdingers, always a stubborn streak in you Doug just like Pebble; it's been some years since Pebble has listened to advice about *anything* in life. . . .

     "I guess the next thing that amazed me that day is the sight of your bedroom, Peb, that stark little bedroom devoid of the frills and flounces of girlhood, denuded of any traditional belongings save for your Books of Common Prayer, your crucifix and that hospice for stray animals you'd built up there . . . every week you managed to imprison a sea gull, some field mice or chipmunk, pleading broken wings or ulcered tails; the room was filled with the sad pink eyes of rabbits gazing out from behind cages, the voices of possibly healthy sea gulls screaming for their liberty. . . . 'You're much better now my sweet' you said to one of your birds and then you screamed back at it in such perfect mimicry of its voice and were so pleased with the fits of laughter that besieged us that you went on to imitate the mouse's, the chipmunk's squeal with equal virtuosity. . . . Olaf your retriever was there, panting excitedly on his mattress, and I asked you whether you were going to be a veterinary and you said oh mercy no a pianist or perhaps a missionary, and Sophie raised her eyes to the sky with an exasperated air and Jeff blew his whistle and said let's get some exercise, Soph be a peach get the basketball give it your . . ."

"Your one oh oh."

"Yes, and Plinker was standing on the lawn among all the cousins, April and Doug and Katrinka, April with her glossy pageboy and mean little overbite and her Long Island way of saying 'That would be so nifty, dearie. . . .' Plinker organizing a clambake for the following day and a picnic sail to Siasconset for the day after, I'll get the big boat ready early in the morning so we can catch the breezerino at low tide; and before I knew it I was on a sailboat for the first time in my life, both Sophie and I, city folk not made for all this smart WASP stuff getting wretchedly seasick in the rising wind. . . ."

In the next weeks, the next years, Edmund would witness the lengthy preparations of Babsie Sanford's empty busy days, the strained, tinkling sound of her laughter as she passed coffee at Sunday lunch, bracing herself for her solitary weekly visit to the Nantucket cemetery. Not allowed to mourn in her own house, forbidden to mention the name of that child who had drowned before the family's eyes in a sailing accident, she would spend many hours of the week preparing a bouquet for her son's grave and spend the afternoon there quite alone, unseen, unheard. The rest of the week Edmund observed her tottering about the business of Sealark in those high-heeled shoes which shackled her movements like little chains, protecting herself from the sun with a multitude of veilings and wide-brimmed hats. Edmund often accompanied her to the Main Street Market early in the morning, when the flower vendors' stalls opened, to find just the proper hue of amethyst and violet gladioli to mix for her Sunday bouquet. Then she returned to the beloved vegetable garden which Plinker seeded every spring to pick herbs and greens before the sun could reach them and wandered sweetly through the house, singing the Anglican hymns she'd learned from her father, a bishop of Boston, making still more flower arrangements for every one of the child-filled, guest-filled rooms, myosotis plumaria delphinium columbine. She was frail and protected like an idol, she painted her sadly smiling mouth a deep shade of ruby red, occasionally she sat on the beach in a large straw hat watching her adopted flock gambol, her hand resting on her husband's shoulder as he accompanied her to the ocean's edge, and that was the way she spent her summers save for those days when she fell into the cyclic depressions she had suffered since the death of her older child.

Babsie Sanford, in the early moments of her seizures, sits on the floor of the sunny living-room trying on a variety of hats and costumes, becoming a heroine of one of the many novels she and Plinker had read aloud to each other when they were first married, when

Plinker was a junior partner in his Wall Street firm and their children were small and perfect; she becomes Catherine mourning Heathcliff, Dorothea chiding the chilling Casaubon. Then she would rise to dance alone in the center of the room, singing her hymns in a high childlike drone, stockings torn, hats askew, her seizures came suddenly. "Would you just go away if you were I, dear Edmund?" she had said one morning as he helped her to carry an armful of vegetables and flowers from her garden. "Would you be able to just trust yourself to the Holy Spirit and *leave* all this happiness?" Within the next half hour Edmund found her seated on the floor of the living room in an ancient ball gown, took her to her room before phoning the Yacht Club to get Plinker home immediately. She was not violent. One called a doctor and kept her under sedation for three days. Everyone in that house was gentle, Edmund soon realized, save possibly Pebble.

Claire at the piano practicing a difficult Mozart sonata as Sophie and Edmund turn the pages. Upon faulting on two successive chords she slams her elbows and forearms violently upon the surface of the keyboard, shouting imprecations, creating cacophonies that make all her animals startle in fright. Many months occur between such outbursts, when her glacially exquisite composure dissolves to reveal a shouting demon whom no parent and few friends can calm. It's as if the Mademoiselles and Fräuleins who'd educated Claire Sanford, striving to fashion the most perfect lady of their careers, had left untouched some unruly darkness that was beyond anyone's control. After an initial temper, or sensing the first symptoms of one, she'd often run into the dunes, the beaches of the island and stay there alone for many hours. Edmund once found her on such an occasion, seated cross-legged like a Buddha on a distant beach, nose to the wind, eyes opening once an hour or so as in a trance. He'd sat in the grass and stared at her, wondering what it would be like to suddenly purge oneself of all anger and rage as she seemed to do in such moments. He asked her later whether she'd been praying; she'd answered it was "more than that," she loved church but the old Anglican prayers didn't satisfy her, after each fit of anger she wished for "a complete and total purgation of myself," she could not further define the nature of what she sought—that particular evening she'd come home with effusive apologies to her father, as she always did after a disappearance, throwing her arms about Plinker and offering a large basket of wild berries she'd picked for him on the moors of Siasconset.

Edmund, Sophie and Claire race up a long dune at sunset. On the beach below Plinker has built a bonfire for his Sunday picnic. At the age of seventeen Edmund will be five foot ten or so, with a nascence of ruddy hair on his slender muscled chest. He strives to win the race after giving his two friends a handicap and struggles mightily up the slope, feet slowed by the deep sand. His hair is the hue of a young lion's mane, there's determination on his face and an ironic smile. Sophie trails Edmund and Claire, laughing and lagging considerably behind. She is sturdy and sleek-limbed, all in her is opulence and delectation of ripeness, her ringlets of hair are hardened by sun and salt to a metallic glint. "You stinkers you're cheating Edmund don't let me down!" Claire is almost up to Edmund, her long chestnut hair waving about like a curtain of silk, as he arrives at the crest of the dune Edmund gives his hand to Sophie while stretching out his left foot to trip Claire; all three fall into the thick dune sand, laughing and pummeling each others' bodies, feasting on the remains of each other's childhood. This could have occurred in the summers of 1946, '47, '48. The island of their happiness stretches at their feet, wealthy and gorse-covered, splayed with the spikes of many churches and hot stretches of wild roses in full bloom. At six o'clock on Sunday evenings Nantucket's oldest church bells play church hymns. " 'Amazing Grace, how sweet thy sound,' " Claire sings in a high clear tone over the shouting of Sophie's and Edmund's voices. And Jeff's, Plinker's voices answer her from the group gathered on the beach below: " 'I once was lost but now am found . . .' "

Edmund becomes good enough to play tennis in club doubles but can never quite manage to beat Pebble. Whenever he leads her three-two in singles her stubborn little chin protrudes in even more determined manner, she returns his strongest serves with a top-spin backhand that sends him flying to the corner of the court, managing a weak dribble which she smashes with such force that the ball bounces three feet over his head, irretrievable. "You never double-fault, do you Pebble?" he mutters as they pass each other at the net. "You never double *falt*," she mimics his trace of foreignness as she runs past him; "why rabbit love I haven't double-faulted since I was six years old." And the phrase charms him as much as her way of saying Madagascar. The few times he's led her four-two she's become all the more tough and ethereal, all the more imbued with those qualities that addict him to her. She goes on to lob to Edmund's backhand, she covers the whole court with a few paces of her coltish legs, she recoups to four-up. She aces him three serves and leads him five-four and breaks his service handily in the last game of the match. . . . But no victory is essential, for Plinker and Babsie waft Edmund in their kindness, Plinker and Babsie have made a vocation of this spot of earth and seem to rule over the very island air which has returned to Edmund the art of breathing.

"I always wondered why they adopted me with such fervor, Peb . . ."

"We were traditionalists, E.R., you were our perfume of Europe, our scent of a still more ancient order. . . ."

"Oh I must have been like one of those exotic animals fed dainties by a monarch, a court jester of sorts with my watercolors and my Voltaire quotes. . . . After all seriousness was suspect at Sealark wasn't it, happiness wasn't a choice but a civility, a distillation of good manners. . . ."

"They force-fed it to me until I almost died of it, Eddem; it was the principal excellence of character they sought."

Throughout his wretched winters Edmund looks forward to the voice of Paul Lincoln Sanford III (vice-president, Clark Dodge and Co., member of the Stock Exchange, chairman of the board of trustees of St. Paul's School, vice-chairman, National Multiple Sclerosis Society, member Knickerbocker Club, Dartmouth Club, Metropolitan Club) booming out grace over the beginning of Sunday lunch.

Almighty Father grace our house as we've honored

34

Thee in Thy tabernacle bless our land with honorable industry sound learning and pure manners save us from violence discord and every other evil way . . .

Bless our summer's work most Merciful Lord and grant us seasonable weather that we may gather in the leisure of our land we humbly beseech Thee to behold visit and relieve Thy sick servant Elizabeth Sanford for whom Thy prayers are desired . . .

Heavenly Father preserve the integrity of Thy chosen land stretch forth Thy almighty arm we pray Thee to strengthen and protect the servants of our government particularly Thy servant Thomas Dewey give him courage and strength in the toil ahead . . .

(At times Plinker asks Jeff to say grace; Jeff is awfully good at grace because as the family says he's "a born educator.")

Almighty and most Merciful God we pray that Thou govern and guide the minds of Thy servants the teachers of this nation bless all those who teach and those who learn and grant that in humility of heart . . .

iii

AGED twelve and fairly short of stature for his age, Edmund decided to play an active role in improving his mother's disastrous finances. He placed the following notice on the parents' bulletin board of the Horace Mann School, where he'd earned a scholarship upon his arrival to the United States:

> Young émigré from war-torn Europe will give private lessons in French, Russian, German at modest charge of one dollar an hour. Phone on weekend nights—555-5942

Still barely five foot two, he dressed in as mature a way as possible and deepened his voice to conceal his youth, not minding if he was thought to be a trifle dwarfed. He prepared his sternest expression as he stood briefcase in hand at his client's door, and would be most severe about students mastering rules of grammar before approaching the art of conversation. ("Being a traditionalist I believe in structure before emotion Mrs. deKay. Say after me, please, *le bras, la tête* . . .") He departed after assigning a formidable load of homework and was extremely stern with students towering a head above him who did not finish their assignments. In Edmund's last three years of high school Sophie Ross's mother, an aggressively warm, bountifully painted woman who proved to be one of his most industrious pupils, decided to take German lessons to aid the Richters' calamitous finances. ("By next Sunday Mrs. Ross I want you to memorize the past, present and future tenses of the verb *töten*, to kill.") Babsie Sanford engaged in Russian lessons for the same philanthropic reasons, a project rendered difficult by her incapacity to follow any consecutive stream of thought. "I forget my name in Russian, dear?" "Elizabeta Ivanovna." "How attractive!" "I've stressed that we mustn't speak any English at these sessions; I've taught you that 'how attractive' in Russian is 'kak ha-ra-scho'; repeat after me, please. . . ." "Cake horror-show." "No, no, Elizabeta Ivanovna, repeat again, please. . . ."

"My childhood? Oh I survived as best I could," Edmund would say in his early twenties, "seeing I was the only son of a possessive, single, extravagant woman. . . ."

"The only son of a Slav of exuberant emotions . . ."

"Oh don't tell me about the Russians," he'd shout out years later when he could bear to remember, "their primal fecklessness, their hunger for extremes; I know more about Russians than anyone else west of the Dnieper, that omnivorous spirituality that's like a case of constant drunkenness . . . their extravagance . . . their extravagance! Let me tell you a story.

"It's one of my earliest memories of the United States. Good Friday of Holy Week. Easter sweets are brought us by two impoverished White Russian princes, friends of Mara's from Munich days, who attempt to support themselves in New York by catering Russian delicacies. Rain pouring. The princes are of indolent disposition and detest all modes of public transport. They've taken a cab from their flat in the East Twenties to ours in the West Nineties, and keep it waiting at the door while they chat with us over tea. Tea in our frugal household remains an elaborate Russian ritual, served in tall glasses, accompanied by blackberry jam and nostalgic talk of how much more flavorful it was brewed in samovars abandoned three decades ago in St. Petersburg. . . . The raisin-studded dome of the golden koulitch and the pearly pyramid of pascha are duly admired, memories are recalled of Chaliapin's last performance of *Boris*; after an hour or so Mara delicately hands our friends a sum of eight dollars. I go out to accompany them to their cab and observe that its meter registers the sum of thirteen fifty; the princes are many dollars poorer than they'd been before they started making the cakes and yet they appear delighted—deeply moved, in fact—by the afternoon's transaction and the visit that attends it . . . this event was repeated every Good Friday in equally whimsical fiduciary style. A parable, perhaps, for the mayhem of penury which my mother also imposed upon our own lives. . . ."

"I love that story Eddem, I don't think I've ever heard it before."

"There are things it helps to only remember later. . . . I'll tell you another one Sofinka. Well you know what a modest living Mara eked out pounding out Ponchielli for you and Peb to do your arabesques to, a pittance really . . . nevertheless our average nightly schedule went something like this: the Shakespeare Repertory Company on Tuesday, the Philadelphia Orchestra's all-Handel program Thursday, Gieseking at Carnegie Hall on Friday, an obligatory opera on Saturday . . . to hell with such fleshly amenities as nourishment, dental checkups, warm clothing, all of that recedes before the meticulous nurturing of aesthetic sensibility; let's limit ourselves to meat on Saturdays and fast on buttermilk all other nights, let creditors keep knocking at the door, *les gens bien* must be capable of humming most major symphonic tunes, spouting poetry in at least three languages, discussing all aspects of theatrical repertory . . ."

"Poor angel, now I understand why you've had such problems with your teeth; you should still watch them, you know."

"Listen here it is 1975 Sofka and I remember as if it were yesterday that musical voice of hers pleading with our landlord, '*s'il vous plaît* Mr. O'Malley a single woman with a child one more week until check comes in . . .' but even at the age of eleven I was a more effective cajoler than she was, having been steeled since early childhood to protect my frail little mother from prehensile hostelers in Munich, Paris, Lisbon . . . 'For shame for shame Mr. O'Malley,' I'd shout, 'expel two orphans and you call yourself a Christian? . . .' yet even such an ultimatum wouldn't deter us from continuing our feast of spectacles, standing in the middle of our filthy little rooms hastily nibbling on a piece of black bread to make the eight-thirty curtain at Carnegie Hall, Town Hall, the Philharmonic . . . you know, Soph, long before I even met the Sanfords there was one ritual I missed in my life more than any other, the sight of a family seated in a proper dining room. How I gloated over the most conventional images of American family life—Thanksgiving covers of *The Saturday Evening Post*, Christmas spreads in *Woman's Home Companion*, ads for silver in *Life* mag . . . Ah for the gleam of a decently roasted chicken, for two forks laid at the ends of a table, for any ritual of stability in the New World . . . Instead of which constant threats of eviction or all heat turned off when the rent went unpaid and we'd resort to the princes' living room, 'Ai ai Alexander Maximovich can you put us up for just a few nights until I receive check from Monsieur Fokine may God ever bless your kindness Alyosha . . .' no penury could deter her from continuing her Sunday-afternoon gambling parties, to which she invited every seedy émigré she knew who could be in some way useful in perfecting my education . . . you saw them there yourself during your occasional visits to our blini parlor, the creeps who'd hovered over Mara ever since we got off the cattle boat, offering their devotion, their dandruff, their decorations from the Crimean War . . . and what did they get along with their flapjacks and their lecherous glances at my mother's beauty, caviar by the tubfuls, do you hear, Soph, the only protein I saw all week . . . let's not even speak of Easter and Christmas Eve, which brought a mayhem of increased rabble off the streets, for each one of whom Mara had bought a tiny present and wrapped it as intricately as a Fabergé egg; since they all brought friends and relatives I was constantly sent into the bathroom to relabel gifts received from guests a minute ago and redistribute them to unannounced visitors; all this made an impression, you see they must always impress, impress . . ."

"Unfair Eddem. Generosity reigns alongside excessiveness in the Slavic soul."

"Don't talk to *me* about Slavs, they've always a need for barbaric display to show off their status, their style . . . actually we might have survived frugally enough without those gambling parties, as if she had anything to gamble with!—on those days I'd escape to the Frick or the Met with my books and watercolors and gloat over the Vermeers and dream of that brilliant artist's career she'd designed for me; I'd stay there till closing time and even then when I came home there they still were screaming, 'Geen, geen,' gambling at preposterous sums like a dollar a point . . . there were those three nights we spent on a park bench to avoid our landlord because the few friends who could have put us up were off catering Stroganoff for some wedding in Bridgeport or playing the yearly chess match up the Hudson at the Tolstoi Foundation; after each of those nights we spent in the park I fainted punctually as I got to school, just before my nine o'clock Latin class, whether out of undernourishment or out of sheer protest I don't know . . . on those Central Park days I'd go to Fokine's from school and watch Mara play Mozart after her work hours, tears streaming down her face, whether out of rage for what was happening to us that week or nostalgia for the brilliant musical career she'd given up for me I'll never know either . . . then we'd spend our evenings at the Automat until the place closed down, oh how she reversed the habitual pattern of parents torturing their children! . . . 'This lack of anything I have to give you will kill me,' that was her tune, 'Ai ai *dousia* when will you ever forgive me for the little I've had to give you? . . .' Every half hour I'd go to the Automat machines and steal us more cups of tea to calm her; I'd found some metal plugs which handily substituted for nickels; God Soph don't talk to me about the Russians' primal attraction to suffering, their love for the fainting sensation of approaching the abyss, now do you understand my adulation for that Sealark tribe? One eternal picnic, childhood returned to me as a gift, the bliss of their repose!"

"Look at the color of the Neva, E.R. . . . ."

"Yes, superb, pure indigo with a trace of zinc white . . . anyhow something usually happened to rescue us just before a final disaster. Mr. Fokine advanced a month's salary or Mara's luck turned and she'd clean up a few hundred dollars at her Sunday gin game, or else we'd meet a protector at a social gathering held by some White Russian group we used to cultivate to get a free bowl of borscht—the Association of the Knights of Saint George, the Association of Russian Cadets Graduated Out of Russia, the Association of Russian Imperial Naval Officers in America, oh how she loved to see me shine at those affairs, you should have heard me! 'I agree with you Countess Schouvalov Tolstoi's treatment of your great-grandfather was not as favorable as some other historians'—'I do think Countess Potemkin that Rimski-Korsakov's importance has been overstressed at the expense of Borodin's. . . .' 'How enchanting your son is Maria Petrovna, what a success he'll be in life. . . .' Here I was, gorgeous little monster humming obscure Monteverdi airs, bowing to women's wrists, impeccably attired in flannel hand-me-downs from some recently deceased White Russian colonel, a perfectly normal quadrilingual child who'd acquired his own peculiar tactics of survival. . . ."

"Yes, all those lessons you had to go through dear heart, even when you were fifteen, we were so awed."

"The lessons! I suppose that's in part what she planned her Sunday largesse for, apart from her own passion for gambling. Barely a guest escaped from her tiny salon who couldn't offer me free lessons in some form of self-perfection . . . the voluminous graduate of the Moscow Conservatory who rapped me on the knuckles for my awkward phrasing of Haydn and threw her arms around me ten seconds later weeping for forgiveness. . . . As for drawing, painting! When I was thirteen she judged the training at Horace Mann insufficient and some Ukrainian card shark who made his living designing de Pinna's windows came to teach me still life, exposing me to a Middle-European style in which threatening bananas and melancholy eggplants were given every possible tragic modulation. . . ."

"What I remember best about Mara are her extraordinary hats."

"Yes her hats, straight out of the St. Petersburg Emily Post, another way of retaining style and caste . . . a lady can't be seen in the street without a hat and every kind of place requires a special texture, color . . . beige felt for weekend errands, velvet for Saturday-morning museum outings, tulle and feathers for the evening and a new assemblage of hats every season so that no one could

41

think we weren't well off, big joke . . . well here she showed an extraordinary sense of economy—have you ever known them to be consistent? We'd spend our Saturdays riding the city's subways to get the cheapest possible fine materials for *les chapeaux;* until I was fourteen or so I was particularly delighted with our search for feathers because their colors were so beautiful; I still have this dream that Mara and I are in this huge warehouse in Queens totally walled and ceilinged with feathers, plumage of hundreds of varieties of wild birds, russet pearl shimmer of turtledove, emerald brilliance of pheasants' neck, a glorious dream . . . and then those egrets and wisps of tulle brushing by my nose each time she turned her head when she sat by me at the ballet or theater in her only black dress, sat there with that haughty bearing of a beautiful woman who knows she's being admired and has no intention of acknowledging it . . . aspiring suitors were always visible, in and out of the theater; how I shook with rage when they grazed their mustaches to her wrists . . . I wheezed and sneezed terribly in any public place and she found this most disturbing to the performance; meanwhile the nose-blowing kid at her side was wondering whether his crazy life was dictated by his mother's aesthetic appetites or by her need to escape the bleakness of her tiny rooms or by her dedication to honing that chef d'oeuvre she wished me to become. . . ."

He'd never forget those nights spent on the park bench, the bowel-deep hysterical yelp of ambulances and fire trucks piercing the darkness as he lay head to head with his mother on a bench they'd found near the West Nineties, the alternating whir of her sleeping breath and of her low quiet sighing and occasional sobbing—he'd pretend to sleep soundly through the night so as not to hear her mutters of remorse, what have I ever given you *dousia* but ruins, dreams—across the fragile forest of the park gleamed the apartments of the very rich, Fifth Avenue, Central Park South, lamplight played on the sooty leaves of the budding trees—while behind him stretched streets strung with the shops where he'd been castigated for his mother's mounting debts, series of shops he'd sworn to never enter again, walking fifteen, twenty blocks to find a new grocery to buy their buttermilk and black bread in—South of him at Columbus Circle the electric ribbon of news blazed out the world's events around the clock, JOHN L. LEWIS ORDERS END OF COAL STRIKE, CONGRESS VOTES TWO BILLION TO UNRRA, BORIS KARLOFF MARRIED IN NEVADA, JOAN CRAWFORD DIVORCES THIRD HUSBAND, HAPPY EASTER, Happy Easter ha-ha—he'd lain there aged sixteen and muttered never never again this is not going to be my destiny and had dreamt of his sporadic life with the Sanford clan—Claire's glacial concentrated gaze as she played Mozart with Jeff hovering over her to turn the pages—Sophie's sturdy legs dangling over the edge of the pool golden eyes twinkling saying guess what's new and exciting Eddem, Barrault's coming to New York next fall and next spring Dad's bringing over John Gielgud—Sophie whom everyone teased about being secretly in love with Edmund performing one of her fabulous swan dives into the pool after saying with her mischievous smile someday I'm going to marry you Edmund someday—Jeff's booming protective voice as he treated them to the horse show every Christmas careful crossing the streets kids careful crossing the street—Plinker's tall heavy body hovering over the vegetable garden as he mulched his beets and lettuces—Sitting at movie houses during Claire's and Sophie's vacations to see *Mayerling* for the fourth time, each of them pretending they'd cried less than the other two—going to church with the Sanfords on summer Sundays watching them share the thin fragile wafer of the Anglican Communion—during those nights on the park bench he'd even missed the uppity athletic little cousins, April, Katrinka, that fringe of the tribe whom he'd never bothered to charm and who still saw him as a dangerous foreign substance saying in their Locust Valley lockjaw you should improve your backhand dearie if you want to play club tennis—he heard the ecstatic graciousness of Babsie's voice as he unveiled some new portrait he'd done of Claire, Claire at the piano, Claire holding an animal under her arm—lying on that park bench all he could think of was oh God let me return to the haven of their order, their repose, their crystal, their rectitude, the neatly aligned knives and forks of their Sunday dinners.

In less critical times Edmund and his mother slept in two small adjoining rooms—Mara's convertible couch in what she insisted on calling *le salon* was surrounded by the armful of curios she'd brought from Europe, a few icons and family photographs, her aquatints of St. Petersburg, Edmund's silver christening cups—she'd never deprived him of her presence for a single night, had never gone anywhere without him except to earn her daily bread, he'd known no separation and no rivals—aged ten as he drifted into sleep he'd considered the possibility of being an immaculate conception as readily as other children fantasize about being adopted, the phrase *causa sui generis* had entranced him in his first year of Latin, Godlike child his own First Cause who might have willed himself—aged thirteen and suddenly grown an inch taller than Mara, his arm gallantly linked through hers as they walked through the Metropolitan commenting on Giotto and Botticelli, he was still not aware that their frugal, precious solitude could ever cease—fathers, who were they, obsolete entities who would have taught him to admire statues and aquariums—a father might have been one of the indolent laggard Russian gamblers of his mother's salon or an American fanatic who would have taught him to sit up straight, throw a ball, be bored—I am the son of no man he occasionally thought with satisfaction.

Every Sunday, in the opaque, incensed darkness of the Russian Orthodox cathedral at Ninety-seventh Street, Edmund knelt before the icons whose large, melancholy eyes resembled his mother's—he stared at the crowd of immigrants who bowed and sank to the floor and constantly moved across the church to cross themselves before another image of the virgin, at the bearded bejeweled priests in pink taffeta robes swinging their censers before the mass of muttering, chanting, seething flesh—he stared at Mara's frail body prostrated on the cold stone floor, in remembrance for beloved dead whom Edmund didn't recall and whom she refused to discuss she lay prone on the floor arms extended to the altar—later they shared the thick fragrant bread of the Orthodox Communion, a basso profundo intoned the dark chant of forgiveness, Edmund docilely knelt by his mother's side, his hand touching the worn cloth of her coat, and wondered about the dead ones for whom she so beautifully wept.

Bare facts: The kind faces that stared at him from the silver-framed pictures interspersed among her icons were those of his grandparents. Flight from St. Petersburg, 1922. His grandfather, a musicologist of some repute, had been able to teach part time in a Munich lyceum. His grandmother had tutored young ladies at the harp and they had both died of typhoid when Edmund was three. Little else: "It's all too old, too sad." Yet also this: Mara had conceived Edmund at the age of nineteen with the aid of a German poet of Jewish origin whose photograph she kept alongside those of her parents and who had died before Edmund was born, aborting her promising career as a pianist; and leaving his son little else but his baptismal name. Or so Mara said. When he passed the photograph of the writer to whom she'd assigned that role (in adolescence he'd compare the mournful, fine-boned face to Kafka's) he'd often salute it with a gesture of defiance, as if to say damn it why didn't you live on at a distance to at least write me the truth?

He only knew that the first Edmund Richter lay shrouded with some curse of art which Mara preferred not to discuss.

Mara had even chosen to derive her son's patronymic from her own father's name, so his full Russian name was Gedmund Petrovich; I am Gedmund Petrovich he'd struggled with since the age of four.

But none of this reticence for what she called life's important issues! Constant discussions over tea and jam with the destitute teachers of piano, violin, painting, Russian history: Mightn't the pain of exile be redeeming to our spirit, we struggle so hard that our soul might become fuller than those of the privileged who've never known any suffering. . . . Nonsense Margarita Petrovna forget such priestly teachings, suffering can only debase us . . . ah no Alexander Maximovich I don't agree, suffering can purify us and refine our vision of the world. . . .

When did it go wrong with poor Mother Russia was it really 1904 and 1917? Or should we trace the roots of the tragedy to the Decembrist disaster of the 1820s? Did the catastrophe begin even earlier, was Peter the villain of the piece when he raped pure integral Russia and gave birth to that Westernized hybrid that made revolution inevitable and landed us on West Ninety-second Street?

Mara would kiss Edmund's paint-stained fingers when he came

home from art class, saying you will save me yet, you will save us all.

That garland of distinguished noble Russian names often held to his ear in childhood Vorontsov Yusupov Dolgoruki Kutuzov Scheremeteff we are distantly related to a distant branch of the Kutuzovs (oh don't tell me about their very special brand of snobbism, their need to hold on to ancient caste systems long ago put in the grave). Years afterwards when he'd have to trace the migration of paintings across Europe to the halls of the Hermitage the garland of names would return to his ear like a childhood refrain, Kutuzov Scheremeteff Dolgoruki Vorontsov.

I had no father to kill no family to hate no milieu to reject he'd joke with friends much later, what an Oedipal void!

Gedmund Petrovich Richter was reared by and for a woman; he'll become one of those interesting late twentieth-century persons who detests the segregation of the sexes, who feels deep loss without the company of women, who'll never find joy or interest in barrooms, poolrooms, men's saunas, team sports or the late-night elation of whiskey poker chips cigars, he's the kind of man who'll spend much time holding a woman's hand saying for heaven's sake let me help you with this problem Claire darling, you've got the blues Sophie sweetheart and I'm going to pull you out of them, Francesca Dorothea Tracy Arabella, you're in trouble trust me I'm your friend.

There comes an age when the son's clinging embrace becomes a light brush of the cheek, when he must start abstaining from the magic of his mother's touch. As single women we are particularly shaken by this severance, we rebecome barren, singularly fragile. A year or two after Mara had introduced Edmund to the Sanfords she began to show interest, for the first time since her son's birth, in the attention of other men.

New York City
April 29th, 1948

Delightful Margarita Petrovna!
I'm filled with happiness at the news of your fiançailles! I hope

46

you'll be eternally happy with Mr. Exter and that you'll invite me soon to meet him at one of your Lucullan Sunday-night feasts! Congratulations also for Eddem's fabulous college acceptance and thank you so much for your note about Smith, I'm going to major in French so as to catch up to you know who! Mama and Papa send their warmest wishes and hope to salute you soon.

In a bourrée of kisses,
Sophie Ross

New York City
May 5th, 1948

Dearest Aunt Babsie,
It is with sorrow that I put this pen to paper, for it is with the principal purpose of announcing the news of my mother's impending marriage. I apologize that I cannot assume anything but a funerary tone for this somber epistle. Voltaire referred to the first honeymoon as La Lune de Miel and the second one as La Lune d'Absinthe. I hope they start with the latter.

Elizabeta Ivanovna, I look on you as one who's been a second mother to me in the past three years. How clearly I remember that first time I walked to lunch at Sealark, how indelibly inscribed in my memory is every gesture of your great thoughtfulness! Gratitude for your note about my scholarship to Columbia; I'm sure the letters which Plinker wrote to recommend me were of immeasurable influence and I hope to grow increasingly worthy of your esteem as the years go by. I'm thrilled about Pebble's own good news about Bryn Mawr (your daughter stinks as a correspondent by the way, owes me a good half-dozen letters in this last term alone). I think she should study a lot of philosophy along with her music, her contemplative side is most curious. . . . As for my curriculum, I plan to major in art history and paint on the side, waiting for the day when I can find an equitable balance between being an artist with a capital "A" and supporting myself without the threats of imminent disaster for which my mother has such talent. . . .

Grisha Exter was actually a tall, dapper, prosperous art dealer of half-Russian, half-Bulgarian origins who had frequented Mara's sa-

47

lon for some years, and for whom she'd broken all precedents by allowing him to escort her, the year before, to the Annual Benefit Ball for the Orphans of White Russian Cavalry Officers. A shock of graying hair hulked over his owlish, handsome face, at which he stared fastidiously in a mirror before entering any room. He claimed to have a doctorate in art history from Heidelberg and carried a residue of calling cards in his wallet, brought from an earlier exile in Italy, engraved with the words Dottore Gregorio Exter. ("The veracity of this distinction, Aunt Babsie, cannot be checked with any more certainty than some historians' claim that Galileo had a mole on his left forearm.") He was widowed, bowed deeply to women with a trace of clicking heels and sold voluptuous eighteenth- and nineteenth-century nudes to New York's growing postwar art market. His favorite expression was "order, discipline above all" and he had an annoying habit of instantly disposing into precise parallel alignment any objects that lay before him—pencils, spoons, toothpicks, pieces of bread. By 1948 Mr. Exter had traded enough Lancrets and Greuzes to own a small brownstone on the East Side on whose ground floor he had an office and a showroom. Fluent in four languages, knowing enough art-buying New Yorkers to have been invited out to dinner many nights of the week as a bachelor, he had chosen so exquisite a wife that he was asked out even more often as a married man. No more of Mara's spectacles! Dinners are where Grisha meets his clientele. Edmund finally had most of those amenities he'd missed during his years with Mara—worn clothes inherited from many a generous Obolenski replaced at Brooks Brothers, teeth decayed through Mara's spendthriftiness recapped by the Park Avenue dentist of a man he hated, punctual meals served by a Filipino houseboy at a candlelit, silver-burdened table—and claimed to despise it all.

Aged eighteen we're still plagued by those adolescent questions about parents, do they make love, how often, how? Sometimes Edmund heard a shuffle of whispers as he came up the stairs at night, a muffled, plaintive conversation. Pausing in the stairway when he returned from a late class a year or so after Mara's marriage he'd heard a long low moan emitted by a voice that resembled his mother's. He shifted his weight, his satchel of books came crashing onto the floor, a door opened and his mother stood above him at the head of the stairs in a luxurious white satin nightgown, braids undone, mass of dark hair falling to below her waist. She'd coarsened considerably since her marriage, that skin once as delicately pale as a magnolia petal had taken on an unhealthily florid hue. She smiled at him with all her old tenderness and a new shyness; *I was worried about you dousia, did you fall?* Her voice was blurred, her body exuded a newly sweet smell, that of a browning flower, an overripe fruit . . . "It's nothing, only my briefcase, the books toppled out. . . ."

Edmund helps Babsie Sanford thread her tapestry needle. The Sealark living room is filled with bouquets of roses and carnations, with paintings of sailboats, retrievers, prizewinning horses. Plinker and Jeff sit by the fire, Plinker gently strokes Claire's head as she lies at his feet with an arm about Sophie's shoulder, looking at an album of last summer's photographs. "Are you happier than you were last summer, Edmund dear?" Babsie asks. "Insanely happy, Babsie dear, how couldn't I be, I've been listening to April yipe out her toilet training theories, satisfying Sophie's insatiable need to swim while Pebble plays her eternal sets of doubles with Jeff . . ." "So you aren't happier? . . ." "And my mother is safely tucked into her new little palazzo with her bordello Louis XV and a man who would surely bore for Bulgaria if the Bulgarians ever had a Varsity Boring Team. . . ." Babsie puts her needlework away. To the end of his life Edmund would remember her eyes the color of dried grass, the tears that threatened to gather in them when she sensed her goal of family bliss thwarted. She smiles, claps her hands. "The Game, the Game," she calls out, "let's play the Game!" "The Game's a super idea!" April cries.

Everyone at Sealark has always agreed that their Game is the world's most amusing one because it brings such fresh and novel insight into people's character. All you need is pencil and paper and six or more to play; Jeff is always assigned to explain the rules to newcomers, for he is "a born educator." Everyone helps to choose a list of questions, like for instance: What would you order as a last meal before your execution? How would you start a conversation if you found yourself stranded in an elevator with Albert Einstein and Shirley Temple? Scribble each answer on a little piece of paper, your niftiest printing, please, then fold the paper and pass it to your neighbor, everyone's on their *honor* system not to peek. When everyone's filled in all the questions Babsie and Plinker will collect all the papers and take turns reading them aloud . . . then everyone tries to guess which player wrote each entry . . . the winner is the one who recognizes the most authors, an extra snifter of brandy for the winner . . . what would you say if you were seated at the Debutante Cotillion between Louis XIV and Toots Shor, between George Washington and Gloria Vanderbilt?

Staring out of the window at the moonlit sound, Edmund nurses his fourth brandy and watches the Nantucket ferry emerge from darkness, white and gigantic, the bride of night, moving with a swiftness amazing for her bulk. All shines so vividly tonight, white steeple of the church the tribe attended that morning, white vessel lumbering towards the Sanford clan so united, so meticulously studious of each other. . . . Edmund takes the first slip passed to him by Katrinka ("Print neatly dearie you tend to be so sloppy"). Query: "Who would you rather have been more than anyone else in the world?" "Machiavelli," Edmund writes. April hands him a slip several questions later. ("You haven't *won* yet this summer dearie.") "What do you hate the most in the world?" the question reads. "God," Edmund writes in large, clear print. Then he sits back staring at the ferry through the spiraling vapors of his English Ovals while Babsie and Plinker start reading the answers.

"Question: 'Who would you choose as your traveling companion if you were to spend six months in the mountains of Ceylon?' Answer: 'Katharine Hepburn.'"

That must be Jeff! How many hands for Jeff? Sophie, Edmund and Pebble for Jeff. Katrinka and Babsie say it's Douglas. Plinker says it's Edmund. Plinker tabulates.

"Capital fun!" Plinker reads the next query. "'What's your favorite pastime on a rainy night?' Answer: 'Sitting up with Tom Dewey at the Plaza Oak Room.'"

That must be Plinker! No silly that's only Jeff or April pretending to be Plinker! Who's for Plinker . . . for Jeff? . . .

"Let's go on, it's all such heaven!" Babsie picks up the next slip. "Question: 'What do you hate the most in the world?' The answer is . . . oh no!" She drops the paper on her lap.

"What is it, dear?" Plinker demands.

"No!" Babsie repeats.

"Are you quite sure you feel all right, my angel?"

"I just don't know what to say."

"What's the *question*, dearie?" April asks.

"What do you hate the most in the world?" Babsie whispers.

"And what's the answer?"

"God."

A hush on Sealark. "Pass me a cigabooo," April whispers to Katrinka. Jeff twirls his coach's whistle, Claire nervously presses her retriever to her chest.

"God!" Babsie repeats. "I mean, who . . ."

"What in heavens are you saying?" (Plinker)

"Someone in the family says they hate *God* more than anything else in the world," Babsie whispers.

"They're just kidding, dearie." (April)

"They're just joking, Auntie." (Katrinka)

"I think it would be a lovely idea" (Sophie) "to separate into backgammon schuettes."

"Or go for a celestial swim." (Claire)

"Don't protect me, Santa Clara," Edmund calls out as the eyes of the tribe rest upon him. "Who in hell but I would say that?"

"Perhaps you're only an agnostic, sporto," Jeff suggests.

"Not at all, dear Jeffrey. I wish my disbelief to have the violence and passion of faith."

"Are you saying you're an atheist?" Sophie asks in an excited whisper.

"And what's an atheist? An atheist is a God-obsessed maniac who witnesses God's absence everywhere, a man with deep religious convictions who truly *believes* in the nonexistence of God."

Deep silence.

"A religion which doesn't call upon you to get out of the armchair

51

or the church pew, why that's the ideal of everyone in this room . . . the usefulness of religion is that it allows you to believe in God without ever *thinking* about Him. . . ."

"I don't mind thinking about Him," Jeff offers. "By all means let's discuss God, fellow. . . ."

But Edmund prefers to hold forth alone. He stands up now, his voice performs exaltedly beside him as if it were stalking the stage like a great bear.

"Your contentment with well-being, to use William James's astute insight, protects you like a carapace from any thirst for transcendence. . . . You're so sure to find him at the hour of your death that you keep him rigorously away from your lives. . . . Only the deepest skepticism can save us from being atheists, and I utterly refuse to be a skeptic."

"What about . . . what about saints?" Claire ventures.

"Saints, dear Disappearance Act, are created by people in *spite* of the Church, and they're made to be devoured by crowds, like angel food cake. But let me finish . . . what is purer than belief in the Void? To be certain that there's nothing is the most pristine faith of all!"

"It's quite clear that the fellow has had too much sun . . ."

"Alas no, Plinker! If I were mad I'd be the genius my mother wishes me to be and genius isn't easily arrived at, one must merit it by serious suffering, by trials firmly traversed . . . genius listens to Orphic voices and writes under their dictation . . . let's put an end to the exalted imbecility of these proceedings. . . ."

He stumbled over his chair and fell, and by the next morning when he woke up with a severe headache he'd quite forgotten the rest of his peroration.

Claire was practicing her piano when Edmund came into the library the next day. She was playing Mozart. He couldn't focus well that morning. His last memory of the previous evening was of being tucked into his bed by the two girls. Her playing was particularly tempestuous; she stopped in the middle of a phrase and stared at Edmund, clamped her arms down on the piano keys with a crash of chords. "You're desperate this year!" she shouted. "Why in heck are you so impossible this summer, can't you be *sane* like us, conform to certain *basic* rules of behavior?" "Oh look who's talking, Mademoiselle Blithe Spirit who feels free to roam the moors for hours at a time while the family turns the island inside out looking for her. . . ."

Without losing her grace of gesture—amazing!—she started flinging books at him across the room. "You and your goddamn artistic uniqueness," she shouted, "you and your damn European individualism!" Bam! he thought, there it goes, our first tantrum alone. "Stop that Pebble will you stop that immediately, you're not used to being talked to are you, they've always thought you were too special, too frail to curb, but I'm not going to stand any shrews around me!" She continued to throw, tears welling in her crimson face. He searched for ways to control her. She turned towards the wall to reach for more books to hurl at him, he ran across the room and grasped her by the shoulders. He shook her very hard, pressed her trembling body against him, felt the arousal which tortured him many times a summer when he touched her. "Why do you attack me like this, Peb, why?" She fell onto a sofa, her hair spread out like a length of brown silk. "Because I love you," she sobbed, "because you're my brother, my best friend, and I want you to be perfect!" She trembled with a soft undulating motion, he sat down by her, put his arms around her, kept his body pressed against hers.

Sounds of Sealark mornings flowing into the room from the summer outside, Babsie humming a hymn as she snipped flowers in her garden, Plinker giving April's daughter a lesson in seashells, here's a limnet sweetheart . . . Edmund cupped Claire's face in his hands, put his mouth to hers for the first time. She responded warmly at first, clutching him to her. "Someday you're going to marry me, Pebble," he whispered, "someday you'll marry me and you'll never have tempers again." She drew away from him brusquely. "I'll *never* marry!" she whispered fiercely. "What if I don't ever want to marry anyone?" "Oh you'll marry Jeff or someone like that all right, that's what they all want. . . ." "Never, never anyone!" "All right then, promise, you keep that promise Peb!" "I swear!" Her swift alternations of mood always alarmed him, he held her shoulder as lightly as he could. "If you promise not to get married then I never will either, ever. . . ." Surrounded with that tribal love he'd so envied she was much more solitary than he. It was the first time he'd come to that knowledge.

Claire is lying on the dunes posing for Edmund. She wears tennis shorts and a brief white halter. She's bent one leg at the knee, as Edmund has asked her to, folded her left arm under her head. It is a year later, they are both twenty years old. They have built a bonfire in the pit of the dune on a windy, cool afternoon in late August. The flames flicker on her bare flesh when the sun goes in behind a cloud. Edmund squats a few yards from her at the grassy knoll of the dune, his sketching pad leaned against a piece of driftwood. She has sat for him like this since the age of fifteen, reading, holding her animals; and the passivity of the act seems to suit her calmer moods. What strikes Edmund most about her body in this spring of her flesh is its continuing childlike delicacy. The legs are long and thin as a filly's, the waist hung extravagantly high. The most singular feature of her face are the enormous eyelids which arch over her pale eyes and give her face part of its haughtiness; he tries to draw those lids, is unnerved by the difficulty of rendering their fragile curve.

"Peb, don't fidget so!"

She stills her head. Her eyes are cast down as if she were absorbed in studying a grain of sand.

He whistles a Mozart aria, struggles to render the delicate slope of her neck. "At times when I draw you I need to destroy you in order to recreate you . . . there's this new idea that realistic art is bourgeois because it's an imitation of reality but when it's good it's anything but that, it's a total recreation. . . . I'm mentally killing you right now Pebble, I'm annihilating you in order to make my image even more perfect than you are. . . ."

She gives a startled, excited little laugh, stares at him with curiosity as she sifts sand through her fingers. He studies the curve of her delicate, arrogant mouth. The underlip is thin and severe; the fully modeled upper lip curves faintly upwards, as if readied for a mimicry, an ironic smile.

"I'm going to need that hand in a second, Pebble."

She puts her hand back on her leg and continues staring at him for a few minutes with her huge crystal eyes. When she begins to speak again he knows that she's about to offer one of her rare moments of unleashed candor, one of those monologues she sometimes indulges in with little need for attention or exchange.

"I'm going to *need* that hand, you absolutely must lord it over all those around you, mustn't you, Edmund, you do love to tyrannize. That's one of the things you relish about my having to sit for you, it's the only time you have me quite in your power, you try to dominate all women around you because . . ."

"Trying to be analytic? So damn unWASP of you."

"Don't interrupt me like that. I think it can be dangerous, such a desperate need for power as you have. Look at the storm you raised when you lost your totally exclusive place in Mara's heart, scenes out of *Othello*, or the way you tease Soph; she's so insanely in love with you she'd go live in Madagascar at the flick of a lid from you and how you adore that, it's the aspect of your character I distrust the most, your need for total control over others . . ."

"A few more hors d'oeuvres for the oral stage."

"Don't always tease me, E.R. . . . You see as a pacifist I have to constantly reexamine all forms of power . . ."

"Power! Dear Clair de Lune, do you realize how much need for power there is in your kind of pacifism? . . . Your need to lord it over the animal kingdom, your utter inability to accept a defeat in tennis . . . that's all the likes of you and Jeff and April can think of anyway, compete compete, you and your cute WASP violence. . . ."

She stares at him, squinting, as if he's drawn a difficult problem on the blackboard.

He whistles again. "Speaking of violence, I saw such a strange show the other day by one of these new abstract artists, a guy called Pollack, Pollock? Nothing but webs of black and white dribbled about bare canvas; if that's the direction painting's going I may have no place in it. Sorry, get that leg up again, Santa Clara."

Only in certain Tanagra statuettes glimpsed in museums has Edmund seen the same frailty of proportion, in those little clay figures with breasts like small hard apples that hold a ritual animal under their arm. Strange creature! Swept by waves of rebellion against the family he craved to belong to, feeling the transience of a tourist in the world which had rescued his childhood . . . Claire the glacial center of his adopted tribe enmeshed in her growing network of world causes; Edmund don't get mad but I flunked bio this term by trying to stop all dissection at college, Eddem please come to a Ban the Bomb demonstration in Philadelphia next Sunday. . . . Her massive urge towards the oppressed, her disdain for the strong, the privileged, her own class. . . . This is what had made her friendship such a privilege, a gift, her aloofness from all she'd been born to, her disdain for most of the alliances of a normal adolescence. . . . Save for her adulation of her father she was rejecting it all as rigorously as she had denuded her childhood room; you never knew how the rich would work out their guilt. . . . He'd recently referred to her revolutionary impulses for justice and compassion as "unique to the conscience-stricken, repentant aristocracy"; she'd given him the same perplexed intense stare she was giving him today, fastidious student deciphering a classroom problem, but now her huge eyelids lowered again, the sideway arch of her neck signaled that she was resuming her blast of candor. "As if it had all been a bed of roses for Mara! You're unfair to her, Edmund, you only started your bouts of erratic behavior when you stopped being the absolute and only center of her life!"

A bored, jaded tone: "I still am, you know."

" 'Still am, you know. . . .' Look at how sensitive you are about it. . . ." She raises her head, shakes her curtain of hair. "I want you to know something . . ."

"And I want you to know that it hurts to have a best friend withdraw the way you do, Claire; you can create hell around you, you and your goddamn notions of world love and peace."

"I've hurt you?"

"Oh Pebble, you know perfectly well you've hurt all those who love you by your withdrawals, your aloofness!"

She lowers her eyes and retreats again, her chin shaking a little. She remains still for many minutes now, posing superbly, unbudging, head held farther down than before, heavy eyelids almost closed; the tension in her limbs makes the intersection of her neck and shoulder more difficult than ever to draw. The ligaments of her neck flow smoothly towards the beginning of the frail collarbone, where they're interrupted by the trite ribbon of her halter top. Edmund draws that transition of neck to shoulder over and over again, erasing after each attempt, never reaching the fluidity he strives for. He curses, takes out his penknife and whittles his pencil, stares at her again; the pose has become strained and wooden.

"Damn anatomical problem that neck-to-shoulder passage. Take off that silly top you're wearing Peb, I want to see your breasts." She makes no motion, does not raise her glance.

"If you move your arms you'll disturb the pose; I'll do it for you." He walks to her and slides his arms under her torso, unfastening her halter. "Listen, I've been doing this at the Art Students League since I was fourteen."

"Doing? Doing what?"

"Drawing from the nude female model. That's considerably better, without those damn straps getting in the way."

Without saying a word she put her arms to her waist, unfastened her shorts and pulled them off. In a few seconds she had lain down again, one arm cradling her head. He continued to draw, stunned by the frail tautness of her body. She had resumed the pose with total obedience, one leg stretched out on the sand and the other leg bent, fully exposing herself. Her pelvis, as flat as a dish of milk, stretched down to a triangle of pale auburn hair. Above her high, tiny waist her curiously large nipples were the nacreous rose hue found deep inside a whorled shell. Her eyes now lay fully upon his with a blank, heavy-lidded, questioning stare that seemed almost drugged. And for a while the artist's eyes she stared at continued to confront her with an intense, disinterested gaze.

He had straddled her and pinned both her arms behind her. The extremely brief resistance she had offered left her hair covering her face. He gently put her wrists together above her head, brushed her hair back and put his mouth to hers. He slid his hand over her pubic hair, gently rubbing the lonely ridge of flesh with his thumb and forefinger. The sun disappeared behind clouds, the light of the bonfire swept over her face. It had the same expression of dispassionate interest with which he had stared at her for the previous hour. Edmund stripped and forced himself against the smooth wall of her orifice, pressing repeatedly against her while she bit her lip in pain. "It's all rather difficult," she said with an ironic smile. He stopped thrusting to put his mouth to her nipples, he continued to rub the ridge that lay like a tiny boat in its sea of fur. He watched her eyes close, her breathing quicken, he put his hands under her buttocks and forced himself against her again a few times with all the strength he could muster. She cried out, her eyes opened, her face tightened and reddened as it did when she was about to have a fit of temper. He continued to thrust, amazed by the exquisite tightness of her orifice, so different still from the ease of the whores he had gone to a few times since beginning college. Her breathing quickened again and she began to share in his movement, thrusting towards him. But her initial pain had softened and disabled him. They lay still in each other's arms. "I'm sorry," she whispered, "perhaps it wasn't precisely the way it should have been." "It was perfect," he lied. He tenderly kissed her eyelids many times, her cheeks, her mouth. And then in a gesture that did not seem to particularly startle her he bent down to kiss her, sweeping his mouth over her bitter little blood.

They searched for Claire Sanford that night as they had searched a few times during her childhood. Riding on top of the fire department truck, Plinker screamed her name throughout the island until the far end of Great Point while Edmund ran through bogs and fens on his own search with her name on his lips; the wind breathed like a lion in the pastures of Cotuit, in the red clay of Sankaty bluffs the wind moaned that she had drowned in the surf. In the middle of the night Edmund slept for twenty minutes in the pit of a dune and then hitched a ride on a truck and continued to shout her name through the stubbly moors of Siasconset. He ran down the beach where Plinker and Jeff had once taught him to catch the surf, where summer after summer he had lain on his raft like a stalking panther waiting for the whitecaps that would carry him most violently to shore. But she was neither there nor in the forest of pitch pines in the middle of Quidnet where he continued to shout all the names he had given her for five summers; My Botticelli, Santa Clara, Miss Elusivity, Clair de Lune, Disappearance Act he called out, clouds of gulls scattering at each outpour of his voice. His breath came short, an alarming wheeze returned to his lungs. He returned to the dune where they had lain the previous afternoon, searched for the indentation in the sand which marked the precise spot where her body had lain and fell into it, sobbing. The morning sun was high and for an hour he lay face to it, eyes stinging from wind and sand. The toll of her innocence, of her crazed search for purity. His guilt. His force. Her submission. Such a simple thing. Thrusting into the virgin rock, sword in a scabbard. Yet she was the one who had made it possible. He was older by three months, he must protect her forever . . . these concerns later lost their gravity when he lay stunned by sun in the lion-colored dunes where they had long held their picnics and their races. Lying in stupor in the sand, staring at the island of his only childhood happiness in the silvery light of the Nantucket noon, no disasters, no serious sins seemed possible. The church bells tolled "Amazing Grace," the horn of the afternoon ferry shouted towards Nantucket, announcing its beautiful vacationers, its plenitude of sand pails and summer furniture, its adulation of childhood. . . . Claire Sanford's disappearance did not last particularly longer than those of her earlier youth. She returned the day after she'd run away from Edmund on the beach, in time for tea, bearing armfuls of plums she'd picked for the family by Hummock Pond. She had just *felt* like spending the night alone in some secret dunes of hers which she'd loved for years. . . . Tears welled in her eyes when she heard that her vanishing had caused Babsie to be put under sedation; she ran upstairs to her parents to offer her effusive apologies, one of her rare bouts of solicitude.

iv

ONE travels to the Soviet Union in 1975 with young marrieds deeply in love, California orchid-growers recovering from painful divorces, aspiring photographers eager to document every Art Nouveau building in Moscow. Some Americans travel there to buy cheaper vodka or lacquered boxes ornamented with leaping Cossacks and melancholy maidens. Others simply come to Leningrad to say they've been somewhere new and sit in dusty blue buses chewing on toothpicks while the rest of their guided tour leaps out to inspect the battleship from which the Revolution's first shot was fired. It is amply explained to travelers in the literature that accompanies their visa applications that they are forbidden to bring marijuana to Russia, change American money at unauthorized sources, photograph airports, bridges, tunnels, power stations or railroad stations under penalty of imprisonment; that it is wise to bring flat rubber sink stoppers for Soviet bathtubs, disposable lighters, ball-point pens and panty hose as tips for hotel employees; that they can under no circumstance travel in the Soviet Union without the company of one of the crisp, efficient government guides who process foreigners through the demanding Intourist schedule. In the twenty-four hours since they've been in Leningrad, Claire, Edmund and Sophie have already visited the modest three-room log cabin where Peter lived while supervising the building of his city, a museum that houses ten centuries of Russian icons, the site of Alexander II's assassination, the innards of the battleship *Aurora*. Sophie, the most restless member of the triad, also wishes to take a taxi on her own to visit the arcade where Gogol's protagonist is said to have ordered his greatcoat, the train carriage now encased in glass at Finland Station which brought Lenin back from exile. "Stop it, Soph, you're going to bring us out of this country on stretchers!" But she shakes her copper curls, laughing and threatening to go off on her own, talks them into choosing one more place to visit; they've loved each other long and are inured to her amazing energy. Edmund and his women take a cab to the pond of Tsarskoye Selo, where Sophie suggests a swim as it's been her habit to suggest everywhere since she was fifteen; but upon the tourists taking off their shoes some guards run up to announce that bathing here is *zaprishchino*, forbidden, what do the Americans think they're doing? It takes Edmund's carefully remembered Russian to assuage the enforcers of the law. So while the rest of their Intourist group visit the Annual Exhibition of Soviet Farm Technology the three friends simply lie in the grass talking about their long adolescence together, and stare at the lake which shimmers at their feet in a phantasm of swans, oak trees, minareted follies as in the effluence of a giant's tranquil breath.

Later that morning they climb into the Intourist bus a few minutes after the rest of its passengers, as they had the previous day. "Late again," one of the guides calls out, "Dr. Richter's party is very often late!" That guide's name is Irina. She has a splendid head of long dark curls and a languid air, is wafer-thin for a Soviet woman, smiles sweetly in between her bouts of reprimanding. Whereas the other guide of Intourist Tour No. 137 Destination Tbilisi-Kiev-Leningrad-Moscow is a squat and handsome man with large imperturbable eyes and a copy of *Pravda* perpetually folded under his arm. Edmund, Claire and Sophie wave greetings to the acquaintances they've made in the past five days and sit down together in the rear of the bus. Ahead of them are the plump, loquacious Zabars, who work on Seventh Avenue and whose favorite vacations seem to be spent in countries whose regimes they can relentlessly criticize—Romania, Bulgaria, Albania, Hungary. To the left is Mr. Jones's group, an eight-citizen-strong delegation of Rolls-Royce dealers from Florida who wear shiny little tags on their lapels saying Silver Shadow, rush onto the bus before anyone else to sit in front for the best view and shop relentlessly, being already burdened that noon with flowered shawls and crates of fragile tea sets. As for Ted Weicker, he teaches political science at a very liberal prep school in the Northeast. He discusses Soviet politics elaborately with his wife and often points out aspects of the Soviet system he finds superior to our own; you've got to hand it to the welfare state not an elderly citizen unemployed look at those fine old ladies sweeping the streets clean as a whistle.

"Professor Richter," Irina says before switching on the microphone for her morning talk, "you will agree that your 1915 Baedeker takes decadent attitudes towards central facts of our history?"

"Allow me the indulgence of my profoundly bourgeois nature, Irina Grigorievna; I promise to be less guilty of deviations after you take me to the Hermitage."

"On Monday when repair is over, Dr. Richter, have more disciplined patience. . . ."

Irina smiles, proudly pats her American jeans, switches on her microphone. "Upon arriving yesterday, gentlemen and ladies, we learn that Leningrad, formerly called St. Petersburg, was founded by Peter the Great in 1703 to open windows towards Europe . . ."

"Venice of the north," Mr. and Mrs. Weicker whisper in unison.

". . . regime of Czar Peter built St. Petersburg at greater human sacrifice than any other city since barbaric times, a hundred thousand men lost in the task . . ."

"It's like the Sleeping Beauty," Mr. Zabar says.

"Like flowers encased in a glass paperweight," Mrs. Zabar agrees.

"And now this morning we are on way to visit Petrodvorets or Peterhof, impressive palace designed to be a country home of Russian rulers, built from plans of French architects, correct, Dr. Richter, enlarged and finished by Italian Rastrelli in 1746. Always take attention gentlemen and ladies as you descend from steps of bus. . . ."

Tourists are recommended to photograph the famous cascades of water which rush down over six steps of colored marble to a majestic central basin. At the basin's center they much admire a gilt bronze statue of Samson tearing open the jaws of a lion, symbol of Peter's victory over invading Swedish troops. We will now visit Peter's little villa Monplaisir, which stands a few hundred yards from the main palace. It was in the emperor's nature to frequently seek escape from the splendor that surrounded him . . . Peter was six feet ten inches tall and suffered from grave spastic fits, possibly epileptic . . . the czar was a big joker and punished any guests who arrived late to dinner by forcing them to drink a liter of vodka in a single gulp, in one gulp! And here is the tankard from which guests sometimes drank themselves to death in this little cottage Peter built to escape the luxury of his great palace . . .

". . . as we depart, gentlemen and ladies, please note again extreme beauty of forty-five gilded statues and of cascade in front of palace. . . ."

Photographs: Claire Sanford in blue jeans next to a gesticulating statue, immense pale eyes cast towards the Gulf of Finland, straight brown hair flying in the wind—Sophie Ross squatting on a park bench holding an ice-cream cone, speckled gold-green eyes squinting in laughter, teeth very white in the strong squarish face— Edmund Richter in faded denims, extremely handsome man of forty-five with longish, slightly graying dark blond hair, points his arm magisterially at the wrestling Samson.

That second afternoon in Leningrad the members of the Richter party plead headaches and excuse themselves from a visit to the Museum of the History of Religion and Atheism to walk arm in arm through the city's streets. Claire and Sophie photograph lime-hued, pale blue palaces, poets remembered in stone or marble at the edge of verdant parks, citizens in worn uncouth clothing standing in lines on Nevsky Prospect to buy a piece of fresh fruit, portraits of Central Committee members strung on banners across the avenue. Sophie still wears her babushka and dark glasses so as not to be recognized too soon by other American tourists as Sophie Ross of the *Good Day America* show. She notes that Soviet teenagers are wearing their hair long, American style, that the overwhelming majority of bus and trolley drivers are women. "Macho attitudes are something else here, Peb," she waves her notebook; "women make up eighty percent of the factory workers and of the medical profession but they're still coopted into a full load of housework and guess what's the only available birth control device, a diaphragm that only comes in one size . . ." Claire keeps straightening Sophie's babushka, which tilts askew when she gets excited by her research.

Edmund walks a trifle behind the women and often hums Russian words under his breath; his first language swells towards him from the lilt of surrounding voices, bittersweet with memories of childhood smells and tastes, of his mother's gardenia scent and steaming kasha. He murmurs returning words like a child caressing a bedtime fetish, words of tenderness, titles of novels. *Dousia*, little soul; *Voina i Mir*, *War and Peace*. Towards the end of the avenue they see their guide, Evgeny, staring at a slender display of Western literature in the windows of a bookstore. He holds a little red umbrella on his arm as he walks towards them, gestures almost forthcoming. "Can I help you, is there anything I can do for you?" "We're looking for a lovely park bench to sit on," Sophie says with her radiant smile. "Preferably with lilacs," Claire adds; "we've been friends for thirty years and we've come to your country . . ." "I would suggest Decembrists' Square." The Russian points towards the Neva with a friendly wave of his umbrella unaccompanied by any change in his hooded gaze.

They choose a park bench near the river. Primness, grandeur, melancholia, solitude of Peter's city, fragility of artifice, beauty frozen and embalmed. Buildings shimmering in the palest light, in the albinic heat of early summer. A pitiless sun hovers perpetually over Leningrad throughout its white nights, its skies remain frozen in the color of tea roses, towards evening the river turns to hues of geranium and crushed mother-of-pearl.

" 'For six months of the year all the Neva's water freezes into a bitter layer of ice,' " Claire reads from Edmund's Baedeker, " 'and

64

the wet hostility of certain winter days induces into Petersburg a mood of Dostoevskian despair.' "

A young man and woman court each other with shy, brief kisses on a nearby bench, four young gymnasts in yellow tights practice their somersaults on the lawn, a child skips rope down the park's graveled alley.

Edmund talks about the gesticulating statues surmounting the roof of the Winter Palace to the right of the square. "They're so measured, Grecian, don't you think, so foreign to this Nordic light, like hostages exiled from some Mediterranean mountains . . . and the austere lines of the long buildings almost glacial, right, so at odds with the sweet tint of their hues, primrose yellow of the Admiralty, pale sky-blue of the Smolny Cathedral . . ."

They've reached that bend of early middle age in which the tyrannic, longed-for past is the immediate seducer and the future looms as fearsome.

Sophie is always the first to face it.

"I've got to break out of the hell of the past ten years, it's been one long backpacking trip for me, a nomad's existence, a succession of hotel rooms decorated in group-sex modern . . ."

"Even after the bezzazz of success?"

"As I was trying to tell you yesterday before you enthralled us with your rap on Pushkin, it's been lonelier than ever."

"It's been a rotten time for me too," Edmund says. "I had very mixed emotions of longing and terror about coming here, certain memories remain painful even after all these years . . . but I've spent the past year living on some kind of a brink, I don't think I can go on with what . . ."

"Edmund, don't fuck up again, don't leave behind the glorious career you've spent twenty years building up!"

"Soph sweetheart let's leave the confrontations till a bit later in the trip, okay?" Claire says softly. "Let's keep away from all unnecessary violence. . . . I think I'm just beginning to pull things together but I came here to be sure I'm going to do it right; I've too often felt on the edge of an abyss, like . . . Eddem, do you remember that day you almost drowned in 1950?"

"How could I forget, wading into the ocean that August evening after one of your disappearance acts, the surf was heavy, I was dazed, brutish, as I swam out each wave rose towards me like a great dark cavern framed by glints of foam . . . I'd no idea how far out I'd gone, I'll never forget those murderous tender arms that braced my shoulders and steered me back to shore while the two of you stood at the water's edge, shouting save him, save him Jeff . . ."

"Oh shit," Sophie says, "just when we were getting up the nerve to talk about the future."

They walk back arm in arm towards their hotel.

$\mathcal{V}$

POSTCARDS:

Florence, Italy
June 27th, 1951

Dearest Sofinka—I've seen few things on this trip I more crave to share with you than the Convent of San Marco, all those cells with Angelico frescoes on their walls, one more glorious than the other, paradisial voices mingling in unison over the city. . . . How's our own island paradise this year? I was torn, torn about the decision to go abroad this summer, but my mother's gracious offer of a trip to Italy is essential to my work and you must all be more relaxed without my twice-an-August acts of desperation . . . write soon my sweet and let's have a family reunion the moment I step off the boat. . . .

Florence
July 2nd, 1951

Clair de Lune—I don't give a damn for the salvation of your soul but if I could capture in one moment of my work the luminosity of the violet-robed angel in the Fra Angelico I stared at yesterday just after reading your quest-for-purity missive I'd be a happy man. It's the one in which the angel bends towards the virgin with a gesture of warning, hand raised in alarm as if to say it ain't all good news kiddo, there's a rough road ahead . . . which brings me back to the theme of your blasted little purity: Until you can name the furies which lurk behind your passion for abolishing all weapons and your didactic avoidance of even Campbell's beef consommé (not to speak of your impatience with most of your fellow humans and your extremely complicated views on keeping your life untainted by sexuality) you'll still have a tough uphill climb to whatever anyone could call salvation. . . .

Rome
July 15th, 1951

Sofinka darling—Must share one of my life's great windfalls with you, I'm faced with the exciting and terrifying prospect of making my debut in the New York art world this fall . . . a chap who runs one of the better little New York galleries came to see my studio class last spring and just wrote a letter offering me a show in November. I hope you all turn out en masse!

Venice
August 15th, 1951

Pebble of the Running Brook—Deep gratitude for the superb Swiss hunting knife you sent me for my birthday; I might just carve up my steppie and serve him for dinner to Maman at Russian Christmas; don't you think that would be one-upping the Greeks? The honeymoon couple whizzed by here last week on their way to Baden-Baden to take the waters, which Mara badly needs, for I must share the painful astonishing news that she's taken to dreadful bouts of drinking since her marriage; can you imagine that beautiful angel taking to booze though she's secure for the first time in her life, she who never touched so much as a drop of sherry until she started her life of idle luxury, it's as if we've had no peace since we ceased to starve. . . .

Lovers, children, heroes, none of them do we fantasize as extravagantly as we fantasize our parents. It may have to do with our need for their immortality. The souls of offspring know what they want,

68

have their own perverse knowledge, nest in layers of deceits, seldom daring to fly out until it is too late. Later, later next year I'll figure her out again Edmund would say, later later there's plenty of time. After his migration to the Sanford clan Edmund would have wished Mara to have a windfall from some White Russian foundation and otherwise retain her life unchanged, pouring tea more frequently than ever for the cake-making princes, intensifying (platonically) her friendships with his teachers of piano and Russian poetry, continuing to stand in line for tickets to her spectacles, continuing to pound out the "Dance of the Hours" for the pliés of wealthy young American beauties. Instead there was the giddy new Mara wandering through the house in florid housecoats, pretending to water her plants, praising her Grisha's fields of expertise (the technique of nineteenth-century aquatints, the iconography of French landscapes), occasionally packing thirteen pieces of luggage labeled G.E. to travel to Baden-Baden, Saint-Tropez, the Paris Ritz. Edmund had moved out of Grisha's brownstone to live in the Columbia dorms the fall Claire and Sophie left for their junior year abroad, pleading easier access to classes and studios. It was not until the day he came in for a morning visit and saw Mara tippling vodka at 11:00 A.M. that he realized he'd avoided being alone with her for more than half an hour in the past year. He began to notice many mannerisms of the novice drunk, repeated pleadings of migraines as an excuse for one more, proclivity for those silver cups of Grisha's which she could pretend at a distance were filled with consommé or juice. It dawned on him that he'd never even bothered to find out how Mara spent her days. She'd severed all ties with previous émigré friends to frequent Grisha's prospective buyers, stopped participating in any charitable Russian causes, read increasingly less. She indulged in numerous new whims—Paris clothes, illustrious resorts, luxurious restaurants (oh don't talk to me about their sudden shifts of temperament, their excessive capriciousness!). "Of course my angel, absolutely everything you want my angel," Grisha exclaimed as he entered her room with his crisp cavalry step after the houseboy had brought her her breakfast tray, acceding gallantly to forty-case lots of vintage champagne, frequent reupholstery of their entire house.

Some months after he'd caught her with her morning vodka Edmund accepted Mara's invitation to lunch on the occasion of her birthday. They meet at "21," where she seems to lunch almost every day with wives of Grisha's clients. ("So *nouveau riche mon chou*" she'd said about that establishment during their years of penury, "not for proper people like us or the Sanfords.") Mara in a Maggy Rouf dress which Grisha had bought her in Paris the previous summer. The aigrettes of her velvet hat brush Edmund's face with bittersweet recall of their Saturday search for feathers. Waiters bowing deeply as she heads for her accustomed banquette, the faint leaflike rancor already on her breath. Mara reveling in the same glossy Brittanic splendor Edmund enjoyed at the Sanfords, oak paneling and gleam of sumptuously aligned silver, splendor of crystal, files of uniformed, cast-iron blackamoors. Mara immediately runs down the restaurant crowd for Edmund; of late her conversation has been restricted to extraordinarily trivial international gossip, who frequents which ski slopes and which Zurich gallery, who's acquired the most amusing butler, lover, chef, plastic surgeon. She starts being very loquacious on her second glass of Pouilly-Fuissé; *a droite*, she exclaims with a sweep of her hand, is a man who owns most of the tin mines of Bolivia, *a gauche* is an English duchess who's about to play the Beast in Cocteau's next film; she'd visited Grisha's gallery the week before last and was most serious about purchasing a Segonzac . . . and at the back of the room, her voice rises in excitement, is a famous beauty married to a Venezuelan oil magnate—the husband is a handsome extremely sad man who only speaks to his cat; a few weeks ago the cat died after the magnate discovered his largest oil deposit to date and he's now the world's most silent billionaire . . . their Paris house is said to have a library with a fireplace of sterling silver, floors of stainless steel and genuine tortoiseshell bookcases . . . that's where this great beauty takes her men now, two or three times a day, on a library couch upholstered in genuine black mink; she'd come into Grisha's gallery recently looking for Degas pastels and had found them overpriced, a stingy bargainer, but he was hoping to soon sell her a little Derain . . . Mara is summing up the room on her second bottle of wine now, "No more Degas," she giggles, "all the oil in Venezuela,

La Belle et La Bête . . ." She stops laughing and stares tenderly at Edmund, not quite focusing, as if his eyes were twin cribs. He stares back priggishly. Reversal of classical tensions, this happens to us increasingly, puritanical children scolding giddy, hedonistic parents . . . she gives an exasperated sigh, pleads with her son to have a zuppa inglese, orders a triple espresso. Is she ecstatically happy in her new orgy of idleness, utterly miserable, shall we ever know?

The tactics of the rival can be cunning. Grisha tries to capture his stepson's goodwill by vociferously approving every opinion or watercolor he brings home. ("*Ton fils est un Chardin,* what order and discipline, *du pur Chardin!*") "*Cher ami,* who do you think is the greatest painter who ever lived?" he asks upon snaring Edmund out to lunch at the Plaza Men's Grill. What an idiotic question Edmund thinks. "Well, perhaps Titian," he blurts out. "*D'accordo, d'accordo,*" Grisha exults, "your answers always brilliant but I've always wanted to know *why* he's the greatest." "Look at those loose, revolutionary brushstrokes, he was the first to liberate painting from the tyranny of line. . . ." "Remarkable, brilliant, thank you!"

"Actually Titian's late period was totally misunderstood for centuries," Edmund expounds at the Plaza another time over a third sherry. "Except perhaps by Rembrandt?" "Precisely," Edmund says to the beaming stranger across from him. "No one understood late Titian until Rembrandt . . . you're spoiling my mother to death," he adds. The pale cavalry eyes stare back, eyes he's never bothered to plumb, has simply overlooked, disdained. "You're indulging her every caprice, encouraging the full extravagance of that anarchic Slavic spirit, that's been your way to keep her totally in your power. . . ." The man's eyes suddenly severe, cynical. "It wasn't an easy life she led alone with you, was it? Can't we have a little charity, *cher ami?*" "You and your talk of order and discipline," Edmund says, downing his sherry. "Discipline for youth like you; as for Mara, let her be, she's finally resting, *elle s'amuse!*"

Sitting on a bus riding uptown to play a tennis match at Columbia Edmund dozes and dreams briefly about Mara's afternoons. She flies over the city like an enormous zeppelin, her newly majestic body painted like that of some tribal statue; she points with her old sweet laugh to all those places in the city where he'd like to find her between the hours of two and six: sympathizing with fellow émigrés at the Tolstoi Foundation, addressing envelopes at the Foundling Home for the Orphans of Exiled White Russians . . . the bus jolts to a stop, he wakes and realizes that she's in none of those places, that she's finally indulging fully in that ancient passion for gambling which she chooses to keep hidden from him, that Grisha will retain his power by letting her continue the vodka, the cards, the desperate boredom that's gnawed at her since she ceased a life of hardship, as if such obsessive temperaments fall to pieces when released from the discipline of survival, can only feed nefariously upon themselves . . . oh Mama you're so good, so educated, can't you get interested in cancer or in the Alliance Française, the extinction of rare animal species, can't you give lectures at the Cosmopolitan Club, there's only one thing left that can draw us back together. . . .

New York World-Telegram, November 22, 1951

> The work of Edmund Richter, a precociously gifted painter who is still an undergraduate at Columbia University, reassures us that the realist tradition is thriving notwithstanding the fashionable new smears beginning to spot 57th Street like an epidemic of measles. Richter's remarkable landscapes—informed by considerable technical skill and lyric precision—are bound to make an important contribution to contemporary art. His oils of Italy and Nantucket are particularly striking, and present the sensuous surface and the attention to detail of a young Corot.

Everyone gave parties. The show sold out. There were fetes for Edmund at the Exters, the Sanfords, the Rosses. At his mother's house, over a lavish buffet of cutlets Pojarsky and chicken Kiev, Edmund asked to renew acquaintance with the genteel companions of his adolescence. His teachers of Pushkin, Mozart, tennis, still life, the cake-making princes and the graduates of the Moscow Conser-

72

vatory mingled with the cosmetic manufacturers and Seventh Avenue designers described by Edmund as Mara's new milieu. In the Rosses' lush interior of mahogany and polished brass ("*nouveau riche* but so warm," Mara always judged them) operatic divas and stars of the Broadway stage raised their champagne glasses to the young painter. And at the Sanfords' apartment at River House, a small black-tie dinner was attended by whatever cousins lived within traveling distance of New York and were not fighting for freedom in Korea.

"Having always been passionately fond of Europeans, I have grown to be particularly fond of this young man who has graced our seaborne domain as a friend—nay, almost as a son—since his fifteenth year, and who like so many Continentals is destined to make a noble contribution to the culture of our blessed country. May we drink to your success, to your wealth and fame, young fellow; I raise my glass to one who may become—nay, I insist, *will* become—the American Gainsborough. . . ."

Plinker has twinkled his glass over the cherries jubilee, tuxedo looming majestically over the candlelit Meissen. At the toast's end Edmund catches a glimpse of Claire hanging lovingly upon her father's words, standing to applaud the toast, clapping. And the arched curve of her back, the rigid regal thrust of her head reminds him of some tiny German figurine that twirls under a glass dome upon the turn of a key. There's something about her adulation of her father, something of the obedient Teutonic princess about her that moment which frightens him.

But ah what triumph Mara has upon reading Edmund's reviews, upon witnessing the sales of his paintings! Mara enjoys a great, brief happiness that winter, for the central goal of her former life (the cultivation of genius) is being fulfilled. "*Il sera Delacroix, er wird Brueghel, he'll be Tintoretto.*"

Five weeks later, at the end of Christmas week, Mara was struck by a cab as she swayed down the street from one of her mysterious afternoons in town, and died three days later of internal hemorrhages, with a minimum of pain.

Edmund stayed with her at St. Luke's Hospital until the end, clutching her hand, refusing to look at the face of the man who thought he had loved Mara. She had been struck in the abdomen and remained in a coma for much of the remaining time.

In a moment of consciousness the day before she died she whispered to Edmund that she wanted him to fix her hair. "Braid it," she said with great difficulty, "the way you did when you were little."

Edmund carefully brushed the burnished mass of sweat-matted hair onto one side of the bed. Working deftly at the first braid, he recalled those Saturday mornings when they had settled in their first American rooms and Mara had let him tie her hair with a bright red satin ribbon which gave her the air of a schoolgirl at a Russian Christmas party. "You're just like my sister this way," he'd said when he was eleven as he'd added a sprig of holly to the ribbon . . . this time he had asked the nurses for some strips of white cotton with which to tie the ends of her hair. And then he had turned her face gently towards the ceiling again, laying each dark braid decorously on the pillowcase. She gave the beginning of a smile. "Thank you, *dousia*," she whispered. Grisha was gazing out of the window, a pearl of tear trembling at the end of his peaked nose. "It was so beautiful, so short," Mara managed to say again to Edmund, speaking very slowly in Russian, her lips straining painfully towards his ear. Precisely *what* had been so short, Edmund urgently wanted to know, what did she consider so beautiful? Life in general? Their love together? Her love with the other one? Had he been too harsh towards her in the past years? Shouldn't he have allowed her the luxury of idleness after those frantic years of scrubbing and scrimping, of plotting his scholarships and his lessons? Couldn't he keep his damn little diligence to himself, continue lavishing affection on this extravagant generous creature whose surface alone had been altered? He started speaking to her but her eyes had closed again. There would be no more words from her; and a few hours later Edmund knew that he must call a priest. Sunday service, to which he'd refused to accompany her since the age of fifteen, about which he'd driven her to tears by deriding it as the opiate of the masses, had been the only unchanged ritual of her new life with Grisha. So a bearded deacon in black cassock and tall

74

square hat came from Ninety-seventh Street and held the crucifix close to her face, chanting for a few minutes about life eternal, anointing her forehead with an umbrous ointment redolent with incense.

Kneeling by Mara's bed, becoming oblivious to his surroundings, as if he were trying to go into coma with her. Conscious only of the lingering warmth of her hand as he keeps it clasped to his cheek, of the occasional pleading of nurses who beg him to eat, take air. Shaking his head angrily at the touch of any hand, refusing to open his eyes or lift his head, remaining on his knees notwithstanding the doctors' urging that he lie down on the cot set up for him in Mara's room. They're gentle with him, do not force. Her husband seems to come and go, sobbing elegantly into a handkerchief, muttering about having to call friends, pressing soup and coffee upon him. No sense of how long the man remains in Mara's room during that last day. A nurse was shuffling sheets, another bustling about the room. It's all over, a doctor's voice spoke softly into his ear. He lifted his head and realized that they had just finished closing Mara's eyes. This was his last vision of her: Mara's brow was deeply furrowed, as if she'd just squinted intently into the sun. The vigorous chin jutted forward more stubbornly than ever, reminding him of those childhood photographs taken of Mara with her mother by some embankment of the frozen Neva, wrapped in muff and furs, already confronting the camera with haughty irateness. Edmund stared hard at the willful features. In an atavistic impulsive gesture he moved his hand slowly over her face in the sign of the cross, three times, in the manner of the Orthodox Church. *"Cher ami, cher ami,"* Grisha was sobbing towards him. But Edmund was already running out into the winter night, not looking at Grisha or even bothering to take his coat, thinking of nothing but his need to retain his numbness as long as possible.

It was a Sunday, shortly before midnight. He ran. He ran shouting down 114 Street, controlled enough to know that he was running on an empty side street rather than on a well-policed avenue and that he had only a few moments in which to give free rein to his voice. "Peb, Sophie," he cried out repeatedly, "Sophie,

75

Peb, where are you?" He turned the corner into Broadway and stopped shouting, ran south and tried to schedule his next several hours. Sophie was abroad with her parents, dining with Dame Edith Evans, John Gielgud. He knew where Pebble could be found every Monday morning at 9:00 A.M. during vacations; his only problem was what to do with himself before he reached her. He rushed down Broadway, aware that he was running at even pace, elbows at his side, left arm raised in symmetrical rhythm with right knee, like a trained runner. Young orphaned desperado immigrant with over-long dark blond hair rushes down Broadway in the middle of a warm winter night past the bookstores where Claire and I searched for rare editions of Emerson in our high-school days, past the New Yorker movie house where a few spring vacations ago I took Sophie to see the *Children of Paradise* three times in one week; every ten minutes or so when his breathing became labored he paused to lean against a wall, staring at the streets of his childhood, let's salute the pharmacies in which druggists refused to sell us cough medications because of nonexistent payments, pay tribute to the Café des Art-istes where the Rosses take us to brunch with shimmering colora-turas. At Fifty-seventh Street he turned left and east and ran through the familiar block of the Art Students League. Stopping for a second in front of the school, where he stared numbly at one of his watercolors exhibited in the window, he realized that he had run with only two or three interruptions for some fifty blocks. He con-tinued sprinting east on Fifty-seventh Street, passing the painfully familiar stoops of Carnegie Hall, the Russian Tea Room, Mara's former ballet school. He ran past the expensive Fifth Avenue stores at whose windows Mara had stared with her curious gaze of envy and disdain during their childhood walks. He swerved south on Lex-ington Avenue, east again on Fifty-fourth Street, and started look-ing for a bar. After passing a half-dozen possibilities he stopped at one on First Avenue filled with men and ordered a double Jack Daniel's, straight up. He drank it slowly, not feeling the fire. It would be weeks before he could face Grisha or the solitude of his student room, the only gesture to live for, the only bridge that could span the abyss, was to fall into Pebble's arms and then, only then, allow himself to go. Until we find her we must suspend all thought and continue to run or else fall into a deep short sleep. He paced the bar as he downed his bourbons, disdaining the men's whistling and appraising, their softly mouthed hoots and whispers. He needed a bed for a few hours of the night and wished to remain precisely in that part of town, near the building where Pebble played tennis every Monday morning of her vacations. After a half hour of refusing propositions he started a conversation with a pale hairdresser who'd accosted him by asking him what sign of the zodiac he'd been born under. "Taurus, like Michelangelo." His companion had spent four years in a Catholic seminary and was presently obsessed with problems of astrology and transmigration of souls. He took Edmund to a comfortable third-floor walk-up furnished with numerous photographs of Greta Garbo. A few hours later Edmund woke before the stranger, dressed quickly, ran out. It was one of those warm January days of springlike haze that precipitate the thawing of December snows. Edmund took up his sprinting pace again and ran to the familiar building by the river.

As Edmund came towards Pebble in the River House Tennis Club she stood alone at the base line of a court, practicing her serves, a basket of balls by her side. He stared at her, wishing for the first time in days that he had some pen and ink. There was a superb curve to her spine as she leaned deeply back on each serve to throw the ball into the air, her torso then swooping downwards with violent acceleration as she brought her racket smashing onto the ball. She was absorbed in the gesture, rehearsing it very rhythmically, pawing the ground with her sneakered foot for a few seconds before engaging in the dual motion of languid leaning back and furious downwards thrust. He watched her through some thirty serves before calling out to her, aware that in her straining for perfection she was capable of repeating the same gesture 80, 120 times in one practice session. And then he cupped his hands and yelled, "Pebble, Pebble." The voice returned to him across the courts, faint and piping, not quite his. And he realized that he could not tell her yet, that he had to remain in motion for a few more hours, even with her.

"Edmund, where have you been, rabbit?" She had turned around, dropped her racket, opened her thin arms towards him.

77

"I've come to play tennis with you," he yelled. She ran towards him and put an arm on his shoulder, stroking his hair. "That's super, why didn't you call me ahead of time? Do you want me to cancel my opponent, she's not due for half an hour, shall I call?" "Yes, yes, please, Pebble." His arms trembled. "Please call, and find me a racket and a pair of sneakers, will you?"

She ran to the dressing room with a skip and a hop, saying, "You look like something the cat brought in. . . . I haven't told you I'm playing some Stravinsky for the first time. . . ." He continued to stare at her body as she ran; she wore the same little white shorts in which she'd posed for him a year and a half before, she'd grown thinner since adolescence, looked more ephemeral than ever. Edmund grabbed Claire's racket from the floor, played the ball fiercely against the backboard . . . "Take that, you bastard," he muttered, talking to death. "And that and that and that." It was the first time he beat her at tennis. He was driven by some force of rage more demonic than any in his memory; the ball is his enemy, the ball is Grisha who had snatched his mother from him and spoiled her to death, the ball is Edmund himself who'd failed to understand Mara and cure her, it's that own grief of his which he must remold into some anger with which he can at least survive. There's no possibility that day of missing the ball. His rage fills him with as much agility as strength; even when Pebble is at net smashing it deep into his backhand corner he manages to return with a deep unretrievable lob, scooping up the ball and keeping it in patient enough contact with his racket to send it flying in a high curve that swiftly dies behind her at base line. His agility causes her considerable amusement, she laughs after many of her netted returns. "E.R., where did you learn that brilliant lob? Who in heavens have you been training with?" He leads her four-three. She rallies, her chin angrily thrust forward, and breaks his serve on a double fault. But in the following game he breaks her serve and the score stands at five-four. "Historic moment my dear," he says at the net as they change sides, beginning to feel a terrible lightness, "I'm going to beat you, Santa Clara." She sticks her tongue out at him mockingly. "Oh no you're not. But I don't know what's gotten *into* you." Changing her tactics, she returns his serves with short, choppy strokes that force him up to net and tries to pass him wide, with deep drives down the line. But he reaches every one of them as if his arms were an extension of his rage. And she can only return two of his serves anyhow. The other three are aces, and he's won the set. "What has gotten into you, Eddem?" she cries with eminent sportsmanship. And she leaps over the net to hug him. But he's run to the back wall and knelt against it, sobbing.

"My angel, what's wrong," she cried, kneeling beside him. He told her. For ten minutes or so he let her hold him against her, his head cradled against her fragile shoulder. As he sobbed and shouted his imprecations he realized that it was one of the few times he'd cried since he'd stubbed his toe at the age of seven, that Mara had protected him from many of childhood's griefs while denying him much of its pleasures. His sorrow expanded, he broke away from Claire and rocked uncontrollably on the floor, his body coiled. When she attempted to raise him off the floor he retreated from her, rocking even more uncontrollably in a corner of the room, attempting to knock his head against the wall. After having shouted for help she offered her self as a buffer zone between him and any surface he was trying to attack, letting him knock his head violently against her body as he attempted to destroy himself.

New York City
March 2nd, 1952

Beloved Sofia Larionovna,

What an unthinkable trip, of course you could never have come all the way from England for Mara's funeral (it's about the first time I allow myself to pronounce or write those words). Thank you for all your notes, and for worrying about me the way you have. Sorry I haven't written yet. This is just about the first time I'm even allowed to write. I've very little memory of the first weeks, to tell you the truth I don't even remember the funeral. I'm told that on top of the incredible asthmatic attacks I was under immense doses of sedation. As you know Pebble took several weeks off from college to take care of me, and between her and Babsie . . . I barely pulled through without needing a psychiatric ward. I myself had to skip more than two months of school, shall perhaps be allowed to resume in a fortnight. But thank God my thesis was already almost finished and that was the brunt of this term's work. Pebble is talking about going to England again after graduation, which worries me. Will you tell me whether she's apprised you of such a plan? Her reasons: the old stuff, "finding herself" away from her formidable conformist clan, et cetera. Well, thanks for writing so often. Sorry I sound so limp, etc. "La chair est triste, hélas, et j'ai lu tous les livres."

Yr. Edmund

New York City
June 15th, 1952

Sofka,

Congratulations on being in love again! Next time I hope you choose a man with a name more interesting than John Dillon, something truly beautiful like Hyman Levine Farina. That way if your endless appetite for broadening your identity involves a rediscovery of your Jewish roots you could change your name back to Mrs. Hyman Farina Levine. Yes, Pebble is going abroad, God damnit. On July 1st. For the whole year. With the craziest plan you can imagine: working as a secretary to be independent from her family while she continues her piano training! So I'm right now a little desperate. As for Babsie and Plinker it's their retirement year, they're going to live in Arizona because the medics say it'll be better for Babsie's nerves. What a good idea for you to work for the Democratic party in California!

Yr. Friend always   Edm.

New York City
June 22nd, 1952

Mon Clair de Lune,

I am drunk, dead drunk, I became willfully drunk so that I would have the guts to write you what I haven't had the guts to write or say à pleine voix for some years; I promise to go to bed and sober up and reread this letter before sending it, but it's the only way I can get up

80

the courage to say that I love you madly, I will never be able to love anyone again, I offer myself to you here and now, do with me what you will, immolate me, marry me, torture me, but the one thing you cannot do is to deprive me of your continuous presence by my side and your continuous power over me. . . . I am at your feet as below an altar, the altar of my expectations, my desires, my ambitions. . . . I hurl my body towards you as a man who throws himself from a burning building, I beg for you the way you beg your Lord for daily bread, all this I could not say when I took you to the ship yesterday. . . .

Next morning: Whew! What a headache! But I'm glad I got it out. What I'm really doing is asking for your hand in marriage, in an outrageously serious way. I don't need to elaborate on bourgeois reassurances such as: The penury I suffered as a child makes me all the more determined to support myself in a consistent manner; what with my assistant teaching at Columbia and the support of a good art gallery I'm as ready as anyone is to offer you a hearty independence from your family, one which would be immensely more helpful to your musical career than the insane course you're presently launched on . . . forgive the inane digression. Let's say that I give you a few months to think about all this, even in the glaring light of dawn I can soberly repeat that you are my life, my blood, my only hope, etc.

New York City
July 17th, 1952

Dearest Pebble,

No need to say how miserable I am at this moment without so much as a postcard. I realize that you're as wretched a correspondent as can be found on this planet, that you're a solitary explorer by nature, that this European venture is one more step in your chimerical search to break with all that's closest to you. I also realize that I may have done something foolish in my letter of some weeks ago. I confronted you with the vehemence of my passion, which is the human ingredient you probably fear the most. I wish to stress that I could remain as chaste in a marriage, if you should so wish it, as Abélard would have

81

remained if he'd been shipped back to Héloïse after his disastrous deprivation. So I'm proposing something quite innovative: a radical extension of friendship into a vie à deux which would enable me to be constantly in the presence of a being as necessary to me as food. . . .

New York City
August 16th, 1952

Sof dear,

So Mr. Farina wasn't up to porridge? How sorry I feel for him! Miss Elusivity has been gone for over eight weeks now and hasn't written a word to anyone, not even to her parents. A good lunch with Jeff the other day, all aglow after his heroic Korea bit, Purple Heart ribbon blooming on his chest like violets in springtime, rather at loose ends for the time being and thinking of going to Oxford for grad work in history. Write soon, dear heart. . . .

New York City
August 22nd, 1952

Dear Claire,

In light of the letter which I posted to you fully two months ago, and of the rather important decisions I brought up in it concerning our mutual destinies, I really find it extraordinary that you have not had the charity or manners to pen a reply. I acknowledge that I'm deeply in your debt, that you saved my life last winter (but then your entire family probably saved my sanity over the course of the past many years). Yet I do not see that a sense of satisfaction about having been admirable towards someone should release you from all continuing decency. I feel right now as if you had pulled me out of the icy ocean only to deposit me on a small parched island with a tree bearing one tiny palm for sustenance . . . that palm being the distant hope that sometime in the next month you might grace me with the nourishment of your words. . . .

New York City
September 8th, 1952

Hey, Frozenpuss,
"Some people fancy they're being natural," La Rochefoucauld once wrote, "when they're merely being boorish and rude."

Yours,   E.

New York City
September 25th, 1952

Dearest Soph,
I really miss you too, very very much. Gratitude for your many heartening letters. What are your plans for autumn and winter? (To answer your query: I'm staying put, of course, to begin my master's thesis and to earn my daily bread, which I do by teaching many charming morons, truly visual spastics, to draw apples.) And so I thrill at the very thought of being reunited with you in the city sometime soon. I'm so eager to see you that if you can't make it farther than Chicago I'm ready to hitchhike out there to meet you halfway! Let me know!

New York City
October 19th, 1952

There's really more craziness in you than I'd expected, Peb, and more meanness, and more smallness. If I don't hear from you in the next two weeks what can I do but capitulate? . . .

October 23rd, 1952

Sofinka
Can't tell you how thrilling it is to know you're soon coming East! Have you made up your mind yet about the exact date of your arrival? If you haven't I command you to. . . .

83

New York City
November 7th, 1952
Beloved Sofinka. It really is ghastly about Adlai but . . . Ecstasy!
You're arriving! I've got to run off to class, just want to acknowledge
the receipt of your beloved last letter and say that I'll be meeting the
Chattanooga on November 22nd at Penn Station, and I can hardly
wait until you rush into my waiting arms. . . .

They began living together the following month.

vi

THROUGH the open window of the Intourist bus
Claire smells wafts of lavender and thyme, she opens her eyes and
sees the calm, massive landscape of Soviet Georgia hulking before
her like a temple, blazing in the still heat of noon, a fragment abandoned on the altar of light—they're driving through tall stands of
birches that alternate with vast fields of red poppies and white nico-
tiana, the bus halts before a drawbridge, a cloud of insects emits a
long, shrill droning that sweeps the ground like a wind—then
there's a stand of pine trees and tall ferns as dark and silent as the
ocean floor; look at that forest so pristine and still Sophie whispers
by her side, it has the isolation I'd like to find someday in Nepal,
Tibet—What a novelty Claire says, that's how I wanted to live for
decades and now you're the one looking for solitude—Sophie is
tired this morning and claims not to have slept a second of the
night, keeps her head on Claire's shoulder; well at least I wouldn't
be giving anyone grief by splitting would I Peb?—That's your first
dig of the week Claire says I haven't given people much of a break is
that what you're saying?—Bet your sweet ass you haven't Peb you
haven't—Explain me to myself Sophie I want you to explain, it
began when I was very little sitting in churches, there were too
many moments when I wanted to leave behind all I knew for a new
life in which I'd feel more worthy—I often think back to a time I

was walking on a beach with my father, I was eighteen, he sat down on a rock and said you're all I've got in the world Peb and you'll be the end of me yet, all I ever wanted for you was to be happy, the tears came down on that large kind face and it was as if a rock were melting before me, the memory's so painful that I didn't recall it until we were all in our middle thirties and I was completing the destruction of that safe world he'd wanted for me—You've always struggled for a total liberation from the world you were born into Claire darling—A search that was Utopian, perhaps harmful to others, right Soph? I spent a couple of decades working on a totally wrong model of perfection, nutty, totally misled!

Georgia is the first leg of their Soviet journey, the bus rambles through a pale golden fire of noon light, the day so brilliant that they seem to be moving across the bottom of a huge crystal bowl and the world's light refracts with myriad force in a great circle about their heads—Sophie has closed her eyes and Claire wraps her sweater around Sophie's shoulders—the Rolls-Royce dealers are asking Irina whether there are bank accounts, zoos, fire trucks in the Soviet Union; "The Soviets are still Asiatics," Mr. Zabar says to his wife, "impossible to understand them in our Western terms," and Edmund is reading to Mr. Weicker out of his 1915 Baedeker— their guide Evgeny sits across from them on the bus dressed in a frayed suit of pale grayed blue, his hair bluntly cut as a sheaf of wheat—if one looks straight into his spectacled eyes they don't so much return a gaze as a fleeting reflection of a grain of world, a passerby; throughout this country Claire has seen many men with his terrified untrusting eyes, with that stare which seldom fastens on the eyes of another human but seems to hover fearfully at some point in midair—Do you remember that first Ban the Bomb demonstration we all went to together in Philadelphia? she says to Sophie, the pickets waving, you and I were cheering the speakers while Edmund was sketching faces of people in the crowd and we kept saying this is serious Eddem please be more serious—Sophie stretches, yawns, you're a walking contradiction Peb aren't you, you attack the idea of power yet you've fucked up our lives by having exceptional power over us—Well nothing's tormented me as much as my relations with others Claire says; for a few decades I didn't think I even needed any others—You preach nonresistance Peb and you're a fighter by temperament, your abhorrence of force is coupled to an extraordinarily aggressive attitude towards life!—Yes yes very complex that all came as a great surprise Soph; pacifists are filled with a lot of inner violence, yet beyond the force of my love for my daughter, for you, for Edmund, I've little to trust in except my nonviolent means; we've always got to see the enemy as capable of conversion, awaken and startle him into openness—look at Evgeny, I know he's been programmed to fear and hate us as the enemy but I'm determined to discover a chink in his armor so I sit here doing a kind of psychic auscultation of him, trying to figure out where the chinks might be—

From the beginning of their trip Sophie and Edmund have noted that Claire has retained her old manner of engaging in long sentences with little need for attention or exchange; she speaks her thoughts out loud, pale eyes staring straight ahead of her, sometimes continuing to talk while her companions have wandered off to study a building, photograph a view. In this she has changed less than any other member of the triad, in this they might be disappointed. This is their third day together and they still delight in discovering the new gestures and phrases of each other's middle age ("that constant clearing of your throat hem hem has little to do with childhood asthma Eddem it's just another dreary academic tic"); they are like vacationing siblings who dramatize the most minute changes in family behavior. Claire's perorations are as interchangeable as ever with her internal musings; if interrupted she will simply lean back against the back of a chair or bus seat and withdraw again . . . for instance, that day in Georgia:

" . . . the only thing pacifists have to work with is their tactic of moral jujitsu, Sophie; once we've palpated the opponent's armor, so to speak, discovered its chinks, we've got to throw him off balance by some act of humility or trust . . . we smile as we pass the machine guns and we carry no armor, we're steeled with a totally different kind of inner guile . . . you know what A. J. Muste said on the eve of World War Two, he got up in Quaker meeting and said if you can't love Hitler you can't love any man, just think how difficult that is. . . . "

"You're making the mistake of considering love as an emotion," Edmund remarks as he comes to sit beside her. "It is, in fact, an attitude."

An attitude! Edmund has always had a way of turning things around on their head, practicing his own brand of moral jujitsu, Claire's holy zeal for humanity in the abstract! The pious luxury of loving enemies! She won't answer him, she leans her head against the back of the bus seat and shuts her eyes; there she goes Sophie says, bye-bye for a while.

" . . . Ladies and gentlemen, we are approaching our destination, village of Mtskheta, earliest mythological home of the Georgian people. . . . "

Irina, the tour guide, has switched on her microphone for her little midday lecture, she's wearing her best American T-shirt and the word Levi's is prominent on her tiny left buttock—The Rolls-Royce dealers lean out of the bus snapping pictures of horses; Irina dislikes ancient history and she sniffs into her tissue as if the mountain air were poisoning her—"This is said to have been first Christian outpost in pagan times until fifth century . . . ai, what else, proud mountain people had military and commerce connections with Greece, Rome, Persia . . . and now gentlemen and ladies before continuing our sight-seeing we're going to take refreshment in typical old-fashioned little Georgian garden. Evgeny Sergeievich, do see that everyone gets off properly. . . ." The group descends into a luxuriant garden filled with roses, dahlias, foxgloves, mallows, every seasonal flower of a tumultuous European garden—they're beckoned to enter the little house that attends it; the owner sits in its dark cool interior, a smiling, aged Georgian with a black cap on his head who offers his guests fruit juices in delicate crystal glasses—Claire sits on a rock outside of the old man's door, needing the air, the mountain view, observing her companions inside— Edmund puts his arms around Sophie in one of those asides he offers when she's depressed, "Oh Sofka this is what Voltaire was talking about, cultivate our eccentricities, our most repressed desires! This is the way I'd like to end my life, painting landscapes and tending a garden as beautiful and useless as this man's"—but Sophie stands still in one of those new moods of gloom and withdrawal Claire can't decipher; in the past day she'd mostly talked about where she'd travel at the end of their Russian trip, which route to take home, "Why don't I fly back via Copenhagen? I've always wanted to see that part of the north, or maybe I'll fly to Italy, drop in on the Rome office and catch the end of the film festival in Cannes; come along and we can rent a boat to Sicily"—then moments of depression they can't decode, her long solitary evening walks; her moments of delight seem disciplined, enforced, like that brittle cheerfulness of her TV appearances which has cloaked her numerous crises, Sophie at 7:00 A.M. the month after her last husband died, flashing to Claire and ten million Americans her extraordinary smile, every curl of her head perfectly sculpted, saying, "Good Day America, more violence last night in strike-ridden Uganda, the Panama crisis is growing to a head"—this creature of total freedom and great solitude who strides through American cities in a turban and dark glasses to avoid autograph hunters; for years Claire had marveled at the tenacity of her affection—Sophie had always been there with her insistent voice, her huge tenderness, her monumental appetites, ah if anyone had the tenacity to get through to the dead Sophie could; in their twenties they used to imagine Sophie broadcasting séances, "Guess who I contacted last night, George Bernard Shaw, John Stuart Mill"—the invasion of Normandy Edmund used to call Sophie's tumultuous entrances, accompanied as they were by a stream of questions and announcements, "Peb how are we going to help the Hollywood Ten, Eddem please explain to me the *ultimate* meaning of Eliot's *Quartets*"—"After the age of forty there isn't much to live for except friendship," Sophie'd announced yesterday and they'd all agreed. "It took me some traumatic years to learn that," Claire said; "you were way ahead of me Soph; for my first twenty-five years I hadn't learned friendship the way other people haven't learned to swim or ride a bicycle; in those years you and Edmund were the only ones whose stubbornness was great enough to claim me, whose voices were tenacious enough to break through my solitude; in the long run Sofka you may have been my humanity"—They were in the sleeping car of a train bound for Tbilisi, 1:00 A.M., Sophie her head in Claire's lap, Edmund lying on the opposite bunk—"Look at it this way," Edmund said, "friendship is freer of deceit than any other bond because there's little power, profit, material pleasure in it"—"What about the free consent," Sophie exclaimed, "no oath or duty, total self-determination!"—"It's perhaps the most pacifist emotion we can have," Claire noted; "look at the Quakers, a Society of Friends"—and then Edmund had come up with something very beautiful, friendship is that state in which we most resemble the society of angels promised us in catechism, in which we can share the truth of our inner thoughts in total freedom and abundance . . . that's just what I came here for Sophie said I sure hope we can start soon and then they'd all fallen asleep.

Vineyards stretch ahead for miles towards a violet mountain—Evgeny sits on a bench a few yards away from Claire, bent forward, self-absorbed, rapping his knee with a copy of *Pravda* which he holds furled into a narrow roll—his approaches to the Americans are meted out in some meticulously detailed program of behavior—"Can I help you?" he asks each time he sees one of his group walking unaccompanied through a Soviet town, "Is there anything I can do for you?" The Zabars assure their fellow tourists that Evgeny spends his nights writing up reports on the Americans but the image ignites no anger in Claire, she sees a creature haunted, hunted by the fears and temptations of survival—the mission lying ahead of her in Moscow might help to save the life of a man who was once as docile as Evgeny; whatever attempts her companions make to keep her from it she's determined not to avoid its complications—one of hundreds of thousands of men incarcerated in this country, Edmund's already warned her, a symbolic gesture, risky, futile—

"Oh I wish I could take home one of those lovely brooms that old woman is sweeping the street with," Mrs. Weicker says. "Ted look what a gorgeous broom!"

"You could eat off the sidewalks in this country they're so clean."

"Soph where on earth did you pick up that odious habit of constantly drinking from water fountains abroad, you're going to get hepatitis!" "Stop always using that word odious Peb, it's so Cambridge, Mass."

" . . . Intourist never tells you what hotel they're ever taking you to on your next stop," Mr. Zabar explains to Edmund; "that's so no one can ever look you up in case you've got friends or relatives in this country; it's the same in Hungary Czechoslovakia East Germany Poland."

That evening on the way back to Tbilisi, Irina and Evgeny have arranged a typical Georgian banquet for the American tourists. It is held at a cooperative farm nestled at the bottom of a pleasant valley. There are vineyards nearby and groves of olive trees shimmering silver in the early evening light. Evgeny takes over from Irina at dinnertime. "Georgian hospitality is renowned throughout our Union for its warmth and old-fashioned charm . . . throughout the nineteenth century our Russian poets came to Georgia to receive inspiration for their verses and restore their health . . . Georgia was our muse as Italy was for poets of the British Isles. . . . " A long narrow table is set in a woodland pasture and laden with many flowers, with heaps of tomatoes, onions and cucumbers, with dishes of Oriental eggplant and cheese pies, with little glasses for vodka and larger ones for white and red wine, with bowls of garlic cloves cooked to such subtle lengths that they attain the crisp blandness of water chestnuts, with abundances of fresh figs, pears, peaches, pomegranates and slender crescent-shaped loaves of fragrant bread. Sophie wades knee-deep in a nearby stream, picking more wild flowers for the table. "These people might be poor," Mr. Weicker comments, "but what a sense of community!" The Rolls-Royce dealers delight in learning to drink their vodka in one gulp and shout many Na Zdarovies to their Georgian hosts. The hosts praise their local wine as the best cure for arteriosclerosis, schizophrenia, impotence . . . the chief source of their astronauts' courage . . . the principal source of the Georgian people's longevity . . . many toasts are exchanged.

"To the health and happiness of our American guests!"

"To Georgia!" (Edmund) "To this remarkable handiwork of nature!"

"To the noble ideals of Western democracy!" (Arthur Zabar)

"To the shared concerns of our two great traditions!" (Ted Weicker)

"To the increase of our mutual trust!" (Claire)

"To your eyes, Clara Pavlovna! To her beautiful eyes!"

"To détente," Sophie drinks, "to world peace!"

"To your beauty, Sofia Larionovna! To her beauty!"

"To our Georgian women! To their tenderness . . . their suffering . . . their patience . . . their fortitude . . ."

("Does he want the shishkebab in his face?")

("Hush, Soph, hush.")

"To the children of Georgia!"

"To the children of America!"

(". . . the little beasts . . .")

("Shut up, Eddem.")

"To the future!"

As they walk back towards the bus after dinner Evgeny stops before an enclosure in which there stands a young buck deer. The animal thrusts its lustrous black muzzle through an interstice of the gate and the young Russian kneels down to caress it. "*Dousia*," he whispers, "*lapachka* . . ." He walks about the pasture stuffing chestnuts in his pockets, feeds them to the deer. Claire stands at his side. "Oh how lovely Evgeny Sergeievich, how lovely!" The animal picks the chestnuts delicately out of the man's hand, rubbing his muzzle against his wrist. "Isn't he beautiful?" the young Russian whispers. "How could one ever kill such a creature? Ah I've never understood hunters, Clara Pavlovna."

Irina claps her hands, calling them to board the bus. Evgeny takes off his glasses, blows on them gently as he continues to whisper to the animal. Claire turns around to look directly into the Russian's unshielded eyes, which still remain boreal and abstract.

vii

On weekends in their New York studio apartment Edmund constantly drew and painted Sophie in the nude. She would remember those years as her life's most perfect moment. He would remember them as his period of odalisques. He painted Sophie in bed in the poses of Renoir's late canvases, a vase of roses by the night table; of Goya's *Maja Desnuda*, arms behind head, breasts trembling warmly in the air. Dictatorial, he did not let her talk, often made her read during the pose so that she would not continually confront him with her questioning gold eyes. She posed with magnanimity, with genius, with a sybaritic abandon. Even when engaged in the most menial tasks there was a tension between the languor of her gestures and the piercing attentiveness of her gaze which made every attitude she struck a painter's dream. Later she would give her poses a self-conscious skill ("Do you want me this way? My arm lower down?") which lost some of their original power. But he would never forget the amplitude and instinctual grace of her movements that first year, Sophie seating herself at a table by the window in just the right Vermeerian light, Sophie reclining on pillows in billowing pants and turbaned head, legs crossed like Delacroix's harem women. The feature of her face which fascinated him the most was the large, fine Roman nose that dominated her

93

softly modeled oval face. It made an abrupt little departure from its bridge, jutted forwards briefly like Giuliano de' Medici's in the Botticelli portrait. It intimated a force, a streak of masculine independence, which had not yet manifested itself in her life. After many odalisques, Edmund concentrated on Sophie's face and painted numerous heads of her, struggling to capture that peculiar still-hidden force of her character: Sophie in a velvet cap, like Raphael's brooding young man; Sophie's copper curls cascading to her shoulders and adorned with a circlet of flowers like Rembrandt's Saskia.

She loved the intensity with which he stared at her when she posed, the crouched taut intensity of a hunter stalking prey from a thicket. She would have wished for that same intensity of gaze in every one of their moments together, for she was one of those women who'd entered life believing in fierce elemental passions, lived through a few brief ones already, sensed that her central tragedy might be to never live such an idyll with an artist called Edmund Richter. She'd waited for him quietly and long—she'd waited for him, to be precise, since the age of fifteen when they'd first met on the terrace of the Sanfords' house, since that moment when she'd come upon him in his outlandishly formal poor boy's blazer, watercolor brush in hand, lifting towards her his defiant and awed immigrant's gaze. She'd accepted the evident centrality of his love for Claire with a cool, complicated patience which had to do with her own adoration of Pebble; she had not so much resented Claire as she had lived in a fatalistic hope that one day the cycle of their infatuations would somehow be broken, shaped anew. Like most women who are capable of long and deep-seated passions she had a genius for secrecy, self-control. Edmund only came to understand her constancy when they started sharing a bed and looked upon it as admirable but awesome in its perseverance. So it was that Sophie could finally be a Muse to her long-awaited artist, breathing as quietly as possible under his heavy intent gaze as she posed, staring with pretended detachment at his chiseled face under its mane of wavy dark blond hair, the high cheekbones which he enjoyed ascribing to Tatar blood, the thick dark lashes which made his very dark blue eyes all the more inscrutable.

If Sophie sometimes fell asleep during an afternoon pose it was because she'd had frequent bouts of insomnia since childhood, a recurring, needling sleeplessness impervious to any medical diagnosis, in which she even had a kind of pride, attributing to it her omnivorous reading of most nineteenth-century novels ever published. When Edmund woke in the morning she'd already be watching for him, mass of copper curls richly tangled on the pillow next to the koala bear that was still her bedtime fetish, exuding towards his awakening senses her faint scent of musk and essence of roses and her radiant smile, springing up swiftly to make his breakfast, clean his studio, perform the menial tasks any of us would perform if we'd been educated to believe that our highest destiny is to bask in the closely reflected glory of a genius.

Glory! He'd never known anything like that adulation for artistic success, performance, fame, which she'd inherited from her family. He often joked that this had been the cause of her insomnia, that since childhood she'd been kept from sleep by fantasies of the great men who lay in store for her. Like her parents she wept whenever she heard applause; he'd never seen anything in his life like the Rosses' reaction to applause; it could be Lukas Foss's Bach Partitas heard on the portable radio they carried to the beach, E. E. Cummings reciting his poetry at the 92nd Street Y, rave reviews of some art show on Fifty-seventh Street, a crowd clapping for Eglevsky's window leap in *Le Spectre de La Rose*; at any of these occasions tears would rise to the Rosses' eyes at the sheer sound or symbol of applause, applause. Edmund compared their adulation of artistic success to servants' infatuation with the alcove secrets of royalty, deplored its effect on the woman whom he now thought of as his most admirable friend. Yet he remained awed by the intensity of Sophie's interest in all that he cared for, the spiritual attunement of a lover whose body foresaw his every need . . . Jewish women, soft-thighed, seldom athletic, dutiful daughters . . . their nutritional reverence for the man of culture . . . Waiting for their artist (dead or alive) with monumental solicitude . . . Muse with legs constantly opened for his enjoyment, breasts trembling over him like bread loaves warm from the oven.

At night he often dreamt of Claire's stingy, Anglican little athlete's body.

Earliest recollections of Sophie's family, 1946: Edmund and Mara, Claire and Babsie visit together for the first time at the Rosses' apartment on Central Park West. The two girls huddling to each other shoulder to shoulder. Babsie: "What a heavenly home you have Mrs. Ross!" "Thank you Mrs. Sanford." Mara: "Ees divine house" (and in an aside to Edmund, "Parvenu, but so sweet"). Camilla Ross: "I hear your husband does a gorgeous business downtown Mrs. Sanford!" Babsie: "Oh thank you Mrs. Ross!" Throughout this ill-matched gathering Edmund stares at Camilla and reflects that he's never seen anyone so extravagantly adorned outside the operatic stage. Her kind, shrewd face is surmounted by an Athena's helmet of brilliantly lacquered hair, bangles clang on her limbs like many cymbals, she reminds him of the finale from *Salome*.

Larry Ross is short, sleek, mustached, plump and lustrous as a bullet. One finger of his left hand is missing, the result of a scuffle with police in the 1920s, when he worked as a union organizer to support his parents while occasionally attending City College. He became an unsuccessful actor, left the stage to work as press agent for a few Broadway and film stars. By the time Edmund has come into Larry's life he's added numerous musicians and playwrights to his clientele and even some novelists who hire Larry to ensure handsomer reception of their work. "Self-made man, former leather-tanner, child of the New York ghetto," the *New York Post* describes him; "Larry Ross has become one of the country's busiest impresarios." His mustache and thinning hair are now groomed twice a week at home while he roars out orders by phone to some minion agent in Pasadena or purrs to directors of the Comédie-Française, his library is upholstered floor to ceiling in the tartan of the McPherson clan, there are signed photographs of John Gielgud, Sir John Barbirolli, Ralph Richardson, Leslie Howard, Sir Laurence Olivier on the Rosses' piano, their immense collection of polished brass—doorknobs, decanters, candlesticks, lamps, mortars and pestles, wall sconces, beakers and salvers—demands an auxiliary force of five domestics before every one of their lavish parties to acquire its proper polish. Resting in the Rosses' library or guest room during the frequent bouts of migraine that follow his mother's death Edmund has ample opportunity to observe the mogul's schedule. At seven every morning Larry reaches for the telephone from his bed, grizzled and swollen-eyed, not from alcohol of which he never touches a drop but from that sheer mania for fame which began to torture his face in early middle age. He first calls London, Paris, Berlin, to be sure he catches clients before their lunch hours and by nine thirty works his way to New York trade, impatient for that exquisitely harassing noontime when he can track down artists in Europe, New York and California in the span of a single hour.

During Larry's hunt in prelunch Europe, Camilla brings him his velvet dressing gown, his *Variety*, his breakfast tray; and several hours later, when he has moved to the other two phones set on the desk overlooking Central Park, she brings him his lunch. From twelve to two Larry is at the summit of predatory joy, interspersing Paris, New York and Los Angeles talents during his manicure, searching through Europe for elusive actors whom he wants on Broadway the next season ("Where is Barrault? What do you mean you can't find him, hunt him down, track him, catch him before the day's over!"). He persuades Paramount to buy the film script of a new novel for which Bette Davis would be perfect; he reassures nervous conductors: "Wait till you preem at the Met, Maestro; you've already got a double page all set to go in *Newsweek*!" In late afternoon, European trade asleep, New York about to fold, Larry Ross is left to savor California until 8:00 P.M., when he emerges from his bedroom triumphant from his day's work and nostalgic for still more. "Oh Camilla *Liebchen*, if we could only crack Japan I could be working until midnight! What do you think about going to the Orient to hook up to the Kabuki?" If they are not entertaining or scouting for talent at a new show that night they dine quietly in front of the television, discussing the day's successes; or they talk about Sophie, apple of their eye, that beloved child of their middle years upon whom they lavished the finest education for art and womanhood available in the United States.

.   .   .

"I'll give you a big party for your next exhibition, Edmund Richter; whom would you rather have at this party, twenty young actors, twenty young sculptors, twenty playwrights?"

"How's our wunderkind?" Larry Ross bellows when Edmund walks into his flat. "How's my Botticelli, how's my Holbein?"

"Monsieur Renoir, I've bought you a warm coat on sale at Russeks, we women know! A wonderful buy, my pleasure! Your poor mother would have fainted if she'd seen you in that thin jacket in midwinter!"

"Sophie, you don't realize what a phenomenon your father was in his time; it's rare we understand parents while they're still alive, that's the tragedy of it, they fall together like pieces of a puzzle only when it's too late. . . . Larry was a prodigy peculiar to our 1950s, one of the first guys who wanted to create a cult of artists in a country which had disdained most artists with Puritan brutality . . . what was his favorite word Soph?"

"Magic, remember Eddem?"

"Exactly. He collected artists' personalities the way other moguls used to collect horses, racing cars, Queen Anne highboys, but for more sacramental reasons, the artist's presence was his talisman, his ride on the silver horse, his only infection of immortality. . . . "

From some celebrities—mayors of growing cities searching for an orchestra—Larry Ross made money. From others—painters, writers, musicians—he was happy to only make transcendence. Even light at the Rosses' lavish parties, provided exclusively by the glow of some sixty candles, has the aura fitting to an atmosphere of worship. Candlelight, much muted candlelight, and the throaty, secretive whispers Larry has coached his wife and daughter to assume in the presence of genius. One cannot stress enough the gracious pious hush, the liturgical reverence, of Camilla's and Sophie's voices when they introduce guests to Larry's collected talent: "Leonid Berman, over there by the piano, is the most exciting person to come to ballet design since Bakst . . . Irwin Shaw, by the window talking to Gertie Lawrence, may be the closest thing to Hemingway in our decade. . . . " Groomed in Larry's art of creative introductions, how adroitly the hostesses pilot conductors towards up-and-coming baritones, William Faulkner towards movie tycoons looking for a Great Writer's script! In these rooms resplendent with bordello textures and churchly lights, the fifteen-year-old Sophie had learned to pass canapés with such poise that the director of the St. Louis Symphony might readily return another time to stare at her plunging young breasts and be snared into a contract with the Detroit Symphony. Sophie, aged sixteen, maneuvering the caviar about the room: "Mr. Williams, *The Glass Menagerie* is the most transcendent *pièce de theatre* I've ever seen!" "Mr. Bernstein, I do think the largo movement of Mahler's Seventh gains unequaled beauty in your hands!" Sophie of the early breasts and golden eyes, how skillfully she'd been trained at the novel glory of seducing artists! And all around her Moët et Chandon pouring, salmon gleaming in their platters of polished brass, Lauritz Melchior and Ava Gardner singing a duet beside a piano strummed by Gian Carlo Menotti, Shirley Booth and Salvador Dali hovering over the caviar, Lucrezia Bori and Truman Capote playing backgammon at a neighboring table, a clipping from last week's *Daily News* prominently displayed next to a brass tankard saying Talent Magnates Larry and Camilla Ross Entertain Lawrence Tibbett and Irwin Shaw in Their Plush CPW Home, Larry bellowing "I'll get you from the Jay Thorpe level of the stage to Bergdorf's!" Camilla Ross emerald-lidded graciously smiling in a mountainous gown of purple brocade whispering "You must return next Thursday, we're having Sir Wildestein, one of England's most gorgeous patrons of theater, and the German ambassador . . ." (a knowing pause) ". . . to the UN."

Editors of *Life* magazine seduced into writing a feature story on the new conductor of the Chicago Symphony, authors achieving a desired transition from Harper's to Random House at the flick of a Larry Ross introduction.

"Head of Philip Morris Corporation, meet the dancing wonder of the City Center Ballet and wait till this little genius hits Kentucky to preem in your auditorium!"

"Publisher of the *Los Angeles Times*, meet the most magic tenor of the San Francisco Opera!"

"Director of the St. Louis Museum, I want you to meet the most promising young painter in America! Just look at that masterpiece by the window, Maestro; couldn't you just reach out and eat that fruit it's so real? . . . "

The artist Edmund's work was most often compared to was Chardin. Pellucid tonalities, lyrically precise rendering, tight lustrous textures. Edmund enjoyed a mastery of the most ancient archaic recipes of the painter's trade; he found the modern world odious for its capitulation to immediacy, facility. He painted on wooden panels of five plies of maple to retain the full luminosity of old masters' gesso techniques. He mixed his own grounds. He began by steeping two and three-quarters ounces of rabbit or hare's skin glue in a quart of cold water; the glue was soaked overnight and turned an opaque greenish-gray as it swelled to three times its volume. It had to be slowly heated in a double boiler; he cooked his potions in the morning when Sophie went to work to spare her the acrid smell, though she claimed it was pleasant; he was ever amused and touched by her accommodations. The glue was poured into a pot containing the chalk or whiting, stirred continually for an hour, strained through several layers of cheesecloth. After brushing the mixture onto his panels Edmund completed the smooth ivory perfection of his painting ground by rubbing it down with several different grades of sandpaper. He used imprimaturas of pale Venetian red mixed with egg yolk, rendered his values in umber and white before applying any further color. His portraits of the ebullient Sophie were brooding, imposing, reflective. "Richter's paintings achieve their classic character by their virtuosity of execution and an emotional detachment remarkable in an artist of so young an age. . . ."

Sophie could not run their ménage without bringing home six bottles of wine at a time, five pounds of peaches, three armfuls of flowers. ("Oh those zinnias against your purple cape, just sit the way you are Soph, don't move, don't move. . . .")
Her college teachers had claimed that she was destined for one of the most brilliant careers of her generation of women "if she could

only focus at considerably greater length on any one of her extraordinarily varied fields of interest."

She swooped with equal appetite upon the latest tidbits of quantum physics, jazz history, Marxist analysis, social biology; her weight had as much variety as her information, her mercurial body waned by scores of pounds as she dove into another week-long fast of grapefruit or papaya. On other days when she sat cross-legged on the floor gorging on her favorite crème brûlée, Edmund saw in her the lustful conniving impulsive child he cherished more than any of her personae, the fat greedy kid who needed to savor down to the last lick every delectable tidbit of opera, friendship, literature, ballet, anthropology, swimming fests, haute cuisine. She was phenomenally industrious; Edmund insisted they share their rent and refuse Larry's magnanimous offers of support; though none of her jobs lasted for more than a few months she'd accepted Edmund's decision that she must "emancipate" herself from her parents. She taught modern dance at a trade school in the Bronx. She previewed shows for a TV magazine. She volunteered at the Upper West Side Democratic Club. She decided she might have a flair for fashion and became a lingerie buyer at Bonwit's. She rebelled against the decadence of that and worked at a welfare center in Harlem. She'd been the star of Ethel Walker's swimming team, she swam fifty laps of an Olympic-sized indoor pool daily to stay in shape. When she'd saved enough of her earnings to stop working for a few months she studied African dancing with Katherine Dunham. "Oh God, Soph, what next," Edmund moaned as she returned from each novel foray with a torrent of praise about its possibilities. "But E.R. you've known since the age of five you wanted to be an artist, the rest of us have to find ourselves. . . ." She took recorder lessons for some weeks and their tiny rooms whined with the flattened notes of "Greensleeves." She took acting lessons and their rooms stirred with the muffled, groping sounds of Method exercises. ("You are a blind girl. Palpate the face of a Greek youth . . . of Cyrano de Bergerac . . . of a baby . . . of a sleeping stranger . . . of your father . . .") One day she rode uptown on the subway and got a job as a reporter with the *Amsterdam News*.

"Now that finally is a *great* idea; you're a born journalist, Soph, you've got a mind for news like no one else."

She had the obsession of all modern youth, she wanted him to remember her as his life's greatest lover. Candlelight, fresh flowers, Coquilles St. Jacques, Pouilly-Fuissé, the art books she collected for him on the coffee table, the wide deep bed, her Tiffany glass shimmering like harem silks, Brahms playing softly in the background, the rituals of undressing, shall I dim the lamp sweetheart, would you rather in the dark . . . She was puzzled by the total readiness of his sexuality and of his simultaneous independence from it; her touch stirred him with ravishing instantaneity, he pounced upon her with such tenderness that she often thought she'd achieved the heat and beauty of ideal passion. But over the months she realized that the impulse had to come from her and her alone, otherwise he'd go to sleep, his eyes staring at the ceiling until they closed. She continued her tactics of discretion, diplomacy: he could have been trying to allay his recent sorrow, dreaming of his own future glory, thinking of the canvas he wished to prepare for the next day, having an occasional thought about Claire, she never asked. Her sexuality was industrious, intense, she studied the newest manuals meticulously to memorize directives for novel positions and sensations, she rehearsed her sensuality like a summa-cum student cramming for exams, she turned and twisted on her artist, alternating largo with moderato vivace as she thrust down upon him at a fabulous variety of angles, riding astride his pensive body like a jockey trying to whip up a steed. She purchased books on erotic Indian temple sculpture, mounted Edmund upon a corner of the bed and moved her haunches fervently upon his as she made him sit up with her legs locked about his waist. She put her mouth to him and circled her tongue languidly about the tip of his sex, one of her most perfect moments was to hear him comment on her artistry, yet one morning she woke up crying. "You never grab me in the middle of the night," she wept, "how can you love me if you don't *wake me* sometimes?"

In the winter of 1953 Edmund finished his master's thesis, "The Concept of Artistic Genius from the Renaissance to Our Time."

102

The artist is the man viewed as most dangerous to Plato's Republic precisely because he partakes of so much Godliness, because his poetic gifts are the result of divine possession and the making of his painted forms so arrogantly imitative of the Creator's own work. . . .

World's most cursed and most blessed, hospital case and prophet, tippler of absinthe and victim of nineteenth-century alienation, he will finally be banished, via the route of Romanticism, to the exile of Bohemia, Tahiti or hashish. Hooligan and seer, heretic inebriate and scapegoat for our sins, he will continue to be held as the complex object of our derision, envy, love. . . .

Most reviews of Edmund Richter's exhibition of November 1954 praised his "masterful control of naturalistic drawing," his "formidable skill for working with veiled transparencies of color." "In an age when the slapdash sham of nonobjectivism seems to be swamping the New York art world, Richter offers a breathtaking reaffirmation of the realistic tradition. . . ." A few periodicals were less favorable. In an issue that featured a monumental Franz Kline abstraction on its cover ARTnews admitted to Richter's virtuosity but dismissed his work as "complaisant oils depicting strong and pretty women in a nostalgically realistic style that could have been achieved anytime in the past one hundred years."

Edmund reacted very poorly to all criticism. Sophie referred to this as his tragic flaw. "They're beginning to want scandal and aimless ferocity, precipitate violence instead of the freedom of discipline! If that's the direction it's all taking I'm pulling out!"

There were always those parties for him at the Rosses. Sophie still cringed whenever he criticized her family. "Wasn't that the niftiest do last night, don't you think Larry Tibbett is sure to buy that big still life of yours?"

"Listen, Soph, one more mention of those artist-gobbling talent mongers I meet at your family's and I'll puke. If I have to sit through one more of those evenings I'm going to pull my pants down in the middle of the evening and play 'Jingle Bells' on your piano with my . . . "

She was an obedient dutiful daughter; he'd singled that out as *her* tragic flaw; she'd avoid his eyes for hours.

"You're the most magnificent model any artist's ever had," he'd say to console her. To placate her he drew her climbing out of a bath and draping herself in towels, as in Degas's great pastels. He often muttered as he drew, it was a habit of his, he sometimes murmured French cynicisms which confounded her. "Damn this business of art, Soph; in all that's useless one must be divine or cease altogether. . . ." When she didn't understand his meaning she gave him one of those smiles that made all other women's smiles pale in comparison; she had spectacular teeth, a little prominent but small and finely modeled, with a cleavage between the two front ones which she adored to hear him say was a traditional mark of great sensuality. He admired the firm ampleness of her flesh, its Rubenesque paleness, her patience. Patience! How often he'd felt her eyes upon his throughout the night (pale, the color of lightning) like the eyes of small hungry animals piercing the darkness one sees in drought-stricken country.

"How's my Botticelli and my daughter his magic model? Have I gotten you tickets to the swellest shows this week!"

Edmund ruefully mused that a season with Sophie was not unlike a season with Mara, minus the penury: Cossack choruses one night, Habima Players from Tel Aviv the next, Gieseking at Carnegie Hall, Japanese puppets, the Vienna Boys' Choir, she cried at them all when she heard the applause.

Once in a while after a cultural sortie Sophie liked to go to Larue's, to the Stork, "Just to see who's new and exciting there."

Sambas, rumbas:
If you're romantic senor
then you will surely adore
Argentiiiiiiina (tsk tsk tsk tsk tsk tsk tsk)
I'll bet an old castanet
that you'll never forget
Argentiii-iiina

When the moon hits your eye like a big pizza pie/
That's amooo-oooooré
When the stars make you drool just like pasta fazool/
That's amoooooo-oooré

Journal American, January 2, 1955—Sophie Ross, beau-
teous strawberry-blond daughter of talent magnate Larry Ross, was sighted at the Maisonnette the other night
with art-world wiz-kid Ed Richter, and rumors that
they'll soon say their I do's are burning the grapevine to
a crisp. . . . Sophie's celeb-hunter dad played a role in
podium-bender Leonard Bernstein's decision to sign up
for another season at the Phil. . . .

Camilla Ross loved to take "the children" with her on her brief
vacations in the sun.

Haiti in 1955 . . . Patou's Joy ("The World's Most Expensive
Perfume") emanating from the women's pink tweeds as Edmund
followed them out of the plane towards Oloffson's limousine . . . Sophie reclining by the pool, ogled by all men in sight,
displaying her majestic milky flesh, the luxuriance of her underarms . . . Edmund sunning himself between the two women, wondering what he would do with himself the following year.

Lying beside Sophie at nights Edmund often tried to recall those
black days after his mother's death when he couldn't even remember the pet name of that other beloved young woman who'd never
left his side. What are those inanimate objects after which wealthy
Gentiles call their daughters, he'd kept muttering during his illness,
Muffin, Fiddle . . . Fern . . . Brook . . . what's the name of
those objects one finds in a brook?

A curious thing had happened in the months of 1954. Edmund
began to draw and paint multiples of Sophie. He could not invent
any more poses for her. He sensed he had explored and exhausted
the total entity of that patient malleable body. He was now painting
her repeatedly in the same identical pose, arm under head, knees
chastely drawn up, eyes not cast down on a book anymore but staring out of the canvas with a haunted, intelligent gaze. He simply did
the same painting over and over and over again, varying only the

tonality of the undercoat—raw umber, terre verte, sienna, red ocher, grisaille. During the week, when she was out working, he used the same principle of repetition in his still lifes. He painted precisely similar arrangements of vase, fruit, tablecloth in multiples of four, eight, sixteen, thirty-two canvases.

                                                    February 1st, 1955

Jeff old boy,

Happy New Year and how are you? I hope your Oxonian studies are all you'd expected them to be; the first thing I'll do when I have the courage to travel alone again is to visit the Ashmolean down the street from you, three Brueghels of unsurpassed beauty right there. . . . I've had a super year selling out two shows and indulging in the prehensile hospitality of the Ross clan. Listen, that talent-gobbling world of the Big Apple is getting to be more exhausting than ever. Consumption of artists a sacrament of success, like fatness for tribal chieftains. Will you eat your artist now or shall I wrap him for you? I've been consumed as artist à la Crème, sautéed with walnuts, boiled and fried (a recipe I frequently have to impose on myself in order to survive). Sophie's sweet as hell and very sexy, whatever that means. I feel like a bejeweled stud, like one of those bulls the Egyptians deified and embalmed near the pyramids of Giza. . . .

So that's how I am. It's seldom that I write you, of course, without inquiring about Miss Elusivity. I received no more than one brief card last year. It's so hard to know how she is, with Babsie and Plinker in Arizona. I hear that Sealark is rented for a three-year term what with Babsie so ill and that she's feebler than usual. News please! Shall we ever see our Paradiso again? Listen lifesaver, stay well and do know that there's always a daybed in our living room for you; we've moved three blocks east to Charles Street, with a large studio skylight this time, quite out of Puccini. . . .

                                        Best always, etc.   Edm.

At times Edmund and Sophie looked at slides of Nantucket together: Jeff in his Harvard-crew shirt, coach's whistle about his neck, masterminding a volleyball game at Sealark. Babsie with a spray of rosemary and zinnias in hand, looking surprised. Eighteen-year-old Pebble embracing her father as he hovers over his vegetable garden, her face nestled in his shoulder. Once Edmund caught Sophie staring at the picture of Claire with an expression of fascination, passion, anger, things so complex he felt too weary to decipher them.

Sixth Avenue and Tenth Street in the late evening when Edmund increasingly walked out for a few hours to be alone: whistling of cabs, garrulous voices from the Cedar Bar, brushes and canvases stacked up in the window of an artist supplies' store as in an ossury. One night he started his first postcard to Claire in almost three years while leaning against a streetlamp. He addressed it Angelface, tore it up, threw it into the trash basket in front of the Women's House of Detention.

He often feared that he forced Sophie to pose as much as he did to allay her devouring solicitude, to halt her invasion of him. So he started their weekend poses early in the morning, made her sit until the moment they had to get dressed for the opera or the Habima Players. When would this beauty exchange the happiness she knew with him for some prolific maternity? He would go to visit her, a decade hence, in some vintage New England mansion. There'd be a plethora of concerts, lectures, aproned maids, savvy young Finnish nannies for her children, first editions, poets in residence, pedigreed Weimaraners, a kind and philanthropic Wall Street husband hovering admiringly in the background. Increasingly voluptuous of body, she would stand over Edmund at the poolside, calling out the year's purchases and accomplishments, her chairmanship of the Connecticut Democratic Party Committee, her rescue of three community theaters. He would lie in the sun and softly whisper, "You plague me with your abundance, you plague me with . . ."

Her smell of rose water and moist animal fur. Her nimble loving hands repairing his shirts, massaging his neck, whipping up delicate mousses in their little kitchen.

At times he adored her.

The threat of her flesh and of his growing anguish on winter weekend afternoons, when the waning light of early dusk forced him to stop painting at four o'clock . . . listening then to Mozart or just talking, his head on her lap, pleading that his eyes were too strained to do anything else . . . he'd seldom known anything as remarkable as her genius for listening; like many men's sisters she was the central anchor of his life and its most perfect constancy; how often he wished that she could have been his sister . . . but such a fantasy would have been offensive to her, totally beyond her understanding . . . so he talked about his fears of being an artist behind his time, perhaps he was a born teacher like they said Jeff was. . . . "No, never, never!" she cried at such prospects and he realized he was threatening something as sacred to her as her faith in great passions. . . .

Early in the spring of 1955 he purchased a Siamese cat. He called it Vico.

"If only I could start everything all over again," Edmund said to himself, aged twenty-four.

During that last year with Sophie, Edmund developed a habit of sleeping away his moments of acute distress. Sleep was his refuge, his haven, his exile from all decisions. Living with this admirable woman plagued with insomnia he could go to bed at midnight and sleep until two o'clock of the following afternoon, paint for a few hours, go to bed and sleep again until ten o'clock the next morning.

Upon his last show he was interviewed by *Newsweek* and several other periodicals. He enjoyed saying things like "Great painting nourishes *the soul.*" Others of his answers were cryptic, ornery, tended to amuse reporters. "You're presently the boy wonder of the New York art world, but don't you fear you might be painting against the tide of fashion?" "The artist's business is with eternity, not costume."

London
Ash Wednesday, 1955
Sophie darling . . . how joyful to put your dear name down on paper again. . . . I just finished writing Plinker and Babsie and telling them how profoundly I'm beginning to miss the States after this almost three

years' absence. . . . *It's been very very hard as you and Eddem predicted studying full time while working, and there have been all kinds of essential political activities taking up my time. . . . Last December for instance I went on a 200-mile Ban the Bomb march from London to Nottingham, the spirit of the crowds was so beautiful, imagine one thousand persons determined to march together that distance, and Sir Bertrand came to address us as we started from the London Mall. . . . However I caught a frightful pneumonia and was laid up for almost three months with it, which is why I failed to send you proper season's greetings. . . . I might have been in very bad shape if Jeff hadn't come to the rescue with a decent doctor, I was so far gone that they kept me in hospital for weeks where I got all kinds of lectures about the dangers of vegetarianism etc. . . . There was that first week when Jeff said it was really hit or miss. . . . Well anyhow don't worry it's all over, it sounds as if you and Eddem are having a celestial time together, I'm presently practicing Schumann but each time I hear Myra Hess play I realize it's utterly hopeless for me to aspire to the art! A big hug to you and our rabbit love and tell him I'll write him myself very soon. . . .*

The quality of Sophie's flesh: on the best days Rubenesque in its sumptuous whiteness, like milk or whey, utterly luminous . . . on other days her flesh seemed to take on the hues of fruit gone too ripe, like Renoir's late nudes, which he had come to detest.

Suddenly at 5:00 A.M. on a spring morning in 1955, it was a Saturday, he ran out of their flat and ran all the way to Fourteenth Street and then up to Pennsylvania Station; he sat down in the first train he saw without having the slightest notion of where it was going, it took him all the way to Harrisburg, Pennsylvania, where there was nothing to do but take a guided tour of the Hershey chocolate factory, he was the only adult not accompanied by a child, it was just a week before Easter and acres of liquid chocolate were being poured into molds of rabbit and egg shapes, he stood over the ocean of brown ooze and wept because he was reminded of Mara's extravagant Easter feasts. ("Every man is born," she used to say, "but outside of Him who else had the imagination to rise again?") He wept thinking of the eggs she'd painted in such delicate silken hues, of the Russian princes sitting over their pascha and koulitch and swallowing small teaspoons of raspberry jam while sipping tea from tall glasses . . .

When he returned the next day Sophie was in bed reading, smiling, bravely pretending she hadn't cried, cheek resting against her childhood fetish.

The following morning he was finally able to write a postcard:

New York City
April 4th, 1955

Sweetest Claire!

Do you realize what a horror show it would be if you didn't take care of yourself and got to the Harp Farm ahead of schedule, can't you just see the hundreds of jerks who would come to your funeral, your great-uncles from Detroit and all your lousy reactionary Republican relatives converging on Sealark, the whole goddamn moronic mob of them Cousin April with her Locust Valley lockjaw saying "yes dearie, it's so nice to see you dearie," and don't tell me that scene would be nifty, kind of neat, delish, swell, keen or crackerjack, it would be strictly lousy, nothing but a floppola. . . . Oh Angelface write me which boat or plane you're taking. . . .

viii

SEALARK'S summer tenants obligingly vacated the house a week early for Claire's late summer wedding, which remained a very small and private affair because of her mother's death that spring.

Standing at the front door upon arriving, Edmund watches Plinker hovering at the gate of the abandoned garden. He has not seen him in over three years, since the weeks after Mara's funeral. Plinker wears heavy spectacles. He has just turned sixty-five. His eyesight is said to have been failing. His face has turned an unhealthily yellow hue that could be the combined legacy of age and strong sun. He stares at the abandoned, weed-filled patch where he used to instruct young ones in the profitable growing of lettuces and zinnias, he looms tall and scowling at the garden gate, cane in hand, as if planning the reconquest of his domain. Edmund starts to walk toward his friend. It takes Plinker a while to recognize him. He puts on another pair of spectacles as Edmund approaches him and the gesture is as grand and lonely as that of a sea captain raising his binoculars to identify a distant vessel. He's recognized Edmund, he hobbles majestically towards him, arms outstretched, half yelling, half growling his ancient jibes and greetings. Passionately fond of young Europeans! Does Eddem remember all the times he'd been sick on his sailboats? Remember that time when he got poor Babsie so upset during the Game? Remember that afternoon Peb disappeared in the dunes and they ended up searching for Eddem too in the fire truck?

Oh does Edmund ever remember.

Well, what else could you have done but let that garden go to weed? What would have been the use of keeping Sealark open with poor Babsie so ill and all the lovely young people grown, and Claire away on one of her crazy searches in England? Thank God, at least that was over, Jeff had brought her safely out of it, that's one consolation Plinker has had since Babsie's death; now Plinker could finally plan his next few years of retirement; they'd rent Sealark for another few summers and he'd go back to Arizona—splendid golf club out there, a lot of fellows of his own kind, knockout place for the glums. And in a few years when the Howells returned from England he could move back to New York, live at the Harvard Club in winter and help reopen Sealark in summer; by that time there might be one or two little Howells to help out with, right? There'd be a new generation to enjoy good summer fun, a lot more beach picnics and clambakes . . .

In his excitement Paul Sanford switches two pairs of spectacles on and off his nose with great speed.

. . . but he mustn't go on about himself like that, how is dear Edmo, is he happy, we've all got to live somewhere, there's breakfast and dinner and so on, is he taking proper care of his digestion now that he's in some ghastly artist's flat? Is he making friends in his new life, always very important to pick the proper friends at his age. . . .

"I wish you were my father," Edmund says.

Paul Sanford takes his long-distance spectacles off slowly and puts on the other pair, staring at Edmund with curiosity. Edmund turns around abruptly and walks back to the house.

Plinker looming at the altar, crying as he gives his daughter away.

Edmund has not seen Claire either since he accompanied her to the *Queen Elizabeth* three years ago. She has not grown any thinner, thank God, and her body is hued that pale tint of honey from her few days' stay at Sealark. Her hair is longer and very lank, surprisingly unkempt for this occasion. Her superb face is as untainted by makeup as when she was fifteen. Even on this day she seems to have given no thought to her appearance.

"Oh rabbit love I've been happy enough in London but do I really have enough talent for the piano to make a career of it? . . . And besides with the world the way it is there are so many other things to be done. . . ."

"Jeff has a small comfortable post teaching at a boys' school in Wiltshire, two hours from London; he's always loved the country life. . . ."

Jeff has tenacity, oh boy does he. Like Sophie.

They stand at the reception line.

Claire wears her grandmother's wedding dress. Sophie, maid of honor, wears a gossamer number shot through with blue-and-green iridescence, like a pheasant's plumage. She lifts her arm to adjust Claire's wedding veil, the two women clutching at each other in a long embrace, the flesh of Sophie's underarms pale as alabaster.

Claire's breath on his cheek as he kisses her: like that of a child being put to bed. "Good luck, cookie," Edmund says. She smiles.

Cincinnati, Atlanta, Boston, Philadelphia, Baltimore, each wedding gift shines roundly on a long table, objects she'd rebelled against since childhood, Spode, lace tablecloths, Tiffany silver.

Edmund, champagne in hand, looking at Nantucket Sound: Would they procreate, could she ever grow large with Jeff's child?

April to Edmund, wry little smile: "What a dull wedding, dearie, this place is dismal with poor Babsie gone."

Sophie: "She's done the only thing Plinker wanted her to do, marrying Jeff."

Someone tinkled at the piano, Plinker perhaps, a bit of Cole Porter. As the piece ended, Edmund saw Claire rise and clap, smiling adoringly at her father, and again there was something rigid, Teutonically obedient about her frail little torso, like that of a toy doll spinning under a little glass dome. She scared him anew then, with her dual quality of obedience and rebellion.

How splendid Jeff looked as they cut the cake! His head had an air of elevation which fairly added to his stature. Shimmering with blue and whiteness, he looked like those perfect young American fathers at the head of the Thanksgiving table whom Edmund used to admire on *Saturday Evening Post* covers in his childhood. Perennial coach, eternal husband, docile consumer of all that's sold to us as happiness. . . . Claire, on the other hand, did not fit in. She was dreaming, staring out to sea as she had when Edmund found her hiding in the dunes of their adolescence, steeped in some communion with God knew what. "We're cutting the cake, Claire," Jeff said. And took her wrist and made her grasp the knife and strike it into the heart of the pearly white mound. He smiled and put his mouth to Claire's cheek. She waved her hand at the camera. There was a look of triumph on Jeff's face which Edmund decided had something brutal about it. He hated him. He admired him. He wanted to kill him.

Edmund took another drink and walked alone to the terrace. Gossamer boats speeding in the harbor like insects skimming a pond, thudding of tennis rackets on the court next door; he hadn't played tennis since that Monday morning when he'd beaten Claire three years ago, he might never play again, he might get successful and play constantly, he might explore the North Pole, learn Sanskrit and Hebrew, it was time to change a life. . . . He stripped off his clothes and dove into the bay. He swam furiously towards the gold-and-black hull of a yacht still called *The Churchill* moored several hundred yards out at sea. That Muse with whom he'd hoped since childhood to share the struggles of an artist's life . . . He was terrified by the helplessness of his desire and of his rage, by the threat of capitulations still to come. I am now obliged to deal with certain unsufferable certainties. Under my masks there's little guile, every betrayal is a little death, I fall upon the thorns of life I bleed, I take a short vacation from pain and have two years of perfect orgasms and fall again on the same thorns, will there be nothing between birth and darkness but a mire of imperfections?

"Goddamn tribe!" he yelled as he swam out into the harbor. "The fucking goddamn tribe has her by the throat!" But this time the water was as flat and calm as that of a child's tub and no one needed to swim out after him. They just went about the business of finishing that rather dull wedding.

114

Buffalo, New York
September 17th, 1955

My darling Sophie,

You've been my beacon, my life, my survival. You've been my manna and my daily bread, the miraculous substance that saved me in my time of starvation. And if I left during your sleep it's because I'm too much of a coward to do it any other way, because I was in a stage of despair and need which transcends any rhetoric of love. I slipped out of our haven somewhat the way I left last spring, went to Penn Station and took the first train I saw without even knowing where it went. Roulette, my little dove, roulette, there's much of the Russian gambler left in me . . . this time I took a few belongings, college papers and dear Vico, and we ended up in this town which I've always associated with the vulgarity of honeymoons in general and of Niagara Falls in particular. Tomorrow I take another train to San Francisco and Berkeley, where I'll start a doctorate in art history as soon as they'll let me. I'm sorry if I haven't prepared you better for this, but you might have guessed by now that I was being tortured by needs vastly at odds with the domestic bliss you so artfully brought me. . . . I may be rationalizing my brusque departure by thinking it was as essential to you as it was to me. . . . There's much growth to come to you and I was always stifling it beyond forbearance, only talking about my own goddamn needs and my uniqueness; you've got to concentrate mightily on yourself after three years spent with a virtuoso of narcissism . . . I'll write soon, I'll write often, oh I know I have a lifetime of explaining to do. . . .

Ever your own   Ed.

Berkeley, California
October 1st

Sweet Sofka,

Here I am holed up in a bleak student room after a long day of washing dishes at the local Howard Johnson's, still on pins and needles waiting to hear about the doctoral program and desperately needing to talk to you . . . having explained why I left the sweetest refuge ever

115

offered me I must tell you why I also had to leave the vocation I cherish as much as life—i.e., why I decided to cease painting.

I'm enough of a traditionalist to believe that the function of religion and of art is to help transcend the pains of life and make bearable the cruelty and senselessness of nature, that the task of the artist is to infect others with his emotions towards reality. And that this function can only be fulfilled by noble, finished, serene works rather than by the increasingly tortured fragments presently dragging the viewer into the maelstrom of our suffering.

But these may be outdated reactionary ideals, Sofka, it's possible that the creation of beauty has become obsolete, that the harmonically complete masterpiece is irrelevant to the fluid mayhem of the contemporary world. . . . Certain things are no longer possible as the devil said to Dr. Faustus. And when I look at the oeuvres of Messrs. de Kooning, Pollock, Kline now thriving on 57th Street I predict that their raw primal violence and celebration of the void will prevail, we're domesticating the outrageous, we've reentered one of those periodic cycles of rebarbarization that recur through history and America's giving the world a dose of barbarism socko this time. . . . I forecast about twenty years of its reign.

Yet you see Soph I hope that my kind of painting may resurface in a few decades, I refuse to indulge in the luxury of alienation, I believe that an art of equilibrium and celebration will recur and I'll wait my turn . . . meanwhile I prefer to make a masterpiece out of my own life, dedicate it to teaching the kind of art I'd have created in a saner time.

This is the only way I can think of surviving in this marvelous country which leaves the artist utterly free to influence absolutely no one.

A creature more superb than you will never again come into my ken Sofka; you've been the most constant, steadfast component my quarter of a century of life. . . .

Berkeley
November 15th
Sofka: I got into the doctoral program that begins next February! And they'll even give me a teaching assistantship which can keep some

116

cash flowing in. . . . I forgot to tell you that in order to get a totally
fresh start I gave away most of the lucre I'd earned from those shows to
worthy causes favored by two of my disappeared Muses—the War
Resisters League and the Tolstoi Foundation. . . .

Berkeley
December 19th

Merry Xmas, my sweet love, I think of you every day. No, I don't
expect any news of you yet, I know I've been a shit; I also know that
time will heal all present pain. I keep thinking of the plenitude I abandoned when I left you; I also think of how things would have developed if we'd followed the luxuriant course of the past years. I remain
content with my decision because of the glum predictability such a life
would bring: I would have ridden the surf for a few years in that talent-
devouring cafeteria of your father's which contaminates rather than
alleviates the artist's solitude . . . we would have led an "interesting
life," which is the ideal of many idiots. . . . Irwin Shaw, Ray Bolger,
Oscar Hammerstein and whatever brilliant professors you pick up in
your varied courses of study would have turned up at our first child's
baptism . . . within a few years I'd be filled with the jaded singsong
of an artist radically out of step with his time. . . . I see myself tragically consuming yogurt to keep ulcers at bay after six hours of teaching basic drawing in some dreary Middle Western college. . . .

Now for a few questions I must ask about you, whose destiny is as
precious to me as mine. Have you ceased dedicating your life to a
member of the male sex? Are you being less generous, more self-cen-
tered with your admirable energies? Have you quit thinking that fucking artists is going to lead you to a higher state of reincarnation? All
these conditions must be met my darling if you're going to find the
happiness you deserve. There are too many rich little Jewish girls
around whose greatest dream is to marry an artist when they grow up
and when they're twenty-one their daddy buys them the largest toy
artist at F. A. O. Schwartz, a six-foot-two artist with real vinyl teeth,
real plastic hair and a genuine corduroy suit; every morning the little
heiress winds up her toy with a big key that fits to the small of his back
and says have a good day dear, off to your studio now . . . unfortu-
nately I've felt just like such a toy in the past year; I'll find you easier to

117

live with when you start fulfilling some of your own considerable talents sweetheart; you happed on a half-Jewish nomad who's got too much rage in his heart to afford being a retail item in your dad's booming celeb factory.

Leaving you I feel like an adolescent who suddenly, painfully must abstain from the magic of his mother's touch, must sever himself from this source of nurturing to achieve his true strength and avoid the scarring of dependence. . . .

More very soon my darling, I'll be watching for your syndicated by-line in the Daily News!

Moderato, with sincerity
Edm.

Berkeley
January 4th, 1956

Beloved Sofia Larionovna,

I miss you as desperately as ever; I feel I owe you a still clearer reading of why I had to flee the dreadful power of your family's protection.

I'll start with the following incident: It was the fourth anniversary of Mara's death last week, and suffering a deeper solitude than I've ever known, determined to suffer through it stoically, I went to Mass for the first time in many years and watched people indulging in the most archaic, ancient desire of mankind, which is to eat the God.

I suddenly grasped, with unprecedented clarity, the power of our unending desire to devour the Godhead and its symbols. How did tragedy and all other art arise? Out of religious sacrifice, out of the universal need to both placate and consume that which is most sacred and to appropriate part of its power. And I understood that it is the artist's risk, precisely because he has a trace of the divine in him, to be in some way destroyed by society.

Take it from there; what happens in a society as profoundly desacralized as ours! It has nothing godly to consume anymore except the artist! Oh Sofka will the world ever resolve its curious ambivalence of love, envy, appetite, hatred for us! What duplicitous ways you've found to destroy us, either by letting us starve (as we did in our noble nineteenth-century garrets) or else by devouring us (as you presently threaten to do).

Well I'll tell you kiddo, I'd rather starve than be eaten, anytime!

What's most terrifying of all is our willingness to sacrifice ourselves for you to resolve your ambivalence, to purge you of your hatred and earn your exclusive affection and esteem. Oh, we'll do anything to forge your love, in life and in death, we'll destroy ourselves in drugs like Verlaine, we'll drown ourselves in booze like Scott Fitzgerald and Dylan Thomas, we'll do anything to satisfy the myths you create for us. . . .

And you wait and see sweetheart it's going to get worse and worse with your dad's spectaculars glamorizing our destruction, we'll alternate being buffoons and media martyrs, Truman Capote will pull his pants down and piss right on television, Irwin Shaw will buy a fistfight with Larry Rivers on the Jack Paar show; by the 1980s the expiatory devouring act will be brought directly into your living room, ladies and gentlemen; artists will commit suicide right on the idiot box to keep your love.

Hoc est enim Corpus meum right on the telly kiddo.

Oh Soph dear Soph I left this racket just in time!

To return to what I wrote you a few months ago:

I hope that my turn will come again; that we shall once more be capable of celebrating the beauty of the created world; and also of preserving our sanity by holding society at bay as a worthy adversary instead of capitulating to its greed.

Until that day I'm using the most expedient recipe yet found for the artist in our times: "Exile. Silence. Cunning."

Part Two

The theme was richness over time.
It is a difficult story and the wise never choose
it . . .

ROBERT HAAS,
Against Botticelli

ix

UPON arriving at Kiev from Georgia, Edmund, Sophie and Claire are taken to see the statue of Prince Vladimir, founder of Russia's oldest city. His statue stands among tall beeches at the site where he once offered Slavs the choice between Christian baptism and death by drowning. At least that is the way Evgeny tells it. Below Saint Vladimir, the Dnieper flows the color of flawed amber, russet beeches lean towards it like penitents from shoals of dirty sand; nothing special here in the way of bathing, Sophie comments, let's not even try it in this city. As they ride to the center of town Irina points to an eighty-nine-room palace built in three days to comply with the whims of the second-to-last czarina, who never set foot in it, after all. Eighty-nine rooms never used, all that money, labor at the expense of the Russian people! A few members of the Intourist group ask if they can visit Babi Yar, burial place of over a hundred thousand persons killed by German occupation forces. Evgeny stands mute at the request, swatting flies with his copy of a folded *Pravda*. Don't even think of it, Irina says, that's over an hour from Kiev, farther than any cab accepts to go, so . . . visit impossible. But Edmund gets a few taxis on his own. And the Americans get to Babi Yar with no problem, seeing it is in the center of the town, ten minutes from the hotel.

At Babi Yar a bronze monument now dominates a majestic ravine in which the victims lie buried. Arthur Zabar takes over as guide: During their occupation of Kiev, Nazis massacred some eighty thousand Jews here and went on to exterminate Ukrainian and Russian resisters. But the site was ignored until the early 1960s when Yevtushenko made it famous in a poem: "There are no monuments on Babi Yar, A steep ravine is all, a rough memorial."

Soviet authorities have tried to suppress the fact that Jews were the first victims to be singled out at Babi Yar. Arthur Zabar thereupon puts on his yarmulke and reads a prayer in Hebrew from a little book covered in white vinyl which he keeps in his shopping bag. The Americans stand heads bowed for a few minutes, staring at the cenotaph. The sight is awesome. The tortuous summit of the bronze monument depicts a prisoner trying to burst from his chains. Even after thirty years the ground at Babi Yar remains brown and barren because of the massive chemical effect of quicklime poured upon decomposing bodies. There are only a few shreds of dried flowers at the monument, Sophie notes; visits must still be very rare, little will ever grow in this terrain. Claire and Sophie pluck blades of grass thrusting through the cement of the walkway and place them at the statue's feet. "Ten minutes from the hotel door to door and they tell you it's impossible," Ethel Zabar says as she replaces her husband's yarmulke in her shopping bag. "According to that party slave who's herding us around it was two hours out of town!" Arthur Zabar exclaims. "What kind of human rights can you expect," Claire asks, "in a country where lovely girls like that are forced to lie for a decent living?"

The next morning they take a plane to Leningrad. As they drive towards their hotel from the airport Edmund recognizes from his mother's aquatints the yellow walls of the Smolny Institute which served as Bolshevik headquarters in 1917. He has a recurring dream of Mara in which they walk down Leningrad's streets looking for her childhood home near the Smolny; they never succeed in finding it; in successive dreams it's been destroyed by Red troops, German artillery, has been superseded by a hospital, an exhibition hall of Soviet farm machinery . . . Edmund wishes to grab Sophie's arm and tell her that Mara's childhood home must be right near here, near the Smolny, but Sophie and Claire are arguing again with Evgeny about religion. A narcotic vagary doomed to disappear, Evgeny says, just as Karl Marx put it! How can you say it's disappearing, Claire protests, look at the babies being christened in your country, the churches often filled! You take the Marx quote out of context, Sophie adds, he called religion "the heart of a heartless world," and only then does he call it "the opium of the people. . . ." Evgeny smiles and compliments Sophie on her interest in Marx. At the back of the bus the Rolls-Royce dealers talk about their newly purchased balalaikas and the pleasures of the trip; isn't it gorgeous traveling through a country where there's no graffiti, no pornography on any walls? Sophie has slept well and is in cheerful mood, banters with the Weickers, who're great fans of her morning show, about détente and the average income of the Soviet factory worker. Edmund stares at the nursery-blue hues of St. Nicholas Cathedral, at the sumptuous lilac tints of the sky surrounding its gilt domes. These days he cannot be exceptionally moved by a landscape or the hue of a wall without wondering what pigments he'd have mixed to render it. "I do not know which to prefer," he recently wrote Claire in a letter which he considered profoundly Slavic, "my suffering before or after the cessation of my art. It is not so much joy which leads us to paint or write but terror of our death, fear of not leaving enough claw prints on the dunes of time; sorrow lies on either side, the act of art is strung between two poles of pain. . . ." The tenderness of St. Nicholas' walls could be rendered in cobalt blue mixed with a very small dose of white, sky would need a trace of cobalt violet, church's marble pilasters have a rose tint prone to alizarin or madder. Dulcet sweetness of Leningrad's hues the most striking first impression; what brutal history is cloaked with a more ambrosial palette, siege of the early 1940s, men boiling leather briefcases into a sticky mass for their dinner, stripping off wallpaper paste to get at its traces of potato flour, more dead of hunger than in any other city in history after Stalin's purges had already carried off millions. Azure palaces, mourning mothers, icy foreheads of starving children, Shostakovich conducting to packed houses, musicians' breaths exhaling clouds of white fog in the freezing concert hall. . . . As the bus rumbles alongside the Neva, Edmund watches the first sun worshipers leaning against the cement of the river's embankment; in this most heroic of cities hundreds of survivors have stripped their bodies and lean against stone walls, eyes closed, lard-hued flesh begging for June's first warming rays; how many summers do they have left, how many do any of us have before it will be decidedly too late to find grace or rebecome what we could wish to be?

"Your mother was from this city, Dr. Richter?" Evgeny's spectacles still shield the curiosity he evidences towards Edmund's party.

"Ah yes Evgeny, my esteemed foremothers were suffering women who taught the harp to your grand duchesses. . . ."

"My parents are dead also," Sophie tells Evgeny, "they ruined my life and I loved them greatly; don't you think most parents have a way of destroying us in some symbolic way . . . oh I suppose you don't subscribe to such Freudian ideas Evgeny Sergeievich?"

"Today gentlemen and ladies we are going to visit Fortress of Peter and Paul. . . ."

The bus is loaded, ice-blue, packed with memories. Irina smiles at her flock, smooths her American jeans, switches on her little microphone. "On way to fortress I urge you please to notice famous Winter Palace Square, largest public space in world after People's Square in Peking. . . ."

Professor Richter is again assured that the group is scheduled to visit the Hermitage Museum on Monday of next week. He is urged to take note of the interior of Peter and Paul prison, forbidden to visit of public until the Revolution and surely not included in his 1915 Baedeker. "One of the first prisoners to be executed there was the only son of Peter the Great, who had rebelled against the czar's reforms and was put to death by his father's own hand. We shall also see the cells once inhabited by Dostoevski, Gorki, Kropotkin, Lenin's brother, Alexsandr Ulyanov . . ."

"What do you propose to do about that dissident, Peb?"

"Everything I can obviously; he's on a hunger strike in one of the worst jails in Russia and I'm trying to reach his friends ahead of time so I can arrange to meet them but I can't even get a phone connection to Moscow. . . ."

"And what precisely can they do?"

"Give me a report on the exact state of his health so we can start putting pressure on to get him out of jail. . . ."

In the heat of the late afternoon Edmund had paused in Decembrists' Square to admire the statue of Peter perpetually defying the pale sky, stopped at a flower vendor's stall to buy fresh tulips for his women. He'd walked into Sophie's room after a brief knock; they were lying in a large double bed, Claire reading, half reclining on a pillow, Sophie bared to the waist, her head on Claire's lap, trying to have a brief afternoon sleep, splendor of two women's flesh joined in ancient affection, sensuality of sheets rumpled in great heat. "What's new and exciting, Professor, what beautiful flowers you've brought us!" And then Claire had started discussing her mission again.

"Since this damn tour only gives us four days in Moscow, I've got to make some contacts ahead of time. . . . The tenacity of this Baklanov, thirty-five years old and he's only been at liberty for fourteen months of his adult life . . . systematic hunger strikes to protest ill treatment of his fellow prisoners, confined to solitary in the freezing winter . . ."

Edmund stares at the Neva flowing beneath their room, darkening violet in the early-evening light. To recreate the curious dark sweetness of that sky, like lilac blossoms about to unfurl! A deep cerulean at this hour. The water a Prussian blue. Two women in black babushkas in an ocher yellow boat in the middle of the water. He toys with the pistil of a white tulip. "Peb take a rest for a change why don't you? Why can't you forget a bit about your missions on this trip?"

"Forget about my missions!" Claire leaps up, paces the room. "When will you ever leave your alabaster tower, Edmund!"

"Now listen you're not going to drop out of our tour and start getting followed by the KGB; this isn't a country in which to exhibit your virtuosity at guilt Pebble; you only have to be here for two days to realize that oppression is as great as it ever was under Peter the Great, who often decapitated two hundred dissidents in one afternoon with his own hands. . . ."

"What cynicism, Edmund, what does that have to do with my conscience, not a tinker's dam!"

Her pale face made more inscrutable by its walls of straight brown hair, for years he'd compared her to a medieval city-state, self-sufficient, impregnable.

"It has to do with the fact that you're a tourist of suffering, my dear, the way I've become a tourist of art, the way our Rolls-Roycers are tourists of Russia, the way Sophie is a tourist of everything. You've been saving asthmatic sea gulls since you were a child just to ease your damn little conscience. . . ."

"Apologies for your own passivity!"

"If I wish to bury myself in the difficult task of reclaiming our friendship on this trip it's my privilege to do so, so don't try to make me feel guilty about being an inactivist who prefers to remain where it was at. . . ."

"Please E.R., please Pebble, let's stop this!"

Sophie languorously brushing her mass of copper hair, pacifying them with weary dutifulness.

"You're both behaving as if we were still at Sealark; I didn't come on this trip to serve as some sort of Security Council . . . let's not be late for dinner again and bring a sweater, Peb. . . ."

Edmund said other things as they walked to dinner through hallways walled in scarlet damask, hung with bright fairy tales and scenes of the Neva at every time of year. You pimp with your purity don't you Peb, you know your problem sweetheart you've been trying to be a saint much of your life but you won't make it because you only love that part of us that can be saved . . . saints are one of my favorite subjects, you can't help but be a specialist in saints when you're an art historian, I collect them, I'm an aficionado. . . . They're tumblers of sorts, people who know how to turn one hell of a spiritual somersault . . . but your somersaults have been abortive Peb, as if you'd lost your balance in midair and landed aslant on the wrong foot. . . . She'd walked ahead of him with her air of being unaccompanied and having no one to listen to; he'd

128

reflected on the dilemmas facing three persons in middle age who've had a lifelong obsession for each other; Sophie had followed close behind them, pretending to be buried in a Russian grammar.

That evening the tourists are taken to see Leningrad's circus on ice. Edmund, Claire and Sophie sit with the clapping Zabars, the delighted Weickers, the gilded Rolls-Roycers among bands of round-cheeked Russian children. They watch seals dueling, clowns and poodles pushing baby carriages, trained bears in sky-blue skates playing hockey games. The youngest bear acts as goalie; he swings smartly at the puck with his little stick when it comes near his cage; when his wobbling ankles fail him the crowd cheers, the circus trainer rewards him with handfuls of fresh fish. There is much clapping and shouting among members of Intourist Tour No. 137 Destination Tbilisi-Kiev-Leningrad-Moscow. "Now you will see romantic ending," Irina promises. In the evening's last act a ballerina in glistening white tutu whirls about the skating rink surrounded by a flock of trained white pigeons. She holds a large hoop through which the birds fly in and out, in and out, like planets gone berserk about the gravitation of a star, briefly settling on her hair, her wrists, her breasts. An acrobat in white satin pants glides into the arena, seizes the ballerina onto his shoulders. He holds the hoop while she makes her exquisite movements through it; the ballerina now circles about her partner like a luminous satellite, hair flying, stretching her limbs into great écartés and arabesques. She stands on tiptoe on the hoop he holds, defying gravity, performing amazing gyrations in the air, and the pigeons become a third planetary circle, still gliding about her body to settle briefly on her breasts, her wrists, her hair. "Three rings of light," Edmund whispers to himself. Which may be nothing but a reflection on the harmony he'd like to achieve on this trip with his life's two loves.

Their favorite time of day in Russia is after 10:00 P.M. For after emerging from the ballet, the opera or whatever other spectacle they have been taken to they receive the guides' permission to walk back to the hotel alone instead of returning by bus with the rest of the group. Dawn through the night, dawn until dawn, in Lenin-

129

grad's white nights the sun follows them like the KGB; when they exit from the theater that night the buildings have sunk into a torpid haze of dark fruit hues, the sun still throws a slice of pale gold across the rooftops of the bloodred Mariynsky, the lime-green Stroganoff palaces. Still silent and trailing behind her friends Claire stops walking and sits alone by the edge of a canal. They are by the church built on the site of Alexander II's assassination, its dark-lozenged brilliance glints like coal in the light of night. "As the czar stepped out of his carriage a second bomb was thrown, the czar collapsed, face splattered with blood, once again as so often in St. Petersburg the snow was red with blood." Edmund stands by the embankment, wondering how long to let Claire brood alone. He walks to her and sits down by her side, his hand on her arm. And she buries her face in his shoulder for a minute. Edmund, Sophie and Claire walk through the city hand in hand again, talking about the islands, the games, the pains of their long adolescence. One detects no other serious tensions between them yet, not too many complications. They have loved each other long, their happiness in being together is as luminous as the white pageant they have just observed. It is the beginning of another beautiful Russian night.

X

On a July afternoon in 1959 Edmund stands in Rome's Villa Borghese Museum with a sheaf of notes scribbling some last thoughts on his doctoral thesis. He has chosen as his theme Titian's painting *Sacred and Profane Love*, which depicts two beautiful young women who resemble each other like twins but differ vastly in costume. The figure at the right of the vast canvas is nude save for a white loincloth, the other protagonist is sumptuous in a gown of white-and-crimson satin; they sit on the rim of a sculptured marble basin towards which a Cupid leans to stir the basin's limpid water. Many precursors of Edmund's labor had spent years of their lives debating the ironic symbolism of the women's vestments—was it the nude figure which Titian meant to embody Sacred Love, the vested one who personified profane and transient lust? (R. von Marle, *Iconographie de l'Art Profane au Moyen Age et a La Renaissance*, The Hague, 1931.) Numerous scholars domiciled in Leipzig or Stanford had dedicated themselves to the single issue of dating the canvas (1514? 1515? Right before or after Titian left the workshop of his teacher Giorgione?) And a few doctoral candidates of Edmund's unbridled ambition had elaborated on the *paysages moralisés* depicted behind the two beauties—dark wooded hill dominated by forbidding fortress brooding behind the figure of Profane Love, serene verdant pasture surmounted by church steeple

131

stretching behind Sacred. (S. Schramm, *Die Früe Bilder von Tizian drucke*, Leipzig, 1920.)

Let's not fuck up with our usual love of confrontation, E.R., don't strive for any revolutionary new views, always a risk as an opening aria . . . also avoid possibility of jealous positivists yiping against subjectively self-indulgent speculations . . . stay quiet, formal, earn the comments "impeccable, irrefutable" . . . just sum up most honorable findings to date and add some stirring insights of your own into Neoplatonism of Titian's vision—

—T's central theme is the tension between two kinds of Venuses, two kinds of love: (1) Chaste Sacred Love, *Amicitia, Caritas*, that higher form of bonding only reached in deep but nonphysical relationships versus 2) Sensual Profane Love, which Romantic agonists later upheld as the central ingredient of happiness——Brief elaboration needed on Renaissance's revolutionary attitudes towards nudity, its rejection of all medieval prejudices against the naked form—by 1515 the nude in art personifies the most exalted and *spiritual* attributes, Friendship, Genius, Soul, Clarity, Eternal Bliss——Include crucial historical background overlooked in earlier studies of *Sacred and Profane*—greatly stress general distrust of romantic passion throughout mainstream of Western philosophical tradition, right until nineteenth century's disastrous glorification of it—up to then friendship rather than love was seen as cornerstone of human happiness—Aristotle: Transience and destructiveness of venereal appetites, capacity for friendship is only measure of human virtue/Cicero: *Amicitia* more valued than either power, honor, wealth/Montaigne sums it up for the Renaissance a few decades after Titian paints *Sacred and Profane:* Love is "an impetuous and fickle flame," whereas the fires of friendship produce "a gentle and universal warmth, moderate and even"—

While traveling through Italy in the summer of 1959 Edmund enjoys staying in those modest *pensiones* in which aging couples, week after week, keep bottles of mineral waters and amber medicines on their tables. There is an orderliness, a delectable monotony about such establishments which reflect the pace of his own recent life. An order from Napoleon Bonaparte issued on the occasion of a soldier committing suicide for love has hung over Edmund's desk in Berkeley for the past few years: "The First Consul notifies his Grenadiers that a soldier must conquer the pain and vulnerability of his passion." Like many of us who've known the ending of an ardent dream he's come to think of himself as steeled and stoic, able to control all future lust. In such moments we may extend our disaffection to the entire race, conceive for the future of our species a Utopian breed that will live in perfect control of all fleshy desires while tranquilly performing increasingly noble mental work. . . . During his years at Berkeley little emotion has stirred Edmund, save the bittersweet memory of three childhood friends he's not yet dared to revisit and the blissful prospect of academic glory. He's already spent much labor on, drawn much applause, for meticulously documented papers on the iconography of medieval ivories, on the disputed meaning of clocks (reminders of life's brevity or symbols of a rising middle class?) in seventeenth-century still lifes. "Recipe for academic success?" he wrote Claire and Jeff shortly before leaving for his summer in Italy. "Charm the wives of those professors instrumental in voting you tenure. Head directly for the silvery-haired, old-school gentleman scholars whose pianos are littered with photographs of themselves with dear B.B. at I Tatti; they still hold the fort, thank God, at most departments from Berkeley to Cornell. . . . Don't omit enrapturing some of the useful faculty wives you might find most dreary, medievalists' spouses bovine with domesticity, blue-jeaned guerillères beginning to agitate for civil rights. Achieve repute for a good table, be noted for amusing little sauces, heed Oscar Wilde's dictum that a gentleman is one who is never unintentionally rude. . . ."

When staying in his Italian pensiones Edmund eats his dinner alone, a book at his elbow; and then walks out slowly into the streets of Rome or Padua, stopping at a café to study closely some architectural landmark and savor the prospect of the assistant professorship which will be his the following fall when he hands in his dissertation.

Upon arriving in Florence he'd checked into his *pensione* and walked to the Convent of San Marco to revisit its Fra Angelicos. He arrived at half past twelve, the convent's doors were closed, he remembered that some museums in Italy close at noon on Saturdays. He sat down on a park bench adjoining the convent, unaccustomed to suffering a flaw in his rigidly structured schedules, and tried to decide where to go next. In the Badia Church some blocks away Dante used to see Beatrice at Mass, in the Strozzi Palace nearby the medical student Savonarola had been brought to God after a severe disappointment in love. Church bells clanged, pigeons gathered in droves upon the statue of a nineteenth-century cardinal that faced Edmund's bench. He observed the preening of males before indifferent, scurrying females, their iridescent green chests and bright rose beaks, the luminous pink eyes that blinked like signal lights in a laboratory. A few young men in blue jeans sat at the feet of two silver-haired duennas, chatting. Italians, their respect for the dignity of elders . . . he and Sophie and Claire would turn thirty the following year, terror of reencountering a past; Sophie might be in Florence this very minute; in a day or two he'd try the *pensiones* she'd be likely to have checked into. . . .

Wisps of cirrus clouds hovered over the city like angel's lungs. An orange bus stopped and discharged a child in green licking on an ice-cream cone, two embracing tourists studying a guidebook. The pigeons flared upwards in a fusillade of feathers. Edmund rose and walked slowly towards the Bargello to revisit Donatello's *David*, feeling sudden loneliness. Shopkeepers drawing down their blinds for the weekend, bare-legged Swedish tourists clanging with metal canteens and cameras, autumnal palette of ocher and mustard palaces simmering in a great August heat. He reached the Bargello through narrow side streets, avoiding the crowds on the main squares. An adoration of the early Sienese school hung in the main waiting room, angels' faces modeled in apple green under the spread of rainbowed wings, mouths open in song or wonder. He climbed the staircase slowly, hoping for the same burst of emotion he'd received from the *David* eight years before.

He walked to the main room and stopped at its open doorway, startled and joyful. In front of the Donatello, a few yards away from him, a young woman leaned against a pillar in a pose of some exhaustion, kerchiefed head held down. Her brooding air made it clear that she didn't see the streaks of sunlight on the gallery's floor any more than she noticed its statuary, that she was engrossed in urgent deliberations of her own. She lowered her satchel to the floor, whipped off her kerchief with an exasperated gesture. Her cascade of copper curls confirmed Edmund's suspicion and he walked swiftly towards her, stood behind Sophie and put his hands over her eyes. She spun around and fell into his arms, her body much frailer than he remembered.

"Angel I just got the letter about your being in Italy, I was about to go to your *pensione!* I've looked for you everywhere, in Modena, Parma, Vicenza!"

"But those aren't the places with important Titians," he whispered, kissing her many times, holding her shoulders at arms' length to better study her face.

"Four years!"

"Why didn't you also write me where I could find you, funny one?"

"I wanted to leave it to Providence."

A few new freckles speckled her marvelous nose.

"Providence has been kind, let's travel together a lot. . . ."

They slept again in the same room for the following three weeks. Edmund renewed acquaintance with the arsenal of objects Sophie carried with her on all trips, he remembered them from their earliest adolescence. Postcards of Chartres, Spanish shawls, harlequin masks, she'd always pack a few of these curios even for a weekend, as if she needed them to anchor her nomadic nature; barely had she walked into a hotel or guest room—Nantucket, Haiti, Florence—she unpacked her magic identity kit, draped a mantilla over a lamp, rearranged furniture, cloaking the most banal room with her intense, domestic sensuality. On this particular journey her first gesture was to shift furniture about again, bring two single beds together, yet how careful she was to remain passive, serene! Edmund would usually kiss her good night with great tenderness after they'd read in bed for an hour.

She fastidiously studied every subtle change in his body, his face. His cheeks were ruddier, his mane of hair made more golden by four years of California sun. He'd grown even leaner and more muscled, tempered his body more fastidiously than ever, his moodiness had neither increased or decreased. Sitting in squares in front of their favorite churches—Santa Felicità, Ognissanti—they talked effusively about their current problems, mostly his. Ah what a life Titian had, it was paradise on earth! Such an artist didn't lick boots in the salon of some whimsical patron, he was often a grand seigneur himself; Charles V made Titian a Count of the Lateran Palace, gave him a knighthood, what have you, rulers from all over Europe paying visits to his studio . . . he wasn't yet quite sure how much biography to put into his thesis, there's that legend about the emperor himself leaning down to pick up one of the master's paintbrushes. . . . The motto on T's coat of arms bore the words "Art is more powerful than nature," the Romantic nonsense about artists' suffering was still a long way off, such an artist dealt in lumber and grain, invested in real estate, gold, jewelry. . . . There's a marvelous description of the freedom with which he worked when he reached his seventies, he used brushes as big as broomsticks and his fingers, even the palms of his hands; Vasari observed that he painted "like God when he created man." . . . He could do whatever he wanted, Soph, they left him alone, they let him work into the fervor and loneliness of great age. . . . She smoothed her hand over Edmund's forehead, reconnoitering the familiar grain of his forehead under her palm, the two small chicken pox scars on his left temple; he often kissed her hand and talked about the course in Renaissance he was about to teach that fall; by the time he was thirty-three or so he might well get tenure, he'd set himself the goal of thirty-eight years of age to be chairman of his department. . . .

136

They made love a few times in the three weeks they were together. Twice they went to Arezzo. Edmund couldn't remember the location of the church where Piero had painted his frescoes on the Miracle of the Cross; it was one of his more petulant days; Sophie kept pointing in the direction of the main square but he complained that she could not read maps, refused to ask directions. They arrived ten minutes before the sacristan was scheduled to close the doors; once in the church he refused to answer Sophie's questions about the iconography of Saint Constantine's dream. "Just look and enjoy them, don't try to explain everything out of existence." He complained that he'd remembered the frescoes better lighted, more grandiose, she understood how intensely he cultivated his moments of high emotion for art, that these were the only passions left to him. Later he stroked Sophie's hair and apologized, gave her the little lecture she'd craved. "That dream of Constantine you were asking about . . . the Tuscans excelled at depicting hallucinations, phantasms, dreams from the beyond . . . the Franciscan Revival, its gospel of unearthly joy was their chief source of inspiration. . . ."

That afternoon they sat in a café while Edmund sketched the fronton of the cathedral. He'd planned to do nothing but finish his thesis during this trip; he'd only started drawing as a way of protecting himself from Sophie's solicitude, aware of that nutritional respect she had towards the act of art. He drew no persons, no landscapes, only architectural details from facades of buildings, friezes and roundels, fluted pilasters and stone rosettes. She checked on his materials, pacing and talking to him while he worked, observing that he drew as meticulously as ever, with the same number three pencil on Arches paper.

"Have I ever learned self-reliance in my past few years as a journalist, Eddem; I love to work the overnight shift while the rest of the city sleeps, live in counterpoint with everyone else, share eight A.M. cocktails with the guys from my news desk under the Third Avenue El. . . . Yes, you're right, it finally keeps me safe from my family's invasions, one more Wagnerian diva and I'd have gone into my own *Liebestod*. . . . Eddem, I'd like to become the first woman

137

bureau chief of a European capital or the first anchorwoman to direct the coverage of a presidential election. . . . I don't care what Kierkegaard says about journalists, you overeducated boob; I don't give a damn whether we'll turn the late twentieth century into one immense voyeurist experience, you're so perverse, you really are, you're the one who inspired me to be a reporter. . . ."

Another day while Edmund drew, Sophie read him a note that she'd just received from Jeff:

"I'm writing to announce glad tidings of great joy. Peb and I are knitting tiny garments! We did want you and Plinker and Eddem to know as soon as all was totally safe. I've got her under wraps, she's seven months along and feeling nifty. The schoolwork here continues to be very satisfactory and we're carding splendid blankets from our own sheep. . . ."

He was squinting at the thick, bristling stones of the Strozzi Palace. She scrutinized his face, terrified at the prospect that it would show pain, equally perplexed to find it impassive, inscrutable.

"Anglican romanticization of nature as vulgar as it's misguided," he muttered, "stinking with baa-baa sheep and bunny rabbits playing croquet on the lawn."

Lying awake in the dark one night during their stay in Florence she compared herself to a hunter waiting before dawn for the most desired brilliant mallard to rise out of the darkling water, then rebelled at the image's violence and the metaphor was wrong anyhow; she had long auscultated her patience, was ready to wait for him for many more years—she often thought she'd absorbed some of Claire's pacifism in her search for great love; her motto was watch everything, mend when you can, lie still when you're helpless—during that stay in Florence she'd pretended to be utterly content with her present lot, her rising career, her new self-reliance—she lavishly praised Edmund for all this; only he could have emancipated her from dutiful filial acceptance of her parents' fame-starved lives—she never shared with Edmund the agonizing weeks she'd spent after his departure to California, her decision to only work night shifts for a few years to make a radical break with all that was most familiar and dearest to her in the city—neither did she share the letters she'd received from Claire a few weeks previously; throughout her pregnancy Claire had had great depressions, seemed unable to leave her house, had barely opened the door to go outside. . . . "I feel more starved and solitary than ever, Soph, stranded in flesh as in quicksand . . . will this be my only future, more cradles, more of my poor mother's carefully nurtured acres of lettuce and potatoes? . . . Soph dearest, do write me often and I'll write back faithfully; I who've always been so aloof and self-sufficient, I need you more than ever and probably more fiercely than you've ever needed me. . . ."

As Edmund fell into his deep easy sleeps he was aware that Sophie might lie awake in one of her frequent bouts of insomnia, humid and superb, still waiting for her once-and-only artist. He kept remembering those last nights in New York a few weeks after the Nantucket wedding during which he'd meticulously prepared suicide at the side of this woman for whom he had immeasurable love and esteem. In between his extravagant orgies of sleep he had outlined diverse plans for self-destruction in order to escape his growing anguish, replace the death by smothering which her solicitude threatened him with. Pills are too messy he'd mutter, drowning takes too much courage, pistols are better, ah, that neat tiny bullet hole in the last minutes of *Mayerling* which symbolizes the impossibility of any lasting happy love. . . . What will become of her? he often wondered in the summer of 1959 as he watched Sophie pacing up and down a piazza while he drew; what would be the fate of this best friend for whom he had such an ambivalence of love and terror? She'd redirected her indefatigable tenderness, thank God, towards the problems of the world. She paced about the streets while he worked, conversing with passersby or reading newspapers with the aid of an Italian dictionary, returning with disparate shreds of information: Italians feared a vacuum in Lebanon, ten thousand Algerian refugees migrated to Tuscany in the past two years, largest atomic plant in Europe about to uproot the sheep-farming economy of the Modena region. You've improved Sofka he muttered to himself as he drew, you're on the right road all right, you're more terrific than ever, but he never told her in so many words. He often castigated himself for his lack of heart.

On their second to last night together he lay on his back, kept from sleep by the knowledge that she was staring at him across space as she had so often in New York, with the piercing eyes of an animal making its way through the darkness. He tightened the sheets around his shoulders and told her he couldn't marry her yet. Oh I know, I know, she whispered, almost laughingly. And how does my Sofia Larionovna always know, what makes my girl so smart? I've learned that's the way much human desire works Eddem, people are always pursuing some great white whale, that which they can never have, the way you're still wanting Claire, the way I've wanted you . . . oh don't pretend that's all passé Edmund, I know just what Peb means to both of us, she's what Captain Ahab was hunting for, solitude, self-containment, perfection . . . that's why I've chased her too, we all want the unreachable; Claire's my closest friend but I doubt if she can ever belong to anyone or anything except those dunes and moors, those causes . . . oh don't worry about me in the least Eddem and don't be disillusioned, you haven't hurt me a bit during this particular segment of our life together . . . I know just what I'm saying Eddem you'll probably continue hurting women left and right as a revenge against being abandoned by Mara and Claire . . . yes I know all about the new Edmund, he's tough, brittle, knows precisely the kind of success he wants and is wearing some kind of mask that he's not quite comfortable with yet . . . oh stop that phony baloney about we Jews being so psychoanalytic, who else knows you as well as I do, how much do women mean to you Edmund, I mean, are you homosexual . . . no of course you wouldn't be lying here beside me if you were totally that; I suppose you consider yourself bisexual. . . .

The musical voice, the lilting diplomatic tone in which she discussed French novels. Dawn had washed the hills beyond the cathedral with a tinge of melon hue. Edmund was dressing, pulling on his shirt.

"I think most artists are narcissists, sweetheart, and even though I may never paint again I'll always remain an artist, I'll nurture my narcissism with utmost solicitude, water it, prune it, give it exotic plant care. It's enabled me to survive through thick and thin. As a narcissist I might prefer to wake up next to someone in whom I see a pond-clear reflection of myself, man or woman. And as an artist I'm rather fond . . ."

He drew the curtains open.

"I'm awfully fond of the sheer aesthetic symmetry bisexuality presents, though I much prefer women."

"I'm flying back to New York tomorrow, Eddem, and leaving New York next month."

He spun around. "When did you decide that?"

"About a minute ago."

"Well I'll be damned. What a monkey you are."

"I want to move around for a number of years, be a nomad again."

He stood over her bed, took her hand.

"Oh, Soph, don't lose what you've gained in the past two or three years, you've become so centered, so strong, you're on the way to becoming everything I'd ever hoped you'd become."

"Thanks for the last minute handout."

"Can't you trust me a little more, Soph? I have so little of your goodness, your greatness of heart, when will you realize how stingy I am about showing my love? . . ."

He pulled at a forelock of her hair, as he'd done to tease her since they were fifteen.

"Cross your heart and hope to die . . . I'm going to sit there in Berkeley hoping that you won't become a Rockette next, or the first woman astronaut."

"That might be cosmic."

"Sweetheart, I'm going to sit in Berkeley waiting for you to become another Marguerite Higgins, promise that you'll continue being even more of what you are now. . . . Soph, you're my best friend, my most trusted love, you're much of the little I have in the world, however rough a time I give you. . . ."

He sat down on the edge of her bed, ruffling her hair. She still smelled of musk, of essence of roses. She brushed her hand over his chest, unbuttoning the shirt he had just put on. He leaned down to kiss her, thinking this is a mystery I'll never understand. He knew again the ecstasy of her mouth enfolding his sex, of her tongue lapping at him like a suckling at the breast. She knew he had loved her absolutely, if only for an hour, which may be the longest it ever matters.

The next day, having several hours to spare between planes on his way back to Great Britain and the United States, Edmund stopped in Rome's Villa Borghese to take a few last notes on Titian's *Sacred and Profane Love*. One beauty shimmering in white-and-crimson satin, the other sumptuously naked to the waist, holding in hand a flaming torch that points to heaven.

—Careful to refute any earlier theses which posit antagonism between personifications of Sacred and Profane Love—It can't be overemphasized that Sacred looks at Profane with unbounded depths of affection—one could even suggest that the Cupid stirring the water at the picture's center could be homogenizing the principles represented by the two women—support Panofsky throughout, stress admirably sane Renaissance view of human emotions embodied in this canvas—relate briefly to disastrous contemporary ethos, we aren't yet prey here to the odious modern dichotomy between deviant and "normal" sexuality, between genital love and "platonic" friendship—Renaissance ideals embodied in Titian's vision present a vastly different view of human bonding—Human affections seen here as a vast rich spectrum in which *Amicitia, Caritas, Eros, Philia* can freely flow into each other, can take on many modulations within the life-spans of persons bonded by great and lasting friendships (see Marsilio Ficino, *Opera, et quae hactenus extetére*, Basel, 1576).

xi

IDYLLIC exile, Edmund's Tahiti! In Berkeley in the spring of 1963 Nobel laureates design new bombs on a hill fabulous with jasmine while whistling melodies from Beethoven's string quartets. Fraternity men still lurch about the campus at 2:00 A.M. singing "Violate Me in the Violet Time in the Vilest Way You Can." Professors with doctoral theses on "The Crystallography of Radium" or "The Phenomenology of Hegel" are giving Mario Savio straight A's on his semester before leaving for their beach cottages in Sausalito. Edmund's seminars are held in rooms redolent with the smell of eucalyptus or (according to his whim) upon lawns aflare with the blossoms of hibiscus and frangipani. Scores of acolytes line up at the door of his office at dawn of registration day to be ensured enrollment in his classes. They delight in his mellifluous delivery and his meticulous concern for each student's progress. They enjoy that mastery of the ironic jibe (inevitably conservative in tone) which enlivens Dr. Richter's lectures and his annotations. Most contemporary art? "Apocalyptic wallpaper." Andy Warhol? "The Leonardo of Boredom." "Syntax is a faculty of the soul," he scribbles in the margin of a paper. "Only the most naive of humans," he comments to another victim of progressive education, "believes that there is something under heaven more important than convention." In this dusk of American innocence Edmund sees

143

only hills dense with vegetal splendor hovering over San Francisco Bay, lemon trees bulging with gold in his backyard and the growing possibility of becoming another Kenneth Clark.

There lives in Berkeley in the early 1960s a tall, blond, suntanned professor who fascinates Edmund because of the sheer abundance of his happiness. Luke Edwards earned tenure at the age of thirty-three, has won every sailing regatta or tennis tournament in sight, is considered to be the West Coast's most eloquent lecturer on William James, has earned literary success by publishing delicately autobiographical short stories which center upon the unexpected felicities of his domestic bliss. As if this copiousness wasn't sufficient! Luke Edwards also claims to have found God. An ordained minister of the Methodist Church, he obligingly holds chapel services one Sunday out of two to enable the university chaplain to engage in his own regatta races. Edmund's friendship with the Reverend Luke Edwards enables him to draw the following conclusion: His own happiness in California is not one whit smaller than that of this creature graced with every attribute of human bliss.

"I've bought a modest little cottage overlooking the water," Edmund tells his colleagues, "with dreadfully mixed feelings about becoming a bourgeois landowner. . . ." The phrase charms persons of all persuasions, but at heart he feels no ambivalence whatsoever. His dinner parties (seductive candlelight, Russian delicacies remembered from Mara's days) are esteemed as the most delectable in town. He forces tulip bulbs, studies antique catalogs, has become a promising collector: Etruscan vase and XVIIIth Dynasty Egyptian bronze bought for a song from an unseasoned West Coast dealer, Tarascan statuettes bartered for a few dollars in Mérida. "I advise charming young San Francisco art lovers on the availability of Seurat drawings," Edmund writes to Jeff's country retreat in Great Britain. "I adore being seen with famous beauties, I've become skilled at many new levels of survival . . ." (it's with Jeff that he fully shares the delights of a worldly success which his other two friends might dismiss with Puritan disregard, involved as they are with their own searches, causes . . .) ". . . my occasional bouts of romantic interest are pragmatic and comfortably brief; last term a sophomore with the breasts of an Ingres sewed marvelously, a grad-

144

uate student with a Botticelli profile helped me cook master-pieces. . . ." When Edmund returns to his sunny cottage the cat Vico pounces softly onto his master's shoulder, rubbing his stubbly whiskers against his neck in way of greeting. He climbs upon Edmund's lap as he sits at his desk correcting papers and gently digs his claws into his master's lap to reassert his presence. Edmund often stares at the animal as it lies coiled in satisfaction on his windowsill, roaring its pleasure at the sun, and compares its furled contentment to his own. Shall we ever know passion again, Pussums? How should we look upon the disappearance of our elemental urges? Shall we say relief, ambivalence, a faint regret?

There also lives in Berkeley in the 1960s a large, garrulous professor of Russian literature who rubs himself against all things Slavic like a chilled animal seeking the fire's heat, and has no other passion in life save for women. John Mirsky is immense and bearded, lives in a state of constant crisis, prefers to engage in all activities in the supine position, and like the characters of the novels he lectures about seems to be forever suffering from some final agony of belligerence and passion. Visiting him one steers between mounds of Lermontov, Pushkin, Tyutchev volumes that threaten to avalanche the visitor like the crumbling walls of a ravine; one finds John lying on his dusty couch moaning his adulation for a newfound love or a newly discovered poem. He lavishes his most passionate monographs on the critical moments of the briefest and most disastrous destinies—the last poem written before Lermontov's fatal duel, the last letters written by Esenin before his suicide. John's been to Russia a dozen times, agonizes each time over the betrayal of his revolutionary forefathers' dreams, swears never to return but reapplies for a visa eighteen months later, revisits Moscow to wallow in the agony of still another disillusionment. His women can be frail, pimply freshmen or voluptuous divorcée flutists, he seduces them into his book-crammed lair for a few months, lets himself be battered by the pains of their infidelities or by the nascent bliss of one of his. And after a tempestuous dissolution reburies himself in his dusty rooms to write a new monograph on Gogol, Gorki, Gumilev. Upon peaks of emotion his large saturnine face erupts in patches of violet like the mauled cheeks of a boxer; turbulent passions or demanding translations manifest themselves like stigmata on his body, making him look as if he'd spent the night street-fighting in the streets of Yerevan. His immense, bearded form looms over all as he walks through campus, and by the triumphant or dejected cast of his head Edmund can always tell whether Professor Mirsky is living the end of another splenetic union, the bliss of a new one or the dejection of a womanless week. This is the way Edmund had met him: standing alone in a narrow abandoned stack of the Berkeley library bellowing out for his own solitary delectation some lines of Mayakovski's: " 'The sea is ebbing . . . The incident is closed . . . Love's boat has been shattered against the life of everyday.

In his lonely womanless moments John lavishes on Edmund his intense affection, bringing him rare Georgian vodka, exotic brands of tea he'd bought a decade ago in Kiev. After recounting the denouement of his last passion he lies supine on Edmund's couch, continuing to roar out more beloved lines: " 'Ah for that woman who brings us delectation/After having fully tortured us for decades . . .' " There are many discussions of love, death, the redemptive power of suffering and passion.

"The older I get, dear John, the more adamantly I support the view that mankind is distinguished from other varieties of fauna and flora by its capacity for total sublimation. . . ."

"*Niet, niet!*" his friend shouts.

"Ninety percent of the power attributed to sexuality is not so much an instinct as the work of man's imagination, his ability to fantasize . . ." "*Irunda*, nonsense!" "But look at animals! Their lack of imagination is the major trait that distinguishes them from humans, and many species only copulate once or twice a year. . . ." "*Oujas*, horrible thought!" "When will you wean yourself from the tyranny of romantic love that's strangled us for two hundred years, all a lot of Wertherian nonsense, dear boy!" "But there it is, big as the Winter Palace twice a day," John bellows.

The cat jumps off the windowsill, rubs against Edmund's ankle, walks towards the kitchen to signify his sense of approaching dinnertime.

"Most lust is a creation of our imagination, a form of literature!" Edmund shouts from the kitchen, stirring his borscht.

"And what else is there to live for save literature?" John yells back.

"I've said *niet* to the tyranny of the imagination, Ivan Maximovich, I believe we may soon see a mutation, a new race of postsexual men . . ."

"Utopia, monstrous reverse Utopia!"

"Will you not agree that the excitement, the anxieties, brought you by the erotic are more important than sex itself?"

Moans, unintelligible splutters of rebuttal in several languages.

Late at night they exacerbate each other's Slavic temperaments, stand on tables to drink toasts.

"Ah if you could only meet that exquisite creature whose betrayal cured me of all lust, Ivan Maximovich . . . I drink to her who has purged me of all future passion!"

"And I drink to the resurrection of every venereal drive in your body, Gedmund Petrovich!"

"To the defeat of the demon of desire!"

"No no, you desiccated monk, to the eternal Venus!" John drinks.

"Ah yes, to the embrace of chaste celestial sacred Venus!"

"You will see, Abélard, you will see!" John shouts back.

It happened this way: On the first day of semester a tall, frail creature with an abundant mass of golden hair made a tempestuous and belated entrance into Edmund's class in nineteenth-century French painting. Standing close to her a few weeks later in her apartment, where she'd asked him for a drink to advise her on Impressionists inherited from her husband's family, he saw her eyes as an unnaturally pale green, the hue of new moss at spring thaw. Within their first hour together Simona made it clear that her husband was in California much less than half the year, and was insatiably engaged in developing new terrain—carving up the Sardinian coast with descendants of the Aga Khan, buying hunting lodges in Kenya, Ceylon. She spilled her life to Edmund with much tossing of her splendid hair, seeming to have already documented

147

herself thoroughly on his, often drawing similarities between their
two fates. Ah she had been plagued by much misfortune! Her mother (Hungarian, an angel) died when she was eight, at the war's
beginning. Her depraved Italian father left her in the care of erratic
aunts, who in turn had her brought up in a series of provincial convents. *Dio* the horror of it, the beatings, the near-starvation diet of
sweet potatoes and sour grass tea! Her first lover—the wretch—at
least served the purpose of financing her acting lessons, which she
was sure would have been her true, brilliant vocation if destiny had
been less atrocious. But at Papa's command she was married for
mercenary reasons at age eighteen to a little count who measured
his descent from the ninth century. She had left him the following
year—he was the greatest bore in Europe—and spent two years in
Paris writing poetry at the keep of an art historian who was finishing a book on Byzantine mosaics. She adored art historians, she
could never stress enough how she believes in Edmund's genius. . . . Later there had been a specialist in eighteenth-century
tomb sculpture . . . anyhow, last year she married the half-Italian
scion to a San Francisco fortune, this man called Craven who leaves
her comfortably to herself with a few servants when he goes para-
chuting in the Himalayas or dives for coral in the most barracuda-
infested reefs of the Caribbean and has already discarded two earlier wives who desired bourgeois marriages. . . .

At least that is the way she tells it. Weeks and months later, as
Edmund cups in his hands the frail face dominated by shrewd jade-
hued eyes he thinks he knows what binds him to her. I am finally
staring at a face which holds some shreds of my own childhood: in
this sun-drenched haven which only glimpses the century's pain
through some crazy course in the history of film she offers me some
continuity with my own past, some shared pool of history and suffering . . . but the green eyes do not stare back with the same
recognition. Simona is seared, unaffectable, living solely for a tenuous survival which she's decided to ornate with as much novelty
as possible, white Jaguars, numerous travels, rare drugs and wines.
In between her trips to shoot rapids in Peru or hunt leopard in
Nepal she prefers to make love to Edmund on a fur rug in front of
her fireplace. Pale long-limbed body, flesh boyish or prepubescent

148

in its frailty, mane of flaming hair spread on a velvet pillow in the light of the dying embers—new items in Edmund's collection of the exquisite. Their meetings are neutral and torrid, unswept by any emotions except her whims for new sensations and his desire to break her will. . . .

"Nou?" John asks.

"Orgasm is another business of the brain, dear one, a way of gaining more information about ourselves. . . . But, oh, how she exploits the frailty of my ego. . . ."

"I know, I know! This creature as obdurate as granite is begging you to sculpt her destiny, correct?"

Will Edmund please help Simona to find her true essence? she begs him; she's always had to live in a loathsome state of dependence on men, it will never cease until she finds that precious vocation she's been struggling to find all her life. . . . Is she an actress, an artist, an art historian? This Sophie he often talks to her about, who helps support her old sick parents so nobly and has just won a big prize for her writing, how did she go about finding herself as a *paparazza*? Perhaps that could be a career for Simona, should she try that next? Only Edmund can help her look for the real Simona Danielli, a daughter of the depraved Roman aristocracy who might only have a few more years to live . . . she expresses these quests in a mongrel mix of languages through the persistent haze of Turkish cigarettes, her eyes glowing with intensity, in whatever moments she is not attempting to enlarge her still fitful grasp of the nineteenth century. As Edmund satisfies himself on Simona's insatiable body he only begins to feel her in his power when the balance of pain and pleasure she demands verges on danger, when he takes her with as much brutality as his body can muster after inhaling rarities that make his heart beat at double its normal rate. In between Simona's frequent trips he sleeps ten hours a night, meticulously supervises dissertations on "Cycles of Martyrdom of Saint Agatha in Italian Painting," "The Iconography of the Railroad in Nineteenth-Century French Art." At the art historian's conventions that annually fill the halls of Hiltons in Chicago or New Orleans, Professor Richter, index fingers delicately joined towards his new blond beard, participates in panels on Caravaggio or presents papers resurrecting the reputation of Guido Reni. ("Richter's trimmed his hair!" young women professors in the audience whisper adoringly. "I liked it better when it was more Byronic. . . .")

Some months after they had started torturing each other Edmund and Simona went to spend a weekend at a seaside hotel in Big Sur which Simona wished to visit because she might eventually interview Henry Miller there; she could begin her career as a *paparazza* that way. . . . Edmund had looked on this stay as an occasion to dissuade her from flying to Katmandu where she planned to join her husband on a two-month hunting trip. With a force of desire which he'd seldom before experienced he seized her many times a day, upon waking, in a quiet sea-lapped cove, before their dinner outings, testing his power over her by trying to make her promise that she would spend the summer in Berkeley rather than accompany Craven to still another nature-depleting trip to an underdeveloped country. But Simona insisted on everything, Machu Picchu and frequent stays at the Gritti and the Plaza-Athénée, she desired her master's degree and her Edmund and her tenuous ability to talk volubly about Courbet; why should she relinquish any of these freedoms for the sake of one brilliant member of a sex she detests, *Sono tutti stronzi!* She seemed to skirt the edge of emotion on the last day of their stay at Big Sur, her limbs twined about him like tendrils of fire about a log, she swore her eternal dedication to his body . . . but the next morning she insisted on returning to San Francisco, where she must pack for that trip to Katmandu.

They returned to Berkeley the day before Sophie was scheduled to arrive for a brief visit on her way back East from Hawaii, where she'd spent the past year writing a series of articles on the fiftieth state. "Statehood is outrageous!" (her last letter). "Do you realize that these blessed islands are blossoming into one of the most powerful outposts of the military-industrial complex . . . American imperialism cloaked by a seductive veil of sunshine and flowers . . . creating one of the most monstrous racist pentagons on earth? . . ."

"How nice to be able to catch a glimpse of you," Edmund had answered the previous week as he despaired over Simona's threatened departure. "It's far from the ideal time for me but I'll meet that 10:50 Pan Am flight from Hawaii on May 12th. . . ."

There are few moments more brutal than those in which a fantasy we have evolved over months, in moments of great solitude, dissolves upon the instant of encounter. Sophie had envisioned Edmund standing alone at the gate of her flight, guarded but smiling, embracing her with that heat of gesture always more ardent than any words he could ever offer.

The tall lanky woman at Edmund's side had a mane of gold hair that recalled the abandoned creatures of Pre-Raphaelite paintings, was dressed in thin floating vestments that gave her a surface of glimmering plumage. Her long pale hands shook slightly, she smiled perpetually, seemed determined to immediately charm the visitor. Edmund chain-smoked and never took off his dark glasses, reminding Sophie of those times in their adolescence when he wished to seem most inscrutable and mature. Sophie decided to remain equally inscrutable. Simona's interest in her seemed to make Edmund uncomfortable. He soon became garrulous.

"The ocean is quite beautiful," Sophie said as they sat down to lunch in Sausalito.

"The sight of unenclosed water is barely tolerable."

"Ah *ottimo, ottimo!*" Simona exclaimed. "I adore the Edmund who hates nature, it is divinely comic!"

"What do you do for a living, Simona?" Sophie asked.

"You never, never ask that in Europe," Edmund snapped.

"What do you do in America, then?"

"Let her be, let her be! She's a little sincere but sweet, so sweet!"

"I'll tell you what she does for a living, Soph, she collects art historians' cocks, the way Catherine the Great used to collect very tall generals. Jewish art historians documenting early Christian amulets, Harvard WASPS writing monographs on Ravenna mosaics, she's had them all . . ."

"Have you been to Caracas, Sofia, or to Bucharest? There's no reason not to go to Bucharest, the Brancusis are magnificent. . . ."

As they gave her a brief tour of Berkeley, Sophie kept asking questions which seemed to bore Edmund and Simona extremely, how many Chicanos had entered California since 1960 she wanted to know, what was the average yearly income of the Chinese working in San Francisco, weren't students at Berkeley beginning to activate for students' rights?

". . . and you have so many independent beliefs; it is wretched to depend on some dreadful male as we are forced to do in Europe, particularly if you hate men as much as I do; presently I am nothing but another bibelot in the life of a man who goes about ruining nature in as many parts of the world as possible; he insists I accompany him on his shooting trips and it is amusing and helps me get rid of my anger. . . . You're beautifully self-composed, Sofia, and you esteem yourself to be very strong, yes?"

"I'm getting there," Sophie said.

Simona flew early that evening to Katmandu. Edmund was co-hosting a party at the Faculty Club that night for a colleague who was leaving for Harvard. When he came to pick up Sophie at her hotel at 9:00 P.M. he seemed to be still another person from the guarded fragile Edmund she'd lived with in Florence, the moody irate one she'd shared earlier that day with the Italian. There was a forced radiance about him.

"We'll be an hour or so late to the party," he said as they got into his car. "That's approximately when I like to arrive to these academic dos. . . . You seem to be in absolutely terrific shape, Sophie darling!"

"And except for the terrific new beard you're a perfect mess, I think."

"What are you talking about? I'm in stupendous form!"

"What are those ghastly things you're chain-smoking? I've never seen you smoke that way before."

"You're mad, honeybun, I've always smoked, I started chain smoking at Sealark when we were sixteen."

"Cut out the macho. What are those smelly black things you and that Italian poison your lungs with?"

"Black Sobranie, the world's most expensive cigarette . . . so listen, out with it, what do you think of her?"

"She's very beautiful, and perhaps not as perverse as you romanticize her to be. A beautiful lost child."

"She's actually *quite* corrupt, and filled with utterly demonic complications."

"She's your great red whale, and I hope she gives you hepatitis. It's slower and safer than a suicide attempt."

By this time she was steeled to her life's search, as he smiled and tugged at a forelock of her hair she knew that he was hiding his surprise at her new measure of impudence.

As she walked into the crowded room with Edmund he immediately became its center of attention, his head stood magisterially above the level of the crowd. He stood radiant and seemingly immense at the door, lingering there as if he wanted to prolong the impact of his entrance; the crowd seemed to turn towards him like many delicate metal filings realigning themselves around a magnet, the sweet domestic classicists' wives with braided hair coiled chastely about their heads, the tall tanned archaeologists with yachting pins in their lapels, the tall sunned English professors who'd forgotten to take elasticized tennis bands off their wrists, they all turned towards Edmund. Sophie suddenly understood that need for instant and forever-assured approval which had led him to early success and early exile; that evening she thought she understood almost everything. He was making the rounds of the room, introducing her as his oldest childhood friend, "the closest thing I have to a sister," "the apple of my eye," "star reporter for the *New York Post*," "my very own house radical," he said another time. He hugged colleagues, kissed their women on both cheeks European fashion, made appointments for the forthcoming week, tennis matches, boating excursions. Time came to make a toast for the departing colleague, it was Edmund, always Edmund, who was asked to make the first toast. "This is not to say that it is impossible for Jonathan to simultaneously retain the deep affection of the Berkeley and Harvard community . . . it is rather to say that Jonathan has a greater capacity to preserve the affection of those two great institutions than any other Rembrandt scholar I can think of . . . I drink to those disciplined savants, to those noble alcoholics of the single object of Jonathan's incomparable dedication who will save our great academies from the growing barbarism of our times. . . ." Edmund does everything with such style, no one can afford to give a birthday party without him in Berkeley because his toasts are so unique, has Sophie seen his little collection of pre-Columbian? Each piece acquired for a song, what an eye! Sophie had to talk for a while to a voluminous hirsute Slavic scholar introduced as John Mirsky. "Grandiose man this Richter," he roared out to her, "the mainstay of my existence, can't you resurrect him, resurrect? . . ." At one point Sophie saw Edmund hovering alone at the bar, hands clutching the rail as if suddenly seized with some great anxiety he couldn't share; he was bent over the bar going "aah, aah," a strange sibilant drawing of his breath; this lasted for a few seconds and then he went to the mirror, ran his fingers quickly through his hair before returning to the crowd his brilliant smile.

As they came into his flat at 1:00 A.M. the cat's soft pounce upon Sophie's shoulder, its intense and immediate recognition of her ("eight years, Vico," she whispered, "eight years!"), gave her a moment of pain. Edmund opened a split of champagne. She lay on a corner of his bed, staring at the exquisite little clay statues on his mantelpiece, blank lunar faces, archetypal arms folded over pure narrow chests. He sat at her feet with his head in her lap, saying the Tarascan one at the right is probably a votive figure, some deity invoked at the time of human sacrifice . . . and then he turned up towards her and before either of them had undressed pulled up her skirt and buried his head in the thick hair of her sex, spread its lips apart with his subtle tongue, a tongue like a muscular flower petal that had a power, a languorous rhythm she had never known about; you are my Orient, this he often said, you're my favorite of all human substances, we'll meet like this as long as we live. Later his tongue and his sex explored every orifice of her body, the night seemed dissected by their flailing limbs, she had the image of insects gone crazed on some drug, mandibles whirling in all directions, mouths screaming for new angles, new chasms, we drone in ecstasy as we straddle the same road or lie furled, receiving bliss from distant hands, the other watches, columnar and vigilant, enjoying the joy he's offering, lying still in the expectation of his own pleasure, our limbs rotate like the arms of a compass, any dawn becomes awesome with the monotony of more desire. There was a new skill and delectation in his lovemaking which saddened her profoundly.

The next morning as he drove her to the airport they were affectionate, matter-of-fact with each other; this also was their manner, to act like two siblings who must discuss some family affairs before leaving each other for a stretch of time.

"Any recent news from Great Britain?"

"Jeff carding his wool and curdling his whey while Peb goes on her sit-ins and ride-outs for disarmament, gets dragged from Trafalgar Square every few months in the company of Sir Bertrand . . ."

"And they're due back this summer, do you know when exactly?"

"Early September. Going straight to New Hampshire, Jeff will be teaching near Concord. . . ."

"Oh God, at that ghastly stuffed-shirt St. Paul's of his."

"Don't knock it, Soph, few such islands of civility left! I've been writing our lifesaver a lot, heartily sharing men's problems. We made a pledge to get very drunk together every seven years; I'll have to look in on them next summer."

"I hope you look in on me too, you may be in for a few surprises. . . . You know, Edmund, I have no idea of who you are anymore and I'm not sure you know either; I've barely known who you are since you stopped painting."

He kept his eyes on the highway, gave an annoyed shrug.

"Art, art . . . in all that's useless one must be divine, darling, and I didn't have that much faith in myself, or in the future. Do you

miss posing for me, Sofinka, you were the most stupendous model. . . ."

"Yes, for some reason I adore to pose . . . how do you conceive
of your future these days, Eddem?"

"I'd like to write a lasting work, quote unquote, on some grand
theme like the nude in history . . . in twenty-five years Harvard
can give me a splendid Italian villa to curate, like B.B.'s . . ."

"*Perfetto.* Your career as a dandy is already off to a smashing
start."

"I'll have a *dueña* to take care of me, a mother figure in mended
cashmeres who paints on velvet. You'll come to stay and I'll pour
tea on a terrace amid rows of cypresses, surrounded by the most
beautiful men and women in Europe."

"You're certainly enjoying your motherfucking power trips over
the local rabble."

He gave her that glance of guarded surprise, threw his cigarette
out of the window. "Yes, three or four years of teaching can give
you the Pygmalion complex if you're any good at it. How about you,
sweetheart? How do you foresee the next years?"

She reached into his pocket and lit a cigarette; she hadn't smoked
one for years.

"I wish to be superbly taken care of. If you knew how depressing
it's been to spend three years as a roving reporter living in sleazy
motel rooms, trying to fall asleep to the screech of Greyhound buses
and the whining of icemaking machines . . . and then the loneliness of the evenings, solitary meals month after month in motel
restaurants watching teenage organists with foot-high mops of
bleached hair play the 'Dance of the Hours' on electric organs, feeling too bushed after a twelve-hour day to walk more than twenty
yards from my bedroom at night. . . ."

"You're so admirable. Why didn't you tell me more in your letters?"

"You're not the easiest person to communicate with anymore,
dreamboat. . . . Larry lost every penny he had and went deeply
into debt besides, some dreadful movie deal he got swindled into,
and Mama had a cancer operation . . ."

They'd sat down at the airport's coffee shop.

"You're even braver than I thought, Soph, tell me more."

"I've often worked until dawn taking on extra free-lance assignments to support them through all this." She became silent, head bent down.

"Why don't you stay over an extra few days and talk it out with me, Soph? Let's go back to town this instant."

"Your kindness smacks of duty. I do think you've got enough to deal with as it is."

"Please, Soph, please stay."

"We've got to do some of these figurings out alone. . . . It's just that it's not a life for a woman, Edmund."

"Well, perhaps it is, for an extraordinary woman."

She started to laugh, knowing it would forestall tears.

"I don't want to be extraordinary yet. . . . All I want is . . . what's that word the Italian uses so well? Repose! I want repose, I want to lie back like an Oriental courtesan and be fed champagne and pomegranates around the clock, servants bringing me fine shawls in the evening, I want to shut my eyes and just live, just live . . .

". . . live a life with *style!*" she shouted, banging her fist on the table.

"Oh, God," he said, "you're going to do something totally idiotic again if I don't do something about it."

Her flight was being called. "Let me go," she said.

And then, as she kissed him good-bye:

"I saw the most marvelous graffiti on a wall in Berkeley yesterday. One of them said The Future Isn't What It Used to Be."

xii

PLEASE note the central floor plan of all Russian churches, Edmund says, always in the form of a Greek cross, four arms of equal length—unlike the space of your Roman rite, which draws the eye in a long directional impulse towards the altar, the Orthodox liturgy focuses on the area right beneath the central dome—and this dome under which the community worships, moving about with uniquely anarchic Slavic fervor, is the symbol of the Dome of Heaven, the dwelling place of God—this central design might be said to express the Orthodox's immense stress on community. . . .

The pathways of the silent muddy town are sodden with recent rain, the church bells of delicately gilded Novgorod seem to have stopped in midcadence; Claire says it's as if some carefully timed poison had steeped into the veins of an entire population and just this morning put it to sleep. Do not even try to go into any church, Irina says, it is all under *remont*, repair, ah, don't ask me why so much is always in a state of *remont* in our country, Sofia Larionovna, you always ask such difficult questions!

The four of them had left Leningrad at dawn that morning. Above the worn brown seats of their train compartment hung photographs of a fiercely bearded Lenin, a statue of Pushkin surrounded by beds of tulips. "Today I am in my playful mood," Irina announced as she distributed a breakfast. "I've spent two nights in my home in beautiful large city and I'm in my most gracious mood . . . I shall give you little quiz. What is the name of the river we're passing on which Leningrad is built?" "Volga!" the three tease her. "Naughty, no breakfast. On what boat was the shot that was heard around the world?" "*Aurora!*" "Good children, chocolate for all. . . ."

The train rumbles towards Novgorod through the flat solitude of the northern plain. Vast fields lined with curtains of birch trees as fragile as the limbs of insects, immense lakes swathed in mauve mist of dawn, their boundaries invisible; I can't tell whether this landscape is dull, Claire says, or whether it has a melancholic beauty I can't grasp. . . . "I'll cheer you with recent Soviet statistics," Irina says. "Every minute in the Soviet Union nine babies are born; women still outnumber men by some twelve percent because of the Great War; our women hold seventy-three percent of positions in education . . ." ". . . and eighty-seven percent in public health," Sophie adds.

"How well informed you always are, Sofia Larionovna!" Irina wears a T-shirt with the words Disco Beat on her left breast, shiny high-heeled black shoes which she keeps wiping with her tissue, a long hunter green skirt with matching jockey cap set on her carefully crimped hair. Claire has said she can't detect a single chink in her armor. Edmund has talked about the narcissism of the new Soviet woman. Irina twists and turns her head seductively at her Americans, pouting and smiling, fingering her curls. "Another point! Our per capita income has increased by twenty percent since 1974, our gross industrial production has risen by twenty percent . . ." ". . . and only ten percent of Soviet women report ever having had an orgasm," Sophie says languidly. There's no telling what Irina ever chooses to hear. She continues handing out cucumbers, buttering slices of black bread. In the past year alone fifty-four million people improved their lives by moving to better apartments. The favorite visiting places of foreign tourists are one, Moscow and Leningrad, two, Kiev, three, Tbilisi, ai ai why you wish to go to sleepy Novgorod is beyond me but it is my duty to make you happy, yes?

159

Ai ai I met the most wonderful Soviet man two nights ago in Leningrad, Sophie says, he was handsome and so much wiser than I. Are you married, Irina Grigorievna, and do you still live with your parents? I live alone with my mother and my *babushka*, we are what do you call, a matriarchy. . . . Are you looking at beauty of landscape, Clara Pavlovna? When you look at fields of Muscovy do you feel Russian, Professor Richter?

Oh yes, yes!

Edmund: Novgorod means "new town" but it's actually one of the nation's oldest cities; in the twelfth century Novgorod claimed some thirteen hundred churches and is said to have been saved by a miracle . . . when the Prince of Suzdal besieged Novgorod the citizens hung an icon of the Virgin Mary on the gates, arrows flew upon it thick as rain but it remained unharmed, and real tears ran down the face of Our Lady . . . so upsetting the attacking army that it fled . . . four centuries later, however, the prosperous town went into decline when Ivan the Terrible butchered half its citizenry to suppress an uprising, choking the river with dead corpses . . . by modern times a population which once totaled 400,000 had fallen to some 850 souls. . . .

Bulbous church domes of celestial turquoise or blazing deep blue like firmament of clearest night, conical domes in the shape of Oriental warriors' helmets, oval domes the flat dark green of forests just before sunrise, freshly gilt domes surmounted by great gold crosses strung to each other by ropes of golden chains, monasteries the hue of tea roses imprisoned in crenellated battlements of bloodred brick, above the locked doors faint frescoes of resurrection, threatening prophet, frail Saint George, Virgin staring staring with terror at the announcing angel. The gilt is freshly blazing, the paint as lustrous as that of a new toy, but all doors are shut, no one in the streets, one single child fishes in the river by a dormant monastery, all dressed up and nowhere to go, Irina says, that's nice American expression I just learn, and rain, rain, go away . . . Irina steps slowly, delicately on the cobblestones of Novgorod, often bending down to wipe her shoes. She moves in the

160

frail sepulchral rain as on a field of broken glass, walking with delicate crablike motions to avoid the troughs of mud. She's proud of the new skirt and cap she inherited the day before from the Zabars after she'd roundly scolded them for dropping out of the tour to visit synagogues. And when she finds a stretch of dry pavement she moves like a mannequin on a fashion runway, with rhythmic swaying of her slender hips, pointing disdainfully to different churches: Monastery of St. Anthony, Church of the Purification, Church of the Assumption, Church of St. John the Compassionate . . . as her Americans photograph domes and towers she paces slowly at Sophie's side, takes a large mirror out of her bag, licks her lips, adjusts her jockey cap, "Sa démarche langoureuse m'ennerve," Edmund says; they sometimes speak French to each other, like characters in nineteenth-century Russian novels. Church of St. Perpetua, Irina waves with her long manicured hand, Monastery of the Holy Spirit, Church of the Transfiguration. We should soon move on Gedmund Petrovich I'm frozen to the bone, I think it's time for a cup of tea, there at left is the nunnery where the czars sent their wives when they were too tired with them, ai ai, what terrible times these were. . . .

You can't go in, you can't go in, the old woman says as she slowly brushes her broom across the steps of the cathedral. The caretaker is dressed in black from high felt boots to wool headkerchief, a bunch of keys clangs at her waist, she sweeps banks of dust and dried grass off the steps of the church. You'll never go in, you'll never go in . . . Why can't we go in little mother Edmund pleads, we'll be very quiet, we'll stay two minutes but the interdiction becomes a chant, a litany, it is forbidden, forbidden . . . she keeps her head down, sweeping at the dust and shreds of dried flowers. Her legs are swaddled in high bands of felt, her kerchiefed head nods in rhythm to the chant, the only sound in the utterly still town, closed, closed, there'll be no going in, there'll never be any going in. He's a professor Claire says, he teaches the history of icons at a great American university, this is our favorite country after America. There'll be no going in, no going in at all the old woman sings joyously; she stands squarely in front of the cathedral door, squinting fiercely at the visitors, all locked up, all locked up forever. Phenomenon of refracted power, Sophie whispers, is she ever proud that she can keep us out. We've made her year Claire says, we've given her a happy year.

Edmund: Well if we can't go in we can at least talk about it. . . . Claire, Sofka, come stand in front with me here—even more than in the West the Slavic Church serves as an icon, an image which shares in the divinity of the archetype it represents— and in this country the Church has always been seen as a redeeming community of love in which the individual is relatively unimportant and helpless—Irina Grigorievna don't fret dear, we'll get our tea, we'll get it in a minute (Ai you're freezing me Gedmund Petrovich, though all you say is remarkable)—The Russian nation has always seen itself as a mystical organism outside of which there is no salvation, Edmund continues; its ancient communitarian roots give us many clues to what's happening here today—the Slavs never recognized Greco-Roman concepts of private property, the generosity, the hospitality you still shower us with today, dear Irina, manifests that unique sense of brotherhood—there was never any room in Russian society for our Western notions of individualism and individual salvation—

All utterly brilliant Gedmund Petrovich but let's . . .

All utterly brilliant but abstract, so abstract Sophie cries out, what in heaven's sake does it have to do with your own life Edmund Richter? When have you ever lived for anyone but yourself, when have you been capable of love for community?

She stands in front of the cathedral, notebook and pencil in hand, suddenly shouting, a gilt dome framing her Titian hair, her angry golden eyes.

All you've been for years is a graduate student of yourself, the rooms of your life upholstered with theses on the iconography of dead game in Early Dutch still life. . . .

Soph . . .

You and your goddamn Tarascan statuettes and your delectable *millefleurs* pattern Meissen.

Look who's talking Soph! As if you hadn't had your share of ultra-bourgeois hedonistic splendor!

162

You and your drugged contessinas, you're as splendid an example of late twentieth-century narcissism as anyone I can think of!

You wear your candor like a campaign button don't you Sofia, have you only come on this trip to lacerate us with your outdated insights?

Don't talk to her like that, Claire shouts at him, leave her alone!

Ever since childhood Sophie and he had criticized each other with brutal clarity but Claire had abstained from any criticism of Sophie, as if she were a sacred precinct of her life which must remain untouched, and now they were both shouting together at him.

Leave Soph alone!

You and your gigs on Chinese bird deities, when have you lifted a finger for anyone since we were in our twenties?

What banal clarity Sofka, why are you throwing me back to what I may have been fifteen years ago? I've come to think that art historians are nothing but glorified undertakers tiptoeing about searching for more corpses to embalm, I've come here to try and transform my life when there's still time and when I turn to you for help you're usually off on one of your solitary night prowls. . . .

I don't believe in the kind of transformation you talk about Edmund, all we can do at this late stage is apply a little aspirin and Band-Aids to our various cancers. . . .

Soph you're the one who seems to have no more need of others whatsoever, which I find morally and metaphysically abhorrent!

Children, children, stop! Claire shouts.

You can't go in, you can't go in the old woman sings, sweeping banks of dust back towards the steps of the church, you see no one will ever go in.

They walked back to the station a half hour before train time and went to the buffet for tea. Its door was ajar and a sign said Open from 11:00 A.M. on. A Verdi aria played on the radio, floating from the little room like a summer breeze. A large blond waitress stood behind the counter, her hair teased and lacquered like an operatic diva's, her lips painted a dark shade of ruby red. She leaned against a vitrine which displayed arrays of radishes and beets, coarse red caviar and smoked fish. The music blared, photographs of Soviet ski teams hung on the walls, the little room was bathed in a seductive roseate light. We'd like some tea, Irina said. We're closed! the waitress called out. Then why are you here? Irina asked. I'm telling you there's nothing! the waitress shouted, nothing to eat, nothing to drink! Then why do you stand there all dolled up with all the lights and music on and that fake food on your counter? None of your business, there's nothing left, nothing whatsoever! The Verdi blared, the caviar gleamed under the rosy lights. Why is there nothing? Irina exclaimed, I want to know precisely why there's nothing! *Remont*, the woman shouted back, *remont*, we're in repair! And why are you forever repairing? Irina cried out, since my childhood I've never heard about anything but *remont*, the Hermitage is in *remont!* My grandmother's heating system has been three months in *remont!* The waitress seized one of her plates with a threatening gesture. Irina swiftly ushered her Americans out of the door and led them towards the train, her needled heels clicking angrily on the stone embankment.

Ai what a situation, what a state we're in Gedmund Petrovich . . . when we can know when our buffets are open then we'll have true Communism.

Once settled on the train she was quiet, and after straightening her hair in the mirror she bit her lip and looked contritely at the landscape.

It's so wonderful to travel in a country that's even more fucked up than ours Sophie said.

Within a few minutes of the train's departure they were all falling asleep.

As he dozed off Edmund thought of all the violent women he'd seen in the Soviet Union, shouting, forbidding, force-feeding propaganda, instilling the little order there was in this most anarchic of nations or perhaps making the disorder even more intense, women beating up their men when they led them out of bars by the scruff of their necks; a few days ago he'd seen a salesgirl bludgeoning a man until blood spouted from his head for stealing a bottle of vodka from her counter, last night in Leningrad the floor attendant had chased him down the corridor of their hotel toilet brush in hand yelling you misbehaved you bad man you left your room without giving me your key, all over the nation women were building, bullying, denouncing, censuring, so it had been in his own frail fatherless life, women inspiring and deceiving him, women beckoning him like unreachable Grails and threatening his life with desire insatiable, women ordering him to be a genius, women working him up to be Titian or ruining his career, women judging him with the great aloof gaze of Byzantine madonnas or with Sophie's furious stare, when all he wanted at this stage of his life was to cultivate a tiny plot of land like that old Georgian's and paint certain exquisite still lifes . . . as the train rumbled on through the stark dusk of the northern plain, Edmund fell into a deep sleep. He dreamt that Irina was walking slowly through the monastery town in her green jockey outfit, her heels clicking like castanets on the pavements of the silent city. She pointed her long painted fingers to north, west, all around, and at each languid wave of her arms golden domes melted into haze, fortifications crumbled, steeples toppled, with the swing of her slim hips church bells were silenced, gold crosses vanished from sight, entire kremlins evaporated into the roseate void of the Soviet evening, the town turned as still as a firmament, as inhuman as the stars . . . after several languorous waves of her lacquered nails all became solitude and emptiness again, all returned to the silence of the eternal plain, all objects wrought by man were swallowed into the brutal Soviet night.

xiii

"THE most puzzling transformation has taken place in our Sophie," Claire writes Edmund early in 1964. "Imagine this: She seems to have entered a brand-new stage of rebellion against the notion of frequenting persons of any talent . . . gone are the promising painters and budding dramatists, the men courting her this year are all hopelessly conservative and very wealthy and dotty about her; does she crave shelter after all these years of pennilessness and solitude? One cannot help but be very moved and a little perplexed. . . ."

A few months later Claire sent Edmund the following newspaper clipping:

> Dorothy Kilgallen reports that Sophie Ross, prizewinning *New York Post* reporter and daughter of former talent magnate Larry Ross, sprung a surprise on her friends yesterday and tied the knot with canned food tycoon Bernard B. Reilly . . . "Beebee" Reilly is rumored to have bought a 30-acre estate in Southampton just last week. . . .

"Mr. and Mrs. B. B. Reilly request the pleasure of your company," so read the invitations that start reaching Edmund's desk in the summer of 1964, "to a reception in honor of Mr. Xavier P. Boyle,

166

president of Greater Lakes Products . . ." ". . . to a soirée in honor of the Uruguayan ambassador to the United Nations . . ." Uruguay? Why Uruguay? Edmund ponders all afternoon as he corrects papers from his Brueghel seminar. It dawns on him the next day that Uruguay is noted for its large importation of some carplike fish, which it is Mr. Reilly's vocation to place in cans. In the chaste months following Simona's final departure, no correspondence more perplexes Edmund than the invitations to Sophie Reilly's numerous parties in Long Island and New York, engraved in florid script on Tiffany's heaviest stock. Edmund even begins to read the women's page of *The New York Times*, in which the Reillys' prodigality is frequently scrutinized. Beebee buys a town house in one of the most exclusive blocks of Manhattan's East Seventies, commissions Sophie's portrait from Larry Rivers and Andy Warhol, pays unprecedented prices for a Sheraton table and a Louis XIV armchair at Sotheby's. Much is made of the Reillys' prodigal travels. They fly to Glasgow for a weekend to premiere an opera; to Peru to pick up several bolts of custom-made textiles for their living room; to London to bid on a case lot of 1937 Mouton-Rothschild, leaving on the *Queen Elizabeth* three days later to ensure their vintage minimum disturbance. Claire seems so enthralled with her Sane chapter and her civil-rights marches, and Jeff with his teaching and his sports, that the Howells don't get a firsthand view of the Reillys until the fall, when a note from Jeff capsules his impressions of the new ménage: "It's like some African principality . . . outlandish dark servants standing at every door just to open it for you, champagne flowing throughout the day, and our old friend wandering about in her finery, not quite as sylphlike as in the last few years, warbling, 'Beebee has the caviar arrived, where are those chandeliers? . . .' "

In April of 1964 one of Edmund's seminars in Impressionism had already been canceled because of a student rally against nuclear testing. The following month he'd lost a class in medieval Flemish to another group protesting the ban on travel to Cuba. The pickets and rallies that proliferate the following fall center about the issue of students' rights. John gets arrested with his students on the very first sit-in. Reverend Edwards is speaking in every corner of the campus about restoring credibility to the community. Throughout the autumn's demonstrations Edmund spends an increasing amount of evenings at home, reluctant to engage in student-faculty discussions in which he's bound to be branded as ultrareactionary. In his free hours he begins to write a series of articles attacking the new vogue for Pop Art and rehearses delicate dishes for himself and his cat—sorrel soup, kidneys flambéed in Armagnac—wondering when he can ever again impress his colleagues with them. Claire's letters only mirror the mayhem growing in his former paradise. "I'm cheered by the prospect of joining the San Francisco–Moscow Peace Marchers when they pass through Boston next month; I'll walk with them for several weeks before going South to register voters, have found a marvelous au pair Irish girl to take care of Victoria while I'm away; Jeff is beside himself of course: 'What will the *family* think Peb?' He's being kept quite busy thank heavens by a local field hockey association which calls itself Marvelous Mothers and Fabulous Fathers. . . ."

In November the Free Speech Movement is formed, several thousand Berkeley students immobilize a police car for thirty-two hours in protest against the arrest of one of their peers. "Our campus swarms with all the accouterments of twentieth-century horror," Edmund writes in the first of his letters to the campus paper, *The Daily Californian*. "We live in a melee of gas masks, clubs, guns, walkie-talkies, motorcycle jackboots, pickets, banners, bullhorns, armed astronauts adorned in garish motel bathroom colors . . . crowds scream and bodies interlock as the world's most privileged children protest their oppression . . . meanwhile a fashionable new breed of youth-adoring professors weep at their students' plight in the midst of liturgical parades that equal the pomp of Seville's Holy Week. . . . Let our young idealists go South and join Martin Luther King's magnificent movement for human equality! What do these admirable goals have to do with the hard-earned freedom owed some twenty thousand men and women of our university, the freedom to teach and to be taught? . . ."

On the night of December 2 some 950 students are arrested after an all night sit-in in Sproul Hall. Joan Baez entertains the crowds by singing "We Shall Overcome," bids them to face their struggle with love in their hearts and leaves shortly after midnight. At 3:05 A.M. the governor of California broadcasts a message giving the police the order to arrest. John goes to jail again. Mario Savio bites a policeman on the thigh while being dragged away.

"Beleaguered teachers!" Edmund writes *The Daily Californian*. "Have we forgotten what our authority represents? We're elected to preserve the only sacred values there are left in our secular society—the sanctity of intellectual tradition, the authority of history. Have we forgotten that the university is the only sacred precinct where those values can be learned, that it is not an ivory tower but an active temple? The only alternative to our authority—and we are capitulating to it today at Berkeley—is the breeding of a new generation of barbarians, of a people without a historical memory. . . ."

Professor Richter pens this letter in an empty classroom after running through the slides he has assembled for that morning's lecture—"After Pollock?"—in his seminar on twentieth-century art. He is the only occupant of the building. A general strike has been called to protest the previous night's arrests. The possessed youth gesticulating and shouting in the begonia-decked lawns outside his window, those once docile angels who'd taken the place of the children he'd yearned to have, are betraying him . . . as he finishes his letter a student runs through the building with a bullhorn announcing that thousands are rallying that afternoon at Sproul Hall to condemn Governor Pat Brown, the regents, the president, the chancellor, the police, the United States government. Edmund packs his book bag and drives to the supermarket. He buys four days' food for his cat and for himself, returns to his flowered cottage in the Berkeley hills, padlocks his doors for the weekend to protect himself from the possible intrusion of ruffians handing out more petitions. He opens a bottle of Cabernet Sauvignon, puts on his recording of Monteverdi's *Vespers for the Year 1609*, places his latest acquisition in sight of his desk—a fine little *sang-de-boeuf* vase, Ming Dynasty. And he sits down at the typewriter to compose his attack on the new art, Vico purring, purring at the edge of the sunny window.

"The phenomenon of Pop Art presents us with still another

tightrope act in the circus of public taste. . . ."

The beloved object has returned (this is the thrust of Edmund's polemic) but in what a monstrous and debased manner! "Museums displaying fenders of wrecked automobiles, papier-mâché bas-reliefs of women's girdles, portraits of Donald Duck, enlarged comic strips, paintings produced by rolling nude ladies in pigment! Cartons of Brillo pads, carefully copied hamburgers, toothpaste tubes and six-foot-high lipsticks!" "Cannibalism of the supermarket!" "Parody, cynicism of perpetual pastiche!" "Art history moving again from tragedy to farce!"

The din of voices reaches Edmund every few minutes like waves of nausea from the protesters' rallying point twelve blocks away. Edmund plugs up his ears with wax and continues writing. With a passion that surprises him, he goes on to defend the Abstract Expressionist painting he'd attacked so vigorously ten years ago.

The president of the university, the radio announces, has canceled all classes and called the entire community to meet at Berkeley's Greek amphitheater. . . .

"Unlike the debased kitsch of current Pop, Abstract Expressionism had embodied most of the values of traditional humanist art: dynamic form, lyric power, a distilled celebration of the glory of the created world. . . ."

Mario Savio was refused the right to speak at the amphitheater and was dragged offstage in front of a cheering crowd of eighteen thousand. . . . The Free Speech Movement has received telegrams of support from Bertrand Russell and James Baldwin. . . .

After finishing the last draft of his attack on Pop Art, Edmund drives to a village on the calm side of the Sierra to avoid setting foot in downtown Berkeley. He mails his article, renews his supply of victuals and sits down at the typewriter again to write another letter to *The Daily Californian*.

"There are no more efficient prophets of totalitarianism than the virtuosos of cheap guilt presently holding toy guns to our heads and forcing us to politicize institutions whose very essence is to stand above politics. . . .

"By biting a policeman on the thigh Mario Savio (self-appointed

Robespierre of our Student Soviet) has earned himself the dazzling new label of 'charismatic leader,' thus debasing a hallowed Greek word to a label for moral parvenus. . . .

"As for the Songstress of the Dispossessed arriving at Sproul Hall in her gleaming Jaguar, it assures us that Berkeley has become nothing but a massive entertainment to the world . . ."

A partial quiescence returns the following spring. Edmund is enthralled by the teaching of his new course, "Stoicism in Seventeenth-Century Painting." His articles on Pop Art have received the kind of controversial attention he's beginning to enjoy—raves from the older generation of gentlemen scholars, vociferous attacks from younger dealers and critics. Every morning over breakfast Edmund proceeds to the women's page of *The New York Times* after glancing at its art critique and book review. He reads with interest that Beebee Reilly has bought a quantity of Sèvres at auction and has built New York City's largest private wine cellar in the bowels of his town house; that Sophie has developed what *The New York Times* describes as "one of the city's most curious salons." (Sophie photographed during an interview, standing by a Ming vase of the feeblest period, something newly round about her face: "Being a hostess is an exciting, demanding, full-time vocation. . . . I've never had a sense of roots until now; don't you think modern society is intensely rootless? . . . Actually I know almost no one in New York, I never know any of the guests at our parties, it's amusing to meet *new* people all the time in your own house. . . .") In May, Edmund was invited to give a paper at an art historians' conference being held in Philadelphia the following month. He accepted with pleasure, and that very day booked a plane reservation for his first trip to New York in several years. He would satisfy his curiosity about the Reilly ménage, attend his convention and later drop in on Claire and Jeff in Nantucket. As Providence would have it, still another invitation reached him in Berkeley a few weeks before he left: "At Home to Celebrate a Birthday: Mr. and Mrs. B. B. Reilly, 125 East 77th Street, June 25th, from six on."

171

The walls were of oak paneling. He stepped upon Bokhara rugs. A black man in white turban opened the door when Edmund arrived at the Reillys shortly after six and ushered him into an immense dining room on the ground floor. It immediately struck Edmund that Sophie could not have engaged in a more violent revulsion against the stark Village flats, the lonely motel rooms, she'd lived in for the past decade. The dining room occupied most of the ground floor and aspired to the ornateness of the most exclusive men's clubs. The Anglophilic opulence of its Sheraton, Hepplewhite, Queen Anne and ponderous silver services summed up all that Larry Ross had aspired to in the 1950s. Nibbling on translucent caviar and radishes carved in the shapes of tulips, Edmund walked about the room with the critical eye of a seasoned fellow acquisitor. They'd managed to paint their dining room a hideous shade of blue. It was awfully hard to mix an ugly blue, but they'd quite succeeded. The Sheraton breakfront might have been elegant as a showcase for Greek pottery, but it was presently filled with a florid Sèvres that clashed conspicuously with the fluting of English woodwork. And he should tell Sophie to apply a duller wax to her Queen Anne chairs, which presently shone with an almost vulgar maroon gleam. . . .

"I'm Mrs. Reilly's chief butler, Mr. Edmund, sir. . . ." Another turbaned black man was greeting him by name and bowing. "Madam refers to you as her oldest childhood friendship; she must felicitate her birthday guests upstairs but she told me that you were commencing a long voyage and asked me to see that you were adequately refreshed as soon as possible upon your arrival." "I'll be up to see her in a moment, I'm having a marvelous time looking at your splendid house." "As you wish, sir. Madam warned me that you are of solitary disposition and might prefer to take a turn away from the maddening crowd. May I suggest that you enjoy a visit to the library on the mezzanine, to which Mr. Reilly has just added a collection of Jack Londoner. . . . You might also study our noted wine cellar, first door to the left in the hall. . . ."

Edmund opted for the wine cellar, which he had already read about in the women's page of The New York Times. "Ah, Sofka, what a sense of drama you've developed!" The arches and vaults of the cavernous space were most carefully copied from engravings of medieval cloister architecture and recalled a stage set for the death scene of *Romeo and Juliet*. Edmund, so admired in Berkeley for his amusing little wines, took time to admire the velvety labels of '33 Mouton Lafites and 1885 Fine Napoleons, the silver tasting cups, marble boards and other refinements of the wine collector's trade which accompanied the Reillys' rare vintages. Edmund began to walk towards the second floor with great apprehension, infinitely dreading the revelation—surely startling—which Sophie's hedonistic new incarnation would offer. Reaching the second landing, still carefully avoiding the din of crowds and any room where he might find her, Edmund continued to climb the stairs to where he assumed he would find the master bedrooms. He stood on the landing and stared at a wall ornated by two portraits of Sophie, one in a neosurreal vein (walking by a tempestuous seashore in Victorian dress, holding a parasol) and another cubistic enterprise in which her eyes descended in mournful triangles to her chin while she strummed on an eggplant-hued guitar. Ah, yes, she loved to pose, but who in heaven's name had advised these outlandish commissions? He must find out more; from the door to the left came the familiar odor of Sophie's rose toilet water; he tiptoed towards it as reverently as an archaeologist approaches a cache unopened for decades. He opened the door, and was reassured.

Only his dear Sophie could inhabit this room, it had a wondrous sense of impermanence, it looked as if she had just arrived or were about to leave, its floors were bare and uncarpeted, her clothes hadn't even been put into any closet but hung from windows in lieu of curtains. The heaps of dusty books piled on the floor reflected the rich fluctuations of her interests—studies of Third World economics and guidebooks to Hawaii, histories of Renaissance paintings and exegeses of Marxist theory, biographies of Democratic presidents and of women physicists, how-to books on losing weight and improving recorder performance. And all about the room were strewn those traditional fetishes of her travels—postcards of Renoir nudes, photographs of the Mont Blanc, Spanish shawls—which Edmund had last seen six years ago in Italy. It was evident that she did

173

not permit any member of her large domestic staff to even enter this precinct of the house. On a narrow, barely made single bed lay the same satchel which she and Edmund had shared during their trip to Tuscany, the stuffed koala bear which he remembered from Sealark and Charles Street. And what happened on this austere little schoolgirl bed? Not much, Edmund surmised, not much. Surprised by the pleasure he derived from this vision, he now wandered down the stairs towards the roar of the crowds as slowly as he could, paused a second at the landing and pushed his way towards the bar. "Large bourbon, straight up."

A dapper, silver-haired man with a black patch over his eye came towards Edmund, hand outstretched. "Ah, you're her dreamboat," B. B. Reilly said. "My wife still refers to you with that euphoric nomenclature. You seem to be an insuperable part of her early life." Here was a household, Edmund reflected, whose men clearly enjoyed using florid language. Beebee spoke a kind of night-school English which seemed to have absorbed large doses of fresh vocabulary without fully digesting them, and cloaked the faint trace of an undefinable foreign accent. "I'm terribly glad to meet you," Edmund said, raising his glass, "here's to your great happiness." "My wife has the most luminous judgment of any hostess in New York and she tells me that you're catapulted towards a meteoric career in the field of art history." "I've just been voted tenure," Edmund said as modestly as possible. "I may not get my full professorship for another two years." "I wish you success in that transcendent enterprise. Your European background must allow you to perceive reality with a detached retina." "Have you been abroad a lot also?" "I often travel for severely transactional reasons. . . ."

Blue eyes. A handsome clean-shaven gent. The eye patch and the impeccably tailored clothes gave him the elegance of a Hathaway shirt advertisement. Sophie'd always been a sucker for good looks. The relationship might be complicated. He didn't understand life. Edmund stood at the living room's entrance and resumed his study of the Reillys' decor. He startled at the sight of a half-dozen more portraits of Sophie hanging over the convoluted marble mantelpiece. Beebee's esteem of his wife seemed to have expressed itself in a need to immortalize her features in as many pictorial styles as were known to the 1960s. And what a choice of artists! What were bestowed place of honor in this room but those currently fashionable monstrosities which Professor Richter was decrying in classrooms and learned papers! Hanging a few yards away over an Empire settee were twelve multiple silk-screen portraits of Sophie by Andy Warhol. By the window, another triumph of Pop Art depicted her in a glaring kitchen, smiling at graphically detailed stacks of supermarket items . . . George Segal's white plaster cast of Sophie seated in a chair, looking like a victim of the Pompeii earthquake . . . Sophie by Robert Rauschenberg, her features outlined against the frottage of a photograph of the World Series . . . ah yes she had always adored to pose! And now she had spent the past year posing for those very idiots whom Edmund was attacking in several distinguished publications, and was about to savage at his forthcoming convention!

Beebee Reilly still stood at Edmund's side, appearing to know as few people at his party as Edmund did. The garrulous guests filling the room seemed as purchased as the newly hung atrocities sullying Sophie's image on the walls; it was a gesticulating, middle-aged, ravenously eating throng dressed with the glittering maladroitness of the Reillys' decor; many women surmounted with hairdos of immense size and strange convolutions ogled each other with inarticulate murmurs and shifted through the room like shoals of perplexed fish. . . . "The Château Lafitte forty-five I've uncorked for my wife's birthday is notorious for its contumelious bouquet," Beebee was saying. "I've devised an unusually delightful way to exhibit our hostess's beauty tonight; I hope you will find the vision as delicate as I do . . ."

Edmund cut the conversation short with as much civility as he could muster, for Larry Ross was hobbling towards him, crippled by a recent stroke, vastly fattened and baldened. Edmund held out his arms to this old protector. "Ah, *Kinder*, who are these dolts?" Larry whispered as he embraced Edmund. "Is this what we sent her to Ethel Walker's and Smith and Mara's ballet school for? What have these people accomplished, they're not creative, they're not famous, they're not even young . . . and you, Edmund, the distinguished art historian, are you going to become the Berenson of our time?

175

Listen, Mr. Renoir, if only you'd stayed around, had some patience, by 1958 we could have had you at the top already, a truly distinguished gallery, the Bergdorf Goodman of the art world like Betty Parsons and if not Parsons at least Sam Kootz; one of his cousins was the brother of one of my big screenwriters . . . and by sixty-two we could have had a one-man show at the Whitney, the Modern, these are great times for artists. . . ."

"That's the trouble, Larry, times may be too great."

All this dying was something wasn't it, Maestro? First Mrs. Sanford and then Camilla, both gone a few years from each other, who else was there to survive? But what a brave little girl he had in his Sophie, what a saint she'd been to them, sharing every dollar she earned, free lancing night after night after her hard day's work to pay for Camilla's hospital bills, and now this Reilly was being most generous too, whoever he was. . . .

Edmund suddenly heard Sophie's pearly laugh ringing through the room; his apprehension and curiosity became untenable. He excused himself from Larry and swiftly pushed his way through the crowds, he walked towards the familiar joyous sound, he reached the middle of the room and saw, from a distance . . . Sophie seated on a Louis XV chair, which in turn was set upon a wooden platform, like a little throne. She had regained some of her adolescent weight since Edmund had last seen her, how much one couldn't tell, for she was wrapped in a voluminous robe of studded tapestry that recalled the vestment of some primitive idol and a regal diamond tiara sat atop her mop of unruly gleaming hair. Seated on a throne, wrapped in tapestries that recalled the sack of Nineveh, the fall of Tyre, there was his Sophie. . . . "Sofka," Edmund called out severely from the middle of the room, "Sofka, what the hell?" She turned towards him and gave him her ebullient laugh, stretching out her jeweled hand with what he recognized to be profound tenderness. "Dreamboat, at last!" Edmund elbowed his way farther through the tuxedoes, the taffetas, the whispers, the rhinestones, the garrulous voices, the tubs of rented caviar, the rented guests, remembering the sad ravenous émigrés at the parties he and Mara had attended to relieve their hunger and their loneliness. Upon this moment of Edmund's return to New York his years

176

in Berkeley filled him with anguish and anger, productive and blazing years, obsessed with acquisitions and honors and exhibitions of his conquests, replete with clever antiques, flamboyant Simonas, papers of great cleverness, lectures of devastating charm. For a very fleeting moment which would only return fully many years later—would then even change his life—Edmund was suddenly flooded with the desire to retreat to a distant place and support himself by humble occupations, mending nets, grinding corn, gardening for others, making sails, anything, anything rather than the rapacity of his past few years at Berkeley or the squalid glitter of the Reillys' opulence . . . but this sense of gluttedness and guilt blazed only for a few seconds. Sophie continued smiling, he came towards her dais, renewed acquaintance with her smell of rose and musk; the fertile odors thrust him into a dual state of panic and desire. Sofka, fellow sufferer on sailboats, beloved model of his brief and brilliant painting career, the most tenderly dutiful and giving of the two or three women who had obsessed his life, she whom he had trusted would become a star of her generation; had he been guilty of not clearly enough showing his love for her, not instilling enough courage? "What do you think you're doing," he blurted out as he stood at the foot of her dais, "will you please get out of that ridiculous chair? Immediately!" "Marriage," she laughed, "just another stage of life's way . . ."

She continued laughing and the fluted sound reassured him a little, perhaps the nomad was resting, drawing strength for future struggles in a rented tent, this travesty might be as brief as some of her earlier excursions, he would make sure it would be her last! Sophie stretched out her arms towards him, he bent forward to touch her dear face, stumbled on the step of her dais and fell to the floor. Our lives are hidden from us, like our deaths, he thought as he lay briefly at her feet. But instead he said severely: "This is impossible, Sophie, impossible! I'll take care of you, I'll kidnap you tonight, I'll do anything to get you out of this monstrous place!"

177

xiv

HALFWAY in the middle of their stay in the Soviet Union, Edmund decides that the whole trip might be a fiasco. Don't kid yourself fellow the recovery of innocence is an idiotic enterprise. We're diving into each other like pilots on reconnaissance missions, insights fitful, sometimes savage, we're trying to turn back to some golden age which may have been more violent than we've dared to admit; the recapture of youth is as brutal as most nursery rhymes, here is a candle to light you to bed here is an ax to . . . In the last evenings of their stay in Leningrad, Edmund starts drinking with Evgeny. Sophie is out walking alone every night, allegedly documenting the attitudes of Soviet women to natural childbirth, détente, abortion; half the time Claire is out searching for Sophie or else she's trying to phone Moscow on her blasted missions. Other members of the Intourist party are equally irksome. Irina keeps chiding the Zabars for dropping out of the official tour to visit synagogues, "rubble of no historical significance." Mrs. Jones has heard that face-lifts are free and wonderful in Russia and wants to come back with her friends to have it done here, Ah yes *remont* Edmund quips by all means have one. The Rolls-Roycers have broken three ashtrays at the Dollar Store after consuming too much vodka at lunch and Ted Weicker is praising the Soviet Union for its low crime rate, where else in the West can you walk alone so safely at night?

Soviet bars close at ten o'clock. Edmund and Evgeny head for one of Leningrad's foreign currency bars, dark chromed spaces filled with the din of rock, with vapors of American whiskeys and tobaccos unavailable to Soviets. Tempted but diffident, Evgeny follows Edmund to these haunts with a stealthy air. The ruby-mouthed Soviet women in deeply cleavaged silks who accompany some of the foreigners remind Edmund of the German officers' molls who filled Parisian bars during the Nazi occupation. . . . Edmund orders a bottle of Black Label and often needles the Russian about the state of his country.

"I've evolved a new theory on this trip, Evgeny, I've realized that civilizations contact each other through their poisons. Take heed, brother, think of the way the Indians were done in by our first colonizers; it's our liquor those poor bastards wanted rather than our alphabets or medicines, just the way you crave our Marlboros and Pepsis and odious music without giving a hoot about our human rights. . . . Look at this Western decadence which you'd all sell your icons for if you had any left; your country reminds me of a fruit that's rotting before it's even had a chance to ripen. Listen, Evgeny, if I were a member of your Politburo I'd be more authoritarian in these matters, more severe . . ."

"Severe?" the Russian repeats loudly over the din of the rock, keeping his spectacled eyes on Edmund.

"Severe, severe!" Edmund cries. "The last thing I'd wish on you is to become like us. If I were one of your leaders I'd safeguard our ancient Slavic values, resurrect our glorious ethnic traditions; oh, I'm an unabashed romantic, I'd only allow balalaikas, Georgian songs, Kalmyk zithers, Cossack dances . . . in old times your craving for debased Westernness was restricted to the upper crust but now you've become one huge beggar's opera; look at how these dens are corrupting your youth with their black markets!"

Evgeny resettles his spectacles with a firm thrust of his fifth finger. "One position is that we're still suffering from the aftermath of the Great War, Gedmund; your foreign currency is immeasurably helpful to our economy."

"One position, brother, is that you're brilliant at finding excuses for every shortcoming you have. Soon the Olympics will provide your next five-year fuck-up plan, no toilet paper in Kiev, all of Leningrad in *remont*, it's the Olympics and so it'll go until 1984. My position is that your beggar's opera is based on that tragic need to ape the West which grew in the isolation of your steppes, and you hate us with that particularly bitter hatred which the imitator has for his model. . . ."

"How can you criticize *us*, Gedmund, when your society is so permissive that your pornography, your media violence, are on the verge of destroying you?"

"Oh don't take us as a model, Evgeny, I'd close it down, close it all down."

"Time may have come for you to start defining human obligations along with human rights, Gedmund. . . ."

"You've put your finger on the American tragedy, dear friend; our honeymoon with spineless permissiveness is over! We're yearning for restrictions, authority, tens of thousands of our kids joining half-crazed religious cults in which they're programmed like robots around the clock; you're seeing in us Narcissus in Chaos, the final wasteland of bourgeois individualism. . . ."

There were many such exchanges, habitually cordial.

"Those two fine women you travel with, Gedmund, you've known them for long?" "Thirty years." "Perhaps you were almost married once to one of them?" "Almost to both of them." "*Colossalnoe delo*," the Russian murmurs, "a colossal feat. The thin darker one, she is always trying to phone Moscow, she has relatives there?" "Relatives of friends, trifles, I wouldn't bother with it in your KGB reports." "And which one is more difficult to live with?" "Oh, don't ask me, brother, they've both become impossible, impossible, perhaps they always were. . . . Do you expect me to live with simple women, without divinities? I'll never settle for a modified rapture . . . let's drink in reckless communion, Evgeny Sergeievich!"

After a half bottle Evgeny offers sparse details of his own life.

During the height of the Stalinist terror his family had stayed up until dawn hours playing cards to assuage their fears of being rounded up by the KGB, going to bed only in exhaustion . . . he'd once been much in love with a teacher of history who became too interested in Polish culture . . . he'd once written a paper on Dreiser at university, he might soon leave Intourist work and take an advanced degree . . . after such moments of candor he picks up his coat and explains that he must go home because his grandmother is waiting for him, his grandfather has a kidney disease, a cousin is arriving from Lvov. "Communists always want to go home," Edmund sighs. Evgeny gives a guarded smile, taps his knee with his *Pravda* as he reminds Edmund of the next morning's tour schedule. Their conversations often end with Evgeny saying, "Ah yes this is Wonderland Gedmund Petrovich." "Wonderland, right?"

One night on their way out of the hotel Edmund and Evgeny pass some members of their Intourist group in a corridor. One of the Rolls-Royce couples is trying to entice the Zabars to have a nightcap in their room. "One more to celebrate this gorgeous country, Zabs, clean as a whistle! No longhair kids standing in Red Square yelling hell no we won't go!" "No Gay Lib," his wife adds assertively. "You think we're crazy, Prof," the Floridian says to Edmund with his wide disheveled smile. "Here's to effete intellectual snobs," his wife raises her glass. The Zabars are trying to be pastoral, proposing Bisodol, urging an early bedtime because of the 7:00 A.M. waking scheduled for the next morning. The Rolls-Roycers' lapels are replete with insignias of Lenin exchanged with Soviet teenagers for T-shirts and gum—Lenin aged four, cherubic and blond-curled as Baby Jesus, Lenin as high schooler, Lenin as fiercely bearded leader. "We too are a Wonderland, Evgeny," Edmund says as they leave for their evening outing.

Sophie burst into the bar of the Astoria shortly after midnight.

"Soph my love, what have you been up to this time?"

"Out for a walk in the Dostoevski district, Edmund; I climbed up the stairs to Raskolnikov's room, saw the courtyard on which Sonya's window looked out . . ."

Claire came in next. "Oh thank God, she's here . . . I was so worried. I saw her walking by the Admiralty and then I lost sight of her in the dark. . . ."

Edmund stared at Claire and continued trying to understand her after thirty years. She stood above them fingering a variety of papers stuffed into her boyish raincoat, her skin the color of clean sand after a storm, looking at the bar with her haughty, abstracted glance. "I may return," she said after hugging Sophie. "I must go upstairs to finish some letters."

"Don't worry, dear heart," Sophie called out after her, "I've survived alone in the streets of more perverse cities. . . ." She downed her Scotch in one gulp, put her arm around Edmund. "Ah if you knew what extraordinary creatures these two are, Evgeny, treasures . . . unearthly . . . or perhaps too earthly. Let me explain . . ."

"Let her explain." Edmund leaned his head back on Sophie's shoulder. "We'll have one of our frequent consciousness-lowering sessions."

"Well I'll start with Claire, it's easier, more brutal. I'm a Slav too, Genia, and I'm inebriated with candor tonight! When we were young I used to see her pacifism as a kind of magnet which could absorb all evil in her own frail person . . ."

"Oh her nonviolence is of sterner ore than any knives, Genia, her silences are bombs with time fuses."

"But later on I saw a few more dangerous things in that purity of hers—it's genuine, mind you, genuine, yet what has it done but trigger us to more and more outrageous behavior!"

They drank. The rock band started playing Presley. Four Swedes sang "Auld Lang Syne" and loudly clapped while their ruby-mouthed Soviet escorts did the Twist in the middle of the room, a drunken young Russian accompanying a group of Danes weaved about the bar yelling obscenities, Evgeny rapped his *Pravda* nervously against his chair.

"Have you ever had anyone like that in your life, Genia," Sophie leaned across the table towards the Russian, "someone whose purity destroys? She's moved by compassion for the world and the lives she's touched most deeply may be ruined!"

"How well you understand human nature!" the Russian shouted with feeling.

"She's ruined our lives hasn't she Eddem, but with such style!"

"Turn off the soap opera, Soph."

"Well you came here for the truth, didn't you Edmund?"

"I'm not sure anymore my love." Edmund refilled their drinks, sat between them, arms folded. "I'm beginning to think that we need illusions even more than truth if the three of us are going to live together from now on."

"Live together? Who said we were ever going to live together?"

"I say so. Right now. I thought of it just now, at this very moment. I think we've totally fucked up going it alone, especially you and I. . . . I'm about to propose it at our next plenary session, propose some revolutionary form of triadic household."

"But you will torment each other so," the Russian lamented.

"The three of us, what madness! As usual you're terrified, you're avoiding your real needs, Edmund. . . ."

"What is he doing?" the Russian shouted over the din of the rock.

"Avoiding, avoiding! It's her alone you want, Edmund, her alone! Why not just grab her now that she's finally free?"

"You are all so Slavic!" the Russian exclaimed.

". . . I need to be more refueled than ever with illusions, Sophie, and I can't abide this hemorrhage of openness. . . ."

"The more Clara tortures you the more she loves you?" the Russian asked.

"Yes, yes, what insights our friend has, she's indeed grown increasingly dependent on us over the years!"

Late at night Evgeny's pale leonine head nodded slowly, methodically, over each word. "How I enjoy your calisthenics of the soul!"

"Love is only one thing, Genia," Sophie said, "it's the willingness to die for the other. . . . I've come to your country with the only two people I've ever known for whom I'd willingly give up my life!"

"Your heroic fidelity to each other moves me so," the Russian exulted. "A toast to her, to the mysterious third one!"

"Yes yes," Sophie cried, "to her who's clarified our lives by the suffering she's brought us . . ."

They drank.

"Do let's toast some more cheerful matters, Gedmund!"

"To the noble suffering of the artist, Evgeny Sergeievich!"

"To the glorious traditions of Russian and American art, Gedmund Petrovich!"

"To the glories of the Hermitage! When the deuce are you taking us there, Genia? . . ."

"Hermitage *remont* is over, Gedmund, we finally take you there tomorrow!"

"To our striving for the ideal man!"

"And for the ideal woman!"

Sophie buried her head in Edmund's shoulder.

"To your tears, Sofia Larionovna," Evgeny drank, "to Sofia's tears!"

"Yes, to her beloved tears!"

Edmund came knocking at Claire's door early that morning complaining of a furious headache; perhaps he might have come to her without that excuse—she hovered at the door's edge in a long childlike white nightgown, rubbing her eyes—the hotel window behind her opened out upon the tuliped expanse of St. Isaac's Square—as he engaged her firm, tense body for the first time that year he was reminded that this most severe of individualists would only come to him at her own pace, her own time, refusing to ever be dictated to or defined by anyone—throughout the twenty-five years of their extremely rare lovemakings he'd learned that there was no frigidity at the core of her abstinent life, that her complex, delicate flesh could be as unleashed as that of any woman he'd known—Radiant 5:00 A.M. light flooded her oval face as she stared at him with pale eyes drained of their habitual defiance or aloofness, filled with an almost sassy playfulness, as if she enjoyed the surprise he had in her unfettering—He put his lips to her face in a ritual sequence he'd begun a quarter of a century ago, first on a cheek, then on each closed eyelid; how maddening she must be to other

184

men because of her ability to control lust, making her rare gifts of it
with freedom incomparable—he'd come to think of sexual encounters as a quest for information executed in a spirit of curiosity and
high playfulness; a line had been haunting him, " '*Je ne veux pas
jouir, je ne veux que savoir,*' " he whispered to Claire that morning—
But this knowledge was denied him, this satisfaction she held back,
her Nordic eyes reflected nothing but an immensely serene affection, the self-containment of a planet—he fell asleep feeling gratitude for a life in which a rich full spectrum of friendship, passion,
brotherly love had been incarnated into each of his two deepest
bondings—when he woke, Claire had already left the room, he remembered with a burst of immense joy that it was the day to go to
the Hermitage. "What a crazy night we had," he told the Zabars
and the Weickers at breakfast, "everyone was drunk, the Swedes
were singing, the Russians were weeping, or perhaps the other way
around, I don't know anymore, you never know in this country."

XV

THE ferry blew its amazing horn before it came into sight. Edmund stood at the Hyannis landing playing the game he'd once shared with his mother, choosing the most magnificent family scheduled to board the vessel. He settled on a Buick whose cargo included six bicycles and a great amount of fishing rods cunningly strung onto the roof, four children, three enormous and anxious Irish setters (he'd always remembered an abundance of setters on the island, as if they were a more trustable token of family bliss than poodles or terriers), a proliferation of barbecue grills, tennis rackets, picnic hampers, and two parents of some beauty impatiently waiting for the boarding to begin. The slender, green-eyed female of the pair stepped out of the car to assess the imminence of the ship's arrival to Hyannis, staring fiercely at nothing in the manner of athletic women. Her setters yapped nervously at a pug on the road, beach towels tumbled out of hampers, her flaxen-haired children were arguing among themselves, the eight-year-old pulled at his younger sister's ear, the child protested with shrill cries, the older girl—a beauty of fourteen or so, the same age at which Edmund had first met Claire—reprimanded her siblings while carefully rebraiding her long pale hair. The mother chided gently also, turning her head towards her brood with a soft laugh, whispering to her husband don't scold on the first day of vacation. As Edmund

186

stood among the fishing instruments, the beach gear, the remonstrances, the Andover T-shirts, the vapors of copulation and nourishment, he remembered how the ferry had looked to him two decades ago; it had glided across the dark water like a blazing caterpillar, metamorphosing into a moth of bridal whiteness as it slid past the lighthouse. But when it rounded the cape this morning it changed from insect to mammal in the space of a few moments, it plowed through the oily sound with the heaviness of a wounded whale, spluttered and spit as it spun on its engines to thrust its maws towards the dock; Edmund lost the image of lightness, bridal whiteness, the ferry had become . . . something else. He had just turned thirty-five this past spring, and in a few weeks Claire would be thirty-five also. The vessel made its final docking, slid into the oily fences of its berth and expelled scores of vehicles—food trucks, early thrifty vacationers returning to the gloom of summer cities—before ingesting its new load. The magnificent family expressed its joy, their setters panted quickly, their blue Buick slid voluptuously into the ferry.

Halfway into the passage Edmund had a talk with a clergyman of extreme black and whiteness—pale eyes, silver hair, white socks, sternly black little suitcase. The priest expressed interest in the fact that Edmund hoped to soon become chairman of Berkeley's art history department and spoke movingly about the Church of il Gesù in Rome. They went on to an amusing conversation about grace; the priest was clearly a Jansenist. "It comes down upon you like rain." He fluttered his dark arms upwards, his long pale fingernails clicking above his head like castanets. The Nantucket coast finally came into sight, offering its beauty like a Puritan woman baring her breast, uncleaned pearls of pale gray houses spread against the harbor, docks filled with coquettish shops which Edmund did not remember there a decade ago. It was shortly before noon when the vessel docked. And stepping alone onto the pier amid the throng of vacationers Edmund decided to postpone his meeting with Claire and Jeff for a few hours. A handsome risk, looking up such friends after six years, he'd been wary of it for months. So he started drifting through the town, peered into Lilliputian gardens and houses that had so enchanted him decades ago, tried to recapture the

187

island's nursery-rhyme spell, walked aimlessly down thoroughfares called Coon Street, Beaver Street, New Dollar Lane. Within a half hour he realized that he was more or less following the movements of the couple he'd studied at the Hyannis landing. They were easy to sight by the splendor of their hair, their children, their dogs. And he proceeded to linger behind them even more meticulously, lurking a block away, feeling like a thief as he watched them act their roles in this theater of family happiness.

How many children there were about, filling the streets! The infant population drenched the air with small sounds of crude and tender timbre, like the din of verbiage in high wind. On tepid threatening days not fine enough for the beach, vacationers parade through such resorts dressed in fishermen costumes of slickers and high boots. It was the Fourth of July (national birthday of a people more dedicated than any other to the cult of happiness) and Edmund wondered whether he could feel part of these happy crowds if he acquired the right props: a child to hold by the hand, a sand pail, a little striped umbrella. He followed his adopted family for another hour at proper distance, admiring the beauty of the children about him, marveling at what it would be like to have married Pebble and be vacationing like this every day of the month, answering his son's questions about birds as he biked downtown for his morning papers, wondering when the wife's period would be over, feeling solicitous about a baby's bowel movements, worrying about the ingress and egress of several earthly frames. Whatever happiness he'd had was of such a different order that he barely felt part of the humanity milling about him. He often felt the burden of his solitude; I sometimes wish we could reproduce alone he'd recently told John Mirsky, like amoebas, like Adam, sculpting part of our bodies into perfect children the way we try to shape our students. . . . Edmund remained a respectful block behind his adopted family as they stood in line at a bakery, procrastinating his view of Sealark for a while longer and wondering what life was about.

The family's mood had become exacerbated. "I'll sock you one if you don't stop yiping," the ten-year-old shouted at the freckled four-year-old. "I shall not have that language in my house, Jeremy," the beautiful mother exclaimed. "I hate islands," the eight-year-old offered. "The children are tired," Father said. "Do we have enough beach chairs, honey?" "Of course, sweetheart." "And towels?" "Yes, yes, love." They received what they'd stood in line for and six mouths gravely bit into six sugared doughnuts. Edmund suddenly felt bullied by the purchasing, staring, chewing crowd; all that was ogled and swallowed in this bureaucracy of repose looked as suspect as its lobster-infested place mats and wooden captain dolls; he'd stared and loitered with others, he'd sat in the sun licking an ice-cream cone and bought a vulgar T-shirt, at two in the afternoon he ceased following the vacationing family and walked back to the ferry landing, he hovered over the ropes by which he'd stood with Mara decades ago at the end of the worst holocaust in human history. And then he started walking towards the Sanford house, trying to recall a line of Sartre's that Mirsky had recently read him, " 'I did not know what to do with my body,' " how did it go . . . ah, there it was, " 'I did not know what to do with my body in the midst of this tragic crowd which was struggling to amuse itself.' "

Claire Sanford Howell has gutted and eviscerated her mother's house, scrubbed it of nearly every vestige of her childhood. Gone is the china striving to imitate the shapes of frogs and various forms of bird life, the painted poodles, sailboats, piglets, roses and carnations, the ducks swimming across green swatches of petit point ponds. All is now limpidly white and unadorned, reminding Edmund of Claire's own pale face when it emerges from the water after a swim. Frenzied chintzes and floral rugs have given way to monastic burlaps and raffias, Babsie's wondrous flower arrangements have been replaced by a few trailings of beach foliage and seashells arranged in geometric patterns upon denuded tables. But the most amazing change of all has occurred on the walls! Claire has turned Sealark into a veritable museum of social protest. The living room, which first undergoes Edmund's scrutiny, literally swarms with photographs of humans marching, picketing, fasting, getting arrested for the cause of peace or of equality. And all is carefully dated and labeled, with Claire's particular brand of didactic care, with fastidious concern for educating the most casual visitor into the various reform movements that have swept America in the past century.

God knows Claire's interest is not new, simply more systematic. Hanging over the mantelpiece is a portrait of the Nantucket-born suffragist and abolitionist, Lucretia Mott, whose burning Quaker gaze is familiar to Edmund from the walls of Claire's childhood room. The air of wasted constancy on the faces of the colleagues who surround her, the stubborn stance of their folded arms, the severe part in the women's flat hair, exude the rigor of purpose that now pervades the house. In 1918 twelve women in large hats clench their fists as they sail for The Hague to plead for the end of all wars, conscientious objectors are herded into a Utah jail. Some years and decades later throngs protest the indictment of Sacco and Vanzetti, Jeannette Rankin is besieged by reporters shortly after she has cast the only vote in Congress opposing its declaration of war against Japan, the civil servant Rosa Parks is dragged to jail after refusing to move out of her bus seat. Amid parades of societies opposed to the vivisection of animals and posters advertising meat-replacing substitutes, Edmund also recognizes Sir Bertrand Russell being arrested in an anti-nuclear sit-in in London, A. J. Muste leading a protest against atomic tests in the Algerian Sahara. As he wanders through rooms once florally serene Edmund is perplexed by this proliferation of humanity being herded through streets and thrust into paddy wagons, this melee of contorted faces shouting for many varieties of liberation. Yes, too many! That is perhaps Claire's tragic flaw. The diversity of causes dramatized on these walls—suffragism, vegetarianism, laborers' rights, animal rights, numerous varieties of pacifism—expresses an almost frivolous abundance of dissenting passions. . . .

Edmund stared out of the window at the unchanged view he'd painted two decades earlier—rowboats bobbing like petals on the glass of the harbor, yachts steered by tall blond men playing captain setting out for an afternoon sail. And when his eyes turned from this serene idleness to the images of struggle scattered about Claire's rooms he felt more at peace than he'd felt for several years. He would realize much later—Edmund always realized things awfully late—the reasons for his surge of pleasure: palpable proof that Claire was not suited for the docile felicity Plinker and Jeff had intended for her, that she resembled Edmund in some mutual complexity of destiny. . . . It was close to four o'clock. Under the arrogantly peaceful face of Bertrand Russell that surmounted the hallway table a note informed him of the Howells' afternoon schedule. He seized one of the bicycles leaning against the garden fence and pedaled to the tennis club.

Edmund could have known that if Claire ever resumed her island life he would find her on a tennis court at 4:00 P.M., and not at base line but right at that net position where she'd spent much of her adolescence, volleying the ball with that swift aggressive turn of her shoulders which he'd always thought of as her most characteristic gesture. This is precisely where he did find her, but the following was less predictable: Right there at net, Pebble was threatening to throw a fit. As coltish as ever and dressed in virginal white, she was shouting at her husband, who was about to start a match of mixed doubles two courts away: "Now for Christ's sake, Jeff, why didn't you give me that message earlier! You know perfectly well that dozens of my friends can be arrested down there at any moment . . . really!" "How many times have you forgotten to give me messages, honey," he said with a cordial smile. "Yes, about some damn hockey game or faculty meeting, not about matters of life and death, what time is it precisely, Jeff?" He was languorously swinging his racket in preparation for service. "Oh, I guess around four or thereabout." "For heaven's sake, I asked *precisely* what time is it?" she cried once more. She threw her racket to the ground and ran off the court towards the clubhouse, pleated skirt waving about her thighs like that of a teenage gymnast, leaving her own doubles matches stranded. "It's precisely two and a half after," Jeff called out after her, "just look at the club clock, Peb!" Edmund had witnessed the preceding scene from some fifty yards away, and was approaching the courts as he heard Jeff say with a smiling apology to his pretty partner, "Sorry, Rose sweetheart, Pebble's constant damn crusade in the Deep South."

Jeff bent down to tie the laces of his sneakers. He kept his head up as he kneeled, radiating his amiable serenity towards the courts.

191

Not one of his three oldest friends, Edmund reflected, had changed so little since adolescence. There was still the beginning of an ingenuous smile on Jeff's lips, an expression of optimism so unaltered that one imagined he retained it in the privacy of his ablutions. Living with this large, sumptuously beautiful man might have been like living under some tall belfry clock which struck each hour with a resounding din to reassure us of the excellent order of mankind. Since adolescence Jeff had stared with equally affectionate protectiveness at boats in the harbor, strangers in streets, children in playpens. And this benignancy was negligible compared to the reverence he offered those persons he might have been the last of his generation to call "the fair sex." "What perfection and grace," his eyes seemed to say when he looked at a handsome woman. "You can be my redeemer, my guidance and inspiration!" "Careful crossing the street," Edmund remembered Jeff saying throughout their adolescence as Claire, Sophie, April, Babsie, ventured towards Main Street on the smallest errand. "Careful crossing the street!" he shouted again in New York City as they exited from theater or debutante dance. Yet there was a strain of nastiness in Jeff which had to do with virtue. Like Pebble he was ever ready to carry the burden of others. But unlike her crusades for voter registration in the South his were the concrete familiar others, childhood friends, blood-kin tribe. And he wished his virtue properly exhibited, his gifts of happiness meticulously accounted for. If the rescued did not collaborate with the rescuing procedures according to Jeff's own ideals of felicity he was capable of sabotaging the whole mission. . . . After he finished tying his sneaker that afternoon Jeff turned again towards his pretty partner with a radiant smile which expressed his capitulation to her charm. The smile waned into a gaze of cynical annoyance as he saw Claire slam the door of the clubhouse. He clutched his racket rather grimly and prepared for service. His afternoon match was ill-fated, for it was then that he saw Edmund and called out to Plinker, who had been sitting in a chair by the court with a small girl on his lap: "Look who's here, Plink, look who's finally come back to us!" And before clutching Jeff's shoulders Edmund saw the old man hobbling towards him too, arms outstretched, accompanied by a girl of six so strikingly resem-

192

blant to Claire as a child that Edmund could have shouted out with the pain of memory.

"So . . . have you come to stare at my happiness, rabbit love?"

Claire was kneeling in her parents' former vegetable garden, digging up clumps of weeds, chucking them haphazardly over the fence.

"People come to stare at each other's happiness in these resorts the way Sunday visitors go to see pandas in a zoo, we're full of families parading their delight like protesters carrying pickets, big signs saying PERFECT AMERICAN FAMILY, BE THE PERFECT FAMILY!"

She continued digging, not looking at him.

"I expect that's the way you expected to find me, sitting on the beach with needlepoint of ducks on a green pond, bustling children about proclaiming our bliss . . . well if you've come to stare at my felicity dear one you should get a refund on your boat fare. . . ."

"I miss Babsie's flowers," Edmund said.

She glanced up at him with a bitter, wry little smile.

"Ah you would miss her flowers, wouldn't you? . . . Well I'm not Babsie and I'm not April and there isn't enough of dear Plinker in me either, maybe I should leave you here to keep housey with Jeff. . . ."

"I'm going back to Alabama next week," she added bluntly. "There's a lot of work to be done in Alabama."

The skin of her arms and legs were like bolts of sand-colored satin. She'd changed little since the brief visit he'd paid the Howells in England six years ago save for the very fine lines about her eyes, which intensified the anger of her gaze. This trace of the passing of time struck Edmund as sharply as a change in his own body.

"A little lettuce, parsley, carrots, I'm seeding it all before I go South again. . . . Plinker would be despondent if he didn't see something growing here before summer's end, just a few goodies to keep them quiet."

"I'm sure you're doing the right thing . . . the garden before leaving, I mean."

"Oh, do contradict me more than that," she whispered. "Aren't you going to dispute me as you always used to, E. R.? Have you come back after all these years just to agree with me?"

As she pulled up a clump of weeds and threw it over the fence he leaned down to avoid being splattered with the loam.

Poor rabbit hurt his paw, Vicky put it in a splint maybe? Plinker was walking from the boat landing to the house, holding Victoria's hand. She clutched a basket in which a tiny animal reposed. Victoria was frail and pensive, with light brown hair and glacial blue eyes that tortured Edmund with remembrance. Plinker's walk was made very slow, more majestic than ever by his gout; he could only see at close distance and from his lawn he gave all passersby the wave of a royal personage passing through crowds in a limousine. That's Uncle Edmund over there, Mummy and Daddy's oldest friend, doesn't Victoria want to give Uncle Eddem a good-night kiss? All right sweets, later.

"Oh I could have continued to play Elgar so beautifully at St. Paul's commencements, Eddem, I could have gone on sitting there year after year seeing that bright ribbon of life go by, hearing a racist headmaster mouth his platitudes about being better Americans let us praise Thee Lord who's given us this wondrous day to send our children onto the road of manhood, Jeff always cried at commencement, those beautiful rich boys seemed to carry his only assurance of immortality, his only faith in the ancient order being able to forever perpetuate itself. . . ."

She had migrated to the other side of the lawn, to the abandoned cutting garden where her mother's parterres had once bloomed in such profusion. "*Achillea*," she muttered, "does best in dry exposed places, like me. *Hemerocallis*, each bloom lasts for a single day, as I do in this house. . . . You know what's wrong with me, Eddem, I've simply never wanted to be like any woman I've ever known in real life. Not like my poor loving Babsie who grew mad in the gathering of flowers or the tragically happy classmates I still meet in the streets of Boston, wheeling prams with the smell of morning sherry on their breath. . . ."

"You were always the quintessential critic."

"Ah, the critic, an old friend of yours, right? He has a nasty gift of mimicry, he's like an immense pair of spectacles through which all of the world's ills are hugely magnified, he's grown so omnivorous that he needs to be curbed . . . or better, anchored to a community of critics. My critic needs group support, that's why he's off to Alabama. . . ."

She looked up at him with that cunning which those who profess unworldliness can wield like a club of stone.

"What about Viola Liuzzo, a woman just like me looking for salvation?"

Fog rolling in from the ocean. Town wrapped in banks of misty brilliance. Thumping of the day's last tennis balls, flap of furling sails from the Yacht Club around the corner. Plinker walking up a neighbor's path in the property next door, teaching Victoria names of flowers that had long since disappeared from Sealark. Lily of the valley, plant pips two inches apart, it's that little thing every pretty bride must have. Edmund recalled Chesterton's description of Saint Thomas Aquinas approaching death: "The confessor, who had been with him in the inner chamber, ran forth in tears and whispered that his last confession had been that of a child of five."

Claire gestured to Edmund as she moved from one part of the property to another; she seemed to want him continually by her side during her tasks.

"And what about you, Eddem? You've had your Guggenheim and your associate professorship, next year you'll start getting honorary doctorates and distinguished chairs here and there, what kind of a future do you dream of for yourself?"

He cleared his throat. He joined his index fingers thoughtfully to his blond beard, Dr. Richter charming audiences from the lectern.

"Well, many things. Having power for instance. Give me two or three years to get the chairmanship of the department and I'll really

195

clean it up, restore all kinds of outmoded disciplines. No more fashionable permissiveness, much stress on classics and iconography . . ."

She stared up at him, inscrutable.

". . . plenty of room for metaphysical speculation that'll bury the positivistic nonsense; I'll make it the best traditional school in the country. I also look forward to being sixty-six; upon retirement I'll move to Venice into a strictly inodorous palace with cooks, frescoes, tapestries . . ."

She burst out laughing with all the abandon of her youth.

"I'll look like a tenor who's too old to make love but is still redolent with charm, I'll wish for conversion each time I hear the organ, the Reverend Edwards already has great hopes for me."

She threw spadefuls of earth playfully over her shoulder and he knew that underneath what he now saw as mayhem she was as resilient as ever.

"Ah Eddem we do need you to wake us from our Puritan earnestness, as Babsie used to say. Now. What about our Soph?"

"Oh I tried hard enough to get her to come up this weekend; between the two of us we might have straightened her out a bit . . ."

"Eddem dear, I worry about her violent shifts of moods, the gloom she was in last year, the manic hedonism of this season."

"I've always thought of psychoanalysis as a science for moral parvenus," Edmund said. "Yet her fluctuations are such it might be a last resort. . . ."

"However," he added pointedly, "she retains the courage of frivolity, as I do."

The one time Edmund saw Claire and Jeff alone together they were discussing matters of the household with attempted civility.

"Beach chairs, Clairsie."

"Do you mind?"

"Not at all, I'll go on the A.M. Also, April phoned, Katrinka has no room for her and she wants to drop in on us next weekend with the children."

"How beastly."

"Now, sweets, it's the family! We'll do a clambake the day she comes, and the next afternoon we can have a nifty sail to Siasconset . . . do give it your one oh oh," he added sharply as he walked towards the boat landing.

"One oh oh," she murmured as she picked lettuce for supper, looking absentminded.

Before dinner Edmund was asked to hold Victoria on his lap. It is possible that he had never had a child on his lap before. It is possible that he had never before closely experienced the smell of a young child's flesh. The texture, the odor, of Victoria's face was terrifying in its novelty. In this flesh of palpitating innocence there was already some principle of procreation which he had never detected—perhaps never dared detect—in her mother's wiry body. He put his face close to the child's hair, closed his eyes, inhaled deeply. In the immaculacy of her hair's fragrance he recalled some moment and texture of his own childhood that had slipped into oblivion, some smell of his own body being scrubbed by Mara. The child turned her face swiftly towards him and he felt the inexplicable delicacy of her skin upon his cheek like the brush of a flower's pistil. The fleeting gossamer joy of her cheek upon his made him feel the somber weight of that splendidly groomed body of his which had never reproduced, which had seldom merged with its highest object of desire, this girl's mother. . . . And who would bring up this superb child? Women were leaving home to find a possible death in good causes, schools were dissolving under the threat of radical idiots, the daughters of women who'd gone mad from staying at home were going mad from being too much in the world. He missed intensely throughout this visit the presence of Elizabeth Sanford, that half-crazed creature of commonplace conversation whose singular contribution (and he suspected it was a gift peculiar to women) had been to bring comfort to those about her. I'm becoming more conservative than ever, Edmund reflected with pleasure.

Before Victoria went to bed Claire embraced her daughter with a tense desperate tenderness and held her very tight. She sat her on her lap and brushed her hair with the silver-handled brush that had belonged to Babsie. How the child delighted in her mother's touch! She had looked distant, amused, in the men's arms all afternoon. But now she sucked her thumb, eyes closed, her head collapsed against her mother's shoulder as if it were the only place in which she could abandon herself to her childhood. After Victoria's hair was straight and gleaming Claire clutched her again and rocked her softly, eyes closed.

Looking suntanned, rested and moral, Jeff sat in his upstairs study that evening writing mail-order houses for numerous articles with which to ornate his denuded house. He ordered shell-shaped night-lights, monogrammed note pads, crème brûlée ramekins, cocktail glasses etched with herons sailing across brilliant skies. He had told Edmund as they'd biked home from the tennis club that his dream was to retire fairly early from the teaching profession and live year round in this part of New England, supporting himself "by some profitable little local commerce." Designing nautical instruments . . . strengthening the local lobster industry . . . he might import some sheep, as he had in Great Britain . . . useless to even mention such projects to Claire, she went berserk at the thought of ever living on the island . . . meanwhile he aspired to make the house as comfortable as Babsie had had it. As Edmund sat sipping Scotch with him that evening Jeff lovingly studied offerings of bowl and whisk sets, wind-chill meters, butter churners, portable weaving looms.

"See, Eddem, the trouble is that I looked forward to marriage more than to anything else in the world! I was going to be a great husband the way I was going to be a great teacher; I wanted to have four children and build a perfect little community. . . ."

"You poor bastard."

"D'you know the single most important thing we're doing in a great school like St. Paul's, Edmo? We're training good husbands, loyal men. What better service can we offer society than to train them for ideal marriages?"

Edmund was damned if he was going to shape students into ideal

198

husbands but it wasn't the right time to differ; he was agreeing with everyone this weekend to keep the household from going to pieces. In Sealark's attic, two floors above Claire's displays of fasting pacifists and picketing monks, Jeff had installed a veritable sanctuary of military values. Walls adorned with portraits of uniformed ancestors—Admiral Howell, strikingly resembling his offspring, leans on his sword during a lull in the Spanish-American War; General Howell of the Battle of the Bulge stands in a field in Flanders, foot poised on a cannon. All about the floor of Jeff's refuge the elaborate collection of toy soldiers from all ages of mankind which Edmund had so admired in their adolescence—silver-helmeted Roman legions shoot arrows from clusters of plastic trees, medieval foot soldiers charge across moats and drawbridges, generals in crimson jackets inspect regiments; and at center stage a two-inch-high Napoleon, hand thrust into his vest, is led away by one of Wellington's blue-jacketed aides-de-camp.

"You know what the schoolboy is, Edmo? He's like a base ore that can be forged into precious metal in the crucible of a great school and then polished to shine with a dull, rich luster; that's why we need to get him as young as possible, to forge his courage and loyalty; one of the masters has a neat way of putting it, Eddem, he compares it to making a perfect martini. You need the right proportions of unswerving loyalty and individualism, the old geezer says, the loyalty of the character is the gin . . . but Edmo the way young anarchists are going today they're getting to be like a ghastly potion of ninety percent vermouth!"

"I know only too well, they're odious."

"I work my ass off to correct the balance, Eddem; I teach three history courses, coach two sports, advise the military history club, I have seminar on sixth-form responsibilities Tuesday and Wednesday night, sex education on Thursday, I take my turn in chapel once a week; teaching is a continuous act of faith . . . like great husbands, Eddem, good teachers are paragons of loyalty and firmness who're capable of exploding in righteous indignation. . . ."

"I strongly believe in anger."

. . .

They sat opposite each other at the table laden with Jeff's books of military history, finishing the bottle of whiskey set between them.

"And what are you going to do about her?"

Jeff opened his arms with a helpless gesture that added to the irony of his smile. He'd always been reluctant to discuss his private life with anyone, nothing Edmund respected more.

"I don't mind if women take over the world, old sport, what I'm afraid of is their values . . . sensitivity to the suffering of unknown hordes, splendid on the private plane but what if it enters the realm of public affairs, forces the masculine tone to pass from the nation?"

"Quite so, a reign of mediocrity, hollow phrases about better worlds!"

"After we get through with animals' rights they'll give us theories about plants having emotions, rocks feeling pain, there's no end to it, Eddem, how are we ever going to feed the planet?"

"Even though I don't have one I'm even more concerned with the survival of the family," Edmund sighed.

The bottle was depleted. Even as an adolescent Jeff had had the most honorable manner of holding his liquor, amiable cheeks flushing, smile widening into the evening until he fell benignly asleep in some chair. Even now when he more or less fell onto the sofa the gesture had a certain choreographic splendor. "Peb and I will make up tomorrow and she'll have a super plan for saving the Congolese . . . where are you going?" Jeff muttered as Edmund paced about his study. "Nowhere . . . I mean, I might take a turn around the block a bit later." "Careful crossing the street," Jeff whispered, and then fell into a deep sleep. Sitting at the table littered with volumes of military history Edmund felt sadness in the felling of this simple complex man. Fellows like Plinker and Jeff were becoming like snow leopards, an endangered species. Edmund had returned to the island longing to taste again of that rich dull luster Jeff spoke about, of that historic order that had nourished his fragile exiled self upon his arrival in America. And if this most stalwart of worlds was crumbling where was the refuge, could the center ever hold? Edmund raised Jeff's feet up more comfortably onto the sofa, put a pillow under his head, continued staring at him by the light of the army lamp that illuminated Jeff's toy battles. There was in Jeff a Puritan Don Giovanni which incited him to aspire to the unconquerable, to climb every Everest of the erotically accessible, even there clearly exhibited valor was of the essence. He'd probably persevered to win Claire precisely because she was so particularly unseductable, and when the process of taming her ran amok his moods might well turn vile. There lay le Puritain Moyen Sensuel, Jeff of the loyal hard-on, Jeff of the dutiful erection; in sleep his profile was almost feminine in its beauty, resembled Donatello's *David*. Edmund looked out the window and stared at the tragic set of New England innocence it had been the Sanfords' and Howells' honor to preserve, at that frozen nostalgia for a purer age shouting through the white spires of floodlit churches. When Plinker and Jeff would be called away the heroic age of America would come to end, age of high ideals and the most elegant hypocrisies. He didn't wish to leave that fragrant face of Jeff's which even in sleep continued to shroud all pains in a benign ironic smile; he would have been happy spending the night on the same couch, coiled in whatever remained of Jeff's certitude.

He went to bed humming an old school song familiar to the Sanfords and the Howells.

"Hath he fulfilled the promise of his youth . . . and borne unscath'd through danger's stormy fields . . . Honor's white wreath and virtue's stainless shield . . ."

"Almighty Father bless our land with honorable industry sound learning and pure manners defend our liberties as Thou has in the recent world upheaval and grace our house as we have honored Thee in Thy Tabernacle in this year of our Lord 1955 . . ."

"Sixty-five, daddy sweetheart, it's all right, all right."

". . . bless all who teach and all who learn among the beloved teachers gathered here today that they may train young souls in pursuance of Thy will and grant that in humility of heart . . ."

"Save us from Communist vegetarian pacifists," Jeff intoned,

201

"help us build mighty fortresses to ward them off." He was in a vile mood at that Sunday lunch; not so much from his headache, Edmund had deciphered, but from the announcement of another of Pebble's imminent departures. The day was halcyon. Victoria was running about in a little apron, helping her mother to bring dishes from the kitchen. Still dressed in her bathing suit, Claire had set the table quite formally with the little that remained of Babsie's silver. In the desolate white dining room ornated with humans agitating for redress, sunlight dappled by the sound gleamed on the same crystal and china as it had precisely twenty years ago. Plinker hovered over the table, leaning on his cane, his mouth open in the bewildered manner of the very old, his eyes traveling from Jeff to Claire to the photograph of Bertrand Russell over the breakfront.

". . . save us from the savers," Jeff continued as he set the roast on the table. "Ban the Bomb Banners, enable us to resist the resisters . . ."

"Mediums, vegetarians," Plinker muttered.

Edmund found Claire's next tactic quite extraordinary. She proceeded to propound domestic information of the grossest common sense: April's toilet-training theories were outdated, not a chance of getting her to listen to Dr. Spock, a string quartet from Boston was playing at Town Hall on Wednesday, the mushroom dish she'd fixed them today came from the *Alternative Commune Cookbook* and wasn't it heaven? Edmund feared greatly what would come next: confrontation, accusation, the pain of history.

"Edmund, you want to be a swell friend to little Victoria?" Jeff was sharpening his carving knife, flourishing it with theatrical gestures that worried Edmund. "Why don't you stick around and help me play dad? When Mommy's here she keeps the vegerino meals coming right on sched, bang bang, but when she's away saving the world it's up to us men to stave for ourselves. Join the club of the bereaved, Eddem, greater love hath no man than to share his family with his friends, the little he has of it. So here's the real grub, and is it delish; Vicky, watch Daddy carve the lovely roast. Thanks for uncorking the wine so nicely, sweet Plinker, I drink a toast to . . . our happiness. Not a chance, let's try again. To the cunning little pacifists who'll save America! Don't knock them E. R. or they'll creep up on you! *Salut! Na Zdarovie!*"

Edmund felt great anger rising. His childhood craving for china, silver, dining rooms, his lifelong love for the solace of rituals, the polonaise of etiquette . . . they were trampling on the torn garments of his youth, whatever there was left of them. He stood up and took his turn shouting.

"Must this family always be going mad in some way? Can't you pull yourselves together and lead this country again as you always have? Where's your stamina, where's everything? You can't even do a proper Sunday lunch anymore!"

Nantucket, Mass.
July 8th, 1965

. . . at some point in that meal, Soph, with that haunting view of the sound unchanged since the day the four of us first had lunch together, I found myself in an argument with Claire that went somewhat like this: Your pacifist friends wouldn't give a rat's prick about watching the world burn, right, they'd let someone else do that dirty little business? . . .

Well, you know perfectly well how she'd retort, she didn't sound that different from the way you would have in one of your earlier incarnations: You desiccated passive academic always locked in your ivory tower she cried, are you saying you believe in violence? Not at all I replied, it reeks of spontaneity. I'm just stating that there's a lot of brutality in your nonviolence Santa Clara, you're being duped by the new manufacturers of liberation, another big business that's about to boom in this country. . . .

Part Three

The perfect interlocutor, the friend, is the one who offers me the greatest possible resonance . . . Friendship could be defined as the space with the greatest sonority.

ROLAND BARTHES

xvi

TITIAN'S *Shower of Danaë* depicts a naked woman reclining on a richly rumpled bed, a wreath of pale braided hair winding between her perfect breasts. Gold, rose, mauve glazes cast on her flesh the luminous grain of time-worn silks, of a camellia on its last days of bloom. One leg is bent at the knee, her head leans back on a pillow as she stares at the shower of golden coins that descends from the sky above her. Her expression is one of rapture, of abandon. Yet the painting is full of doom, russet shower bursting upon Danaë from a somber thunderous sky, Godhead manifesting itself not in a beneficent stream but in some awesome explosion. And at the right of the canvas an aging woman servant greedily holds out her arms to catch the falling gold, her sear of vice and rags hovering like another storm cloud over the maiden's sumptuous flesh.

Edmund stands before Titian's *Danaë* on a June morning in Leningrad's Hermitage Museum. Let Dr. Richter write an ideal last paper in which he'll elaborate on the ambiguous symbolism of this spilt radiance, gold and sperm, greed and grace, man spending his sperm or his hard-earned coins, sky god spending itself in a rain of gold. Previous instances in which an effusion of riches is a sign of grace: shower of coins blessing Hänsel and Gretel as they fall into their innocent sleep; Grimm brothers' *Sternhaler*, wealth of gold raining down upon the pious orphaned virgin who offers all her clothing to the poor; the young hero of still another German folktale soars above his city on a giant bee, dispensing golden showers on all the marriageable girls of his province. One could speculate on the roots of such legends in primeval agricultural myths, in the ancient rites which call on male gods to fructify the fields of female earth. Teutonic legends merely Nordic variants on Zeus's rain of gold and the mysterious events of the Immaculate Conception, Danaë was even seen by some medieval scholars as a prefiguration of the Virgin Mary. And so the cloudburst of coins descending upon Titian's reclining maiden (this would be an amusingly farfetched aside of our discourse) could be compared to the fertilizing beams of grace that flow to Mary from the angel's palm in paintings of the Annunciation. "Dr. Richter will give his last lecture of the century tonight on 'The Iconography of the Shower of Gold as a Prefiguration of the Word.'" One could stress that in earlier depictions of the Danaë myth (Correggio's, Gentileschi's) Danaë stretches out her own hand with considerable greed, seems as guilty of cupidity as the elderly attendant hovering by her side. But this is where Titian shows his psychological cunning, transposes all avarice unto the hag who hovers over the rapturous girl, purifies his heroine into a symbol of amorous and celestial grace. . . . Also! Essential to elaborate right here on the splendid Oedipal elements of the Perseus-Danaë tale: Danaë's father, ruler of Argos, warned by oracles that he would be destroyed by his own grandson, imprisoning his only daughter in a brass chamber to preserve her virginity; sky god's divine rain piercing through the fortress wall to conceive Perseus, the redeemer king, Perseus later performing heroic feats to protect his mother's chastity, destroying her tyrannic captors with the head of the Gorgon Medusa whose sight turns men to stone, "Snake-haired creature fought and won through lurid air on strident, whirling wings . . . "

The city of Leningrad glimmers a floor below the windows of the Hermitage; sharply etched buildings washed with pale hues of confectioners' colors, familiar from the aquatints hung about Mara's bed in their tiny New York rooms; the walls of the General Staff Headquarters across Palace Square are the pale yellow of fresh butter. Edmund had looked away from Titian's *Danaë* for a moment and realized why the image had long mesmerized him: the very tale of his adolescence, fatherless Edmund and chaste much-courted Mara whose marriage led to her destruction. A curiosity about his father's identity had recurred periodically throughout his life, like bouts of very mild malarial fever. It's odd that you don't wonder more about who he was, John Mirsky had once said. Well perhaps he was another salesman of fake degrees from the University of Heidelberg, Edmund answered, like that creep my mother fell for in her blini parlor. Do you realize that you can only joke about it? John had persisted. . . . Some years ago, shortly before dying, Grisha had finally given Edmund the key to his father's identity. The first Edmund was a gifted but unsuccessful painter who had killed himself with laudanum out of fear of not making his proper mark upon the world. It was as dreary and simple as that. He had never even been a writer. The epiphany had explained Mara's long-suffering silences, her awesome nurturing of her son's gifts, her determination to bring him early fame so as to enjoy its fruits during her own short life. The revelation had strengthened Edmund's disdain for any form of suicide, existential, too chic, bad literature! Genius wasted, talent spent. His father had just been . . . a shower of sperm, a man spending himself in a shower of golden talent. . . .

Edmund goes on to pace about the ornate gilt-ceilinged galleries of the Hermitage. Earlier that morning Intourist Tour No. 137 had been guided through chambers surfeited with marble surfaces and precious stones, through doors flanked by caryatids and columns of jasper, malachite, lapis lazuli. " 'Everything in St. Petersburg is colossal, innumerable,' " Edmund had read to Claire over breakfast from a nineteenth-century traveler's diary. " ' . . . the costliness and glare of the courtiers' apparel, and a profusion of precious stones, create a splendour of which the magnificence of other courts can only give us a faint idea . . . many of the nobility are almost covered with diamonds yet the same nobles sleep on the floors of their palaces to avoid the vermin of their beds, have a great part of their estates pledged to pawn shops. . . . ' "

Impatient to reach the galleries of European painting, Edmund had walked restlessly that morning through rooms of pink marble where Moorish fountains cascade into alabaster basins, had stood before a twenty-seven-yard-wide map of Russia whose cities and rivers are indicated by rubies and emeralds. The Rolls-Roycers exult over the quantity of gems, the Zabars ask Edmund studious questions about French influences on nineteenth-century Russian art, the Weickers photograph every portrait of royalty in sight. The Americans are particularly elated by Fabergé's eight-foot-high sapphire-studded gold clock in the form of a peacock which makes a total revolution of its wings upon the striking of each hour. " 'Once outside nature I shall never take / My bodily form from any natural thing,' " Sophie whispers to Edmund as she stands in front of the blazing bird. " 'Once *out of* nature,' " Edmund rebuts, she's still getting it wrong after thirty years; "give me the next lines, sweetness. . . . " " ' . . . but such a form as Grecian goldsmiths make / Of hammered gold and gold enameling . . . ' " He kisses her forehead and wanders on. The Hermitage contains 1050 rooms 1170 staircases and fourteen miles of floors and galleries, Evgeny calls out; Dr. Richter is advised to strictly follow the order of the guided tour. Edmund goes to stand before a Memling which he suspects is false, searches for Claire. Standing by a window he sees the gold needle of St. Paul's Cathedral rising ethereal towards a mother-of-pearl sky, Claire passes him by with her abstracted gaze, flat brown hair hanging straight as a schoolgirl's; at times he wishes he could drink her, ingest her so as to know her from the inside of himself. Shreds of their early life return as he comes back to stand before Titian's *Danaë*, Claire at the Sealark piano playing *Für Elise*, sunlight pouring into the room from a gull-filled sky while Sophie trims his hair with Babsie's gardening shears, Jeff radiant with heroism brings him hot broth every hour, it's the day after Edmund's almost drowned and the household has gathered about him and caters to his every whim; in the next room Plinker growls out orders to his Wall Street firm over the phone . . . another point to make about the image of Danaë! Ambivalence of money, gold's demonic attributes never enough stressed, outward sign of inner grace as well of lowliest corruption. The foulness of riches, Midas choking on his fortune, finding death in it. Luther had gone further than anyone else in associating wealth with excrement and Satan, "Money is the word of Satan," "*Simia Dei*, ape of God." Gold equals grace also equals defecation. The prophet of Protestantism receives his first illumination in the privy of his monastery at Wittenberg, later envisions the Apocalypse, the Second Coming, as a rain of gold that turns to fecal filth. Ambivalence of the most potent symbols, shower of gold that is both sinful offal and symbol of God's love!

"Gentlemen and ladies," Irina calls out, "we are now entering the great rooms of Hermitage's Dutch paintings, collection begun by Catherine the Great with help of French philosopher Diderot. . . . "

Much greater stress on grace in Rembrandt's version of *The Shower of Danaë*. The iconography of coinage disappears, Rembrandt dematerializes gold into pure light, transmutes the shower into a blaze of radiance which streams in from the upper left of the canvas. The northern Danaë does not lie in the erotic pastoral loggia of Venetian nudes but on the alcoved bed of a proper Dutch interior; contrast her modesty, her Puritan reticence to the brazen hedonism of her Venetian counterpart . . . the torso of Rembrandt's figure is half raised on a folded arm, she greets the effusion of light not with the voluptuous abandon of Titian's maiden but with the serene, surprised gesture of an Annunciation scene. The cloudburst of radiance pouring down upon her seems to bring happiness to all; the aging servant at Danaë's side is devoid of the greed of her own Venetian counterpart, stares at the spilt radiance with the obedient awe of a worshiper at Mass. Light! No ambivalence there, an element of redemption wherever you turn, Australian shaman gaining his magic powers by swallowing rock crystals, Augustine, the light Grace pours into our inner eye. . . .

In the early seventies, trying to ease Claire through her convent phase, Edmund had used the term secular Pelagianism to stress that her current search for grace could be delusory, that she could find whatever she wished to call salvation by returning to the palpable political suffering of others. Which she'd eventually done beyond the call of duty; such was the nature of the errand they'd debated a few nights ago and a myriad of her other dedications. In that austere period of her sisterhood he'd told her that grace could lurk on many levels, in the hard decision, the clear memory of a mother, behind every closed door of the courage to be. He had confided to Claire that if he were ever to paint again (this desire was then just nascent) he would have to find many new sources of fortitude—a new wellspring of trust in himself, a new fund of trust in others, a disdainful indifference to most criticism, a vastly purified life lived far beyond the pale of that public scrutiny which he had come to think of as demonic. To paint again would require some upwards mobility of trust, rebecoming as unwary as a small child, shed of all fear of foolishness, trusting all, believing in love and loveliness, believing in the spilt radiance of belief.

Edmund begins to walk out of the Hermitage after having mustered the courage to tell his two loves, two Muses, about a curious decision: On this particularly light-flooded morning he will tell them that he's about to radically change his life again. Sophie will have a fit, he can already hear her, at your level of success, achievement . . . Edmund smiles at the travelers assembled with him in the Rembrandt gallery and feels a happiness he hasn't known for decades.

"What's so new and exciting, E.R.?" Sophie whispers as she comes towards him.

"He's manic, marvelous this morning"—Claire taps his elbow with her notebook—"pouring forth pure sunshine."

"Our own dear tyrant, what's come over him?"

"Are you suddenly happy, Edmund love?"

"Happy? He'd need a Nobel."

"A superb new insight to share with your classes next term?"

"Oh, I'm not giving any more classes. *Finito*, I'm quitting, I'm leaving Berkeley."

"When," Claire says excitedly, "precisely when did you make that perfectly extraordinary decision?"

"Quite some time ago, it's precisely what I came here to talk to you about."

"You're totally out of your mind" (he could have said it for

Sophie, journalists are so predictable), "when anyone's at the top of their . . . "

He doesn't hear the end of her sentence. He's spun around and is walking swiftly towards the museum's exit. He's placated Evgeny with declarations of urgent bodily needs. He walks through a gallery hung with quattrocento masters he's dissected for decades of classroom lectures: note the drapery language, the bleak featureless landscape which emphasizes the monumental isolation of the figures. He pauses once with reverence before a Fra Angelico depicting the Virgin and Child flanked by Saint Dominic and Saint Thomas. The sun is God's sun and light stems only from the saints; for Fra Angelico there is no nature independent from God's hierarchy. Self-absorption of Angelico's figures, incorruptibility of their inwardness, saints as well as artists know that loneliness is the central condition of their vocation; how clearly this is stated in their fiercely lowered eyes, the isolation of their gestures . . .

He resumes his swift walk towards the Neva, passes through the palace's barbaric expanses of marble, jasper, malachite, walks by a bronze life mask of Peter the Great—eyes dilated as those of a Gorgon, brutal face set upon a monstrously thick neck—standing amid the vulgar gilt of caryatids. The artists with whom we've communed this morning have achieved most of the goals of heroism and religion, they've forced us to remain perpetually in their presence, they've conquered death; in these rooms the suffering of history is temporarily eased, time the destroyer is imprisoned and held at bay. . . . All of art is one gigantic guerrilla expedition against the chaos of experience and the silence of death. . . . "Orpheus dismembered will continue to sing, his head floating down our rivers . . ." The artist works on the faith that he contains in himself the source of his eternity, still engages in that communion with the immortal which is said to have passed away with the waning of the gods. . . .

That was one way of putting it, E.R., not very satisfactory, too much of the old Romantic tripe. Divinity of the creator, artist as sacred vessel—bane of our existence! Debased Faustianism, elitist ooze, Kraut metaphysics doled out in seedy art schools . . .

213

Try again, Richter.

I want to be more of what I could have been.

Edmund walks to the embankment of the Neva and stares at the swiftness of the river's flow. He climbs down a flight of stairs, stands a foot above its eddies. The Neva swirls in tortuous currents from some icy lake many miles east of the city, flowing senselessly to lose itself in the glacial waters of the Gulf of Finland. Edmund opens his trousers and relieves himself. The little arch of gold vaults triumphant over the stone embankment, descends into the innards of Russia's most brutal river. Edmund spends himself graciously into the pool of his unknown forefathers, he sheds years of pain as he flows into their victories, their passions, their unknown sins. He watches his arabesque for a felicity of time and when it subdues he feels great loss, great regret, that such moments of joy can not last for an eternity. His bliss flies above him in a dazzling troika, a flock of swans echo his delight on the black water, the Sphinx of Russia laughs all about him with bared fangs, all noise ceases on the Neva; the corrupt world waits for its absolution, tail lowered, like a guilty dog, all sleeps for a while—humans, palaces, canals—and then bells begin to ring again over the city's golden fleece.

Edmund turns back towards the green-and-gold immensity of the Winter Palace, stares at the great bronze statues that stand atop the ice-green roof. Their arms are raised in various gestures of command, pleading, exhortation. Edmund is still for a few moments until he sees his friends flowing through the portals of the Hermitage. Flanked by the chattering Zabars and the photographing Weickers, Sophie and Claire walk slowly onto the quay of the Neva, their arms about each other's waists.

"Freedom, *svoboda!*" he says as he hastens towards them.

"Dear God" (he also knew something similar would come out of Sophie), "what a country he's chosen to find that in."

xvii

HE heard Spanish being spoken, toilets flushing, dogs barking somewhere next door. Sophie was wearing a turban. A large parrot hovered over Edmund, staring out of a mean yellow eye. This was New York? A man sat by the window, smiling, peeling carrots. Sophie had lined up seven large canvases against the wall by the fireplace, they were her paintings, damn it; here he was impotent before his life's passion and she was dabbling away with excruciating freedom, even with a measure of talent. . . . It was 1969. What was life about? He already had a headache. Edmund leaned back against the pillow on Sophie's bed and inhaled his joint. Sophie seemed to have divorced and remarried and was wearing a turban. He also saw organic cookbooks, amaryllis plants in various stages of phallic splendor, effusions of batik, a tyranny of mirrors, pillows and tatami mats strewn about the floor. All was precisely as it should be. Claire was serving a two-week term for civil disobedience in some D.C. jail and Sophie was shacked up with a body-freak Off-Broadway star who was peeling carrots of bright cadmium orange. Two months ago she'd notified him that her radio program, *Tell It Like It Is*, was being syndicated to thirty-seven stations and that she'd started going to the Art Students League at nights. America was going mad. This generation thought it could master, domesticate everything. The mirrors lining Sophie's living room reflected myriad areas of the parrot's plumage, shimmering panels of cobalt, alizarin, chrome yellow. It was 1969. Why was he lying on batik sheets?

The room thrummed with that same brand of feminist rhetoric he'd heard on Sophie's program all the way to Berkeley. "Someday I also want to write a novel which expresses sexual experience from an intensely female point of view," she was saying. "Mailer and Henry Miller piss me off; I mean how do they know what it's like for a woman to have her first orgasm or suck a man's cock?"

"If you can't talk like a lady at least talk like a gentleman," Edmund muttered.

The actor wore a gold chain with a small squat Buddha around his neck. He had dark glasses and long wavy brown hair and a Chagall-blue jacket with gold braid on it, like the prince's in *Swan Lake*. The actor was quite famous. Edmund had seen pictures of him in a half-dozen publications in the past year alone. He'd seen him in *The Village Voice* doing a *Cherry Orchard* in modern dress, playing the schoolteacher in SDS costume. He'd read about his performance of a sleep tableau in which he lay naked for twelve hours in an environment of red silk. Sophie finally had an artist of her own again! And in the corner of the room stood her new easel, surrounded by dozens of fresh lustrous canvases. She smiled at Edmund radiantly, hair more Titian-sumptuous than ever. Her breasts hung splendid and braless under a T-shirt which said Liberate the Presidio Seven, her hips were swathed in a lamentation of African cotton. She stretched her arm up rhythmically, as if practicing one of her old dance exercises; dark soft hair stood like a small forest in the snowfield of her underarms, her ancient floral odor wafted towards him with the precision of new lilacs. Come away with me he wanted to say, erotic sister, beloved companion of my happiest days, come away! Shared studios of our youth, plaster casts, the paisley shawls we'd draped under vases of fresh roses . . . She stretched her arm still higher; her perfume pulsated towards him along with the torturing smell of his abandoned oil paints.

"Well what do you think about my paintings?"

"They're interesting." He inhaled, deeply this time. "Watch your edges."

He was a donkey, flying through the room, braying. The actor's shoulders had grown a tender hue of crimson as carrots mounted in his bowl. Today, today! the parrot screamed. Edmund finished his joint and leaned back on the bed, peacefully looking at Sophie's canvases. All was spherical, orbed, drawn with remarkable precision and executed in excruciatingly fleshly hues, sometimes dimpled with what seemed to be a proliferation of nipples. Abundance of genital shapes, dark chasms surrounded by delicate labial convolutions, crimson clefts, violet orifices, botanical curiosities honeycombed with the fluting and thrumming of biological tissue. . . .

"You're sure painting with your ovaries on your sleeve. Powerful sense of design. Are you two planning marriage?" Edmund feigned a yawn.

"Institutionalize the rape and bondage of women?"

"Legal whoredom!"

"So. No nuptial benediction," Edmund murmured, relieved.

Edmund squinted at the paintings and at the titles labeled on the edge of their frames. *Rosa Luxemburg, Let It All Hang Out, Homage to Eleanor of Aquitaine.* Cathedrals of convoluted tissue, femaleness offered as some primeval covenant. Serrated, revolutionary labia bulging with assertive tendrils (*George Sand*). Shy pearly labia nestled in collars of elaborately drawn lace (*Homage to Emily Dickinson*). Fleshly labia palpitating around assertive central slits (*Charlotte Corday*).

She said: "You're threatened, aren't you?"

"Uhh . . . why?"

"Let's be existential, Edmund, one of the reasons you're so threatened by my imagery is that women have an infinite capacity for orgasm."

"Uhuhhh."

"Uhh, uhuhhh, a new academic tic of yours. Not only can we have eighteen orgasms in a row, honeybun, we can also fake them."

"Really. Good luck, my precious darling. Just watch your edges. That saturated yellow at the extreme right of the canvas . . . "

217

"Always talking about form, Eddem, is that your only karma? What did you think I was going to paint, fields of daisies?"

"Today! Today!" the parrot screamed.

"The problem of avoiding emotional strain can only be cured by the praxis of nutrition," the actor was saying. "I see in you the fatigue, the banal metaphysical fatigue of a man still striving to find himself . . . it can be allayed by daily intakes of lecithin in normative doses, and you'd better check on your glycogens . . . "

They had sat down to dinner.

". . . glycogens are the existential component of our biological spectrum, they tune, they vivify, they turn the body of despair into the hope of the future. . . . The American diet elevates innocent stupidity to a form of suicide, pure Thanatos at six P.M. across the fifty-two states. . . . "

"You could only have found him in California," Edmund muttered to Sophie when his host went to the kitchen for the next course. "I've come East to escape that monstrous state and see the two loves of my life; one's in the pokey and the other's telling it like it is with a Sausalitan carrot freak. So rising media star Sophie Ross is preaching the gospel of self-revelation, playing high priestess to our new nudism of the soul. . . . "

"You're so pathetically closeted!"

"Closeted, Soph! My closet is my haven, my most precious refuge, my repressions are truly collector's items! You've become infected with the cult of openness, sweetheart, that diet of absolute candor you feed me on your program and off it is ruining the culture as fast as anything else. . . ."

The first phase of grass always made him talk very quickly, he packed his words in as fast as he could in apprehension of the torpor that followed.

"Civilization, dear Sofia Larionovna, depends on ceremony, which is the veiling of the truth . . . listen, honeybun, since we have a minute alone I'll tell you a little story. I had a lover last year who tortured me with her passion for unadulterated candor—a fe-

218

tishist of the authentic . . . she insisted on disclosing every detail of her life and I've never been as miserable, Soph, never. . . . Whether she picked up a hi-fi repairman or shared a bacchanal with a triad of stoned sociologists she described her encounters with the sordid detail of a botanist's journal. . . . I threatened to leave her; since she didn't have the imagination to lie I begged her to deceive me, that's how tedious these unsolicited accounts became. . . . I insulted her, I told her that I didn't ask of a lover to be faithful but simply to remain interesting—all to no avail; for a year I lived *folie à deux* with this voluptuary of the sincere. . . ."

"You never did give women enough space," Sophie said.

Garlic course after garlic course was arriving. There had been a gazpacho as thick as ketchup, stuffed peppers in which whole cloves of garlic lay enthroned like pearls. In between his trips to the kitchen the actor noted that Pliny had listed garlic as the finest recipe for longevity, that Eleanor Roosevelt's doctor prescribed three cloves a day to retain memory. Sophie and her man hold up their bowls with both hands and make a small bow of the head to each other at the beginning of each course. Edmund asks which ashram they've picked that up in but by that time everyone's having trouble hearing each other. Miles Davis is on full blast. There's been much wine. The grass is catching up with Edmund. "Listen to those drums!" the actor says to Sophie. She raises her eyes to the ceiling with a knowing smile. "It must be like this every night," Edmund says; "is it like this every night?" His voice floats faint and piping above him, he's as detached from his voice as the melodic line of the trumpet is aloof from the saxophone's, the harmonic strains of tomato and pepper each draw their slow separate strings across his tongue, other voices float polyphonically above his head. "I'm driving down to the Sunday demo in D.C. for Clairsie's birthday," Sophie says; "a bunch of us from Women's Strike for Peace are going to stand under her jail window and sing happy birthday; that kid has her shit more pulled together than anyone I know. . . ." "Garlic doesn't admit the possibility of overdose, it's been proven that Bulgarian garlic eaters don't get cancer. . . ."

"Gene is thinking of doing a modern-dress Hamlet which he'll intersperse with recollected fragments of his own analysis, and then he might do an Othello for The Living Theatre in which . . ."

"We must discipline our ego to keep our ideas to ourselves," Edmund hears himself saying. "Whoever is ready to say anything is ready to sell anything he says. . . . "

They nod their heads to the music, throwing specks of garlic to the parrot.

Oh they haven't heard Professor Richter's sermonette on the decline of the West, have they? This is the peak rush hour of the Western gods, and is the traffic ever heavy going out of town! Yes he's used to being labeled reactionary, he's even been attacked on his own Viconian grounds . . . Vico—the seventeenth-century Neapolitan philosopher, after whom his cat is named. . . .

They all laugh loudly for a minute, spilling wine.

Vico prophesied that we've got to return to an age of barbarians before we can resurrect our gods; well that's where he breaks with Vico, resurrection isn't as sure as Vico thought.

Vico, Vico the parrot calls out.

What did they think?

He realized that he'd spoken in Russian for the last few minutes and that Sophie was holding a monologue. Crack them open she was saying about the celebrities she interviewed on her radio program, lob to their backhand, make them reveal themselves when they're off guard . . . the jazz was so fabulous that she was thinking of becoming a jazz trombonist next . . . they all laughed, spilling a lot of wine on the floor. The actor was serving something called consciousness three pudding. Carobs, dates, nuts, cinnamon sang polyphonically upon Edmund's tongue. "I'm like, like . . . man, laid back, I'm really together," Edmund tried. But his tongue slowed down, clogged on its nourishment, seemed to take an infinity of time to simply cross his mouth, ground for sound but could only emit single words that flashed with great solitude somewhere above his head. "E.R., remember that poem we used to say as kids?" Sophie slurred tenderly, " 'Once out of glory I shall never take . . . ' " " 'Once out of *nature*,' " Edmund slurred back.

" ' . . . my bodily form from any worldly . . . ' " " 'no, *natural* thing . . .' " A wave of dates rose in his throat and he suddenly desired to be totally alone, he only wanted to enter a small dark room and enjoy his state of profound idiocy by himself, he wanted to climb into his night-night and cover himself up and hug his solitude, his urge for solitude was as overpowering and demanding as the call of an imminent bowel movement. His hosts were still dipping wooden African spoons into consciousness three, shaking their heads to the music as he rose to leave. For some agonizing minutes they stood at the door embracing him and promising eternal affection, pledging to take him to a Sufi farm in New Jersey the next time he came East, planning to travel with him to Nepal, to Algeria, to Greece as soon as the colonels would leave, at the next demo they'd all three share a room together in D.C. . . .

Edmund went back to the Westbury Hotel and started assembling every lamp he could find in his suite. Then he surrounded his bed with them. He was consumed with fear that someone, anyone, might come in and disturb his private, precious imbecility, the lamps would be his sentinels, his guard of honor, he found lamps mounted on ceramic statuettes of red-shirted polo players, ardent Italian lovers. He had to address a convention of art historians the following morning and he'd taken two rooms in the kind of hotel that his mother and he had aspired to decades ago and he was only beginning to afford, the kind with pearly doorknobs, careful imitations of Louis XV chairs. He went to bed and floated in his new luxury, enjoying his haze of idiocy, relishing the calm of a room which had admitted no novelty or change in over thirty years, there were footsteps in the corridor, people threatened . . . he got up once more before falling asleep and assembled the lamps more tightly around his bed, lamps mounted on simpering eighteenth-century shepherdesses, winged Hermeses . . . he fell asleep. He had a dream about his mother:

They climb the stairs of a great warehouse, they enter an immense room totally walled and ceilinged with feathers of hundreds of varieties of wild birds, goose and guinea hen, peacock and snipe, feathers thickly laid on, not an inch of space between three-inch-

221

thick layers of plumage, russet pearl shimmer of turtledove, emerald brilliance of the rings about pheasants' necks. Amid this splendor walk four or five enormous creatures of upright carriage, covered head to toe in plumage, some dun as owls and others of resplendent parrot hues; they speak a language unlike any he's ever heard, a soft cooing and gurgling, a tender chortling as kind as the flow of water over polished stone; they point to diverse areas of the wall or ceiling. Mara gurgles and trills back to them in their own tongue, the most resplendent and desirable feathers lie on the ceiling so Mara grabs his hand and they fly through the width and height of the room, smoothing their palms over the wings of many a silken bird, hovering at length to caress the gleaming plumages, they swoop from swansdown to shimmering egrets to bronzed guinea hen. . . .

Edmund woke up brutally at the sound of his alarm clock, bright morning sunlight New York 1969, he'd flown across the United States for the purpose of giving a paper on Tintoretto that morning and seeing his two great loves, his two remaining Muses, who were nowhere to be seen as he remembered them.

xviii

THE visitors' gallery in the chapel of St. Agatha's Abbey was set at the left of the apse. When Edmund wanted to attend an Office during his visits to Claire he came in well before the appointed time, loving the mystery of the space at its most tenebrous, before any candles were lit. Shortly after she'd entered the monastery he'd gone to hear None, the Office preceding the nuns' afternoon work period. A thin white curtain had remained drawn across the wooden choir screen of the chapel, fluttering in the summer breeze like a moth's wing. And from behind it there emerged the frailest, most ethereal chant imaginable, the nuns singing the Alleluia of midday on a single spectral note, perhaps high E . . . the timbre of their voices was supplicating and expressed a certain helplessness . . . the single tone of their litany floated wraithlike above the sounds of nature proliferating outside the small chapel, blackbird proffering its liquid trill, guard dog barking . . . The pale incantation lasted for ten minutes, the candle was blown out, the room was once more dark, a band of women in dusty gray work robes and muddy boots streamed out of the chapel and went out again towards their fields, their sheds, their kitchens, to continue their task of survival. . . . Claire had told him that her favorite Office was the Matins sung between the hours of 4:00 to 6:00 A.M., which was exclusively dedicated to the singing of the

223

Psalms. Once in a rare moment of insomnia Edmund rose at four to hear Matins and was perplexed by the thought that throughout the world tens of thousands of his contemporaries were still dedicating over five hours a day to chanting sacred litanies—Matins, Lauds, Mass, Sexts, None, Vespers, Compline—"simply singing in celebration of the ground of being," that was the way Pebble had put it . . . perhaps if he let himself go and thought of sacred life as simple celebration, thought of the Lord as a great Will diverting Himself in the garden of His creation, the meaning of her present life might become clearer to him . . . the world and time could be the dance of the Lord in emptiness, and the silence of the spheres the music of a wedding feast . . . there is a painting of Zurbarán's which reminded him of Claire when he stared at her standing at the back of the chapel, one of three lay sisters coiffed in a simple veil, her beauty more impassive, more imperturbable than ever, the perfect oval of her face, the slightly arrogant mouth . . . it was in this state of stubborn self-determination that she had realized her fullest and most complete womanhood . . . on another occasion some sly beckoning of her eyes led him to go up to the altar at communion time with the handful of worshipers from the nearby village who came to daily Mass . . . he walked up to the altar and closed his eyes, remembering the icy ting of the Communion spoon on his lip in the Orthodox church, in the Eucharists he'd shared with his mother . . . now the wafer lay tasteless and fragile on his tongue as a single snowflake; he felt nothing and went back to his pew.

In the tempest of opinions and regrets that followed Claire's exit from the secular world (*"Folie mystique!"* exclaimed Cousin April, who had left her second husband and taken a string of courses at the Alliance Française), the central trait of Claire's character was curiously overlooked. Except for Edmund, no one took into account her excessive will to autonomy, her lifelong struggle to liberate herself totally from the privileged world she'd been born into. History's made it clear, Edmund would say, that most persons striving for sainthood or the monastic life are endowed with a perfectly remarkable will to power; why else do

224

they so frequently pray for humility? Yet even Edmund admitted that the timing of this decision was extremely singular. Throughout the 1960s thousands of men and women had been leaving the traditional religious life to work for precisely the same secular causes that had been obsessing Claire. Nuns who'd been forbidden to read anything beyond the collection of saints' lives on their convent bookshelves were telling their students that picketing was a form of praying and attending weekend seminars on revolution. Benedictines who had written on the contemplative life for arcane theological journals were protesting the Vietnam War with acts of civil disobedience and singing hymns over piles of burning draft files. It is in February of 1971, at the height of this rebellion against all traditional premises of salvation, six months or so after her father's death, that Claire went to live as a lay sister at the Abbey of St. Agatha, a community of cloistered Anglican nuns in eastern Minnesota.

For several preceding years she has engaged in a ritual that has already caused much consternation to her family: Claire Sanford Howell, progeny of all that's most decorous in American society, has been repeatedly dragged away by policemen in antiwar demonstrations. There is a core of austerity in her that adapts with an assentment almost perverse to the rigors of prison life. By 1970 she's been arrested twelve, fourteen times. She comes into a cell, takes off her shoes and sits cross-legged on the prison floor. The night's visions sway about her in a haze of absolution as she observes the cold animal rage of women's eyes clutching the bars of their cells, the pistols slung on the hips of jail matrons patrolling the corridors, the graffiti on cell walls saying ARISE AND SHINE YE SISTERS OF THE WORLD. In the late sixties Claire had engaged in civil disobedience with a nun who convinced her that "in witness to the poor" they should refuse bail and choose instead the alternate penance of five days' imprisonment. She henceforth refused bail at all her arrests and deepened that sacrifice with a water fast. (Edmund gently scolded her, in a note from Berkeley, for "indulging in that greed for personal salvation which might be the most obnoxious greed there is.")

225

With questionable precision, psychologists have tended to divide humanity into the healthy souls who are content to be born just once and those problematic "twice-born" spirits driven to search for redeeming conversion. One of the intricacies of Claire Sanford's character is that she doesn't belong clearly to either category. There is little issue of conversion or "rebirth" in her decision to leave the secular world. She's never entertained, for instance, the fashionable Anglican custom of turning to Roman Catholicism. To the contrary (as she enjoys stressing in her letters) she's being more faithful than ever to "the rock bottom of our own tradition." Her decision seems to be forged in that iron of the soul which drives most reformers and revolutionaries to return to earlier levels of purity and rigor. In the months preceding her departure for the convent, for instance, Claire spent much time reading medieval history, concentrating in particular on the great abbesses of the early Middle Ages. This obsession had also been instigated by one of the many priests and nuns she worked with in the antiwar movement— a Franciscan who lectured spiritedly, during an all-night vigil at the Pentagon, on "Women's Autonomy in the Religious Orders." And if Claire ever came close to a state of trance it might have consisted of some historical meditation on these paragons of female independence. Women of such forceful presence that they became fabled for stilling storms and taming wild beasts, founders and administrators of great separatist enclaves, females so powerful that they didn't allow bishops into their monastic settlements! Saint Melania, converter of Byzantine emperors, Saints Thecla and Lioba, girls of noble birth who left their families to escape unwanted marriages and ended their lives as contemplatives in mountain retreats where they healed and taught the hundreds who came to them. Women saying no to the dictates of family, leaving marriages that enslaved them to the cycle of childbearing, pioneering enclaves of peace and learning in the chaos of barbaric forests, defying the patriarchal order, creating the truest semblance of equality offered women in the West. What transcendence, what a release from the tyranny of nature, Claire would write in one of her letters to Sophie! What a splendid improvement on our pathetic new concepts of women's liberation!

"I never did like the Reformation," she wrote in her P.S. "What an erosion of our autonomy, what a blow to women's right to truly determine their destinies!"

On a clear morning in 1971 she'd pack a small bag of personal effects and leave her home in Concord with a long letter to Jeff (two impeccable carbon copies had already been mailed to Edmund and Sophie) announcing her decision to go and live, for an indeterminate amount of time, at the Abbey of St. Agatha in Four Rivers, Minnesota.

There were two separate letters for her twelve-year-old daughter Victoria: one to be opened before her departure, another one a year hence.

She didn't claim to have heard any voices, sensed Presences, experienced transports. Her departure for Minnesota seemed as calm and measured as the little notes she'd written to herself since childhood, those neatly labeled exhortations towards self-perfection scattered among the pages of her Book of Common Prayer and her cages of recuperating animals.

The first visit Edmund made to St. Agatha's occurred some three months after Claire's departure, and was preceded by several communications concerning the behavior expected of him at the abbey guesthouse, where relatives and friends of the nuns were allowed to come for limited four-day stays:

"Be advised that the abbey lodge is open to visitors for only a few hours of the afternoon, and for good or for worse that's where we'll have to meet. I asked the mother superior for visit permission a few weeks ago and it's been granted. . . ."

"Your essay on Van Der Weyden's Deposition sounds like an ideal project to work on here, and if I told you not to bring your darn typewriter I'd feel as if I were ordering Kenneth Clark not to write. So yes do bring it, but only use it in your room with the doors closed so as not to distract other guests who seek the meditative silence we promise them. . . ."

The abbey was set in heavily wooded Minnesota terrain, several hours from the nearest large town. And the guesthouse where Edmund came to stay for his visits with Claire was situated at the bottom of a steep hill a half mile or so from the abbey proper. The rustic dirt road wound upwards through several stands of pines, then through sloping fields edged by laurels and apple trees. The abbey church loomed before the visitor at a sudden turn of the road when one least expected it, its small gilded cross outlined darkly against the setting sun. Edmund had arrived on a halcyon evening in late May for his first visit, feeling great need to look at the landscape which Claire was confined to seeing day after day. In an expanse of valley within the monastic enclosure he glimpsed well-tilled fields of corn and wheat, thriving vegetable gardens and fruit orchards, pastures dotted with Hereford cows. A frail, high strain of women's voices emerged from the chapel, they must have been singing Compline, the last office of the day. Mallows, day lilies, buttercups, blazed in the small field at his side. On a summer evening like this twenty-two years ago he had kissed Claire for the first time and felt her resistance, that mineral resistance to the expected which was the core of her being. A beaver shuttled swiftly, silently across a nearby pond, carrying formidable amounts of twigs towards his dwelling, his canine face emerging sleek and intelligent above the umbrous water. He dove repeatedly to prepare the terrain of his habitation, floated several large balls of mud across the pond to heap them upon his dam, his paws often scrubbing his face as if to sanctify it for a new bout of work. It appeared to be the first sunny evening after a stretch of rain, the air was filled with the fervid buzzing, gathering, soaring of spring insects. Edmund picked a few wild flowers to take to his stark room in the guesthouse. Before walking downhill he stared once more at the serene enclosure in which Claire had chosen to continue her struggle for self-perfection. In this tiny community as closed and self-sufficient as the beavers' pond nearby, what a challenge it was to curb one's drives of greed, envy, pride!

Before going to sleep he started a letter to Sophie, who the year before had begun a vigorous new career as television correspondent. She was presently on a long-term assignment in Jerusalem, where she was living with a journalist named Amos. O Protean contemporary women, he began as he sat down to write, free to metamorphose until the end of their days . . . (he always strived for a dramatic opening when writing to Sophie.) Polymorphic creatures tackling vows of chastity at forty, struggling with doctorates in sociobiology at fifty-six, dropping their first acid at sixty-two like Mrs. Tillich. . . .

"O brave new world," he continued his letter, "that is seeing the Odysseizing of women, the Penelopizing of men."

"It was in November or so of 1970, Eddem . . . I was standing with some nuns and priests in a small room in a black section of Boston; we were having a Eucharist in preparation for an action on the nearby draft board. . . . The room we stood in faced a black tenement, a backyard full of boards, rags, trash, debris, buildings that looked as if they'd been struck by a series of bombings . . . it all had a quality of occupied territory, as if the people in that building were captives living under some foreign rule. Only one room in the tenement looked lived in, and at its window sat a woman hugely swollen with some disease who fanned herself with a newspaper and held a wasted, screaming child on her lap. . . . The Epistle reading that day had been from Corinthians Two: 'I've been in danger in the towns, in danger in the open country, in danger at sea, in danger from so-called brothers . . .' And as I began to think about these lines everything in my field of vision suddenly took on a curious and intense existence of its own. That is . . . everything suddenly appeared to have an immense interior *space*, to own an individual life as precious as the whole universe. To save that woman and child, to go out to them and not only feed them and get them work but particularly to give them the courage to live on seemed as important and quite as difficult as stopping any war. . . . Eddem, this wasn't a vision I insist, it was something simpler. . . ."

She had moved towards him an hour ago across the parlor of the abbey lodge with a merry, rolling gait. And he was both startled and perplexed to see that she'd never looked so well. Her cheeks had gained a startling new ruddiness. She had even plumped out a little bit. ("Hi, cookie," he'd said when they'd embraced. What does one say? He hadn't known precisely what to say. "You're looking so marvelous! What a marvelous place!") Her erect posture, her crisp walk, had something newly determined about it. Dressed in a surprisingly contemporary long gown of brown serge, a lay sister's simple white veil floating about her head, there was his Pebble walking towards him with a radiant smile. . . .

"I do want to stress the difference, Edmund; in that moment in which I seemed to make my choice there was none of that sense of unity or merging mystics report, none of that business of All Things Are One . . . no, the absolute opposite, everything stood out with a fierce and glowing individuality. And E.R. you know how much guilt I've been burdened with for years, guilt for the very fact of surviving and being *blessed* with much; perhaps that's why I didn't even feel worthy of the happiness I could have had with you . . . well, in the surrendering I experienced that day, the guilt was . . . as if melted, melted. Burden of condemnation gone, darkness lifted."

"But, Pebble . . . allow me an indiscretion. You had no vision? You don't call that a vision?"

"No, it was rather . . . an abandonment and a return. At that moment in the bleak room I stood in, the stillness was marvelous, and I felt both . . . both deeply anguished by our *helplessness*, and supremely happy because I was *accepting* that helplessness. There was very little theology you know in this moment of mine. Simply a willingness to capitulate. An increased sense of Christ being the center of course but . . . that's too private to talk about. A passion of acquiescence."

There was a bright new caroling quality to her voice, she spoke with the oddly emphatic phrasing he remembered from her adolescence.

"You are peaceful," he whispered.

"I looked around at the men and women praying with me that morning and was filled with fear for . . . oh, this is hard to explain, Eddem."

"Don't always go so fast, Peb. We've plenty of time, you know."

"Well not so much, only until Vespers. . . . Looking at them I was filled with emotion not so much for what they were at that precise moment, more for where they'd come from. Here they were preparing another of their amazing acts of protest, more courageous and self-giving than anything that's been done in the Movement . . . I'd always sensed that it was the meditation and witness they'd lived for centuries that had enabled them to undertake these actions, and suddenly I had a great fear that their contemplative force was waning, shedding its power like a battery, that the world's ordinariness was contaminating them too much. . . ."

There was a silence. He found it hard to talk to her because he'd very quickly sensed that she was still celebrating her isolation, that she was apprehensive about talking about her child and that this must be saved for the last; he'd sensed a lot. He cleared his throat as he tended to do in the middle of a college lecture, looked out of the window. Claire flung back the flat brown hair that hung under her veil, a defiant gesture unchanged since childhood.

"Oh you're still puzzling," she cried out, "you're still wondering, confused about me, aren't you . . . all right, this is it, Eddem. The reality of my need for the sacred suddenly became greater than my need for any proof of its existence. And so I needed to bear witness to it, okay?"

This was delivered with such force that he was compelled to look deep into her eyes for the first time since the beginning of that visit. The pale eyes had changed greatly, he couldn't tell how at first. Lost their anger, he decided now. On the wall of the abbey lodge behind her chair were affixed the same stark little directives that confronted him daily in the guesthouse: WE WELCOME YOU TO THE ABBEY AND ASSURE YOU OF OUR PRAYERS . . . SHORTS ARE NOT PERMITTED ON THE GROUNDS OF THE MONASTERY . . . ST. AGATHA'S SERVES THOSE SEEKING MEDITATIVE SILENCE.

"I knew that I had to take a radical new direction in life, and this in the space of barely a few minutes, Eddem. . . ."

"Like in Somerset Maugham," he suggested. She waved her hand impatiently, stood up and paced the room.

"Hardly as colorful. You're probably trying to define my experience, darn it, everyone out there is always trying to define every-

231

thing. No, I simply had a sense of urgent crisis about this being my last chance, my last possible chance of acquiring peace and strength. The universe remained as meaningless as before and even more hopelessly charged with suffering, yet more charged also with some sacred fullness . . . above all it occurred to me that all could be right if I stopped trying to do it all by myself, if I finally ceased to resist and subjected my will to a greater one. . . ."

"Ouf, that was hard," she whispered, "that decision to surrender."

"You of all people."

"Oh it was a struggle."

At night during his many visits to St. Agatha's, Edmund read from the pious biographies that studded the guesthouse's bookshelves. He always brought his own work with him but was curiously unable to proceed with it, as if Claire had not yet clarified some aspect of her presence here which he must still persevere to decipher. During those study hours in the evening he kept coming across curious relics of the pietistic 1930s and 1940s, accounts of W. H. Auden's conversion, biographies of St. Thérèse de Lisieux by Clare Boothe Luce. ("Preciousness of every hidden soul in the economy of the universe . . . law of conservation of charity as the center of the comtemplative life. . . .") He would bring Claire tidbits of his reading during their afternoon visits, as if to reassure her that he was taking a small step into her world.

"I read the most marvelous story about Elizabeth of Hungary last night."

"Tell."

"This sainted queen had for confessor a tyrant, which I would define as a man without imagination. He was perceptive enough, however, to discern that the penances imposed upon Elizabeth in the confessional brought her into a state of joyful exultation. . . . So he searched and searched his mind every Friday afternoon for penances which might bring her a proper dose of pain. He finally came up with a real zinger, he forbade her to help the sick and the poor. But this is where she parted with him and with the system of obedience she'd adhered to all her life, she went right on helping the sick and the poor. . . ."

Claire leaned forward intently towards him; she observed him during those visits with a depth of concern she'd never given him before. "I think you should travel more, dear one, go to Europe; I feel you're in a rut after fifteen years of Berkeley."

"You've turned psychic in your seclusion. But let me finish with Elizabeth. Another order of nature takes over . . . a snowstorm screens her as she makes her nightly trip to the sick and the poor so that her disobedience may not be observed.

"The story may exemplify," he added pointedly, "tyrants' excessive zeal against all forms of satisfaction."

There were many days when she'd meet him in the abbey lodge after having come straight in from working in the fields, hair tousled, dust in her face, nails still dark with mud, eyes more serene than ever. Her peevishness, her old resentment towards her family's garden . . . Edmund constantly saw many young, clear-skinned women walking about the monastery compound in sneakers and farmers' boots, their long gray garbs cinched with thick workmen's belts of heavy leather. Some had come from their beehives, others from their vineyards or cornfields Claire said, they carded their own wool, wove their own cloth. She often pointed out some nun's name as they said good-bye at the abbey lodge door, that's Sister Patrick, there's Sister Stephen, Sister Jerome. "I find them infinitely seductive," he once wrote Sophie, "like everything that's veiled."

"Sophie's gone through another metamorphosis," Claire announced one day.

"Dear Lord, not in a kibbutz."

"Oh it's for the best Eddem, just listen . . ."

Whenever she had a new letter from Sophie she'd welcome him in the abbey lodge with a joyous wave and immediately begin to read it aloud, quite admitting to her craving for news.

. . .

233

"Let's say I'll just talk about the eyes of these people who've lived through three wars in ten years" [Sophie wrote]. "Like most men in this garrison state Amos's green eyes have a very controlled anxiety, they're the eyes of a man who's had to be both a soldier and a monk, whose body has been struck or grazed by shellfire many times since the War of Independence, and they're still not as disturbing or disturbed as the eyes of those who live in the northern kibbutzim under a constant barrage of fire. . . . Last week for instance Amos and I drove north to document some articles on the Lebanese border and I'm still obsessed by the resigned, beaten-down gaze of the twenty-five-year-olds to whom a machine gun has become a fifth limb. . . ."

Claire paced the room while reading, interrupting to open the window with a brusque gesture.

"I can't forget that moment last week when we walked into the dining room of a settlement two miles from the Northern border and Amos tapped the shoulder of a young man sitting alone at the table, he slowly turned his head towards us and there was so little expressed pleasure, so little recognition in that gaze that I assumed he was barely acquainted with Amos . . . the young Israeli just continued to silently eat his soup, staring at us with those exhausted aloof eyes, yet a moment later I learned that he was one of Amos's most ardent fans, the one who constantly writes and phones to invite Amos to this kibbutz. . . . When Amos started to question him about the rocket attacks of last week his friend's eyes lost some of their weariness, grew almost angry as he barked back, How do you expect me to remember last week's shelling from the one before, or from the year before that?

"Well how else can I put it Claire darling, there's little talk about anything but the possibility of survival in this new Sparta, one only lives for whatever work and love one has, all's very austere and meaningful . . . at first I was confused and overwhelmed by this state of

234

*siege but recently it's led me to totally reorder and redistill my exis-
tence, face up to the brevity of life, focus on a single task. . . ."*

"What a miracle, Eddem," Claire exclaimed, "and what a serious
writer she's getting to be!"

"If she survives it she'll finally start having the glory she's always
dreamed of."

"No, no, totally different from the passive man-given success
she'd wanted as a kid, this glory will be her own!"

It struck Edmund as interesting that Claire's seclusion led her to
observe others more attentively than ever.

"Tell me this," he began another day (her costume, the room, sometimes imposed an uncomfortable formality
upon him).

"Are you planning . . ." (the question was irrelevant at that precise moment but his need to ask it was immense, a fear as ancient as
his love swept through him) "are you planning to take vows?"

"Oh, no great need! I'm not good enough for that! As long as I can
lead their life a bit, participate in their witness. They're the rock.
I'm just . . ." She searched for the image.

"I'm just a barnacle."

The humility of the reply affected him. He turned towards the
window, stared at the amber pond where he often sat in the evening
watching the family of beavers at their work.

She would sometimes break off their talks, at the appointed time
before evening Vespers, with a terse, pithy phrase: "Sin is just a
messing up of your priorities."

That child, that daughter of hers! Once or twice a
year, whenever his work brought him to New England, Edmund
made a point of taking Victoria out to tea. She was as pensive as
ever but had grown sturdier, was not as fragile of body as Claire had
been. Her large eyes were as cold blue pale as her mother's. The
ephemeral touch of her adolescent cheek upon his when they met,

the nascent rebelliousness of her talk, thrust him into a panic of affection and remembrance. There are people who don't care about discussing matters such as good and evil, Victoria'd once said, and they truly bore me to death. Like who for instance darling? My aunts and cousins of course, all they do is win tennis tournaments and give themselves airs going out to look for persons of the opposite sex, which is so gross. You might belong to a new generation of mystical celibates, Edmund said, a grand solution to the population problem. You know perfectly well that many people get along without all that nonsense, Uncle Edmund; my generation is strictly into friendship, anyway. . . . Uncle Eddem, do you still believe in romantic love? she'd asked him warily from behind her curtain of light brown hair. Oh I've pretended not to darling he'd said fiercely, you see I've had rather little of it.

The funny thing, he often thought when he came to the convent, is that Claire's never been so available to me. The monastery enclosure guarded, imprisoned her for his sight like the net posed over an insect. During the days he spent at St. Agatha's he experienced the delight of the lepidopterist who triumphs after years of searching for an arcane species and can stare tranquilly at his prize for hours, admiring in loving closeness every detail of mandibles and rainbow scales. Yet he knew that his love was bound to be all the more arduous because its object seemed to grow more perfect under his close scrutiny. She reversed that habitual process of human passion which wanes with the melting of distance and of dream; in her new peace and candor she was becoming, to his sorrow, increasingly marvelous. Is there something peculiar about the persons who love only once in their lifetime, he also worried, are the once-in-loves as singular as the twice-born? Is it a glandular condition, could it be dictated by early deprivation of the mother's presence (Freud, Leonardo's lovelessness), is there only one human Muse for each artist's life? Are such persons more prone to depression, happiness, sodomy, nationalism, pyromania, anorexia, are they better or worse athletes? He imagined people in his part of California forming consciousness-raising groups for the once-in-loves, associations as garrulously introspective as those for the drug-deprived, the homosexual, the adopted.

"It also happened to me in a jail cell, Peb . . . a locale which you barely associate with my decorous right-wing behavior. But I'm more radical than you think I am, my love. If I hadn't become much of an activist it's because I'm much more of a cynic than you are; the antiwar movement had always reminded me of doctors putting Band-Aids on a cancer that needs radical surgery; I've come to think that the whole culture has to be rebuilt from the basement up, priorities revolutionized, massive humanistic socialism established if such a thing exists. . . . Anyhow, I was hanging around a demonstration trying to keep my dear Slavic friend John Mirsky from getting busted for the tenth time and they rounded up the whole lot of us and I got dragged away at last, thinking mightily about you, to the strains of one of those detestable hymns that have their proper place in church. . . . I'd been finding little meaning in anything that year, a medal at the College Art Association for my book on Caravaggio, honorary degrees from Brown and Vanderbilt, letters of corroboration or protest with flattering frequency from the readers of my articles . . . I could accept honor after little honor and feel numb, indifferent, blah; I'd turned down visiting professorships at Harvard and Chicago because the only reason I'd have moved would have been to be nearer you or Soph but you were both so nomadic there was no hope of ever catching you anyway; I could see no alternative to continued steeping in the poisoned juices of Academe . . . until the day I sit in a jail cell staring at a graffito that says what do we want freedom what do we get bologna sandwiches. A tall blond page boy out of Botticelli walks in and lies down on the bunk opposite mine and starts berating me for not signing some damn faculty petition that had been passed around the previous week . . . he'd started in art history and had switched to pol sci because it was more 'relevant' quote unquote and I dug into him for that . . . the memory is dim now because I was so extraordinarily taken with Toby's presence. Oh I'd had several decorative persons in my life in the past decade as you know, average fare for a

237

department chairman, pert grade-grabbing sophomores wanting to squeeze me dry of every inspired thought on Degas, divorcée potters with a proclivity for interminable foreplay . . . it had been pleasant, it had been lonely in turn. And suddenly here is a Botticelli facing me in a cell, holding a copy of Regis Debray in hand. . . ."

"And you had Pater?"

"Close, Peb, close. Ruskin. An idiotic ideological argument ensued, what's appropriate reading in these times of crisis and so forth, Toby was clearly baiting me; you're sitting back and letting society rot Professor while mouthing inanities about the stones of Venice. He lay on his bunk orating, orating as from a soapbox, and suddenly leaned down to seize the book from my hand. As that pale rather beautiful hand traveled towards me I put my mouth to it and bit him, as satisfying as planting my teeth into a peach in a moment of hunger on a hot day . . . thinking as I did, what barbarians these times have made of us. There was the taste of blood on my tongue, and in his eyes an air of startlement that verged on amusement, pleasure even. Those eyes were a curiously dark brown, like water at night, so dark that you couldn't distinguish the iris from the pupil, which would make his periods of drug ingestion maddeningly difficult to deal with in the next months we were to spend together . . . a time devoted of course to reforming his character in my perennial Pygmalion fashion. Oh how readily he turned from the rigors of his Trotskyite student cell to the sybaritic pleasures of my little Pouilly-Fuissés while retaining the luxury of his Marxist rhetoric! You must know the I Want Everything generation as well as I do, they want the revolution and the palazzo; you'll do well in Italy, Toby, I told him the week he left, you'll get taken to cell meetings in chauffeured Alfa Romeos, Rolls-Royce radicals of the world unite. . . . Of course there were the sweet good moments too that would flood me with regrets for months after we quit, so much that was malleable, splendid about him; much occasional sweetness, and that long slender body wandering naked about my house with the insouciance which it's been the genius and the depravity of this generation to cultivate; the moments when I stared

238

at his face below mine, as into the mirror of my own lost youth. . . ."

"But we're babies, Edmund! You keep talking as if we're so ancient! I feel I'm at the very beginning of the best life I'll ever have!"

"That may be an agreeable asset of being one of the twice-born, my dear; as for myself I feel decidedly ready for reincarnation . . . well, bless me sister if I have sinned, just a recent installment from the epic of my tragic flaws."

"I've told you before, E.R., I think you need a change," she whispered.

How soothing, after all these years, to have her advise him! In 1973 Edmund would accept a visiting professorship to a New England college, having carefully determined that Minnesota was equidistant from California and Massachusetts.

"How is she?" Claire had whispered towards afternoon's end during the very first visit he'd made to St. Agatha's. Her face had tightened with pain. A vast expanse of her new armor (faith, serene obedience) was shed in that moment.

"Victoria's unbelievable," he said. "Demonically independent, like you." He was trying to pace his visits to alternate with Victoria's, who came every three months or so. He always tried to add a new fillip of information. "She's doing particularly superb work in Latin this term."

Claire's eyes widened with interest, amusement. "Latin! Right up the old family tree . . . Jeff's been good enough to write often, and she writes all the time . . . are you absolutely sure that she's very well?"

"Oh you know how impeccable Jeff is." "Impeccable. Otherwise I couldn't possibly be here." "Don't rationalize," Edmund said severely.

Her eyes cast down, undecipherable.

"She's beginning to look at boarding schools," Edmund continued. "She's drawn to Milton, and lately to St. Paul's, of course . . . you might have heard that they're taking in girls beginning next year, going co-ed."

239

Her eyes fluttered briefly in merriment. "Oh I wonder how Plinker would have felt about that desecration."

"Are you absolutely sure she's very well?" she'd ask at the end of each visit. He'd reassure her, she'd smile and let him go with one of her funny little koans.

"As for myself, I desire nothing in particular, which means I'm *really* well."

Four Rivers, Minnesota
February 1972

Well, dear Jeff, after having tried radical dissent she's trying radical obedience, which can come to more or less of the same thing. Her "crackerjack plan for salvation," as you call it, does seem to be a tough, old-fashioned way out of modern quandaries, but I beg you to honor her decision (if only in the spirit of history) as one of the more imaginative alternatives a liberated woman can find in our time. . . .

You keep falling into the dangerous trap of labeling it "self-abnegation." In our present tornado of carnal propaganda we seem to forget that celibacy is not necessarily a form of self-denial, that it's equally served throughout history to enlarge our secular powers and achieve the full potency of our selfhood, that it's been as much practiced by the tribesman readying himself for the big hunt or the warrior preparing for an important battle as by the shaman, priest or hermit. . . . Her "love affair with God," as you so cutely phrase it, is by far the most radical act of independence she could engage in. You forget how devilishly consistent she is, dear fellow; only the devil is more consistent than she is. . . .

Jeff! In the recent past when Edmund stood in an airport on the way to one of his conferences he had seen Jeff waiting for a plane, waiting for a woman. . . . Jeff kept his hands in his pockets as he smilingly waited, as if nervously fingering handfuls of loose change . . . the trousers of his perennial Brooks Brothers tweeds were cut on the short side, in the manner of the 1940s, and underneath their cuffs there stretched an area of immaculate athletic

240

sock. . . . Faint gray now streaked that excellent head of short-clipped hair and gave him an added air of venerability. . . . Jeff the ever-ready groom, Jeff the king of honorable sensuality stood there expectant, smiling, fair, and over the years Edmund came to associate Jeff's particular cut of Brooks Brothers trousers with the loneliness of early middle age, the peculiar restlessness of its flesh, the incandescent furtiveness of Puritan adultery. . . . On the first instance the woman who appeared looked strikingly like Cousin April. Her hair was sleeked into a smooth glossy pageboy, as in the 1944 graduation pictures taken for the Miss Hewitt's yearbook. Her fair athlete's face was both lined and warmed by frequent sun and her pink lips opened in a photogenic smile as she clutched Jeff's arm. Edmund imagined that in his school-bound life at St. Paul's, Jeff could only have met these women at commencements, faculty-parent teas, parents' weekends, soccer matches . . . Edmund never greeted Jeff on these occasions, knowing the extent of his friend's moral delicacy, his stated probity . . . he'd usually duck into some restaurant to buy cigarettes, find a phone booth, do anything to respect the zeal of Jeff's search for happiness. . . . These women, this charm-braceleted chorus line of Jeff's middle-age felicity, sometimes carried beach bags embroidered with sailboats and pussycats, or stepped off the plane from a sunny Southern provenance still wearing short golf skirts, brief socks with pom-poms. . . . What better reassurance could Jeff have of the ancient order than these slender Junior Leaguers with faint crow's lines and gleaming eyes whose braces barely seemed to have come off their teeth? . . . Edmund enjoyed visualizing people's domestic interiors and he imagined them at home, admitting Jeff to their bower while their husbands were on business trips, their children away at camp or boarding school . . . there might be a curved oval dressing table with starched white organdy ruffles like the ones that April and Katrinka had had in the forties . . . some childhood fetish—a white and woolly stuffed dog on a floral bedcover . . . the fetish would lie on the floor of the pink and flounced divorcing woman's bedroom as she tossed in bed crying with joy at Jeff's hungry, competent love-making. . . . Once in New York a colleague had enticed Edmund to have a drink after a lecture and he'd actually seen Jeff with

Katrinka at the Waldorf Skylight Room; his palm was placed on the small of her athletic back as he steered her towards the dance floor with the same rolling, confident sailor's gait with which he'd moved through Larue's, the Stork Club decades ago. . . . Katrinka had recapped her teeth, remarried twice, lost some of her over-bite . . . in the last years (so Edmund had gleaned from Sophie, who always knew everything) Jeff had confined himself to shuttling back and forth between these two companions of his youth, April and Katrinka, Katrinka and April . . . a year after Claire had left for Minnesota he saw Jeff and April at the corner of Fifth Avenue and Sixty-second Street, outside the Knickerbocker Club, at the exact same spot where he'd seen them in the late 1940s when he accompanied Claire and Sophie to some coming-out par-ty . . . April was tanned and fitter than ever and had a barrette in her hair and wore a mink instead of a panda and was saying in her clearest Locust Valley lockjaw, "What a nifty idea, dearie, we'll fly to . . ." The cuffs of Jeff's Brooks Brothers suit rode frugally high over his ankles and they were buying a little bag of roasted chest-nuts from the street vendor, precisely as they had when he'd glimpsed them on the same street corner a quarter of a century ago.

"Who won Wimbledon this year?" Claire once asked during one of Edmund's visits to the monastery. "I think it was Kodes and Billie Jean," he answered. And then continued: "Nixon should be prosecuted; if only Bertrand Russell were still around to start a proper tribunal for war crimes, there should be another Nuremberg. . . ." He remembered that he was using the same phrases she'd used five years ago. She was fingering a daisy and looking absentminded.

"I've realized here that any politics not grounded in spiritual sub-stance will dissipate into failure," she said, "will even breed its own violence. . . ."

"Dear one!" Edmund leaned forward, flecked a speck of dust from the sleeve of her stark serge gown. "Didn't you know that everything begins with mysticism and ends in politics to begin all over again in mysticism?"

He had little idea of how traditional her beliefs were, whether the nuns questioned her concerning their catholicity; she preferred not to discuss such "dogmatic" things. The few definitions she made had a limpid, brutal simplicity.

"How do you pray?" he once asked. "I mean, this has always struck me as the most difficult. How do you name Him, or It or whatever?"

"No matter. You have to name yourself first. Then it just comes."

"And what . . . what if that fails?"

"Oh dear, you worry too much!" she laughed. "No matter! If you don't find it in prayer you might find it in your own true work."

On one of his last visits to Claire, Edmund stopped at the pond neighboring the abbey on his way back from Compline and watched the beaver at his work . . . the animal was shuttling back and forth across the water with large branches in his mouth, depositing them upon his dam. . . . Each time he waddled onto shore and hovered near Edmund for a few seconds, as brown and lustrous as the water that was his home, before diving back for further tasks. The intricate steering mechanism of his forelegs, whirring about like propellers . . . The animal rose before Edmund one last time at the edge of the pond, monumental in the mystery of his work, his compulsion . . . and then as the mist rose over the darkening orange dusk he dove into the water again for his daily recreation. He swam about in large slow circles now, not fetching or carrying anymore, moving about in pure play, no purpose, all pleasure . . . once or twice he lashed his tail out upon the water with a flat broad motion, exploding the darkening pond into high white sprays and spumes . . . then dove under and came out again and swam again long into the night in wide meditative circles, having become his own contemplation, his own survival.

xix

THEY begin their wait for Lenin's tomb early in the morning. On their second day in Moscow members of Intourist Tour No. 137 line up in pairs as docilely as schoolchildren by the west wall of the Kremlin, Sophie clutching Claire's arm. They stand behind hundreds of Soviet citizens, all patient in the burning sun, moving inch by inch towards the sepulcher of the embalmed leader.

The expanse of Red Square looms before them, spelling perpetual vigilance, sided by crenellated ramparts, surmounted by numerous watchtowers—slender as minarets, peaked like caps of Mongol princes, punctuated with belfries, sentry boxes, dungeons, turrets, lookouts. All color in the sullen capital converges prismatically at the heart of Soviet power, the battlements' brick is the color of clotted blood and dormant fire, at the far end of the square the green and blue protuberances of St. Basil's domes bristle like a bouquet of lapidary fruit.

And at the center of the russet battlements: rich frozen rose of the mausoleum's tiered granite, militiamen in forest green guarding its massive doors, gleam of silver-plated bayonets.

As the Intourist group starts to stand in queue, slender young Russians approach them, softly beseeching American coins, cigarettes, offering for exchange the star-shaped medallions of their belt buckles or more insignia of Lenin; they whisper with the humility of beggar children, they brush swiftly against a foreigner and go on to another so as not to alert the soldiers guarding the visitors' line.

On their first morning in Moscow, Claire, Edmund and Sophie had risen at dawn to drive about Moscow by themselves. Their cabdriver was a cheerful, ruddy-cheeked man who talked effusively about Russians' love for Richard Nixon. A good friend of the Soviet people, Brezhnev's favorite Western leader! Perhaps they haven't been told what's happened yet, Claire quipped. Do you have a boy or a girl Sophie asked, do you love her very much, according to your last census sixty-five percent of Russian families have no more than one child, where does your wife work, how far away do you live from the day care center?

During their long queue for Lenin's tomb members of the Intourist group try to talk among themselves. "Listen to this!" Ethel Zabar reads from her guidebook. " 'Rushing upon Europe for the last time, Asia stomped the earth and left us the Kremlin.' " Sophie: "Genghis Khan with the atom bomb, that's what this country's about, advanced technology mixed with total primitivism. . . ." Ted Weicker: "Oh, now listen, the effects of science are just as disastrous everywhere. . . ." A soldier guarding the file of visitors sternly puts a finger to his mouth. Irina and Evgeny mimic him with a parental smile, repeating that everyone must stand silently two by two, in pairs, when waiting to visit the mausoleum.

At times Sophie leans heavily against Claire, eyes closed, her head buried in the shoulder of her friend's coat. She can't sleep at all in Moscow, she turns down the Zabars' offer of Valiums, she complains about the grimness of walking alone in Moscow. "What a labyrinth, what a nightmare. You go along Gorki Street and within ten minutes you've circled back to the same sagging glory-to-Lenin sign you started from, and these resigned, contentious crowds shuffling about, all you smell is solitude and fear. . . ." In Moscow the three travelers have become more detached from each other, the triad tends to split into its separate tones, Claire on her Amnesty errands, Sophie on her solitary walks, Edmund taking long sleeps in the afternoons and wondering where to live the following winter; a language has also grown between the two women from which Edmund is excluded; sensing Sophie's depressions Claire often studies her face, brushes a lock of hair from her forehead, hugs her with the same sudden tenderness with which she'd hugged Victoria as a child.

Waiting in line behind his friends Edmund stands next to an aging Ukrainian whose face nestles like a hazelnut in the folds of her flowered babushka. "She's come from Kiev to see Vladimir Ilich one last time," Edmund translates to Sophie in whispers; "the last visit she made to Moscow was in 1925, the year after his death; she says he was ever so beautiful then but lately she hears he's not looking so well anymore. . . ." Sophie asks whether the old woman's widowed, how much pension she receives, and then the stern young guards silence them again.

The previous morning they'd taken several subways to sectors of the city quite other than the one they wished to reach to make sure they weren't being followed, then after taking a train to the Scheremetevo Station they'd walked a mile from the subway stop. They were on their way to visit a mathematician who might get Claire in touch with Baklanov's mother.

The family they visit lives in two small rooms filled with every vestige of Western freedom, with photos of Hemingway, Gandhi, Martin Luther King and Osip Mandelstam, with icons, crucifixes and photographs of beloved exiles, with ancient wooden dolls and single unmatched teacups preserved since before the Revolution. Every gram of precious space is filled, every scrap of matter is saved, stored, gathered against the loss of memory. The apartment is steeped in the odor of dust and sour milk and constantly refried leftovers, the tiny kitchen teems with relatives and friends perpetually dropping in to share the information of survival, your cousins may be in trouble this week, my brother's arriving from Leningrad tomorrow and will come to see you at three o'clock. Yogurt brews on the sideboard, a four-day-old mess of kasha stands on the stove, the room is filled with the grease of their perennial waiting, Edmund remarks that it all reminds him of Mara and his earliest childhood.

As they walk through a park after their visit Claire talks about the Russian dissident she's set out to help: "The sheer tenacity of this Baklanov, first arrested at the age of twenty for being in possession of some obscure banned novel . . . three years in a psychiatric ward, and when he comes out what does he do but organize a demonstration in protest against the Sinyavsky-Daniel trial. . . . Back in prison for another two years, then after one year of freedom he's locked up again for transmitting medical reports to the West . . . twenty-nine years old by this time, sentenced to twelve years, and do you know what he says at his trial? 'I regret that in the fourteen months of my adult life in which I was at liberty I've managed to do so little for the cause of freedom. . . .' We started sending messages to Baklanov's mother through Boston Amnesty last summer to help her publicize her son's struggle, she wrote Helmut Schmidt, Kurt Waldheim, the Red Cross, a month hasn't gone by at Amnesty without some communication from her. . . ." Claire walks slightly ahead of Sophie in the flower-budded park, head bent, hands locked behind her back, with that isolation of purpose they remember since her childhood.

"Back home we have a joke," Edmund whispers to Evgeny as the Intourist group moves slowly towards the mausoleum. "One day Lenin's body is gone from the vault and the guards find a note on the pillow. It says 'Returned to Zurich to start everything over again.' " The Russians's boreal inscrutable gaze, perhaps hiding amusement. Edmund focuses his camera on the domes of St. Basil's. The Spassky Tower merrily chimes the eleventh hour. The soldiers guarding the mausoleum door change again in frozen ritual, two new men goose-step alongside the sepia wall, stride up to each of their colleagues at the door, present bayonets, spin on their heels, take their place at the entrance of the tomb. As the visitors' line moves still closer to the mausoleum the green of the guards' epaulets becomes even more raw and brilliant, a green out of nature, Edmund whispers to Sophie, the rawest chemical viridian; they're close enough now to hear the soldiers' boots swish against the wool of their greatcoats as they goose-step back along the battlements of the Kremlin wall.

The evening before Edmund, Claire and Sophie had taken the subway again to visit with still other friends of Baklanov's. Their hosts had laden their kitchen table with an abundance of miraculously found food, filled it with whatever shreds of cheese and cookies they'd found in their cupboard, a relative appears with a bottle of wine, another with a can of mussels, more friends come bringing bread, the table soon fills with food miraculously gathered. I had a Russian mother, Edmund tells his hosts, there was this tradition for us also that not an inch of the tablecloth could show when we had visitors, we lived in great poverty but those may have been the happiest days of my life. "Truly he's had trouble having faith in anything since," Claire remarks. Edmund looks up at her, frowning.

"There are two paths to liberty," the daughter of the house says. She is short and powerful, a sociologist whose permit to teach has been revoked. "The path outside, in the open, in society, and the inner freedom which we struggle to retain when we're deprived of our public freedom."

"We live in a state of domesticated desperation but we retain an inner freedom which no despots can destroy," her mother adds, turning to Claire. "The human spirit must struggle so hard here that it might become fuller than yours."

"What nonsense, my dearest!" one of her sons exclaims. "There's nothing uplifting about our suffering; we console ourselves by searching for redeeming features when there's nothing to it but animal fear and pain."

"Whether there are listening devices in our homes is beside the point," the daughter of the house continues. "The fact is that our fingers constantly point to the ceiling and we're afraid of ever opening our mouths."

"It's up to us to help you out of your suffering," Sophie whispers at some point. "We wish to share it with you."

"Of course you do," the daughter of the house says gently. "You

248

Americans have an admirable way of wanting that which is uniquely our own and unshareable."

Claire would tell Edmund, on their way back to the hotel, that these were the people who would take her to see Baklanov's mother.

They had noticed a curious detail about the dwellings they visited in Moscow: The entrance door to each apartment was padded on the outside with a thick substance of quilted leather, like the padding of walls in insane asylums. Sophie had seen this as a symbol: The interiors behind these doors, she said, were havens of sanity and goodness from which the mad official Soviet world was isolated as in an immense security cell.

"Her son and husband died in World War Two," Edmund is still translating to Sophie from the old Ukrainian at his side, "she's a retired teacher, she says it's the last time she'll ever see Vladimir Ilich. . . ." As it approaches the bronze door of the Lenin mausoleum the visitors' line quickens, begins to be swallowed more swiftly into the tiered structure of rose granite. And before they know it the tourists stand directly next to two stern young guards at the tomb's entrance, who hold their faces high and their eyes skywards as if to evade all human gaze; all becomes increasingly glacial as they approach the door, even the soldiers' flesh seems made of some substance new yet unorganic—marzipan, the plastic of new toys. One walks through high bronze doors, two more guards stand at the head of the stairs bayonets thrust forward, fingers covering their lips to impose silence, then there's nothing but the shuffling of feet down a long black porphyry stairway, a mighty whirring of air-conditioning machines, the moment is very brief and frozen, one is herded swiftly through a small luminous room, the serpent of humanity circles silently around a brightly lit glass coffin, inside it lies a very small bearded man in a black suit, his face very pale, his delicate hands clutching a book; Sophie would remember the suit as being made of velvet but this would be denied by Claire and Edmund; before they know it they're climbing up another staircase through the sanitized darkness, herded by lapidary soldiers holding fingers vertically across young faces of peach hue.

They reenter into blinding sunlight and move through the avenue of fir trees at the back of the Lenin mausoleum, filing past dozens of obscure generals and presidents of councils memorialized in busts of stone.

"Incredible, I can't believe it, death taken as archaically as that, trying to preserve his spirit by keeping his body intact, pure Pharaonism at the heart of the world's most technocratic state . . ." Claire's voice is high, excited, and they know she'd launched into a soliloquy. ". . . pure Pharaonism, the leader's spirit continuing to guide the people as long as his body can avoid corruption. . . ."

"We have joke too," Evgeny says, coming up to them beside the modest bust of Stalin set among other effigies of forgotten leaders. "Under capitalism man exploits man, under Communism it is the opposite."

"And you know Edmund this all reminds me of you," Claire continues with her way of not listening, "reminds me of what you've been for these past twenty years dear heart. . . ."

Sophie was already gone and Claire had turned away from Edmund that morning with a quick step, striding towards the subway. Edmund had gone back to his hotel room and gone to sleep. In the past year he'd vastly increased his capacity to sleep away his moments of annoyance or confusion. "I demand an explanation of that perfectly outlandish statement!" he'd first shouted at Claire as she'd begun to cross Red Square. But she'd just blown him a kiss and continued walking, calling out, "I'll see you tonight. . . . Let's have a drink after dinner."

She was faithful to the appointment.

"A group of glorified undertakers tiptoeing through the morgues of history in search of more corpses to embalm . . . that's what you said art historians were, right?"

They were sitting in the foreign currency bar on the ground floor of their hotel. He kept staring at two Soviet women across the room with Cupid's-bow mouths and deeply cleavaged blouses of blue silk who reminded him again of Paris in his childhood, wartime, the German occupation.

"Are you really strong enough to change your life again, Edmund? You've wanted to freeze, arrest the past, history's been your cop-out, your second mother, your only Muse . . ."

"All the other Muses were out of town."

"But now that you've decided to paint again the Muse will only return if you have faith, and true faith can only exist with a considerable measure of doubt, and you've never accepted the necessity of doubt. . . ."

A rock band thrummed in the room and he lightly cupped his hands over his ears to hear her better.

"To have faith in God, in love, in art, is to have faith in something that is infinite. And therefore faith must be uncertain because its infinite object is being received by a finite being. . . ."

Her eyes blinked twice, slowly. These were tough issues. She'd never let him get away with anything.

"The element of uncertainty in faith can't be removed. It must be accepted. The courage of uncertainty is what you need, you haven't taken a risk in your life, you've always wanted to be dead sure of your fame, your eventual glory, your immortality. . . ."

She slowly rubbed her powerful hands against each other, as she had in their conversations at St. Agatha's.

"Anyone who's dead sure is dead, Edmund. Where there're daring and courage there's the possibility of failure, the risk must be taken.

"Otherwise you'll only paint sentimental little seascapes or fashionable empty abstractions," she added with her old bluntness.

Their conversation was brief. They hugged each other good night and went into the desolate maze of their hotel corridors, both searching for their own rooms.

During the last two days of their stay in Moscow they walked out every night to stare at the amazing sight at the center of Red Square: Guards in unearthly green standing at bronze door. Blinding cones of light pouring down from the Kremlin's sien-

251

na battlements. Tiered temple of frozen rose denying the finality of death.

One night as they stood in front of the mausoleum watching the changing of the guards the militiamen stationed in front of the Kremlin walls started shouting orders, chasing all pedestrians off the center of Red Square, Claire grabbed Sophie's arm, scores of citizens dispersed like docile cattle, a moment later a limousine swept like black lightning into the space habitually forbidden to all motor vehicles, it was immense and gleaming, its windows curtained. A gate suddenly opened in the bloodred battlements, the vehicle sped swiftly across the stone lake of Red Square and dove into the darkness of the Kremlin's might.

XX

CLAIRE appeared at Edmund's door on the Williams campus one winter night holding all of her worldly possessions wrapped in a square of burlap, having left the convent the day after Jeffrey Howell's death. She had first flown directly to Boston to be with Victoria and came to Edmund four days later in the middle of a heavy blizzard. She would succumb the following day to a severe bronchitis complicated by pleurisy. She was dressed in one of the nun's habits she'd worn for three years, some inches hurriedly chopped off with a pair of kitchen shears, wearing nothing over it but a thin sweater which Victoria had forced upon her that morning. She hadn't phoned him because she "refused to disturb his difficult schedule," the bus stop was three miles from his house but she was "used to a great deal of walking." Shivering in front of the fire as Edmund heaped blankets on her, Claire had sat with her chin resting on her knees, staring at the fire. Her shoulder blades were fiercely outlined under the folds of her altered serge dress, there was a bluish, cavernous cast of exhaustion or undernourishment under her eyes. The anguish of losing one we've not loved well can be more painful than the death of a great love.

For the following weeks she knew only the outline of Edmund's face hovering continually over hers in the blur of her fever, heard only the hoarse, grating voice of Edmund's aging cat, the soft thud of his cheek rubbing against her bed. She woke in and out of her haze of fever to see him sitting in an armchair by the bed correcting students' papers or moving about her as soft-footedly as his cat. He hovered above her one last time late at night as he came in to bring her a mug of hot milk and adjust her bedcovers. She always pulled the quilt on the wrong way, he chided, short side down, she was determined to get chilled again, didn't know the first thing about home comforts. Every night he hovered over her in his frayed blue robe as she was falling asleep; he adjusted her quilt and lifted it high with a wide impatient gesture; it fluttered over her like a canopy, a benediction before coming down with a gentle fall to which she grew so accustomed that on the evenings when he worked late and she'd already fallen asleep before his last visit she woke at dawn with a sense of loss.

A man in early middle age whose thick mane of sandy hair faintly showed the gray beginning to lace it; tanned, stubborn-chinned face; those deepened lines between nose and finely chiseled mouth which increased her own sense of time's passing. From her captive point, immobilized at the center of his world, Claire began to observe Edmund gyrating about her. He had the domestic obsessions of an only son who's survived the love of a penurious, possessive single mother, he saved leftovers for soups and frugal stews, loved all childhood smells and tastes, believed in ancient remedies for every bodily ill—inhalations of tincture of benzoin, hot porridge in the morning. "Another cup of broth Peb dear, please lambkin, I want you running marathons in a fortnight. . . ."

Jeff Howell had died while searching for his own stability, conversion of life. The plane he was traveling on crashed in a snowstorm in the woods of New Hampshire. As Edmund reconstructed it, he had boarded it to rejoin the estranged wife of one of his colleagues at St. Paul's, a loving blonde who rode a great deal and much admired him, and for whom he'd even begun to think of the possibility of divorcing Claire. Jeff had remained fairly happy to his last days. After Edmund had begun his visiting professorship at Williams College the preceding fall he had met Jeff for lunch several times in the vicinity of Boston, halfway between their two schools. Jeff had spoken glowingly about Victoria's performance at boarding school, summer life on the island, his yearly voyages abroad. The last one was to the Galápagos, the scale of its birds was amazing, there were many stunning mating habits to observe in the animal population. . . . Victoria had a summer job tending the flower stands on the island's Main Street, the purple gladioli Edmund always looked for were more glorious than ever. . . . They'd often had huge beach expeditions with April's and Katrinka's tribes, scores of them ranging from the ages of five to sixty going out to the clam beds near the lighthouse and bringing the clams home and everyone giving a hand in making a fine linguini sauce and watching the ferry come in against the sunset . . . shall I ever want that happiness again? Edmund wondered as he joined Jeff in a second martini.

A heavy snow had fallen upon Massachusetts the month of Claire's return and remained undisturbed by thaw, their landscape was stilled for weeks in the brilliance of a deep New England winter. As Claire regained her health Edmund was struck by her reluctance to make contact with the splendor of the world outside his rooms. When her fever had ended she'd spent hours by the fire, reading, mending his clothes, writing daily letters to Victoria. As she grew still stronger she began to glide wraithlike across the floors of his apartment, working quietly, talking little. Every domestic duty—the dusting of his books, the kneading of a bread dough— seemed to be savored with meticulous fervor, with the calm of a litany.

She had a way of keeping her eyes averted from the window during such tasks, avoiding all view of the outdoors.

"You can't imagine the glory of the landscape, Peb, let me bundle you up and drive you out for just ten minutes, we could go to the village and surprise Victoria with a lot of books when she comes home this weekend. . . ." (Ah, that word to use with her at last, "home.") "Do you mind going without me dear heart?" "As you wish."

He often ran his fingers through her thin brown hair.

• • •

As Edmund came home from campus and saw Claire profiled in his window, drawing a sewing needle with swift high strokes, he sometimes recalled his youthful visions of future happiness. Claire and Edmund continuing to live on the island six months of the year, Edmund painting eight hours a day in a large skylit studio facing out to sea. . . . Two children at the most; after a few years they'd move to a large city most of the year for the sake of good schooling . . . half of a brownstone in the East Twenties, two golden children growing, a guest room upstairs where their godmother, nomadic Aunt Sophie, could come to stay in between her reporting trips. . . . "All juvenile, corny, not as interesting as it's turned out to be." They were in a three-room flat on the edge of the Williams campus, on the top floor of a shabbily genteel Victorian house which they shared with the chairman of sociology. Edmund was teaching seminars to wealthy students who didn't know the difference between Bacon and Bakunin and participating in discussions of interminable tedium on whether to add a course in Carolingian architecture to the next year's curriculum. Claire was a frail, haggard woman with traces of admirable beauty remaining in her face and roughened field worker's hands of almost masculine power. Had the failure of her lifelong urge for self-determination, always aborted by men, by Jeff, partly broken her will to recover? Throughout her convalescence she took brief naps throughout the day in odd places of his apartment, on a blanket by the fire, curled up at the side of his desk, with the abandon of an enfeebled animal.

Their first domesticity.

His boots scraping on the doorsill as he came in from the snow, bringing the logs for the evening fire. He came in with more wood than he could carry and threw it on the hearth with a wide brusque gesture, shattering splinters onto the rug. She brushed them off, chiding gently. "Why always so rough, you'll burn the house down. . . ." "I'm really very brutal." He had a habit of squatting on his heels in front of the fire for a good while to make sure that it didn't flare up too high.

256

On cold nights she forced him to take a long hot bath before going to bed to help his arthritic knee.

Vico was now almost nineteen, a Siamese cat with eyes of lapis lazuli unclouded by age who hunted for heat throughout the winter. His voice had become an almost soundless call, a hoarse grating yawn accompanied by an immense opening of jaws which Edmund compared to those of the beasts in Assyrian bas-reliefs. When he settled on his blanket in a corner of Claire's room he lowered himself ever so slowly, first one arthritic limb then another, holding his breath as if to suppress a groan. He wreathed himself lamely about Claire's leg as she rose every morning, purred his gruff note of thanks as she bent down to caress his head. "I'll go berserk when it's the end of him," Edmund said. "I'll get you one you may love almost as much." "Oh never, he's the only one who's taken the time to know me well."

He slept on a folding cot in his study, had given Claire his bedroom at the beginning of her illness. He had frequent nightmares and she came into his room when he cried out in his sleep. During these visitations he burst out in short, subhuman cries, his body trembled with a long tremor like that of an animal dreaming. She loved to see his body hulking under its lair of covers, a dark blue, breathing mountain. Soon I must help him, she kept telling herself, eventually I must rescue him, fearing that these phrases were akin to Saint Augustine's O Save Me God But Not Quite Yet.

Some years ago when she'd left for St. Agatha's she'd often meditated upon those Irish pilgrims of the Dark Ages who'd set out on sea journeys with no particular destination in mind, aiming solely to abandon themselves to Providence. They'd floated as randomly as possible into the Atlantic, entrusting themselves to the hazards of storms in hope of being led by His Will to a solitary place where they could find a new level of grace. During her stay at the convent she'd maintained this same sense of submission to Providence, of random journeying. And she was filled with both anguish and a singular new peace during those winter months of her return as she lay sheltered in Edmund's care. Well now she might have to chart a course again. Well yes she might, with his help.

She saw all about her the carnage of her battle for self-perfection—the lonely success of Sophie's middle age, her child's uncertain future. Jeff.

O Great Spirit, she'd often whispered during her illness, give me the humility to finally understand others as well as they've loved me.

"Love in middle age!" Edmund wrote in one of his frequent letters to his friend John Mirsky in Berkeley. "A process of hulling, husking, denuding, fleecing, decorticating our early dreams, a stripping away of illusions so radical that we create a new dialectic of the passions, a romance of the real."

Claire and Edmund often talked about how life had to be lived in the years that followed the forty-five-year mark: A massive process of centering, focusing, zeroing in. She: Confine yourself to small but intense acts of compassion, use the little stuff rather than the big stuff, Saint Thérèse de Lisieux said.

He: How to find a way to survive on those fringes of society which are the only proper place for an artist and yet survive.

He muttered often about the dark times ahead, the imminent rebarbarization of the West. "It's later in history than I thought, Peb; what a Pollyanna I was a decade ago, the university as a temple of the intellect, my foot . . . temple's in ruins, heap of rubbish accommodating gigantic festivals of the ego; those pals of yours at St. Agatha's may have the right idea, sever most ties to the marketplace, set up your own islets of salvation. . . ."

Claire finally observed (this was all discovery, discovery!) the full anxieties of his forty-fourth year.

"Dad may have been saintly," Victoria said, "I'll miss him till the day I die. But to be absolutely frank I approve of Mamma's life more."

The hair was a shock of light brown silk, like her father's. The pale blue eyes had the guarded irony of Claire's.

"What do you mean by saintly, sweetheart?"

"Well they're the ones who think human nature is very perfectible, who have utterly peaceful characters and love people with great ease. Mamma isn't saintly, she's trying to be a saint, which is a very different matter. . . ."

"And what do you mean by that?"

"She's one of those people who probably carry more evil in them than most others and have a low opinion of human nature and are the great workers for change . . . that's what makes her so difficult and interesting really."

She had recently turned fifteen. Her life's singular events—her mother's absence, her father's death—had occurred when she was just old enough to grapple with them. She had a way of masking her brooding moods with a clever, disturbingly precocious conversation.

"Mamma sees so much evil in the universe that she has to work much much harder at being perfect. It's a path I understand well because I too believe myself to be profoundly evil."

She bent her head, nodding tragically. It was two months after her mother's return. They were walking in the Williamstown woods picking early wood violets as a bouquet for Claire—another attempt to induce her out of doors. On the earlier weekends she'd come home from school Victoria had stayed at her mother's bedside staring at her with intense curiosity in between long bouts of reading aloud—they'd spent March on Teilhard.

Victoria bent down to pick a fern. "You see that's the fascinating thing, Eddem. Goodness is much more of a mystery than evil. In Bible class at school they only talk about the mystery of evil. Well the irony is that it's *goodness* which is much more of a mystery."

Edmund paused in his flower gathering. Was this precociousness in matters spiritual an inherited trait? Would one be able to breed generations of theologians and mystics by proper selection?

"What I'm most grateful to Mamma for is that she taught me to take utterly nothing for granted," Victoria said during another walk. "Daddy took all that society offered him with open hands, without ever saying the no no no that's essential to a genuine life; he was much easier to live with. . . ."

"And what are you going to be like?"

"I wish to be difficult too, Uncle Eddem. I trust a few people

259

implicitly like you and Mamma and Aunt Soph about idiotic matters of everyday survival, but about absolute concerns—what's the good life and so forth for me—oh, no no, only I can tell what's best."

There was a silence. Pity the young men growing up in 1974, Edmund thought.

"I mean, what else is feminism about? The true feminists of the future have to go in my mother's direction and have total control over themselves, refuse to be brainwashed by the propaganda machine of the sexual-industrial complex. . . . Eddem, can you pray?"

"I wish I could. But I'd better just concentrate on taking care of you and Mom. It's the duty of men of action to take care of you contemplatives when you fall into the ditch."

That put Victoria in a state of considerable merriment. As she was able to indulge her passionate affection for her mother this grave child began to laugh more often, with abandon.

"So you think of yourself as a man of action! The dissenters in convents might be much more active in the world than you are because they're truly radical critics of it."

Occasionally her mother's former arrogance announced itself.

"Imagine anyone accusing contemplatives of not being useful! Those placid yes-men in the regular world have the usefulness of suckers."

"But don't worry, Eddem," she added, "you're a born educator."

"Alas."

"Edmund," Claire often said, "I wish you'd paint again."

"You sound like Sophie used to. . . . I'm not boring enough to be an artist these days, darling, I believe in old-fashioned things like giving pleasure. Have you seen what's being exhibited today, Peb? The aesthetics of tedium, ladders and rods of steel set at ninety-degree angles to each other, a hundred and forty-eight little black dots set out on white canvas, films showing one idiot eating a doughnut for ten hours, oh, *ils vont trop loin, tu sais!* How I miss

those tornadoes of self-indulgent paint I yiped about too impetuous-
ly two decades ago, the primal energy of Pollock; today it's the new
Puritanism denying us pleasure in any form, as if Jonathan Edwards
had been recalled by séance to rule the art world. . . . The shocking became so boring that the only next step was to make the boring
shocking. Collective boredom as the newest species of terrorism, of
psychological hijacking. . . ."

"But you're too afraid of not being instantly loved!"

He drew a little bit for the first time in two decades. He began by
drawing Claire's hands, her feet. Her blunt-nailed hands were
rougher, more powerful after her arduous years away. Her feet were
unchanged, the bare delicacy of Botticelli's *Primavera*. He drew
Victoria reading, his cat Vico drinking the noon sun on window-
sills. At first the pencil was like some clumsy rock in his hand, recal-
citrant, unyielding, he recalled with pain and longing the days when
it had been like the nimblest and swiftest of his limbs. Over the
weeks it softened like a piece of clay warmed by pummeling. He
still muttered as he drew, as he had in his twenties.

"There's nothing more presumptuous than emptiness Claire darling. Contemporary art has succeeded in finally killing off the
Muse. The rude French began it all, of course, with the vogue of
insulting and boring the audience, Duchamp, Dada . . . we're living in a solipsistic Museless world whose vestigial religion is the
cult of Nothing, at whose shrine the proper liturgical response is a
yawn . . . nothing to do but create enclaves where we can thumb
our nose at fashion and resurrect, shelter, nourish, surrender to our
Muse. . . ."

If she'd ever marry him (this was once said in a playful bantering
tone) he'd have such a powerful live-in Muse and paint with such
ferocity that he might even refuse to go out of the house, be just the
kind of recluse she'd become in the past months.

Perhaps, she replied in that cryptic little manner she'd acquired
at St. Agatha's, an artist is simply a person who's invented an artist.

They'd learned from brief, desperate letters the
previous year that Sophie's Israeli husband, Amos, had died from

shrapnel wounds suffered during an assignment on the Lebanese border and that she was returning to the United States. Then after some months of silence she had written them to start watching the MBC ten o'clock news. And one day Sophie's radiant smile began to appear almost daily, her hair abundantly teased, her face painted with the most lustrous art. And Claire sat in front of the set as if that beloved face were rebuilding her bridge to the world outside of Edmund's rooms.

These were the years when former Vietnam activists were re-channeling their energies into the issue of human rights. Sophie began to forward to Claire the literature she received from Amnesty International. And while still convalescing Claire pored over dossiers relating to imprisoned Soviet dissidents, Brazilian priests.

When Edmund missed the seven o'clock news because of a task at college she complained about the frivolity of Sophie's assignments. "I wish they'd give her more important news, Eddem; they had the impertinence to assign her a birthday party for aging lions at the Bronx Zoo, a woman of her brilliance!" "She'll fight her way out of that very quickly," Edmund predicted.

A few months later Sophie was promoted to the position of anchorperson for the weekend nights and they never wanted to miss that. "More violence tonight," Sophie would begin the program with her lustrous violet smile, "the Near East crisis is growing to a head, police readies for confrontation as looting grows in Newark's slum areas and a Brooklyn church is ransacked by three masked men. . . ." When will she ever find time now to come and see us? Claire and Edmund complained. Wouldn't it be lovely if the three of us could have a vacation together? Claire said. One of these days soon we must take a long trip together Edmund agreed.

One day while sitting by the fire Claire knew she must unburden herself of an emotion which had grown to immense proportions since her return. Can I dare tell him, she wondered, shall I ever dare. She feared that if she didn't have the courage to offer him her new knowledge the essence of tragedy might work itself out between them also—tragedy, the process of learning things too late.

262

For weeks the words were ready to rise in her but the ancient, ancient reticence kept holding them back—she was quieter than ever, staring a great deal at the fire, the aging cat Vico stalwart on her lap— Certain things are harder than ever to say in this time of ours, she finally said one night, our world has increasingly shunned sentiment in favor of irony. . . .

This makes the writing of novels and the expression of great loves most difficult, he agreed, not to speak of painting decent paintings.

Then her words came out with startling simplicity as he sat on his heels watching the nascent fire in his supple, primeval farmer's squat. "I've meant and meant to tell you," she said, "that I love you so much I'd gladly die for you. Anytime." She'd quickly returned to her reading. He'd shot her a swift, almost suspicious look, the glance of a primitive tribesman startling at the sound of a foreign tongue.

"I'm sorry," she said.

"Don't be." He rose and walked to the window.

And now it lay behind her, a flat, calm object, her proffered life.

One day in late April when Victoria was home for the weekend they finally got Claire out of doors. They'd teased and teased her, saying she wasn't good enough yet to deserve being a hermit, and on a fine warm Saturday she'd finally stepped out the door, blinking at the sun, her arms linked through both of theirs. Edmund knew how bold that simple step could be. He knew that the greatest gift he'd ever received—the passivity of her winter's bondage—was coming to an end.

They finally took possession of each other (Claire and Edmund) during a great spring rainstorm when the wind so buffeted the windows that they'd sat by the fire making believe they were at sea on a Europe-bound schooner, hearing the surf pounding against the porthole of their cabin. . . . Later that evening as he engaged her fragile body and assuaged his life's fiercest appetite, knowing for the first time her potential for joy, he cast away a burden which he had borne most of his years. And this act of possession thrust him into a new age as distinct from his past life as his adolescence had been from his childhood, serving as a rite of passage as well as of fulfillment.

Under his touch every moment of her body miraculously grew to pleasure like a grain of sand swelling into an acre of the earth.

Yet he knew that no search for joy could ever guide her life. And that the certainty of her love, for a time, would continue to depend on the extent of his proffered freedom.

Whereas she sensed that if he had his will he might take her to an enclave quite as distant and arcane as the one she'd just returned from, as deeply secluded as his long, solitary love; that the exile he'd impose upon her might be even more irrevocable than the one she'd once chosen in total freedom of the will.

And so when he let her go after having strengthened her into renewing her freedom, feeling as if he were letting go some bright shining bird that might be his soul, it was only in a spirit of very distant hope.

XXI

VICO old friend you're my talisman you're my life force how's this for an image Pussums you're like that Golden Gate Bridge right over there, you're the chain on which the beads of my life are strung . . . so hang on sweetheart the only thing I'm going to do this winter is see you live to the age of twenty, I've set myself that goal the way I used to say I'll finish my thesis by the time I'm twenty-six, by thirty-five I'll be chairman of the department, our agenda isn't tainted by the impossible little brother there's a handful of you who've even made it to twenty-two, twenty-three, it's sheer continuance we want, the older we get the less words matter, sometimes I even want to forget to read and write, I only want to growl with you and babble and whisper like the aspen leaves in August and do some modest magic again, describe the tongue of a hummingbird a night of love the mirages over hot asphalt explain youth and old age . . . Edmund is spending many hours this winter sitting still with the cat on his lap. For two decades the Siamese has hunted the sun's heat in the window of Edmund's apartments in Berkeley or Williamstown, vigilant whiskers taut against the sky, blue-gray flanks as still and solid as mountains in the distance, the most constant landscape of Edmund's life; but this winter it's safer and more consoling to hug the cat close flesh to flesh. So for many hours the two sit together in front of the window or the television watching life go by, Vico in Edmund's lap, deadly petals of the paws furled inwards, occasionally raising his steady blinking eyes towards his friend's face; staring at those wells of speckled gold and azure Edmund often tries to assess the meaning of this winter as if he were observing it from the cat's depths, he's never been very good at seeing things from anyone else's point of view, he studies the blue cisterns filled with a knowledge unanswerable to any man and tries to measure in them the hours of his life. You've seen me in a lot of incarnations haven't you old friend, young Werther copping out of art because it might ruffle his damn little ego, Professor Richter grooving on his Pygmalion act, then the demons swept over us didn't they, something hit us, something snapped, yet we're not that badly off Vico, look at those pretty girls going down the street with their book bags what are they going to do but study sociobiology, buy five-piece bedroom sets, betray their husbands, love Beethoven, bang dishes in the kitchen, go into orthodentistry at forty-six, remember nothing about their childhoods but a little pond they fell into at the age of five and a patient, mysterious animal like you . . . Vico's silken tail waves like a metronome, he greets the touch of his master's hand with a hoarse brief call of thanks. And after a few hours of sitting this way before the window or the television they go back to bed and go to sleep.

Upon leaving Claire and returning to Berkeley the preceding spring Edmund had decided to change his life. He wasn't yet sure how he wanted to change it. So he'd walked to the grocery store, bought a stock of canned goods for himself and the cat and taken to his bed. Upon waking in the morning they have their breakfast, watch television for a while and then move to the window to enjoy the late-morning sun. They sit facing south, Venetian blinds tilted down so as to get full sunlight yet not be seen from the street. And when the cat has warmed his flesh, signaled well-being with faint rhythmic roars, Edmund carries him to the pillow that's lain for twenty years at the foot of his bed, he gets in between the sheets and sleeps again until the afternoon. Upon waking he reaches for a book on his night table to take a few notes on his current project, "The Wane of the Muse in European Art." The two bachelors then repeat their gestures of the morning. They go to the sun at Edmund's western window, stare towards a view which had once struck Edmund as the world's most sublime, ethereal bridge spanning the blue bay like a bracelet of bright bone, magnolias and centennial firs burning in the glow of a faithful sun. They watch students and teachers pause at the street corner, biologists carry bags of Finast potatoes, sociologists wheel prams; splendid young 1970s women often strike poses of great languor by the mimosa tree outside their window; waiting for the traffic light to change they take out little mirrors to study pearly teeth and restiffen lashes, they're buffed and spruced like poodles just out of parlors aren't they Vico and look at how politely they're talking smiling to each other again, the young have regained some of their manners that's one thing you can say about them, they've dallied back to their fraternities to attend to soufflé recipes and the perfecting of their orgasms, listen Vico sweetheart one must honor the extraordinary variety of tactics humanity devises to survive despair, others might have increased their proclivity to liquor or to Mexico but we've chosen to sit, to dream, to sleep, I assure you I'm utterly sane old Pussums, I've never felt more composed emptier more calm, I feel little, I desire nothing, I suffer not at all, this afternoon I'll write a sentence about the modern artist's sensuous union with nothingness or his celebration of absence, all rage has left me, I feel generous, vast, drained, like those folk who change into their cleanest clothes and rearrange furniture before turning the light out one last time I want everything about me as orderly and still as I am, I'm in tune with the times for once, bravo, Faustian man is dying; there's little to rescue and even less to invent so live in the wind young folk, lots of sambas, smiles, sailing races, wine-tasting fests, breathing exercises, lots of compliments to the ladies and please let's call them ladies again. . . .

Towards evening the cat gently paws at his master's sleeve, clambers down from Edmund's lap, moves slowly towards the kitchen with the stiff, dignified gait of his great age. They eat. They prepare for bed. And before going to sleep they watch Sophie give the ten o'clock news. There she comes Vico, our switchboard to reality, pretty scary being watched by ten million people every day, look at our beauty with the Titian hair. . . . "More violence tonight as thousands of citizens rally for protest in strike-ridden Uruguay," she

267

says with her marvelous smile, "back home John Wayne goes into surgery . . . a birthday party is held for Siamese twins who were separated five years ago . . . Wall Street averages show industrials up one point two . . ." Edmund's head begins to nod again when Sophie's voice goes off the air. He stares satedly at the art objects that fill his room, the *sang-de-boeuf* vase by his bed, the Tang scroll on the wall opposite him, a pre-Columbian statue acquired in the early sixties stands on the desk, prize of his collection, eight inches high and monumentally inscrutable. ". . . Now for a station break . . . Wannamee Village/Florida's most beautiful old age community . . . Year round tennis courts heated swimming pools a rich and rewarding social life . . ." Edmund returns to his exile of sleep.

        At summer's end Toby, the most beloved and rebellious student of Edmund's 1960s, phoned to say that he had married and had just returned to live in Berkeley, could he bring his wife for tea? Edmund said he'd be enchanted and closed his eyes and tried to imagine an ideal woman for Toby; he thought of the Meissen cups standing on his mantelpiece and these gave him the image of what he hoped her to be: fragile, orderly, floral, a woman of Mozartian translucence, a voluptuary of the domestic whose linen closets would be neatly stored and labeled, filled with sachets and pale blue ribbons. He fancied Toby and his young wife constantly shopping together for crass little delicacies to fill their nest with, comparing eggcups and the swell of wine goblets, ah yes such a woman could confine Toby as severely as a cup's function is confined by its form and glaze; he saw her as the principle of order that would tame this figment of the sixties' wildness, this imagined couple were a symbol of the exhaustion of the West, our growing lassitude must be accepted with the most serene acquiescence, Toby of the long matted hair and Ché Guevara buttons who'd stood in torn sandals at Sather Gate shouting about the creation of new worlds is coming home with a little beauty who's rechanneled his ardor into the choosing of place mats and tea services and better quality of air. . . .

        Toby's wife came and was precisely the way he'd hoped she'd be.

She was dressed in hues of off-white as delicate as the barks of birches and was equally fragile of line. Her pale hair was neatly rolled into a bun all around her head, she said Professor Richter I soon want to study the middle period of Fragonard, she drank from her teacup as if it were a magnolia leaf and asked if she could bring the baby for a visit. A few weeks later, at the beginning of term, Edmund disconnected his phone and ceased to answer doorbells, responding solely to the communications which his friends Luke Edwards or John Mirsky slipped under his door. He presumed that Toby and his family had moved into a neighboring block, for several times a week as Edmund sat behind the Venetian blinds with Vico they wheeled the baby down the street; they'd glance up at Edmund's window, squinting and frowning with curiosity. And Edmund would watch them until they became specks on the bright Berkeley street, would watch Toby's long now languid body ambling in the sun as he wheeled home the little luxuries of his new world, would stare at the pale hair through which he'd loved to run his hands when it fell to below the shoulders, now cut to a helmet of tight curls like those of the Apollo Belvedere.

"In Ethiopia we have evidence of thousands of executions of political dissidents and systematic use of torture—" (so a letter of Claire's reads) "three thousand persons alleged to be sympathetic to the opposition shot just last month—many of the victims ranged in age between eight and twenty—bodies publicly exposed in Addis Ababa every night—we know of instances of children denouncing parents to break out of their captors' hands—methods of torture include the tying of heavy weights to male genital organs, insertions of red-hot iron bars into the vaginas of nine-year-old-girls, etc. . . ."

She must sit up night after night in the bleak little Boston flat she'd taken after they'd parted and she'd found work with a human rights group, photographs of dissidents strung above her desk, attempting to continue that course of self-denial which had marked her life . . . at times Edmund addresses an envelope, writes Dear Peb on the top of a piece of paper and keeps it on his desk for several days out of fear that one adverb might upset the tenuous

269

half-promises they'd reached in the spring. When he allows his pen to touch paper again he writes something like this: "I'm increasingly grateful for my new sabbatical and the essay on the Muse is going quite well—reversal of attitudes towards the artist's melancholic temperament particularly fascinating to trace in the early Renaissance, the medievals had equated melancholia with sloth and condemned it as one of the seven capital sins—but the Humanists resurrected Aristotle's view that melancholia is the Muse's inseparable companion, a noble trait gracing all men gifted in the arts—"

There are times when Edmund sinks even more deeply into his languor and fails to get dressed, remains in pajamas for days, catnaps all over the chairs of his undusted room rather than make the effort of walking to his bed; his friend John thinks this is all sublime, sublime. "Your ego is . . . utterly diminished in your inaction, yes? The Will abolished! A passivity . . . almost mystical in nature!" (Volcanic splutters, barely intelligible groans of admiration.) "Ah I've got it, I've got it dear one, the saint as slob, or perhaps the slob as saint. . . ."

John's sexuality has abated with his increasing flesh and his Slavophilia now centers on twentieth-century Russian poetry. He comes to lie on Edmund's couch to groan out his disillusionment with love, with the Soviet Union, with the academic life, "To sell our thoughts like farmers at market, phooey, how vulgar! Our terrorists of overactivism, our Stakhanovites of awakedness, I yawn at the very thought of their vigilance. . . ."

"What's the use of striving anymore, John, when the laboratory of the twentieth century is closed, everything's been seen to death, look at the pluralistic decadence of our art world, social realism Postimpressionism Abstract Expressionism photo-realism Minimalism floating in a broth of torpor like alphabet noodles swirling in a baby's bowl. . . ."

"Listen to Mayakovski's prophecy, Edmund, 'There's less and less love, less and less daring, and time is crashing into my forehead . . .' "

.   .   .

270

"Good Day America, this is Sophie Ross at MBC with a special report from our fiftieth state where the sun is blazing at a gorgeous eighty-seven degrees and the beach forecast is for safe gently swelling surf, we're here to bring you a scoop on the biggest new industry in Hawaii. . . ." [Sophie on Waikiki, orchid lei around her neck, stray lock of hair seductively blowing in the wind.] "Now what would you guess is the biggest cash crop in our seven-island wonderland, fellow Americans, pineapple, sugar, citrus fruit? Guess again. . . . You've given up? It's marijuana . . ."

Edmund watches carefully for the scheduling of Sophie's special reports; he keeps the cat on his lap throughout most of the day and they're watching increasing amounts of television; the stillness of his body at those moments seems to heighten Vico's comfort; towards Christmas the animal began to drag himself very slowly about the house, there's a great shuffling of covers, a few stoic groans as he gets up on his rheumatic hind legs and limps forwards to perform his ritual greeting, rubbing the rough stubble of his whiskers against his master's cheek.

"Marijuana is now a billion-dollar cottage industry fostered by rebellious Hawaiian labor unions who're just plain bucking federal authorities; the tall green weed is even grown on terraces and condominiums throughout the fiftieth state and in some buildings five out of seven residents are grass farmers. . . . Here we are in the Honolulu office of State Senator Neil Abercrombie, who's been urging his legislature to decriminalize the cash crop. . . . Neil, what reflections do you have on this lucrative new trade?" "Uh, it's Hawaii cowboy style, Sophie, part of the frontier ethic of doing your thing; it's being sold at every street corner, we haven't even got enough room in our jails for our offenders . . ."

Cradled in Edmund's arms before the set Vico resorts to his old jokes, pretends to sleep and suddenly flips over on his back to paw the air at imagined birds, feigns vigilance towards a buzzing fly, expresses contentment by that slow blinking of the eyes which Edmund sees as his way of smiling.

". . . Back at MBC studio this morning we also have Dr. Murray Kempner of Columbia University, author of the recently published book *Keep Off the Grass*, and his views might conflict sharply with those of Senator Abercrombie." [Sophie back in New York, in chaste white cashmere.] "Marijuana's a grave danger to all human organs, Sophie, particularly the reproductive, a disaster to our future generation of offspring; we have conclusive evidence that the sperm of men who're light to medium smokers doesn't develop properly and that the surviving offspring of female monkeys fed marijuana during pregnancy are hypotrophic and hyperactive. . . ."

"Are you still lying around week after week, Edmund, going through an acute phase of male climacteric?" Edmund's torpor seems to concern Sophie and she returns his phone calls punctiliously. The fluctuations of her moods from manic cheer to depression increasingly alarm Edmund; she often blurts out her reprimands in a flat, Valium-drugged monotone. "I diagnose it as acute anomie . . . early senility and advanced agoraphobia complicated by a total collapse of the will. . . ." Or else, in one of her more exultant moods: "Treasure! What's new and exciting in the life of sloth?" "I just phoned to tell you that you're my pipeline to reality." "Are you really all right, darling?" "Yes yes." "You didn't see my special on Jeremy Thayer, that prof who experimented with psilocybin in the sixties, highly controversial, watch for it, we're rebroadcasting, you know I'm always there when you need me." "Yes yes, you're always somewhere, honey, I hope you're getting enough sleep." "I love you and everything."

The last time Edmund has seen Sophie he'd behaved miserably. Claire was still in her convent, Sophie had recently returned from Israel, she'd flown to see him in Detroit where he was attending an art historians' convention. Edmund had found this event depressing. Three thousand men and women were there with stick-on

272

labels saying Amherst, Wayne State, University of Florida, they swarmed through the halls of a large hotel in search of teaching positions, they were writing more and more about less and less, they catnapped in corridors waiting for interviews, these hordes of academics encamped with their dissertations on "The Iconography of the Harp in Sixteenth-Century Bas-Reliefs" and "Aztec Symbols of Parturition" looked like the hostages of a plane hijacking bivouacked at some Near Eastern airport. Edmund had fled the convention right after giving a paper on Caravaggio, driving to the airport hours ahead of time to wait for Sophie in a bar. There was something noble about her newly chiseled face which reminded him of a grave young matron in a Roman frieze, which both confused and seduced him. Her Israeli husband had died that spring, three weeks after their marriage. He saw new little lines at the corners of her eyes during dinner and kept turning to a mirror to scrutinize his own face while she talked. A pregnancy at forty-three, always risky at that age, yet she'd thought of keeping the baby but soon after Amos's death she'd decided on an abortion. . . . Edmund disliked listening to such things, he'd talked about Caravaggio. "Can you imagine any man more radically different from the cautious academic I've become than this ruffian revolutionary genius, Soph, this first of the bohemians who lived like a bandit in the slums of Trastevere, this *artiste maudit* whose biography is chiefly derived from the police records of his time . . . You've suddenly become a woman," he interrupted himself, "and I've remained a messed-up kid." She listened as carefully as ever with her newly tragic, guarded gaze, looking at him at three-quarters, as if posing for camera. He needed to bathe in that rich intimate presence of hers which after almost thirty years had gained something of the marvelously incestuous; it was a time when one impulse of Sophie's might have settled all, might have brought him that constant and predictable happiness which he'd been denying himself, but she was guarded, steeped in her recent sorrows. . . .

He'd felt all this very early in the evening and had become extremely drunk. He'd driven her about the unfamiliar city in a rented car, insisting on one last drink, and they'd ended up in a homosexual nightclub where a pale young male in rhinestone-stud-

273

ded G-string gyrated on top of the bar amid a crowd of braying men. Edmund had played the pinball machine, drinking whiskey with beer chasers. He'd leaned over the machine like a jockey, shouting at the silver ball that sped through its maze of electric-blue machine gunners and motorcycle racers, he jerked the handle sloppily and the ball kept ricocheting off the walls, dribbling slowly into its nearest exit; Sophie stood by him sipping on a glass of wine, looking absent; he remembered later shouting imprecations at his own arid virility, at the silver missile that never reached the delicate ovarian channels between the rich round globes. In their hotel room he was too drunk to make love and fell asleep for a few hours. Dawn light flooded her body as he woke next to her and he was dazzled by the familiar milky splendor of her skin, the youth of a body steeped lifelong in pleasure—he'd not had a woman for some months and returning to her was like returning to one's childhood home after a long absence, imbibing the mystery of history and desire in the smell of a centennial lilac bush—he was grateful again for her subtle hands, her courtesan's suppleness—they lay breathing in each other's arms as they had ten or twenty years ago in Florence, Nantucket, New York— " 'Three hundred men between your thighs,' " he whispered, " 'embracing all love turned false, again, again . . .' "—her familiar "Where's that from?"—"Catullus . . . a page or two before he says, 'Friendship is here, my heart/Richer than love or passion' "—he realized with guilt that he would wish to have her like this until the end of his days, occasional, unbinding, more refreshing and torrid than any bodily substance he knew—in the past she used to say "three years," "ten months," naming the passage of time since their last lovemaking with an accuracy he often hated—but this morning she simply stared at him with those great golden eyes, stared at him with a new desperation he was terrified of plumbing—"What sumptuousness you are," he said, "you are my Orient, oh no more metamorphoses Soph, just give me more of what you are today, I'll never have enough of what you've become. . . ." He fell into a brief sleep thinking of all the men who must have known her in the past decade, creatures not worthy of touching one inch of her glorious skin, scrupulously fashionable men with water beds, sleek lofts in SoHo, exotic new therapies,

triple alimonies, odious new theories of expanding their consciousness, they jogged, they fasted, they consulted nutritional healers,
they sat on executive boards of Esalen, they worried about children
who'd joined Fascist cults, they tried Tibetan meditation, they believed in open marriage, late twentieth-century monsters, virtuosos
of the psychobabble of the self, America, America . . . When he
woke again Sophie had already left the room, the city.

Such things happen suddenly. A day came when
Vico couldn't raise himself off the bed without Edmund's help.
Edmund woke later than usual and wondered why the animal had
failed to bring his morning greeting. He raised his head towards the
cat and met his gaze. The animal's silken bluish flanks were
stretched out behind him with great rigor, he stared back unflinch-
ingly through those azure eyes that had become increasingly speckled with gold in the past year, like the turning of leaves after great
frosts. How easily the cat breathed when he cradled against Edmund's breast and they lay very still in bed! Edmund now took all
his notes that way; on the days Sophie didn't do the *Good Day
America* show he tried to catch the five-minute roundup she occasionally gave at noon by keeping the set on throughout the morning.

"We've got a gorgeous ten-thousand-dollar kitchen
work center complete with radar range for you lady if
you spin the machine right . . . why, you're crying, oh
don't cry lady just spin it again sweetheart, come on let's
go after that ten-thousand-dollar spin. . . . SHE'S
GOT IT! SHE'S A WINNER! A WINNER! There are
some more prizes coming this morning on *The Price Is
Right*, folks, the winner of the next game will receive a
free two-week stay at the Corfu Hilton so stay tuned for
our station break . . ."

—get your early copy of the spectacular up-and-coming
best-seller *Too Young to Die!* Stories of thirty-two superstars who died in the prime of life—Marilyn Monroe,
Bobby Darin, Freddie Prinze, Billie Holiday, Jack Cassi-

dy, Sal Mineo, Judy Garland, Elvis Presley. . . . What did them in, what was the nature of their anxiety? Get your mail-order copy today special prepublication price twelve ninety-five—

The noon mail arrives inviting Dr. Richter to offer this or that lecture, partake in symposiums and seminars; Edmund amuses himself by rolling up each letter and aiming it into the wastebasket across the room; if it lands right the last third of our life will be okay Vico, if it misses it'll be a mess, hey, look who's out this morning, Dick Stoddard from Classics, another honest suntanned scholar another alcoholic of the single object, "Augustan View of Providence as Reflected in First-Century Numismatics" was his thesis I believe, admirable citizen, what nobler task than to turn the new frat brothers into coin freaks, and there's Mrs. Toby her tummy out like Cranach's Venus again what do you think of that Vico, she's off to envy neighbors and birds, talk on the phone for hours, wipe away dust, curse the government, love Rachmaninoff, moan at the touch of a beloved, grouse about the rain, remember nothing about her childhood but a mysterious pair of eyes like yours. . . .

"Religion doesn't cash itself in like science or art history, fellow," the Reverend Luke Edwards says during one of his visits to Edmund's room. "I do think this more than deserves your passionate attention, you don't seem to accept the *is* of God's presence because you're so hung up on the *must be* of proof. . . ."

"Are you offering me mystery, Edwards? Now mystery *is* something I've great need of in my life." Edmund shuffles languidly across his room, the cat cradled against his chest, dusting his possessions.

The reverend leaps up from his chair in the hope of another conversion. "Yes yes, that's where it's at, fellow, part of the magic of Christianity is that nothing is ever totally understood, got to recycle that, Edmund. . . ."

Dr. Edwards has drawn closer still to God since becoming university chaplain and his culinary skills have become so noted that Dione Lucas occasionally phones him for a recipe. He's credited for

returning to the Christian fold many students who'd been seduced
by Oriental cults, and he looks upon Edmund's reclusion as a co-
vert, unacknowledged thirst for Deity.

"I believe you do have faith, Edmund, but you have it at a very
low temperature . . . got to unpack this, Edmund, the grand strat-
egy of the world religions has been to diagnose the flaw in ourselves
and point to some deliverer who'll overcome it in the future . . . don't you sense such a flaw in this outstandingly slothful
new phase of your life?"

"The future seems too ethereal to merit primary concern."

"But neither are you dealing with the present, fellow; it's this
refusal which the Church has always condemned as sloth, one of the
seven deadly sins, you know the Bosch. . . ."

"There's nothing less real than the present, Reverend. Today's
news wraps tomorrow's fish."

Edmund sits at the window, staring at the bay hung like a surplice from a cloudless sky. Laughing co-eds walk by, hair scrubbed
into curtains of silk. The wife of a biochemist researching crystals
does a headstand in the neighboring backyard, suntanned legs twirl-
ing like mandibles on an emerald lawn.

"In a truly imaginative metaphysic, Edmund, man can become all
things by suspending understanding, the existential cash comes
with an abandonment to mystery, Edmund, not with proof. . . ."

"This notion has met with less than universal acceptance."

The chaplain comes close to losing his patience. "Well, do phone
if there's anything you need . . . 0800, year of Charlemagne's cor-
onation. . . ."

Have a nice day Edmund calls politely as the door slams, best
wishes to the department. Sleep is a very busy condition Reverend,
more active you can't get, God sends us songs in the
night . . . shall we capitulate to his demands for emotions gaseous
and overflowing Vico, got to unpack this Pussums, the self is what
hurts, the solution to the identity problem is get lost, is there life
after birth as the Buddhists put it, some things are not quite true
but are too good to be wrong, has our turn come at last, what do you
think little brother, or is it forever too late, the exile is long, cunning
we're running out of . . .

Edmund wakes up at night to see that the cat is properly covered, tightens the blanket about his flanks as we would a child's. Sophie is away for most of February. In March, Vico turns twenty.

"I'm thinking of calling my essay 'The Demon of Noontide,'" Edmund writes Claire, "a term Chaplain Edwards tells me was used by the Church to describe that aridity of the soul which plagues monks in the midday hours of contemplation."

One day as they sat looking at the street the cat seemed to try struggling off Edmund's lap and he understood that Vico wished to lie on the windowsill again. He placed him on a pillow in his ancient position, turned towards the sunny street, but the animal continued struggling, asked for a different angle of vision, opened his jaw in a noiseless call to say all was not right yet. Edmund turned him the other way, his head towards the room. And Vico finally lay still and stared back in peace, his new golden eyes blinking with gratitude. It was as if he'd chosen Edmund's room as the last sight he wished to fill himself with. His pain was swallowed in the determination to be stoic—so Edmund saw it—his eyes were a sacred cistern of knowledge even unavailable to him.

In the last days Vico's eyes would remain closed for long moments of time, he opened his eyes in a new way, not upon the call of a voice or the din of conversation which John brought with him but as though to simply look at the room for a moment before closing his eyes again; to remember the room better or simply to see that it was still there.

He died on a day in late March when John was reciting Mayakovski: "'The poet's word is your resurrection, your immortality citizen bureaucrat . . .'" Edmund had looked towards the window. There was a clenched finality about the way the animal's eyes were closed. He'd covered the animal with its little blanket, not able to carry him to the backyard. It was John who had to do it for him. They carried him there some hours later, they buried Vico in the backyard under the mimosa tree. The nightmares Edmund had that night were not so much dreams as distorted visions induced by malefic spirits. Every art object in his room writhed and pulsated with a Satanic agitation, the cabbage plant in his Tang drawing swelled like a corpse in water to monstrous size, leaves dismembered, tendrils floating about the room like scum on pallid lakes, the Meissen cups shattered into dust, dissolved into a fine colorless powder that choked him like a smog; at early dawn the delicate little pre-Columbian statue he kept on his mantel began to advance across the room, her white lunar body increasing to human size as she came nearer; in her original state her arms had been crossed over her breasts a few inches above the primitive triangle that indicated her sex but now the right hand raised itself off the pure narrow chest, arm broken at the elbow in an archaic angle of sacrificial gesture, the idol loomed close above him, lunar, absentmouthed, machete raised over his bed . . . he woke crying out, turned the light on, stared at the tiny statue calmly standing on the mantel, the empty pillow at his feet, saw about him the room of a fastidious scholar noted as a connoisseur of the admirable, a gatekeeper of the exquisite; he went back to sleep still haunted by the statue, its association with rituals that preceded the existence of recorded time, rites of atonement testifying to our dread of all that is feral, he reflected on the primal terrors which have led us to domesticate animals such as Vico since the beginning of speech, creatures providing a link to the lowest most implacable forces in the chain of being, beasts which could bring an illusion of safety to the natural jungle of our minds, the solitude of our forests.

He phoned Sophie the next morning. He'd thought of announcing a grave illness and then decided against it. He simply phoned to ask her whether she could come to Berkeley in the next few days. She was in one of her elated moods, she'd just returned from Alaska where she was doing a special on the pipeline, she was compassionate and loving, she sobbed briefly when she heard about Vico; when Edmund's voice failed him she asked him whether she wasn't being supportive enough. But she simply couldn't find time to see him that month, she was off to Jerusalem again the following weekend to interview Begin, then to Geneva to interview some Iranian dissenters Claire had told her about. . . . "Try hard to fit me in, sweetheart," Edmund said, "I'll ring you at three tomorrow." "Don't phone me until after five, at three I have a cardinal."

She called back five minutes later. "Edmund love, if you truly need me you know perfectly well I'll drop it all, I'll leave everything for you at any time, all we've got is each other, I've been more depressed in the past years than at any other time in my life. . . ."

"Damn it, Soph, speak up sooner, I never know what's on your mind anymore."

She paused. "I've learned to repress, to hide, the way you always told me to, Eddem."

"You know I'd give up my life for you anytime, don't you?"

"Maybe I'll take the next plane."

"No no no, you've got all that . . . Soph, I may need you even more in a few weeks."

"Promise?"

"Absolutely sweetheart."

"Really sure?"

"I'll do all right."

"You know I love you and everything."

He wrote to Claire, telling of the cat's death and then continued: "It's clearly Dürer's great engraving *Melancholia I* which offers the first modern concept of artistic inspiration—the cult of melancholy (and later alas of boredom, of the void) now begins to absorb the ancient Muse—"

Every four or five years over the past three decades Claire had sent him an utterly memorable letter.

I feel that notwithstanding much public concern (Soph, Edwards) over your present phase of silence, stillness, you've spent one of the most fruitful and healing winters of your life. What they call your passivity, indolence, etc., may be nothing more than a stripping of yourself greatly needed to return you to essentials. It's as if you've worn a series of masks for twenty years, darling, masks of the hardened cynic, the bureaucrat of academia which have nothing to do with the creature inside. The danger with any mask is that it may force one's true features to emulate it, it's urgent that we remove masks before it's

too late, before our features have hardened into them irrepara-
bly . . . you've been a translation of yourself, Edmund dear, and I
look forward to reading a more real you very soon. . . .

There's a conference on the abolition of the death penalty she has
to go to in early May, then she must see Victoria through her
exams, wouldn't it be splendid if she could talk him and Soph into
getting together for a few days sometime later in the
spring . . . just think, twenty-five years since that's happened,
she'd consult Soph as to dates, etc.

On interview programs which follow Sophie's occasional appearance on *Good Day America* severe gray-haired wom-
en with doctorates in sexology advise teenagers to pet to orgasm
rather than go all the way; doctors of the male sex angrily protest
that petting will never be a substitute for genuine penetration; fifteen-year-old girls speak movingly of what it's like to come out of
the closet as a Lesbian. On the soap operas that lie like a lonely
plain between the morning shows and Sophie's evening news
Americans still seem to have many dreams and aspirations, some
Americans confess deep love for each other in candlelit restaurants
upon the occasion of a thirtieth wedding anniversary and others
worry about their daughters going out with porn photographers; an
amazing amount of the soaps revolve about the sagas of adulterous
doctors. There's one particular show, *General Hospital*, which mes-
merizes Edmund because of its fastidiously elemental passions. The
first time he watches it Monica is about to give birth with great
danger to her life in a country house isolated by a violent snowstorm—her doctor-husband (Eric) is trying to get through to her by
ambulance in the company of a colleague (Alan) whom Eric suspects is the real father of the child about to be born—one of the
three women helping to deliver the baby in the snow-stranded
house is Alan's barren wife (Leslie) who is also a doctor—During
Monica's arduous unsedated labor Dr. Leslie hears Monica scream
out the name of the baby's real father, Alan, Alan, I'm giving you
the son you always wanted—both doctors, cuckold and adulterer,

281

arrive to the young mother's bedside, the baby is safe but Monica's life will remain in danger for some time, stay tuned for the station break—

—Buy the *Star* for Jeane Dixon's special column! Jeane Dixon predicts again! Marriage for Princess Caroline of Monaco, trouble ahead for the pope, Teddy and Joan on the splits . . .

"I believe you might be heading towards a nervous disorder," John says softly one morning. John tries to distract Edmund by giving him a refresher course in the Russian language. He brings his tape recorder and a set of cassettes he'd made twenty years ago with the help of a voluptuous specialist in Lermontov. "This is Professor John Mirsky and this is my friend, Tamara. Good morning comrades! *Zdrastvouitie tovarishtchi!* Repeat with us . . ."

Whenever Edmund sees Sophie's face on the screen she infuses him with a small yearning for the outdoors, he gets out of his pajamas, dusts his possessions, goes out to buy some food. He savors every second of his excursions because the effort of deciding to go out is very great, he stands a long while at each traffic light, he looks carefully from side to side like a child just taught to cross the street alone.

On warm evenings other exiles to California drink wine on their verandas. The bay lights up in the distance like a surplice of velvet studded with a thousand little stones. He likes best those days when Sophie has an extensive interview with a personality deemed controversial. What cool, what aplomb, his Sophie is indomitable, she can handle anyone! He finally catches the interview with Jeremy Thayer she'd aired the previous fall.

"Good Day America, this is Sophie Ross at MBC greeting you on Wednesday April second; we have a very special guest with us this morning who's come to celebrate his sixtieth birthday with us, Dr. Jeremy Thayer. . . . Good morning, Dr. Thayer! Dr. Thayer, you've had a long varied career which began with a distinguished teaching position in the University of Michigan's biology department, you went on to be the guru of the turn-on, drop-out generation after your pioneering research with psilocybin, commonly known as psi. . . . As you look back on your long career, Dr. Thayer, how do you think you affected the generation that's just coming of age today?"

"Sophie, I probably encouraged, abetted, stimulated, prompted, aided, incited, inspired, persuaded more people to grow than any other human being in history."

"It's said that you yourself have taken some six hundred psi trips since you began to research the drug, is that correct, Dr. Thayer?"

"That's right, Sophie, I think I'm one of the smartest people in the country today. . . . I'm writing three or four books a year, I'm challenging the Judeo-Christian ethic, I'm helping people all around the world to get rid of their guilt. . . ."

"Now, Dr. Thayer, I want to show you a photograph. Here's a photograph of a handsome twenty-two-year-old college student, Nick Nordlinger, who jumped off a windowsill to his death after experiencing the drug which you were preaching to America . . . Now behave yourself, Dr. Thayer, you're going to stay right in this studio, you're not going to get up and walk out, behave yourself, you're sixty years old today, Dr. Thayer. . . . Do we hear a phone ringing . . . yes, we hear a phone ringing, it's the phone call we were waiting for from Phil Nordlinger. Phil Nordlinger, what part did psilocybin have in your son's death? Dr. Thayer, please . . ."

"That's ghoulish, I won't let that killer Nordlinger answer such a ghoulish question. . . . Nordlinger made fun of millions of kids, he even got to the White House and cooperated with the death machine which hundreds of thousands of young Americans protested with the help of my drug. . . ."

"That aging hippie . . ."

"You got to the White House, didn't you, Mr. Nordlinger, it's Phil Nordlinger himself who killed his son. . . ."

283

"Gentlemen, we must pause now for a station break. . . ."

—*Too Young to Die*—Biographies of thirty-two entertainment superstars who died in the prime of life . . . George Gershwin, Rudolph Valentino, Carole Lombard, Cass Elliot, Mike Todd, Hank William Buddy and others . . . walk with them from their humble beginnings to their tragic ends, enjoy reading about their ups, their downs, their traumas . . . call toll free for this luxury volume at half price—

"Tell us this, Phil Nordlinger, did you feel responsible for your son Nicholas jumping out of the window?"

"The first thing I say to parents who've lost their children, Sophie, is stop whipping yourself, get rid of your guilt . . ."

"It's Phil Nordlinger himself who killed his son, you got to the White House, didn't you, Phil, I've had enough of this. . . ."

"Please stay seated, Dr. Thayer! You're sixty years old today, Jeremy Thayer! Yes of course, do as you wish, Dr. Thayer, good-bye, Dr. Thayer . . . to round up the show . . . oh I hear the tears in your voice, Phil Nordlinger . . . there were no health centers, no early-detection centers yet, were there? . . . I hear the tears in your voice, are we ever going to beat the drug problem, Phil?"

"People want to be happy, Sophie, so they'll keep on taking drugs, even aspirin can be a dangerous drug, Sophie. . . ."

"Phil, thanks a lot for being on the show, you're a real pro, Phil, thanks a lot . . . that's all for today, ladies and gentlemen . . . what would *you* do if your kid were smart and well-behaved and belonged to the Ku Klux Klan and couldn't graduate? Tune in tomorrow for Sophie Ross at MBC. . . ."

—Oh Delite/Dynamite/Diet Rite/

"Monica, we're not going to lose you . . ." "Please,
Alan, if it looks like I'm not going to make it you tell me,
okay? . . ." "You're the center of my existence, Monica, if you don't want to live for my sake then try to live
for the sake of our son. . . ."
—We created Enfin, elegant, sensual, so French, the
fragrance of the year—
"Alan, your wife told me that you talked things out,
did you tell her that you love me?" "Yes I did, Monica, it
was rough. . . ." "I was afraid it was all over between
us. . . ." "How could it be . . . are you going to cop
out on us or are you going to hang in?" "I love you, Alan,
it's wonderful to say that. . . ." "I love you too, Monica. . . ."

Edmund saw Toby and his wife go by his window again every
few weeks, she was coming to the end of term, swollen-bellied in
the splendor of the April sunshine.

He saw other men and women wheeling children and groceries
who were writing theses on the dynamics of Borromini's ceilings,
on the development of early Slavic polyphony.

He wanted to paint again.

It was a day in April when he hadn't been able to reach Sophie for
three weeks; she hadn't answered his messages so it was evident
that she was out of the country. On the jacaranda tree outside his
window a cuckoo was counting the hours of his life; he asked several
questions about himself which he couldn't answer alone. He didn't
want to alarm Sophie and Claire. He wanted in fact to disalarm
them. He wished to sound utterly composed, quite healed, almost
formal. He took out some pen and paper and this is what he
wrote.

Berkeley, California
April 14th, 1975

Sophie, dearest nomad,
I'm aware of the variety of places you might be in as I pen this
missive. Woody Allen's arms, Giscard d'Estaing's dining room, docu-

285

menting the reforestation of Wall Street from the top floor of the World Trade Center—You may wonder why I'm suddenly writing after weeks of trying to track you down by phone at every Hilton I could think of between Caracas and Amman—It's in hopes of seducing you with the following proposal—Why don't you, Pebble and I take a trip abroad sometime soon to celebrate three decades of that lifesaving course referred to as our deep and lasting friendship?

After all, Sofka, here we are turning forty-five, a threat to be confronted head-on; there's no period that requires more choice; I'm beginning to think there's nothing much more to genius than an enormous talent for choosing. . . .

To hell with restraint, with theory, he decided in midletter.

What I wish to recreate between us, Sofka, is that ethereal summit of candor which only friendship can offer and which is more drastically needed than ever in mid-age, that desperate time when we must cease to be cannibals of our own hearts, must take the risk of total truth-telling in order to make the last third or fourth of our existence bearable, must recenter our lives upon the only human bond in which the tyrannical cycle of self-deceit is broken . . . at our age there's little else to live for, I'm asking for the brutality of mirrors and the fearlessness of angels at this proposed meeting; oh, I'm asking for a lot and I refuse to take any less than a radical stripping of each to each . . . think about it.

Forever, Edm.

Sophie's secretary phoned to say that Ms. Ross had just returned from Bucharest with a severe bronchitis and was writing back to Dr. Richter that very day.

> New York City
> April 21st

Darling, funny that in focusing on the problems of our shared age you center on the issue of truth whereas I've been zeroing in on the problem of facing death, of saying okay you bastard I'm grateful for every scrap of time you throw me but it's time I confront you head-on, dare to stare straight down your jaw, let's not fool ourselves Eddem the fear is central to me; since Amos's own death I've been unable to fight my way into any of the courage I need to survive without totally drugging myself with work; I haven't taken a day off in four years and I'm terrified of what would happen if I do, so I need to give a little thought to the prospect of your truth-in (what a flip-flop you've made on that one by the way.)

Love always   Soph

The letter alarmed Edmund, but was followed two days later by another one:

E.R., I've decided it's a great idea, I'm lonely as hell and need some radical doses of sister/brotherhood! Do you realize it'll be the first time in a quarter of a century the three of us will be together for more than a day? I'm already dreaming of all the places we could meet in: Kenya (to catch the wildlife there before it totally disappears), southern Morocco (stupendous architecture, greatest hash around) or what about Scandinavia, Iran? Listen, I'm game for anywhere as long as we can be together!

Miss you miss you   Soph

Boston
April 28th

Dear heart,

How superb that we've agreed to do it. However Sophie angel there are several countries on your list that I've grave misgivings about; I know you journalists are supposed to be objective but Iran has one of the most repressive regimes in existence, as for Kenya I wouldn't think of touching it until they ban all shooting of wildlife . . . let's think some more.

Loving you always   Peb

287

Berkeley
May 1st
Sofka/ A brief P.S. to add that Peb also vetoes Morocco for obvious political reasons, has been on Gelusil all weekend just thinking about it. As for myself I boycott Scandinavia; nothing to look at except the boobs of all those odiously liberated blondes and at my age I'd rather get my hard-ons from Tintoretto. So let's give it more study, my sweet.

Je t'embrasse   E.

Roma
May 10th
Shit man between Peb's pacifist ecology and your macho aesthetics are we ever going to decide on a place here we are in an age of limitless jet travel and we can't find one city to meet in is this supposed to be a parable on modern freedom or something? Just a jet-lagged gripe between assignments.   S.

Berkeley
May 12th
Chère Bedouine,
How would you feel about the Soviet Union? Peb may veto that too damn it on the other hand she might decide she can do some good there, let me know—   E.

New York City
May 16th
Dearest both/
The Soviet Union really puts me off you can only go there with Intourist and that's totally run by KGB goons who OD you on propaganda and spy on every step you take. . . .   S.

288

May 18th

Dear heart—I think Eddem's plan for the Soviet Union is magnificent—Nevsky Prospect, the Hermitage, Tolstoi's childhood home!
And if we hurry we could get there in time for the white nights.

Peb

New York City
May 22th

Peb, Edmo/ Just back from Tijuana and want to say that the USSR
suddenly strikes me as perfect; weather is reported very variable there
in June so pack plenty of sweaters and don't forget solid folding stools
for the museums.

Love you love you can't wait

S.

xxii

SOPHIE stood on a parapet above the Moscow River, her hair flaming like a monstrance in the light of a streetlamp. She raised a leg in arabesque, stretched a hand over the water. Edmund ran towards her on the embankment, not daring to call her in fear of startling her into a fall. The colonnaded palaces of Tolstoi's time flowed past him in a ribbon of lemon light, he saw her turn on one leg very slowly, as if practicing her childhood dances, extend another arm towards the livid river. He reached the parapet and crouched a few yards from her feet. The muddy wash of the Moskva lay twenty feet below them, he looked up and saw her pale cheeks, closed eyes, the dazed face on top of the wavering body. The current was extremely swift. He feared startling her and didn't know whether to leap up and seize her by the waist. He crouched there for a moment, wishing he could die for her. Her hair flared again in the light of a car that cruised down the embankment. Edmund shouted for help, waving at the car; he saw the beginning of her fall, she fell towards the water sideways, with considerable indecision, as if she'd continued trying to grip the parapet but had lost her balance after a brusque movement. Then he heard a low thud upon the water, darkness. He climbed up to dive in after her, strangers' arms held him back, shouting at him in his mother's tongue. A few minutes later there were sirens, more cars.

. . .

After Sophie lay safe in a hospital bed he sat by her side in a room the hue of dusty sun-parched mint leaves. A smell of archaic herbal medications recalled moments when Mara had bent over his own childhood illnesses—valerian, belladonna. Many photographs hung on the walls on either side of the narrow windows; he held her limp hand and stared at the pictures. Ice-grizzled skiers saluted the Soviet flag in some northern outpost, smiling Tatar women in mountain landscape chiseled at frames of cloisonné metal, Buddhist temples rose by the side of Lake Baikal. Claire was away that day visiting Baklanov's mother. Edmund had told the Soviet police that Sophie was an expert swimmer but had not realized the dangerous swiftness of the river's flow. Every hour impassive women doctors came into the room to check Sophie's pulse. Edmund waited for the stirring of her hand in his, stared at the pictures of the brutally vast land. Volcanoes in Irkutsk, a soccer game at the Minsk tractor plant, poetry-loving physicists hold a reading of Mayakovski in Siberia, "The poet's word is your resurrection, your immortality, citizen bureaucrat." Sophie's face had been scrubbed of makeup and she had a white cotton bonnet on her head, resembling the child who'd plunged into Nantucket waters beside him. Towards noon her arm began to twitch, her eyelids flickered. Edmund rose to sit at the head of her bed, stroked her forehead.

"Why why why?" he whispered. "You and your sacrifices, Sofka. . . ."

"Do I look old?"

"Don't talk yet . . . when will you start living for yourself, Soph, when will you cease having enough goodness and craziness for all three of us?"

"I can so talk . . ." He leaned his head close to hers, listening for the slurred, sedated words.

"In fifteen years we'll all be sixty, Eddem." Her head nodded in sleep every few minutes but there was an indomitable will to speak.

"This isn't the way I want an end, Eddem, I don't want one of these solitary northern ends, I want a Mediterranean thing, I want . . ."

291

He paced the room when she dozed off, returned to stroke her head as she found words more clearly.

". . . I once heard Amos describe his grandmother's death, she lay in bed with dozens of offspring and relatives about her and in the last hours each of them held on to some part of her body, all those warm hands clutching you, we three have had lonely lives."

"And where would we be without each other, Sofka? Sofka, will you please explain why?" She waved her hand impatiently.

"There was always in you and me a terrible slowness, Edmund; we're the kind who resist understanding, Claire seized her knowledge early and used it as a tool to control everything and everyone about her. . . ."

Edmund rose and stood by the window, trying not to listen to her too closely. For the past three weeks he'd been able to shed both solitude and restraint; bombarded by the presence of his two women he'd felt the rational fabric of two decades dissolve, the sum of his life lay about him every day in a rich jumble of pieces whose growing multitude alarmed him; it was like staring at several trunkfuls of archaeological shards being dumped into a pool of muddy water at his feet. This is precisely the information I came here for he thought upon waking every morning but I don't dare dive for it yet. . . . The city lay before him with cartographic clarity. In this bastion of atheism there isn't a place from which you can't see a church Claire had said. Nursery-hued, often flaking, mostly closed, churches heaving through desolate cement like islets of candied Orient, like flowers thrusting through carpets of decaying leaves. The hospital looked down upon the oldest settlement in Moscow, that Arbat whose serpentine streets still bore the Oriental stamp of its Tatar builders. The great fire of 1812 had spared a few islets of European grace; colonnaded palaces on which Tolstoi had modeled the Rostovs' mansion flared like single daffodils in the cement iceberg of the modern city. . . . "Prepare yourself for a nation that seems to have been singled out for suffering," John Mirsky had bellowed out as he saw him off on his trip, "for a people that looks on its suffering as its vessel of redemption. . . ."

"Just think!"

Sophie woke from a brief sleep, coughed lightly as she spoke.

"Eddem, just think how little Peb ever *desired,* and yet everyone every detail of everything was completely taken over by this mist-wreathed nun of ours, while you and I were always desiring but never having. . . ."

Almost drowned twelve hours ago, she lay there dumping more shards into his well.

"I'll tell you what I want said at my funeral if someday I really pull it off right, Eddem, I want it said she embodied something of humanity's search for total freedom, her honesty was exquisite."

He sat on her bed, kissed her forehead.

"But you and I may have confused freedom with license, Soph; I'm finally seeing that license has to do with the liberty to pursue goals and aims, whereas freedom . . ."

"Oh, do tell!"

". . . is something else. I don't know yet."

"Well, let me know when we're seventy, okay? All I know, Eddem, is that it's hard when people who've been fighting beside you for a long time splinter off and you must find someone else to fight on with; that's hard at our age, when there may be so little time left. . . ."

She dozed off again. Edmund continued staring at the drab terror of Moscow. His numbness of the early morning was disappearing. He felt ineptness rather than anger or guilt. Throughout the trip the women had been subtle and variable, instruments so finely tuned that trying to fathom them he'd felt like a thick-fingered plumber tinkering with one of the capricious delicate fountains of the Hermitage. The best metaphors he'd found for the mysterious chemistry of great friendships had to do with processes of distillation, information. I go to my friend steeped in the turbid dirty water of my self-ignorance and he/she will give me back to myself crystal-clear as spring; I've dived into the muddy depths of my passions without success and my friend will by some alchemy refine it, guide me towards the shards; without a friend I remain morbid, undecipherable, a garbage heap unto myself. For three decades Sophie and he had excelled at brutally distilling each other but Claire had always abstained from criticizing Sophie, had protected her like a lioness from his attacks; her candor of the past few days may have been too sudden . . . the previous evening after returning from their visit to Baklanov's friends the three of them had talked late into the night. Claire kept broaching the idea of their eventually living together; this is our last chance to kidnap you from your hideous life, Soph, to brainwash you of that idiotic industry which is working you to death, we need you to set our lives in order. Sophie had pretended to be amused, oh you alcoholics of purity you're mad if you think I'm going to hang out in some frugal little community of salvation; when will you realize that I'm not really one of you, that I want every gaudy little American bauble ever dangled before me, penthouses and awards from the Newswomen's Club of America and lunch at the Four Seasons, the whole bag, what do you think the Ross education was about? Leave me be with the only illusions I have left she'd cried out the night before in the bar of the hotel.

She woke again, her voice returned to normal.

"You don't even need me as a critic anymore."

"What on earth do you mean, silly girl?"

"Nietzsche's phrase about the ideal friend being the beautiful enemy, the most vigilant critic . . . you're both so well now that you don't even need me as that!"

At dusk a doctor said that Edmund could take Sophie back to the hotel the following morning.

"You and I have been followers, Eddem; we've always been determined by the measure of someone else and she never was."

But in the past few days Edmund had felt that some nefarious imbalance of three decades had been broken, that he was standing splunk at center, in immense control. So he rebutted:

"I've ceased to follow anyone, Soph, and you can cease too."

He may have spoken too sharply. Her voice rose with an anxiety which he didn't want to hear.

"The kind of thing I've just been through today comes after a crisis and not during, Eddem, when we've ceased fighting not during the fight, when there's nothing more to be done. . . . I had to live with the two of you for this long fortnight for the first time since we were twenty to fully know . . ."

"For Christ's sake, you could have kept me so many times, Soph,

294

how many times! That winter we met in Detroit . . ."

"Shut up, Edmund, I want you to be happy with her! Be happy with her, can't you give me what I ask of you for once?"

"You've lived with your body, Sophie, and this is a tale of passion, isn't it . . . which has little to do with the flesh."

"For once!" she shouted. "For once give me what I want!"

He would always remember the triumphant timbre of that voice, the hair tangled with sweat lying like a pool of brandy on the hospital pillow. Then she cried a great deal. She was brought some broth, a pill. He would remain by her bed until morning.

"It worked in part," she said as she fell asleep for the night. "It may have worked a little bit, your big Slavic truth-in."

On the day before flying home Edmund, Claire and Sophie took a cab to a small monastery they wished to visit in the outskirts of Moscow. They sat on the grass on a June Sunday in the park attending the main church. Sophie was still a little weak, she kept her head on Claire's lap, never letting her eyes off her face. The alleys were filled with women who dozed in the morning sun as they waited for service to begin, they lay on benches with paper bags that held their day's nourishment, radishes, hunks of bread.

"Little's been known about Volodya Baklanov for six months, save that he's increasingly weakened by his fasts," Claire began; "his mother has been living like one of those hunted creatures of the thirties, kept alive by a few friends who're staking their own freedom to take care of her. No phone, threats to intensify reprisals against her son if she continues sending messages to the West . . . to lessen the risk of being observed she'd decided not to transmit any more messages but somehow she's come to trust me. So yesterday when I rang her doorbell there was no problem, her friends had received the message that I was coming. . . ."

Claire closed her eyes for a second and as she opened them again Edmund saw them as weary and skeptical as those of the aged women dozing on the benches. The church they sat by was the most beautiful he'd seen in the past weeks, a paschal whirl of titanium white surmounted by domes of gold-speckled cerulean. On a small colonnaded porch of the monastery a young monk in a brown robe stood very erect, hair tied back in a long braid, staring at the fields ahead.

"Immediately to the left of the door was a dark room that looked like . . . like a kind of shrine. Several people seemed to be sitting around someone, I couldn't see well at first; I went into the room and Madame Baklanova lay there propped up on pillows surrounded by little offerings her friends had brought, bits of Western medicines and magazines, candy, old clothing. Her face is as sallow as that of some relic yet her eyes are very blue, very kind and lustrous and not even angry; she has a gastric ailment which requires very special medication and she obviously doesn't dare go to any hospital for it . . . she'd received a message from her son just two weeks ago and the news is as bad as we'd expected; he's fasting again and this time seems determined to fast until death or freedom . . . she didn't complain, she only stated, stated the facts. And then she gave me her radiant smile and we talked about the icon over her head, she said that her kind of Christianity isn't based on atonement or sacrifice because they've already taken place, when she prays she already tries to find the joyful communion with God she'll have after death, she compares it to the trusting joyful games children play with their fathers. . . . She also said this, we mustn't let our suffering *ghettoize* us, she used that word, we must always remember those who suffer even more than we do. . . ."

"But it's impossible to leave them this way," Sophie whispered. "What's to be done?"

She still lay on the grass, her head on Claire's lap. Claire gave a small laugh, almost cynical.

"What's to be done? We can only work gram by gram, one drop of saving at a time. All the information on Baklanov's condition is right on me; I took notes and threw them away after coding them; I've also a petition to the West signed by several Russian scientists who're staking their freedom again asking for Baklanov's release. . . ."

The benches had emptied. A drone of voices was flowing from the church. Claire, Edmund and Sophie walked towards it. They entered a dark space seething with women moving about and prostrating themselves before many icons, a file of bearded priests in pink taffeta robes wound slowly around the iconostasis, gold and precious stones flamed from their domed hats and massive crosses, from the cupola above a Christ gazed down impassively, right hand raised in warning or in judgment. On a table in back of the church worshipers had heaped offerings to the monastery, farm produce, bunches of apples and hunks of bread; there was no focus and no center to the celebration, only a seething crowd of women in a state of anarchic fervor who bowed and sank to the floor and moved about and constantly crossed themselves, who muttered snatches of prayers or sang a phrase of litany before stopping to kiss the icon of some saint and move across the church to another one; in midroom the central image of the Virgin was gravely wiped by an attendant between the salutations of its visitors; Claire leaned against a wall, supporting Sophie's head on her shoulder, eyes fixed on the image of Christ above her head. In the scant dusk of candles the pink-robed priests continued to wave censers about the blazing screen; this fragrant heavy cloud of muttering and chanting and prostrated flesh, of poverty and abundance, of a spirituality as dense and anarchic as the lichen of the ocean floor, recalled to Edmund the Sundays of his childhood, Mara kneeling on a stone floor in Manhattan praying silently for beloved dead whom she refused to share; he walked to midchurch towards the icon of the Virgin, approached the bent melancholy face, leaned towards her chiseled tranquil eyes, brows furrowed by hieratic lines of suffering, chaste mouth turned downwards in hopeful sorrow, gold leaf blazed about her columnar neck like God's holy fire; he put his lips to hers and in a gesture as alien and familiar as the genuflections of his childhood he crossed himself three times, in the Slavonic manner. Sophie's eyes remained closed, Claire watched him with interest. He'd never forget how easy it was, for a moment, to believe.

"Your intelligent traveler books his trips to the Iron Curtain well ahead of time," Arthur Zabar said as Intourist Tour No. 137 Destination Tbilisi-Kiev-Leningrad-Moscow boarded a bus for its farewell banquet. "He'll be careful to plan much further ahead than for any capitalist country."

"Arthur studies the travel pages of the *Sunday Times* the way others read the financial or theater section," Ethel Zabar explained.

"We're already booked for Czechoslovakia this fall and next spring we're scheduled for Hungary," Mr. Zabar added.

"New York is going to seem so dull after this trip," Mrs. Weicker remarked to Mrs. Jones, "don't you get bored in America?"

"Brazil is next on our schedule unless some smart lefties get the upper hand," Mrs. Jones said. "There are several Rolls-Royce dealers in that handsome country; we'll get a dandy reception but I doubt if you can beat the Soviets for sheer *joie de vivre.*"

"These Iron Curtain countries seem so hospitable and warm," Mr. Jones said, "and we just loved the food."

The Rolls-Royce dealers were thrilled with their purchases. Mr. Jones alone had bought three stuffed panda bears for his grandchildren, four fur hats, several Ukrainian flowered shawls, many painted wooden dolls and a twelve-piece set of imitation Popov china, three of which he'd broken at the Dollar Store after consuming his luncheon vodka.

"Pay attention, please, to beauty of sunset on ancient walls of our Arbat," Evgeny spoke into his little microphone, "built by Tatar hordes who occupied Moscow in twelfth century."

As they drove by the Bolshoi Theatre, Sophie was photographing a flock of ravens settling on the head of the statue of Karl Marx. Edmund was murmuring to Claire the winged, aerial names of the Kremlin churches: Annunciation, Assumption, Archangel.

"We have thirty-two other theaters in Moscow with permanent companies and large repertoires," Evgeny said, "thirteen concert halls, two circuses and one hundred and nineteen cinemas. Our Soviet people are passionates of art."

"It is raining!" Irina exclaimed. "Rain is a very good sign, it is sign that city is sad to see you leave and that you will all come back soon again."

" 'Good night, Irene, Good night Irene,' " the Americans sang, " 'we'll see you in our dreeeeeeams.' "

"Let's buy the girls electric samovars at the Dollar Store right at

298

the airport," one of the Rolls-Royce dealers said to Mr. Jones. "Hey, great idea," Mr. Jones agreed.

"I hope you're feeling better, Miss Ross!" Mrs. Zabar said. "We certainly look forward to your special on the Soviet Union on *Good Day America!*"

"Have you ever seen little children so well taken care of, beautifully dressed and nicely mannered?" Mrs. Weicker exclaimed. "Look at those little people over there in the smart blue suits and red ties."

"They are members of our Young Communist League, Mrs. Weicker, and we have even younger term of honor; we call our babies Oktiabristi at the age of two or three as soon as they can recognize portrait of Lenin."

"How too dear!"

"Such an effusive, warmhearted people," Mr. Weicker remarked.

"Never known such dolers out of claptrap as these Soviet guides," Mr. Zabar said as they stepped off the bus.

"Both repellent and curiously moving, like much in this country," Claire commented.

A floor show accompanied the abundant farewell banquet held at a restaurant specializing in Central Asian cuisine. Muscular sword-dancers in Cossack costumes were particularly applauded, a mournful redhead in sequined gauze sang "Volga, Volga, Beloved Mother," a Siberian rock band played "When the Saints Go Marching In" on electric guitars. Evgeny was immensely enjoying his last talk with Intourist Tour No. 137. "All through our long history Russian people have enjoyed arguing about what is love, what is death, what is God." "I have admiration for your great Dreiser but I also confess passion for John Updike."

After much vodka the Americans fell upon the ample, brutal Soviet fare of pickles and potatoes, lard and cucumbers, grilled mutton and smoked fish. There were many toasts.

"To our struggle for the future of democracy!" Arthur Zabar exclaimed.

"To Muscovy, this remarkable handiwork of nature . . ."

299

"To our shared goal of mutual trust . . ."

"It is with a joy tinged with sadness that we look for the last time in the eyes of our American friends . . ."

"To our women!" Edmund drank.

"To our artists and poets," Evgeny shouted towards Edmund, "magicians of our tribes!"

After dinner Edmund, Sophie and Claire receive permission to walk home alone through Red Square. Sophie walks in the center, her friends' arms around her waist. All seems ice and flower in Moscow's durable lacquer night. They watch for the last time the spectacle at the heart of Soviet power: tiered shrine of frozen rose denying the finality of death. Marzipan-cheeked boy soldiers guarding the temple's entrance. Single red star of the Spassky Tower blazing over all like a threat of eternity.

"Les passagers d'Air France en provenance de Berlin sont priés de se rendre au guichet des controles . . ." "Passagieri Alitalia en partenze para New Delhi sono pregati embarcare immediatamente . . ."* "Is this the flight to Istanbul?" "No this is Air Congo 673 to Beirut. . . ."

The Moscow airport was mayhem. They'd decided to stop in Paris on the way home to see the Matisse show. Claire and Edmund had tried to talk Sophie into taking an extra week's vacation, flying home with them and going on to Nantucket. Edmund had to find himself a solid warm house there for the winter. That's where he'd determined to spend the following year, they needed Sophie's advice, her sense of life's comforts. But Sophie was adamant about going right back to work, she'd fly to Paris with them for a day and go on to Monte Carlo where she must do a special on the film festival.

On the bus that drove them to the airport Edmund had started writing postcards to Berkeley which he planned to mail from Paris. For his friend John he'd chosen photographs of the poets' statues which dot the squares of Moscow: Curly-headed Pushkin, hand inside vest, brooding against a backdrop of new lilacs; Mayakovski striding with clenched fists, trousers waving in sculpted wind.

"In the monolithic despair of certain Russian lives there's not even room for love," he wrote, "only for a certain kind of fierce, passionately self-sacrificial friendship; there's no way they could conceive of the *self* here the way we do, for with enough communal suffering the self breaks down, becomes an untenable entity of speech, a myth . . . one leaves Moscow saying I want to wake up from the nightmare of their history. And yet I'll miss this country as much as I dread it because of the massive spirituality which continues to thrive in its people like random flowers thrusting through cement; they haven't begun to be tainted, for instance, by that tragic disease of the West in which sexuality has replaced man's fate. . . . Was it Dostoevski who said that Russia exists only for the purpose of teaching the world a lesson?"

". . . Claire, by the way, may have played a modest role in the eventual release of Baklanov . . . ah yes that may be my Claire's vocation, to greet the resurrected. . . ."

"From July on, dear John, you can reach me care of General Delivery, Nantucket, Mass. Things are falling into place. You're welcome to share my solitude up island anytime you want. . . ."

Just before customs they walked one last time through the desolation, the stained and brutal bleakness of Soviet public rooms, past dour distrustful guards and surly-eyed women hovering over arrays of gaudy wooden dolls.

"We'll see you very soon again, Gedmund Petrovich! When will you return to us, Clara Pavlovna?"

"Ah, you lie so sweetly I could kiss you, Genia! It may be years before we're allowed the luxury of a reunion."

They hugged in parting at the airport. The Russian put into his embrace a heat which he'd refused to put into words.

"To your wonderful eyes, Sofia Larionovna . . . to your splendid gaze, Clara Pavlovna!"

"We'll see you in a thaw or two, Evgeny Sergeievich."

There was a delectable sleekness, efficiency, comfort, about the Air France craft which their bodies had not experienced for the past several weeks. Perfume flowed in fragrant washrooms. The seats were cloudlike. "*Ce soir nous avons les papillottes de veau Vacheron, une escalope bien fine avec une pointe de mou-tarde et d'echalotte . . ."*

All was succulent, fresh, sumptuously spruced and perfectly functioning, Edmund commented, and seemed a wasteland of the spirit.

Sophie went to the back of the plane to interview the Air France steward about his impressions of the Soviet Union. Claire took Edmund's hand. "I need you," she said. "We're about to have the best years of our lives."

He had not time to express his startlement at her gesture. For as their engines began to whir there was great commotion on the runway a few hundred yards away from their Air France craft. A cageful of snakes about to be boarded onto an Aeroflot plane (Sophie surmised they were destined for some zoo in a distant northern province) tumbled out of the truck from which it was being loaded. The cage's latch broke upon falling, several dozen beasts writhed swiftly unto the ground, the running brook of terror spread with extraordinary speed around the Soviet plane. Carfuls of Soviet soldiers rushed out of the hangars, sirens blowing; they attempted to stake in the animals with makeshift fences but the cloaked power of the dust evaded the barriers, continued to slither in all directions of the runway. There was much shouting, much commotion. The Air France craft lifted up on angel wings before any of its passengers could learn how the problem was solved. Edmund looked out at forever, across the land of his mother's birth.

xxiii

THE island air is both dark and brilliant. The lengthening shadows of autumn haunt him. In late afternoon Edmund sits in the November sun reading Vasari, Kierkegaard. During weeks when he or Claire have been ill they don't leave each other's side. Wrapped in blankets on their terrace they sniff at the last essence of afternoon light, argue gently about the call of birds. Listen to the redwing. Not at all it's an oriole. I don't need to even look at it love, it's a male redwing. Claire has taken up the piano again, goes to Quaker Meeting. They often wake early and walk in certain moors to watch geese rise on heavy wings, assembling into the tumultuous v of a flight south. We're still young she'd said one day, this is a spring, in some sort of way we've always wanted each other. It must have been July for the wild roses were in full bloom on the lion-hued dunes, the beach on which he used to draw her when she was eighteen was steeped in the slow fermentation of the rain. He'd stared with love immeasurable at the slender high-waisted body that had always reminded him of some archaic clay idol, she'd bent down to glean a seashell and he'd admired the high young breasts which wrinkled now about the nipples with the savageness of time, the fragile skin of underarms grown even paler with their age. They'd decided to repurchase Claire's old family house from its present owners, at first it seemed as simple as that. Claire is thoroughly attentive to Edmund, she is often tired. She takes much care of her kitchen, she tends the herb corner of the garden she once detested, she works hard at making Edmund's life as pretty and safe as possible. At times her fierceness seems broken. At times he worries that she's lost that part of her he used to love the most. My exile may finally be over he often says. Every few weeks in July he walks to the ferry landing to watch the ship disgorge its burden of summer happiness, its plenitude of cribs, collies, rackets, playpens, golf bags, picnic hampers. The tribes seem smaller, the one-child family predominates, the father is often absent or else he is alone, coping with the hurried fastidiousness of the divorced. There are fewer families and more solitude, there are many single men, single women, or else men with men, women with women. Edmund watches it all like a native now, with a trace of resentment; they're invading my paradise. He walks back from the ferry with his groceries through files of coquettish clapboard houses celebrating the chaste peace of our country's youth, amid the din of many voices celebrating summer. He looks forward to October when the days grow brief and the shadows long, when the haven of his adolescence seems his alone as it sinks into the solitude of its winter. When they first moved back to the island Claire and Edmund shucked scallops in winter to help earn the down payment on Sealark; they stood deep-booted in freezing warehouses plunging their hands in buckets of hot water as they struggled with the tough grimy mollusks' shells. We survive with little news and no gossip Edmund writes John, we're admirably estranged from reification hypotheses, polemical desiderata, metalanguage and alienating hierarchies of values. I'm living in my first permanent embrace with a woman and a soil. With much emotion and painful slowness I paint lemons, peaches, roses from my garden, luminous tankards of water. Muse equals Great Mother equals infinite faith and patience. I'm like a paraplegic relearning to use his limbs, like a rider mounting a fierce Arabian left wild in pasture for many years. I'm not saying this seclusion is the best for me, it may be deathly, I am a plodding patient man, slow to come to understanding. We miss our dear Sophie, to whom nature is a one-night stand, and who keeps threatening that we'll soon feel nostalgia for nervousness. . . .

                In the first years Edmund is often melancholy. He works in a shed behind Plinker's old vegetable garden, refusing to show his paintings to anyone but Claire. He is certain of her love but is terrified of his own uncertainty, of the risks he is posing to himself. Am I finally saving myself from the black velvet of universal emptiness, from the night and murk of nonbeing? He lays his grounds with ancient craft so they will survive for centuries, once again slowly heating rabbit's skin glue in double boilers, slowly stirring in chalk to make the gesso with which he primes his canvases. On his more melancholy days Claire brings him lunch in the studio, suggests a stroll in a moor where she's walked many times that month but which always soothes him. What does he really think of as she watches him shuffle up the path under the lowering winter sky, bringing in wood for the evening fire? The continuing threat of failure and nonbeing? The futility of all art in our time? The particular futility of his own? Edmund's somberness is as opaque to Claire as her new docility is mysterious to him. He knows that something precious has left her life and he knows that she'll never admit it. In his youth he'd thought that upon marrying Claire he might finally decipher her with total clarity, read her as closely as the palm of his own hand. But one day during her convent years she'd told him that such knowledge could never exist on earth. She'd quoted Saint Augustine, We too, dear ones, will someday see each other's hearts but later, for now we yet bear the darkness of our flesh. So only when the thugs of eternity come after us, Edmund had said. She'd preferred such words as Later, Afterwards. At times he is resigned; opaqueness, mystery nourish the greatest loves; must be accepted, even hallowed. The more you love the less you understand. The game of reality and appearance done away with, a mystic impulse, my ignorance becomes knowledge, I know best that which I do not know.

All art is a joke anyhow he says as he opens a bottle of wine for supper; it's all an illusion anyway, there's little to work for but the peace of life.

Just look at those poppies.

Nothing like them is there, three years and they've never stopped budding.

Next spring we must try some anemones.

They didn't leave the island more than twice in the first few years.

Plinker's tall body often haunts Edmund by the gate of his vegetable garden, stooped and yellow-faced, rake in hand. The garden is now mine, Edmund's. I've come to claim it for you. I've come back to give your daughter precisely the happiness you wanted for her. I most love this spot of earth in early winter when I can admire the persistence, the tenacity of things, the parsley persevering under its hoar of frost, the obstinate succulence of turnips wrenched from the ground with heavy spades. The world outside seems ridden with trivia and impatience. I admire doggedness, upagainstness, permanence, slowness, any patience as long as mine. As he works his garden Edmund often remembers a decaying Italian villa in which he'd once stared at a row of sculptured torsos overgrown with mosses and lichens, suspended in metamorphosis between animal and vegetal nature, and that's the way he feels on many days, increasingly rooted and blurred into his first and last terrain. Sometimes I'm afraid of rusticating, of becoming totally overgrown by the tenacity of the soil I've chosen. The refuge might be dangerous but I am leading a most beautiful life. I may have chosen life over art again. I have chosen a kind of quality of quality.

Six of one and half a dozen of another.

When Claire walks back from the country store every night at dusk she stares at a stand of pines that looms with particular starkness at the last bend on their dirt road, pines bristling and opaque against the peach of winter dusk. He is the shape and doom of my life. He's the vessel into which I've chosen to pour myself in order . . . to survive? No. In order to simply pour myself. He's like the medium with which through which the artist struggles to find his meaning. He has become my only meaning. He is as inevitable as the fact that these pines will loom over the dormant meadow until the day they're cut down. I am drained of much indignation. As a child I'd felt anger at the great feast days of the Church because I'd thought they'd bring some miraculous transformations of the cosmos which never came, well they never came. No more need to stress my separateness, to strip my rooms of all but the bare essentials. Surplus is our common fate.

She goes to Boston for a week a month to continue her work in human rights.

They believe in the family. Victoria comes up frequently from Harvard, where she plans to take a degree in theology to become a minister of the Episcopal Church. Our pursuit of freedom has become excessive, Victoria says, we've sacrificed communal duty to an excessive preoccupation with individual liberty, classical libertarianism isn't working, we're stuck again, never forget what Mom learned at St. Agatha's, hell is oneself, not others. . . . oh God not again Claire whispers, I couldn't go through it anymore. Edmund teases that Victoria will become the first woman bishop.

Back home Claire often sits in the library compiling documents about the torture of dissidents in Peru, Afghanistan, Iran. Above her desk there hangs a photograph of Baklanov and his mother, both restored to health since finding asylum in the West, standing at the entrance of a German university where Baklanov now teaches. Lying in their bedroom Edmund hears the scribbling of her pen on paper, as patiently persistent as a litany. He continues to find her quieter, more mysterious than ever.

Claire loves to look at Edmund's body as he stands naked to the waist in their garden, a body as finely tuned as it was at twenty-five, helmet of gray-streaked dark blond hair curling about the muscled neck, firm torso of a man who's been relatively frugal with the joys of the body. One night as she knelt beside him tending her rosemary plants she thought she saw the stand of pines advancing towards her, an umbrous army of verdure, resignation, permanence, she knew again the depth and enshacklement of her new happiness.

He seldom talks about art anymore except to say: Complicity in the evils of the age is the artist's greatest sin. The artist must address himself to a clear but distant viewer, an angelic viewer whom he cannot merely seduce or entertain. In this most tempting of decades he's the one who must impose the greatest rigor, the most severity on himself to survive.

There are days when he makes himself a bowl of Cream of Wheat and goes to bed at 6:00 P.M. too depressed to read or talk. And it takes all the force of her love not to be angered by what she calls the artist's vice of melancholy; on such days she refuses to have his anguish affect her, he becomes like a swollen limb of her own body bordering on gangrene, she refuses this infection, she does not lance his pain with questions because she's learned that there are archaeologies of the unsaid we make silent pacts to not disturb. On such days he resents her chosen distance as she sits in the library writing more letters about strangers suffering in distant places. From her desk at the window she occasionally stares out at the tragic stage set of her island's innocence, at a frozen nostalgia yelling heavenwards through sparse white spires of New England churches, at the primordial ocean water in which her brother drowned plying the rudder of a sailboat in her tribe's deathly urge to compete, she stares at this town she began to detest as a child but which Edmund had insisted on recalling her to, as another husband had before him. This is how they want to get infected by my so-called purity, my pedantry of virtue.

At some point during such evenings Claire manages to talk about the birds she's seen that afternoon or to praise Edmund's last painting, to bring more herbal tea into the lair of his seclusion, to be precisely what he's wanted her to be for now thirty-five years; and through her shrewd bringing of new joy, her carefully choreographed resurrection of his faith, he recovers with remarkable agility. He sits at the breakfast table the next morning smiling again, deep blue eyes the hue of lupines on a sunny day, saying that soon he might be ready to show his paintings to someone else than her.

She is new to the art of helping those she knows and loves, not even rusty but new. Her vocabulary is limited. The laboratory of the twentieth century is closed she repeats after Edmund, the cult of constant innovation has passed. There's little or nothing to invent anymore she writes Sophie, all is permitted now, he can paint any way he wishes and be loved again; soon he'll regain the glory he abandoned in his youth, you'll see!

After a few years they worry that their island sanctuary is being despoiled. Community theaters, pottery and watercolor and yoga and ballet classes, various other forms of the 1980s' striving for self-improvement proliferate in the vicinity of the old Town Hall. Young men with scraggly beards weep in coffee shops after their consciousness-raising sessions alongside angry girls in frayed jeans and granny glasses. Coteries of art lovers move to the island in alarming numbers and give fawning parties for exurbanite novelists who celebrate the occasion by insulting everyone at hand. Glamorous divorcées from D.C. who've slept with everyone in public office are remodeling lobster shacks on the old wharf in odious hues of primrose yellow. Trust-fund hippies in scalloping gear winter on the island to play fisherman, and say "I'm going to America" when they take the ferry to the mainland. Falseness seems to pursue us everywhere Edmund complains to Sophie during one of her weekend visits. We face a historical quandary she replies; our cities are increasingly difficult, more and more of you purists retire to the vacuum of the countryside, where you claim to enjoy nature and complain that you do not rub enough against other humans to create meaningful art.

Claire and Edmund now pick up TV magazines that come free with purchases of groceries over ten dollars, they study them for the scheduling of all of Sophie's special reports, they read interviews in other publications that describe her solitary but excessively busy life, her "monastic dedication" to her "phenomenal career," her arduous backpacking vacations to the wilds of Ceylon or Nepal, the macrobiotic diets she engages in to ensure the perpetual freshness of her skin. "The alarm rings at 4:15 in Ms. Ross's Sutton Place penthouse but the star newscaster is already awake, hair freshly washed for one of her special reports on the *Good Day America* show, sitting under the dryer with the early-bird copy of *The New York Times*. . . . ." In 1980 Sophie realizes one of her many dreams, she becomes the first woman to be anchorperson of a presidential party convention.

—"It's now clear that Senator Kennedy will stay out of sight until the end of President Carter's speech . . . will stay out of sight until the faithful gather for that family picture on the podium which might provide next week's magazine covers. . . . You don't need to be an expert on body language to expect a rather frigid meeting up there; even if they end up raising their arms together it'll be a pretty empty gesture at this point, like the sound of one hand clapping. . . . Let's switch now to NBC correspondent Jim Pettit who's covering the Kennedy headquarters for us at the Waldorf-Astoria. . . ."
—"That's not exactly a small compact fuel-efficient car the senator's getting into, Sophie . . . but there he is getting into it . . . Ted . . . Joan . . . the three children . . . the limousine is pulling out of the Waldorf-Astoria . . . we can hear the sirens that'll accompany the senator through darkened Manhattan towards his rendezvous with destiny at Madison Square Garden. . . . Back to Sophie Ross now at Central Control."
—"Thank you, Jim. . . . While we're waiting for the vice-presidential nominee to begin his speech we'll have a few words with Governor Babbit of Utah, who's kind enough to visit with us at Control Headquarters. . . . Governor Babbit, Jimmy Carter has a long grueling campaign ahead of him this fall, a rough uphill fight, how would you define the principles for which his Democratic party platform stands?"

—"We've always been the party of ideals, Sophie, we're the party that's always looked to the future. . . . Ideals are like stars . . . you reach for them but you can't touch them with your hands . . . you follow their light the way those fearless seafaring men followed the stars that guided them to their destinies on dark desert waters. . . ."

—"Governor Babbit, don't you think a lot of people are going to leave this convention hall feeling it was a smoke-filled room with a lot of rhetorical smoke screening in it? . . ."

—"The party's more united than you think, Sophie . . . it's united against a common enemy, against big money and deceitful propaganda, the American people aren't going to believe the lies that go into that propaganda. . . ."

—"Thank you so much, Governor. . . . We're quickly approaching the acceptance speech of the vice-presidential nominee, Vice President Walter F. Mondale. . . ."

—"We Want Fritz / We Want Fritz / We Want Fritz /"

—"Thank you . . ."

—"We Want Fritz / We Want Fritz/"

—"Thank you thank you . . ."

Every day Sophie keeps in shape by swimming a hundred lengths of the Olympic-sized pool at New York University, where she received an honorary doctorate last fall. She keeps her personal life extremely private. It is possible that she doesn't even have one, that she works as hard as she does in order not to miss having one. Sophie is one of the two or three American women most in demand as commencement speakers in our nation's colleges. She has taken up needlepoint to calm her nerves. Her birthday and Christmas presents to her close friends and to her goddaughter Victoria remain extravagant. She has recently reread all of Balzac and Trollope. She is now able to sleep five or six hours a night at a stretch. She loves to come up to the island on weekends because few people watch the news there; she can relax and take off her babushka and dark glasses. The days she shares with them on the island are among the happiest of the Richters' year. Several million Americans are said to be affected by Sophie's opinions. She often jokes with Claire and Edmund that she has a recurring nightmare in which she dreams of being precisely the opposite of what she is, there are many children depending on her in this dream and she must cook for fourteen every day and is constantly running out of food and everyone is perpetually shouting at her asking her to feed them more, feed them faster. . . .

Edmund Richter's first exhibition of paintings in twenty-five years was held in New York to considerable critical acclaim. It was written that Richter's work embodied our current return to humanistic values in many of the arts, that it was the work of a man who believed in communicating his emotion about the beauty of the created world.

Critics praised "the muted, radiant surfaces of his lyrical still lifes," "the angelic chastity of his humble objects." Once again they compared him to Chardin: "Richter captures the poetry of domestic existence." They expounded on his rigor of form, on his avoidance of the nostalgia prevailing in much of the realism presently returning to Western art.

It was noted and admired that he was extraordinarily slow to produce. "Behind the tranquil splendor of his canvases one detects agonizing and laborious hours, a pugilistic struggle with the medium throughout which the artist must retreat, correct, must stand for hours in an agony of hesitation."

Eager art dealers, plump and spectacled, come to the island to offer Edmund more exhibitions. They sit in the studio by the sound over wine and Greek olives, greedily eyeing the half-dozen paintings he's finished that year.

He explains that he's always believed in an art of equilibrium and celebration and has quite simply waited his turn, that the greatest happiness is the longest in coming.

Interviewers describe him as "a man of tranquil contentments who believes that sanity is the most profound moral option of our time."

It is noted that over his easel there hangs a comment of Chardin's made to Diderot shortly before the painter's death: *"De la douceur, messieurs! Avant tout de la douceur!"*

"So what's next?" Edmund writes John Mirsky. "I'm acquiring a reputation that'll give me ulcers again, a dealer I can't trust, art collectors who want me as the main course on their dinner party menu, reviewers who'll soon shoot me down once more, jealous colleagues who'll wish I'd OD'd on shooting up, punk-rock groupies in Nazi uniforms with paper clips on their eyelids at my vernissages . . . the jackal viewer is ever ready to hound the Muse to death. Next year they'll accuse me of slamming the door on the twentieth century and of not dealing with questions raised by post-Lacanian structuralism . . . oh, I can't get rid of my distrustful nature, Ivan Maximovich, and I've always been dead right."

More dealers come, smiling, eyeing. Hyenas in syrup, Edmund says. Edmund and Claire rent a small weekend cottage up island, no phone, an hour from town. There they take walks in the gorse-covered heaths where he'd long sought her as a child, through gentle violet undulations scattered with bayberry and shadblow, glossed with the gleam of golden aster and sweet arrowroot. This must be the love of oldest age, she thinks, to worry each time he comes in ten minutes late when he's taken an afternoon walk alone; to feel amputated each time he walks a half hour by himself.

The contemporary artist, Edmund tells some magazine, runs the risk of destruction because the world still believes there's a trace of the divine in him. And society has nothing else godly to consume.

"Don't be so old-fashioned, gentlemen critics, do us a favor and dedivinize us, cease torturing us by seeing us as the elect! We're simply makers of documents, more meticulous craftsmen than most."

"I resent it deeply," he tells Claire one morning over breakfast, "when many persons have access to my state of mind."

Sometimes he fears he's been too infected by her purity.

They continue to be happy, as far as one understands the meaning of that word. They save their money to see Victoria through graduate school, enjoy a few trips abroad. If history permits it they will often return to Russia. This is their dream, to return to the country where they resolved some of the difficult alchemy of middle age.

They also talk of leaving the island to live still farther away, to a place still more distant and pristine. They're not sure where to move to. It's hard to decide these days.

Every evening at ten o'clock Sophie's face glows towards them from under the liquid midnight of the stars. "Give me twenty-eight minutes," she says, "and I'll give you the world."

ABOUT THE AUTHOR

Francine du Plessix Gray is the distinguished author of *Lovers and Tyrants*, *Divine Disobedience* and *Hawaii: The Sugar-Coated Fortress*. Her work has appeared in *The New Yorker*, *The New York Times Magazine*, the *New York Review of Books* and other publications.